ALL TOGETHER NOW

ALSO BY HOPE LARSON

Madeleine L'Engle's
A Wrinkle in Time: The Graphic Novel

Compass South (Four Points Book 1)
Illustrations by Rebecca Mock

Knife's Edge (Four Points Book 2)
Illustrations by Rebecca Mock

All Summer Long

ALL
TOGETHER
NOW

HOPE LARSON

Farrar Straus Giroux
New York

Farrar Straus Giroux Books for Young Readers
An imprint of Macmillan Publishing Group, LLC
120 Broadway, New York, NY 10271

Printed in China by Toppan Leefung Printing Ltd.,
Dongguan City, Guangdong Province
Cover design by Molly Johanson
Series design by Andrew Arnold
Interior book design by Rob Steen
First edition, 2020
Colored by Hilary Sycamore and Karina Edwards

Paperback: 10 9 8 7 6 5 4 3 2 1
Hardcover: 10 9 8 7 6 5 4 3 2 1

mackids.com

Library of Congress Cataloging-in-Publication Data is available.
Paperback ISBN: 978-0-374-31365-4
Hardcover ISBN: 978-0-374-31162-9

Our books may be purchased in bulk for promotional, educational,
or business use. Please contact your local bookseller or the Macmillan
Corporate and Premium Sales Department at (800) 221-7945 ext. 5442
or by email at MacmillanSpecialMarkets@macmillan.com.

September

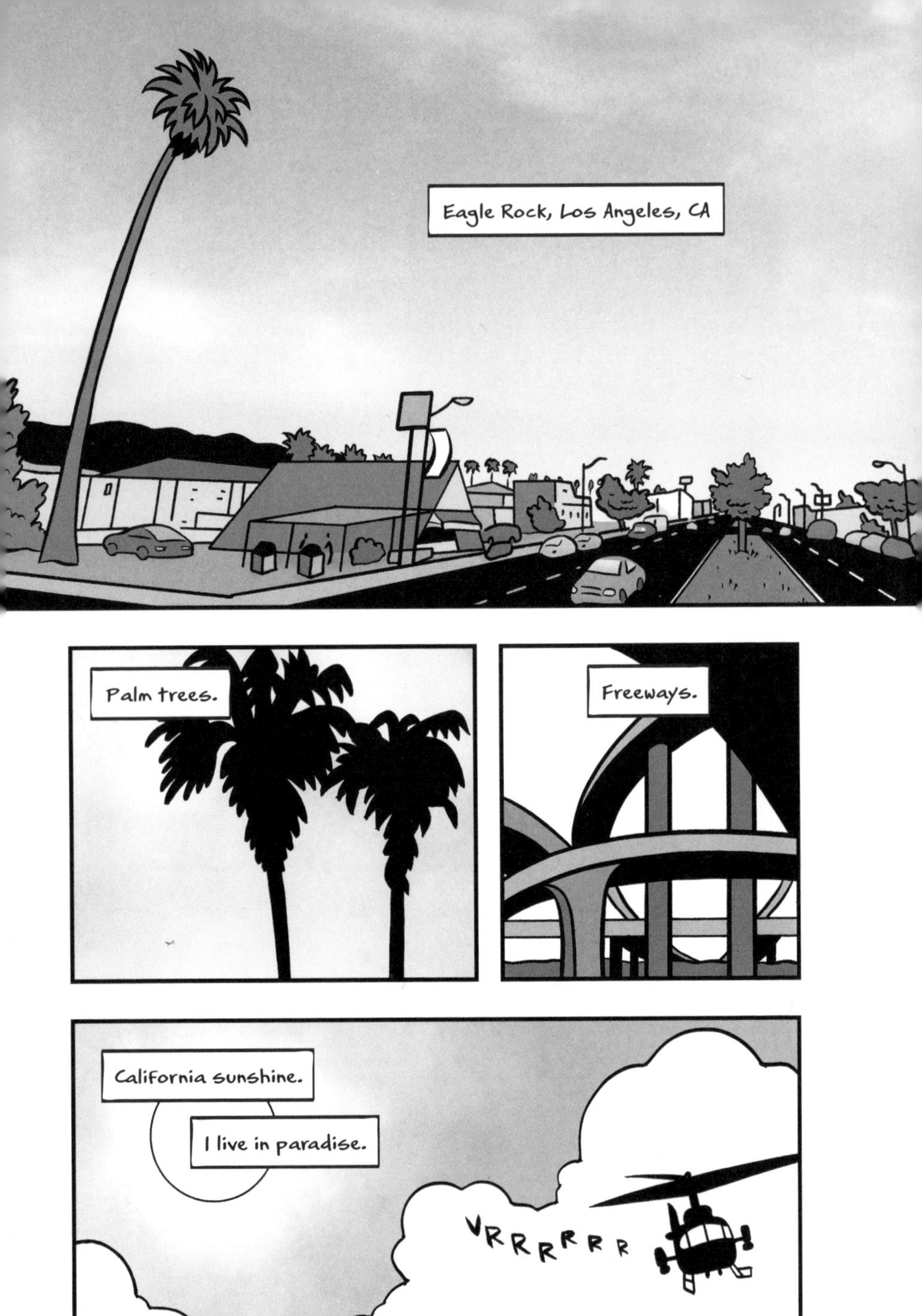
Eagle Rock, Los Angeles, CA
Palm trees.
Freeways.
California sunshine.
I live in paradise.
VRRRRRR

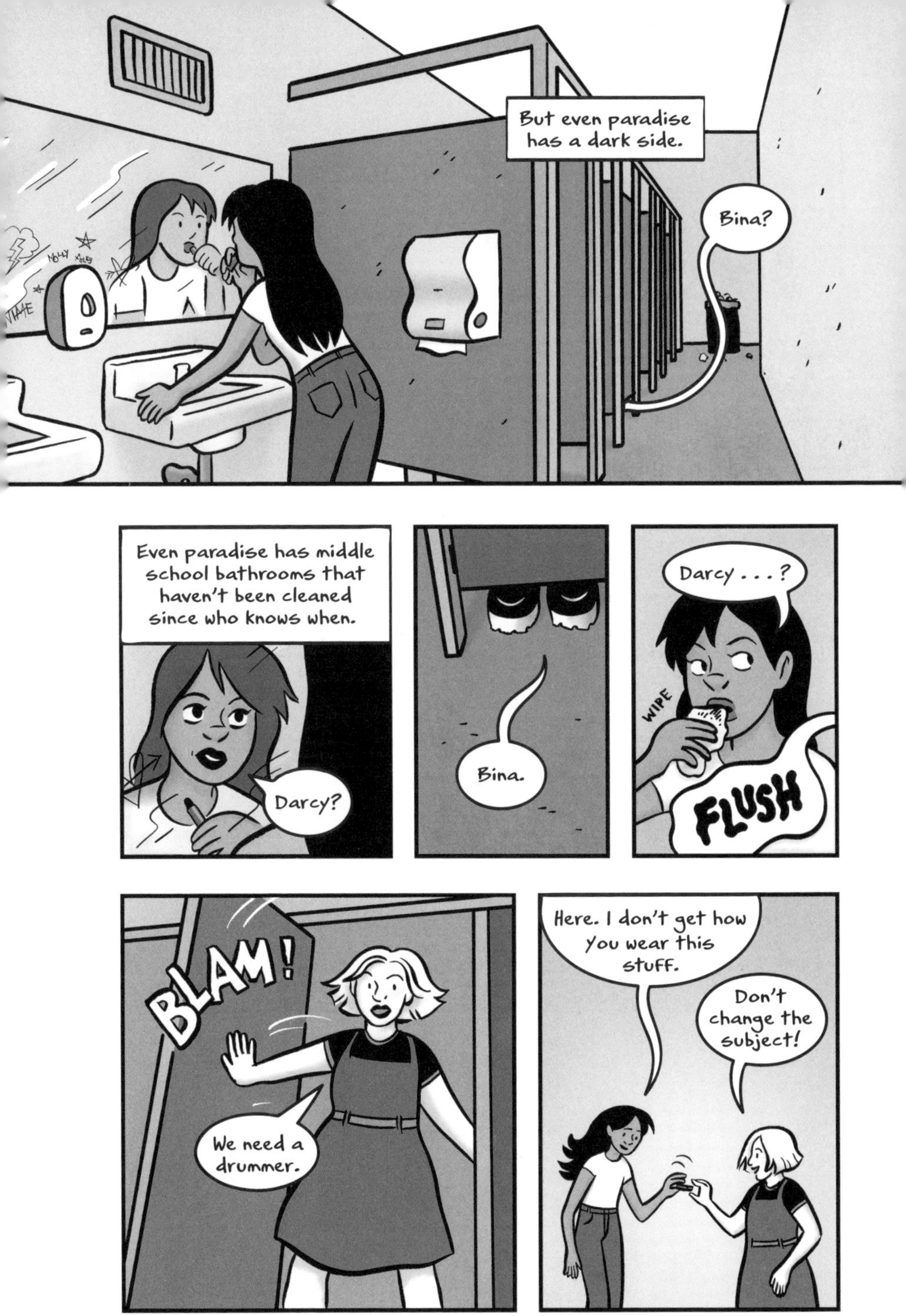
But even paradise has a dark side.
Bina?
Even paradise has middle school bathrooms that haven't been cleaned since who knows when.
Darcy?
Bina.
Darcy . . . ?
WIPE
FLUSH
BLAM!
We need a drummer.
Here. I don't get how you wear this stuff.
Don't change the subject!

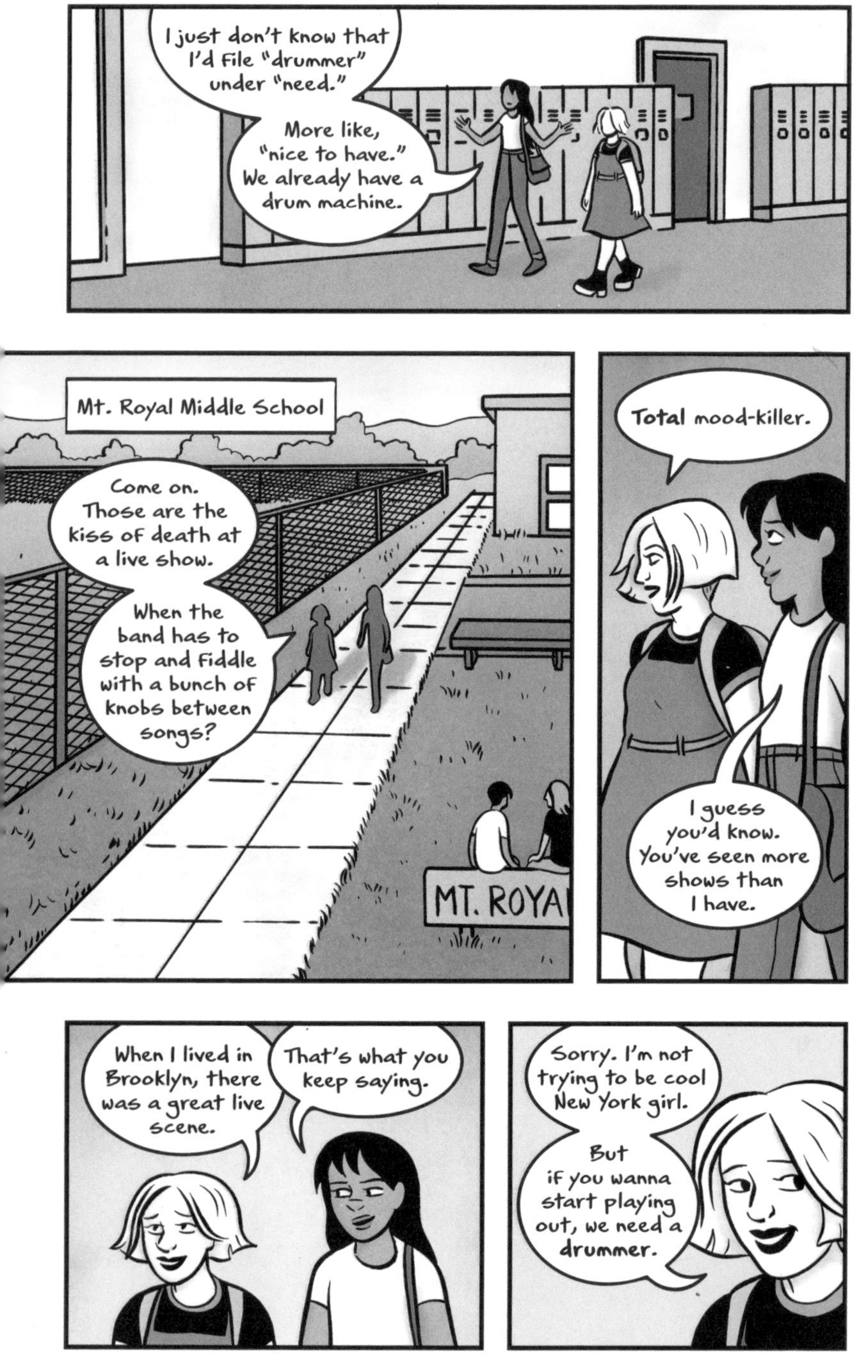
I just don't know that I'd file "drummer" under "need."
More like, "nice to have." We already have a drum machine.
Mt. Royal Middle School
Come on. Those are the kiss of death at a live show.
When the band has to stop and fiddle with a bunch of knobs between songs?
MT. ROYA
Total mood-killer.
I guess you'd know. You've seen more shows than I have.
When I lived in Brooklyn, there was a great live scene.
That's what you keep saying.
Sorry. I'm not trying to be cool New York girl.
But if you wanna start playing out, we need a drummer.

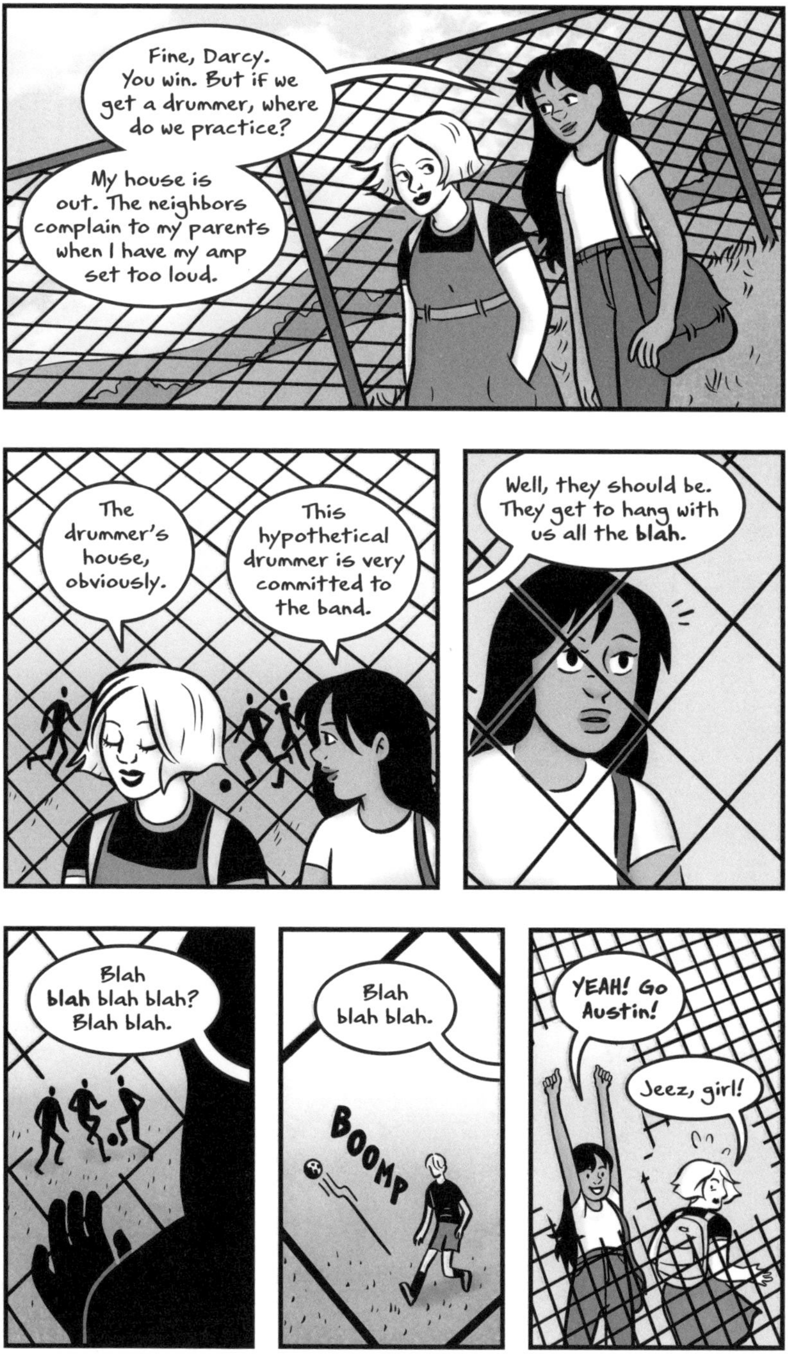
Fine, Darcy. You win. But if we get a drummer, where do we practice?
My house is out. The neighbors complain to my parents when I have my amp set too loud.
The drummer's house, obviously.
This hypothetical drummer is very committed to the band.
Well, they should be. They get to hang with us all the **blah.**
Blah **blah** blah blah? Blah blah.
Blah blah blah.
BOOMP
YEAH! Go Austin!
Jeez, girl!

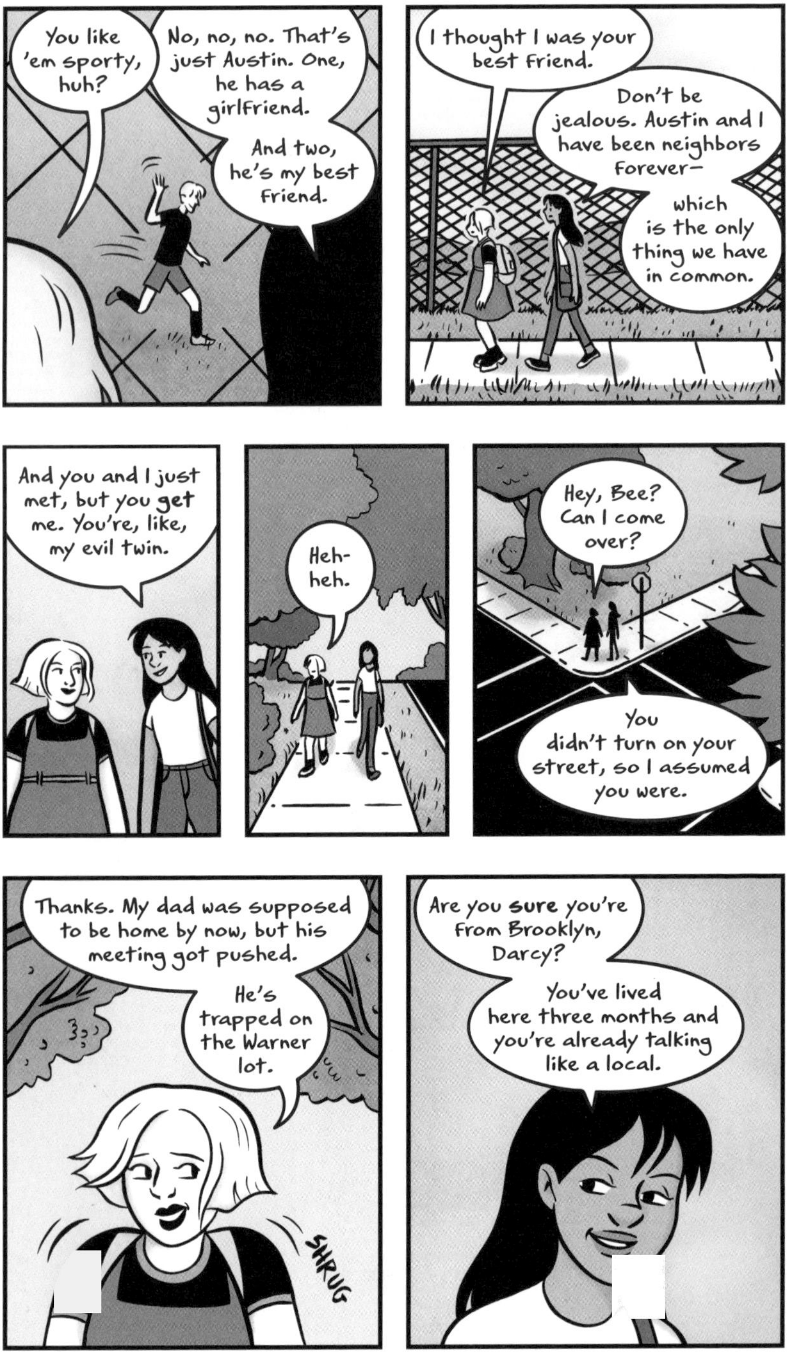
You like 'em sporty, huh?
No, no, no. That's just Austin. One, he has a girlfriend.
And two, he's my best friend.
I thought I was your best friend.
Don't be jealous. Austin and I have been neighbors forever—
which is the only thing we have in common.
And you and I just met, but you get me. You're, like, my evil twin.
Heh-heh.
Hey, Bee? Can I come over?
You didn't turn on your street, so I assumed you were.
Thanks. My dad was supposed to be home by now, but his meeting got pushed.
He's trapped on the Warner lot.
SHRUG
Are you **sure** you're from Brooklyn, Darcy?
You've lived here three months and you're already talking like a local.

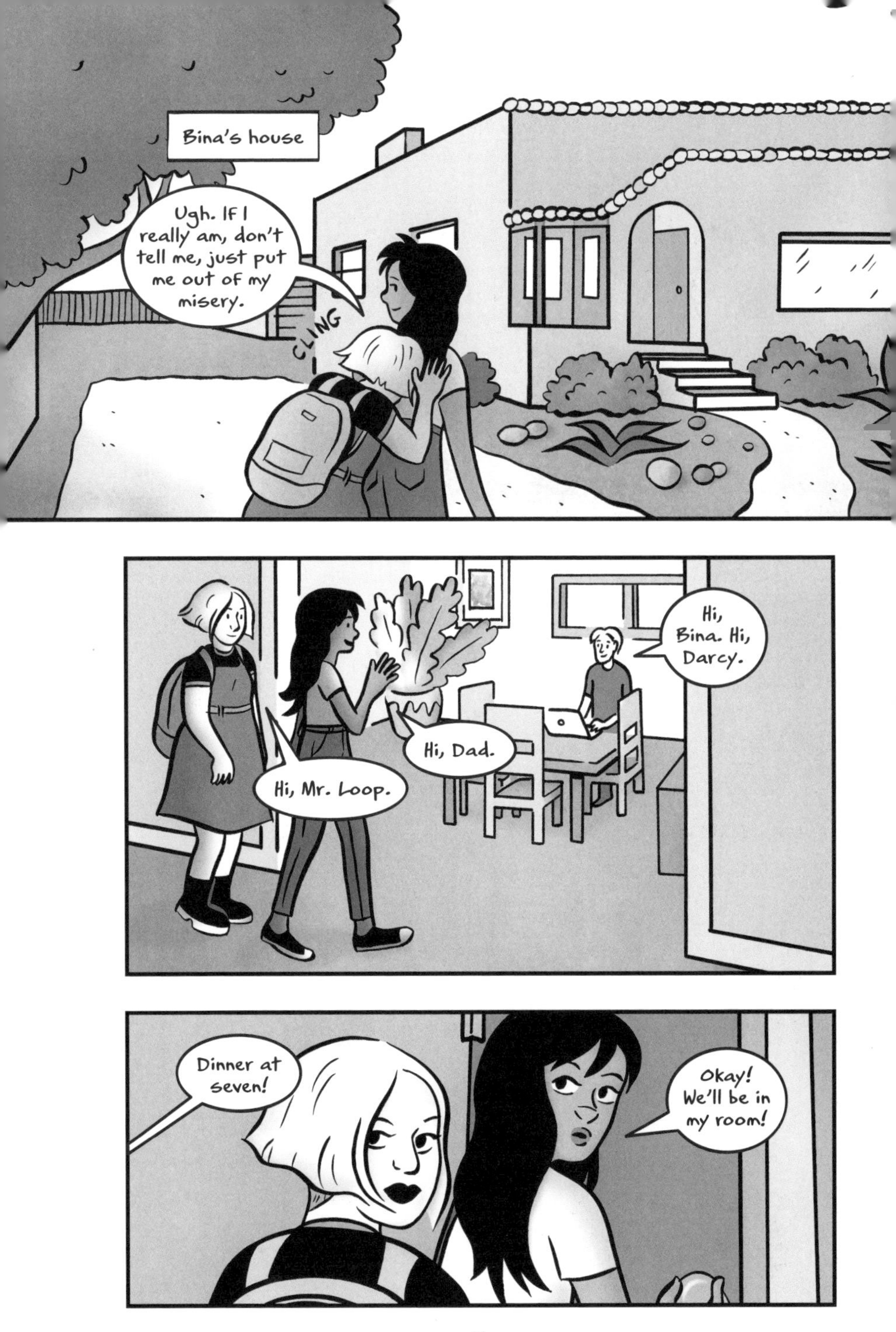
Bina's house
Ugh. If I really am, don't tell me, just put me out of my misery.
CLING
Hi, Bina. Hi, Darcy.
Hi, Dad.
Hi, Mr. Loop.
Dinner at seven!
Okay! We'll be in my room!

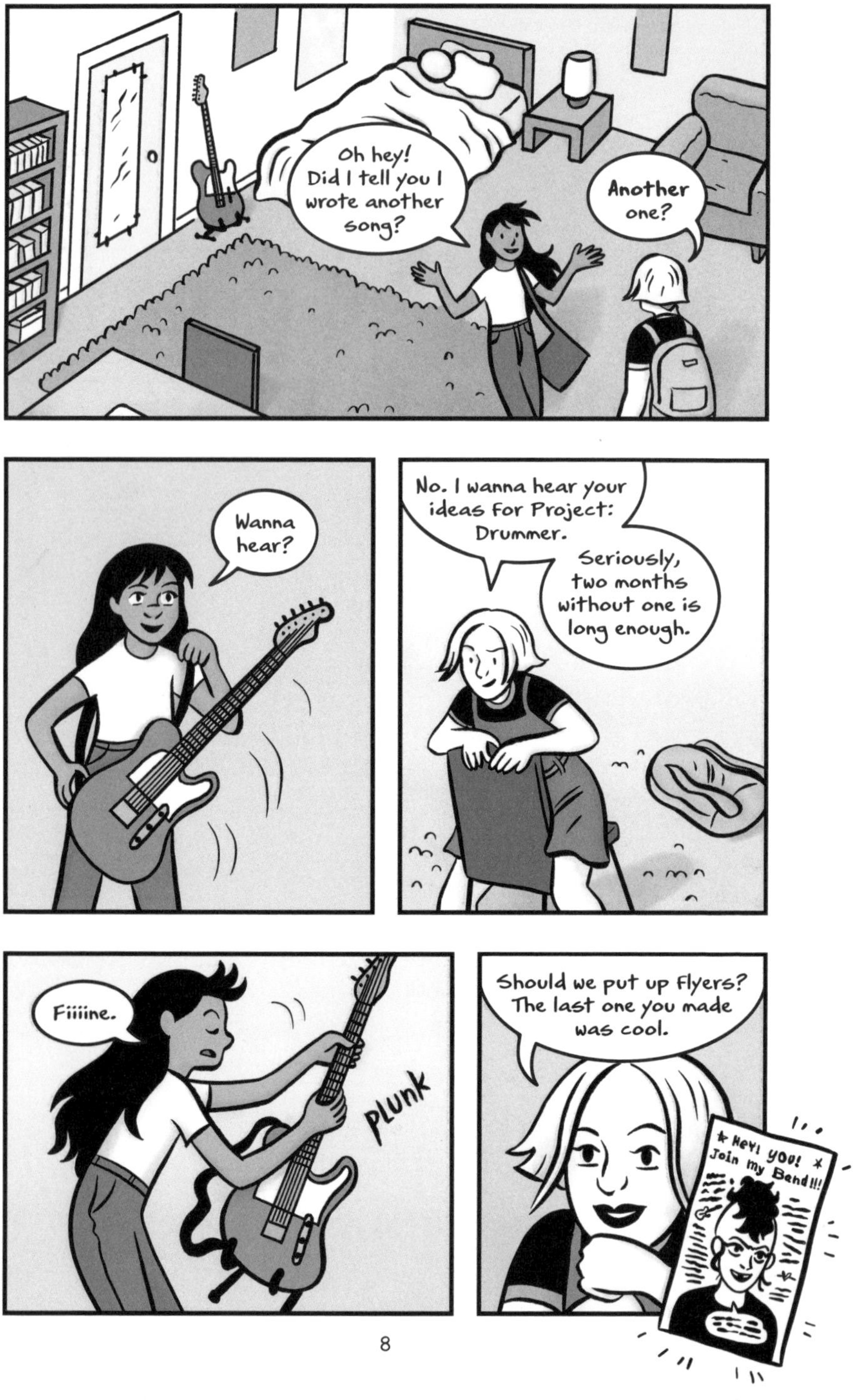
Oh hey! Did I tell you I wrote another song?
Another one?
Wanna hear?
No. I wanna hear your ideas for Project: Drummer.
Seriously, two months without one is long enough.
Fiiiine.
PLUNK
Should we put up flyers? The last one you made was cool.
HEY! YOU! Join my Band!!!

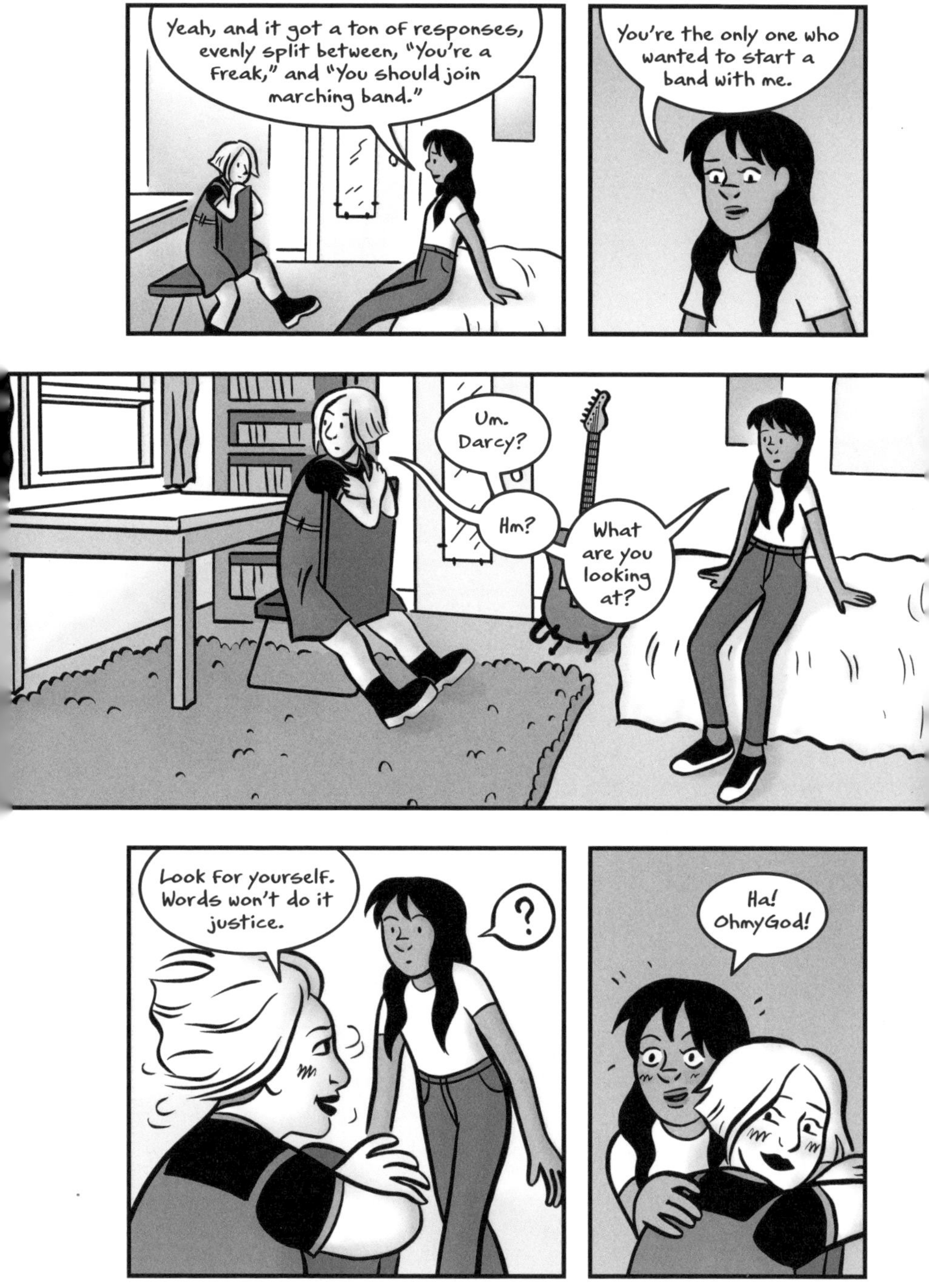
Yeah, and it got a ton of responses, evenly split between, "You're a freak," and "You should join marching band."
You're the only one who wanted to start a band with me.
Um. Darcy?
Hm?
What are you looking at?
Look for yourself. Words won't do it justice.
?
Ha! OhmyGod!

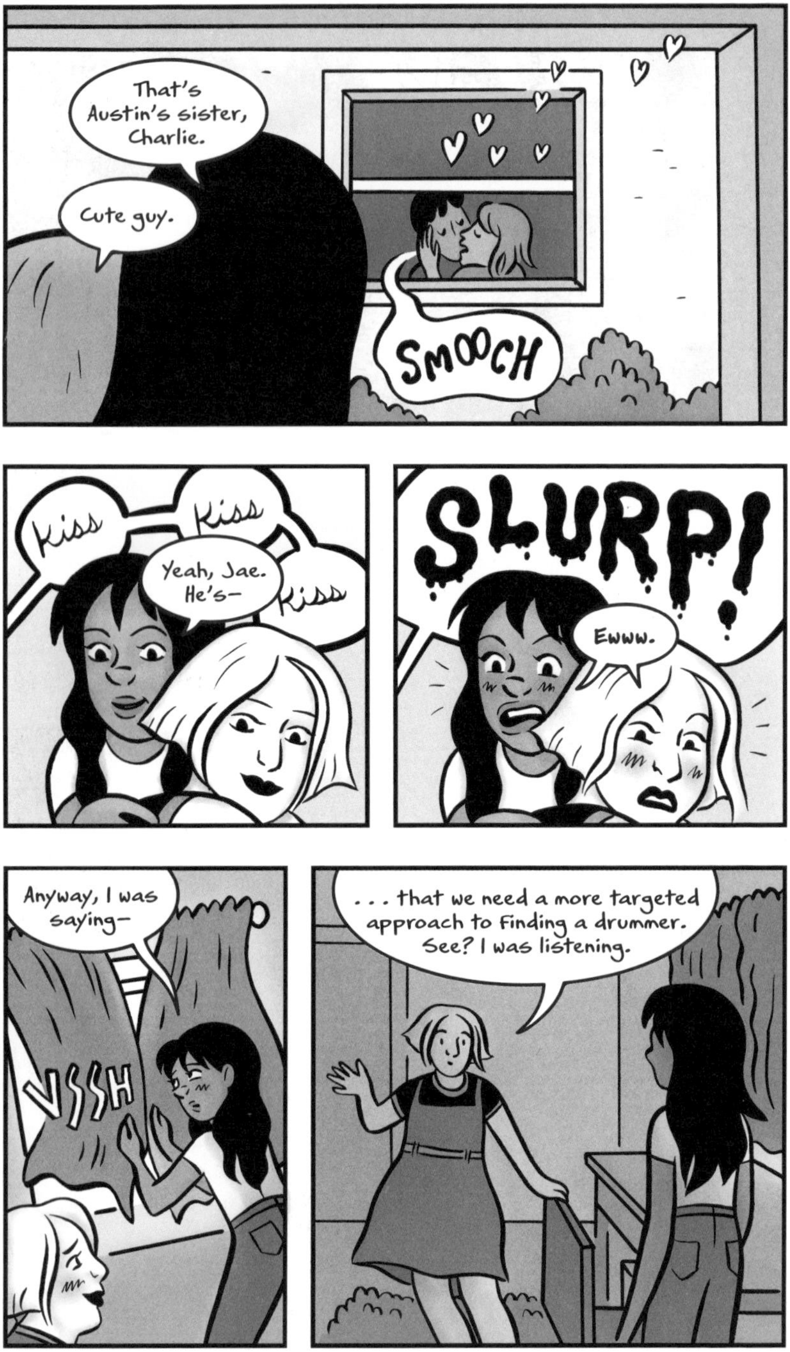
That's Austin's sister, Charlie.
Cute guy.
SMOOCH
kiss
kiss
Yeah, Jae. He's—
kiss
SLURP!
Ewww.
Anyway, I was saying—
VSSH
. . . that we need a more targeted approach to finding a drummer. See? I was listening.

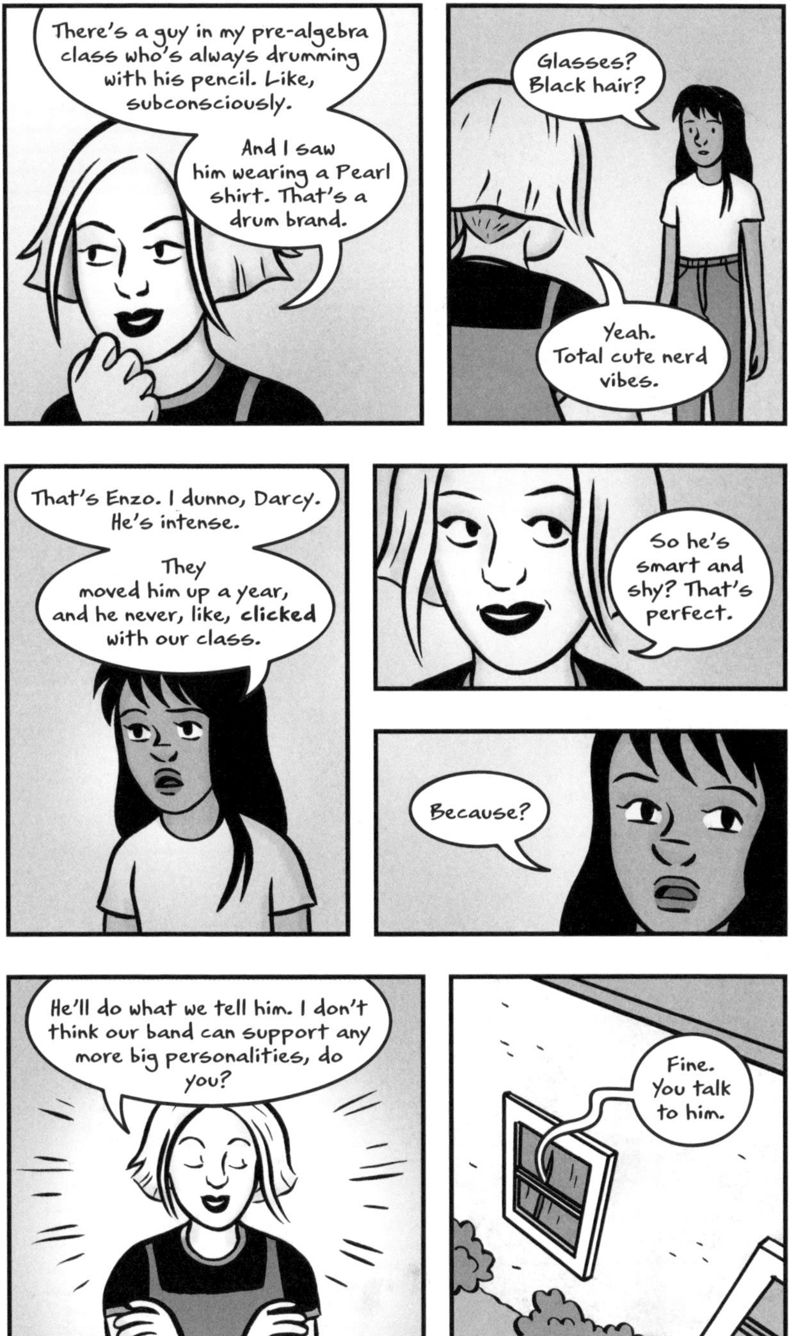
There's a guy in my pre-algebra class who's always drumming with his pencil. Like, subconsciously.
And I saw him wearing a Pearl shirt. That's a drum brand.
Glasses? Black hair?
Yeah. Total cute nerd vibes.
That's Enzo. I dunno, Darcy. He's intense.
They moved him up a year, and he never, like, clicked with our class.
So he's smart and shy? That's perfect.
Because?
He'll do what we tell him. I don't think our band can support any more big personalities, do you?
Fine. You talk to him.

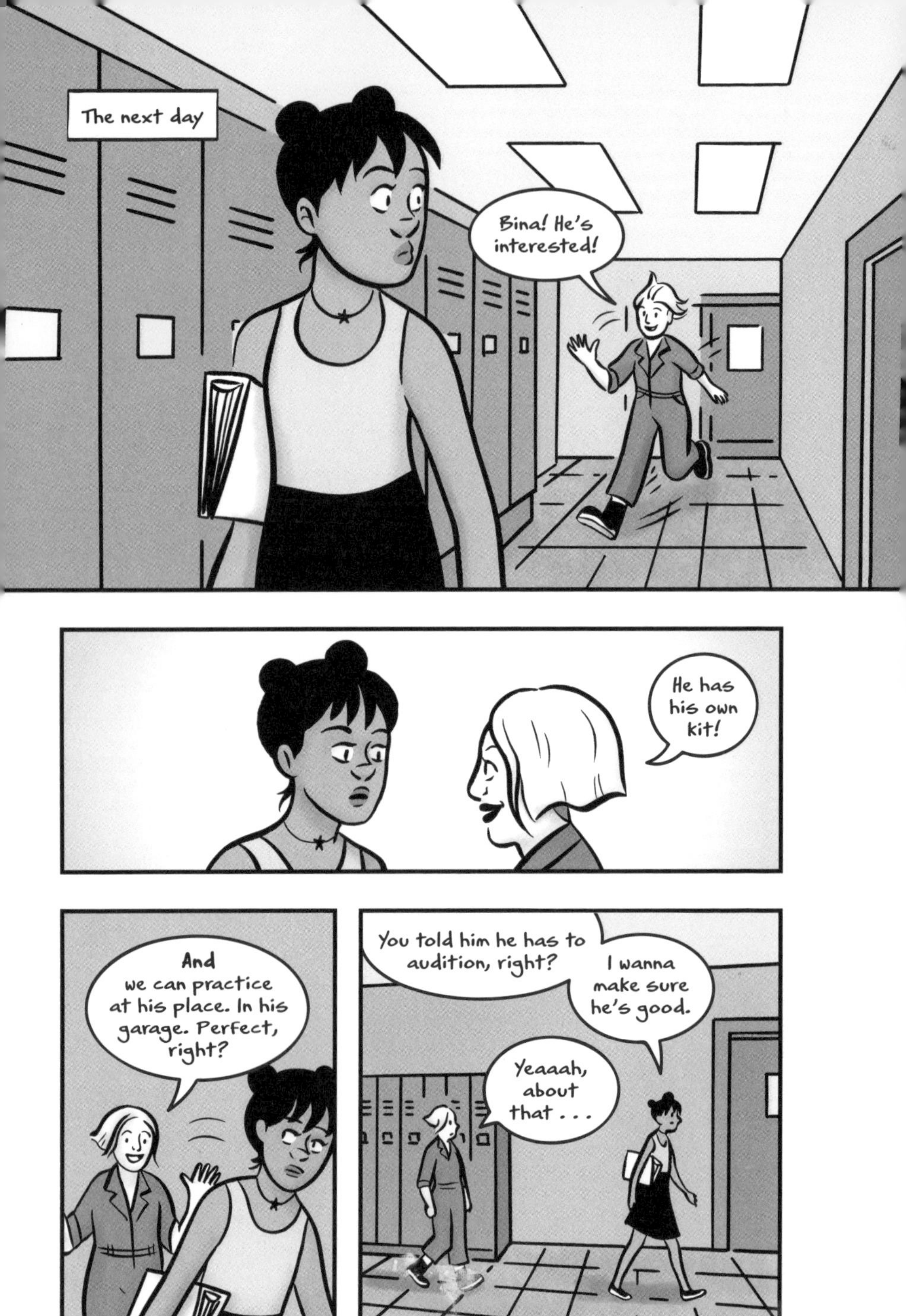
The next day
Bina! He's interested!
He has his own kit!
And we can practice at his place. In his garage. Perfect, right?
You told him he has to audition, right?
I wanna make sure he's good.
Yeaaah, about that . . .

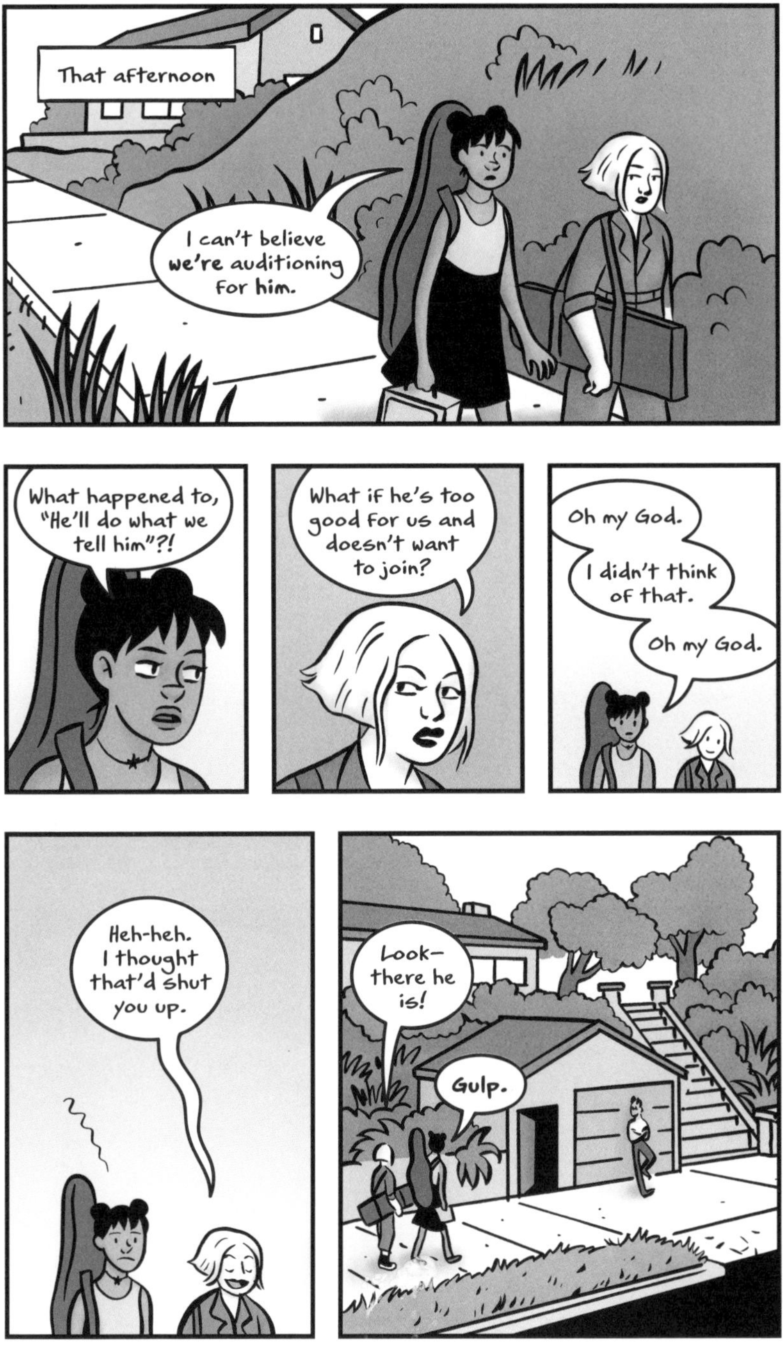
That afternoon
I can't believe we're auditioning for him.
What happened to, "He'll do what we tell him"?!
What if he's too good for us and doesn't want to join?
Oh my God.
I didn't think of that.
Oh my God.
Heh-heh. I thought that'd shut you up.
Look—there he is!
Gulp.

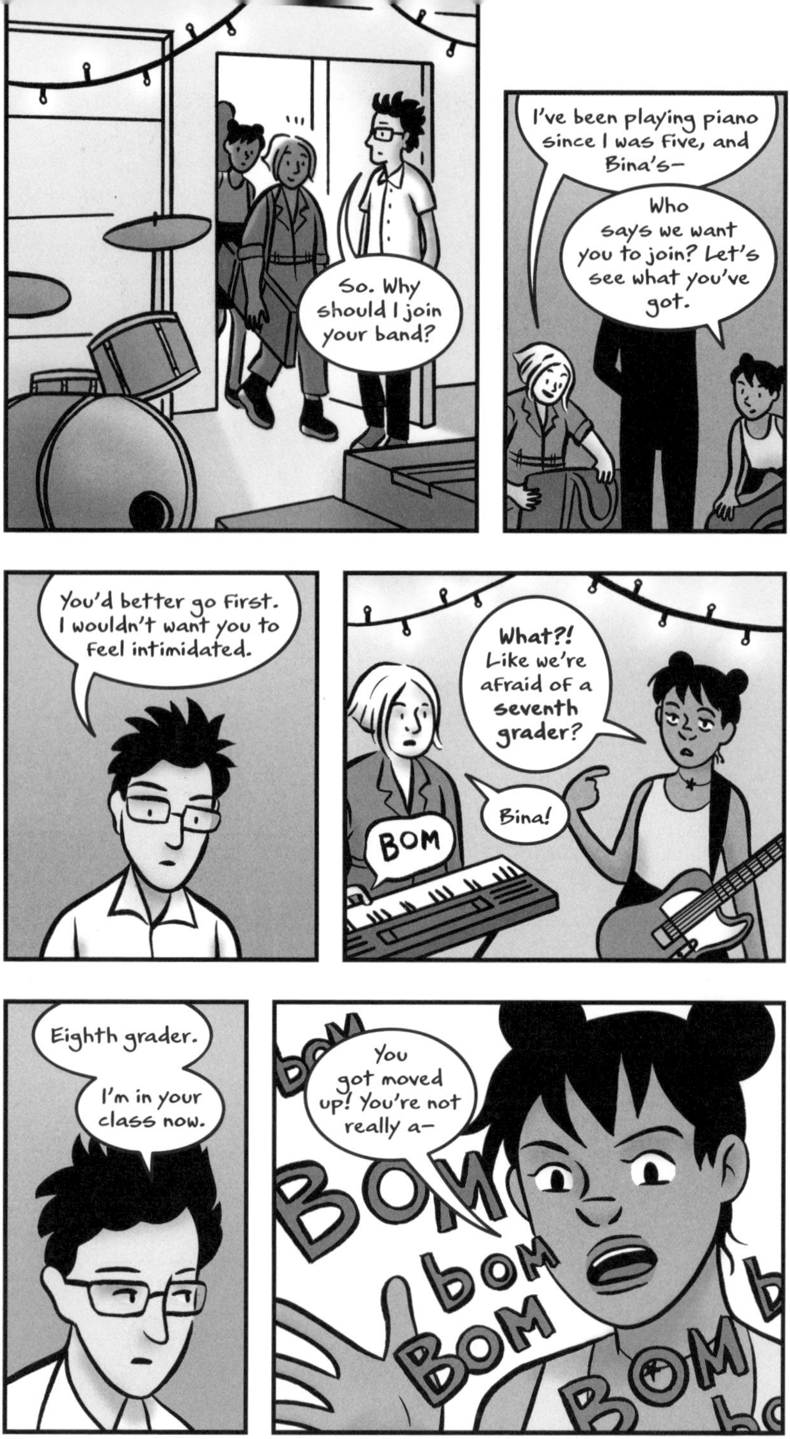

So. Why should I join your band?
I've been playing piano since I was five, and Bina's—
Who says we want you to join? Let's see what you've got.
You'd better go first. I wouldn't want you to feel intimidated.
What?! Like we're afraid of a seventh grader?
Bina!
BOM
Eighth grader.
I'm in your class now.
You got moved up! You're not really a—
BOM
bom
BOM
BOM

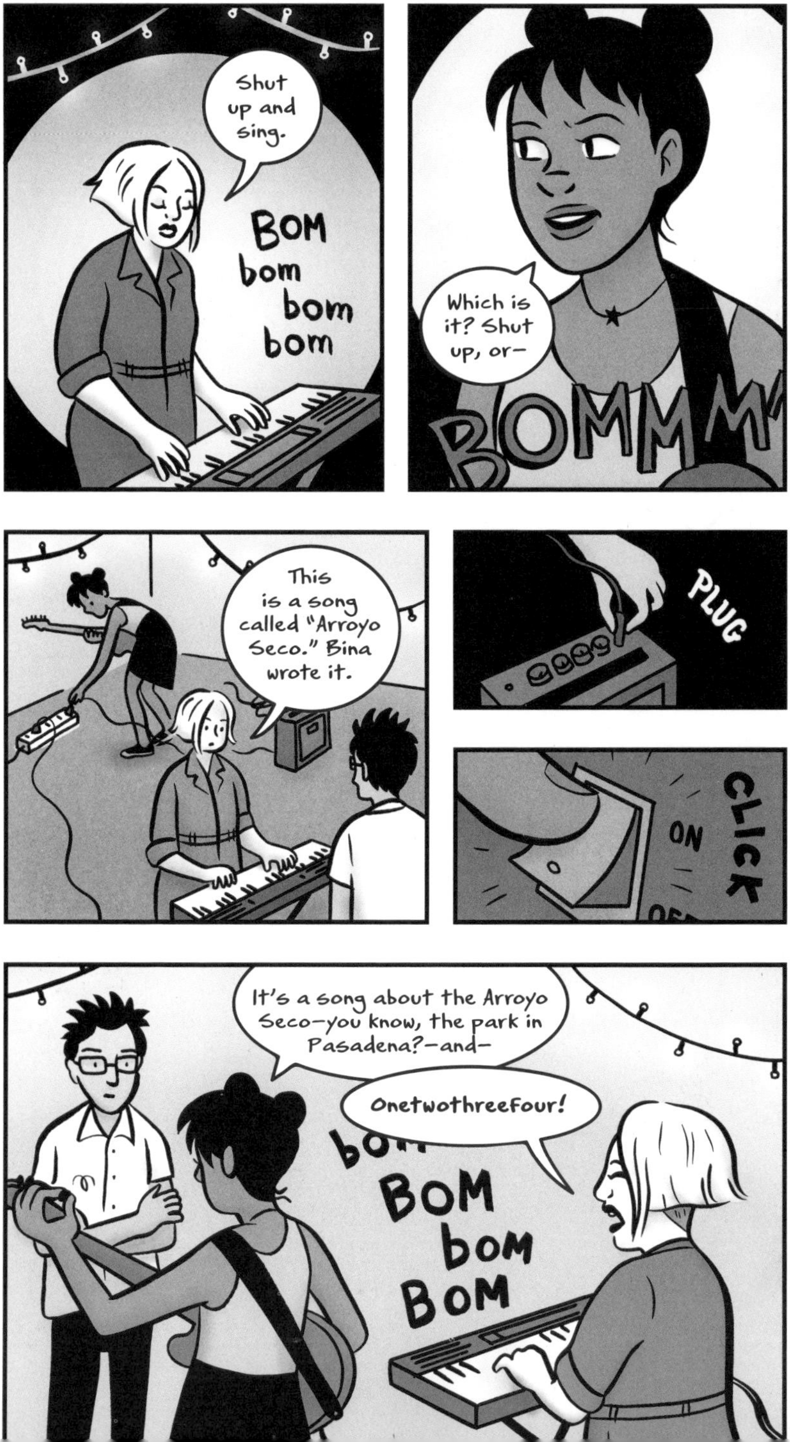
Shut up and sing.
BOM bom bom bom
Which is it? Shut up, or—
BOMMM
This is a song called "Arroyo Seco." Bina wrote it.
PLUG
ON
CLICK
It's a song about the Arroyo Seco—you know, the park in Pasadena?—and—
Onetwothreefour!
BOM bom BOM

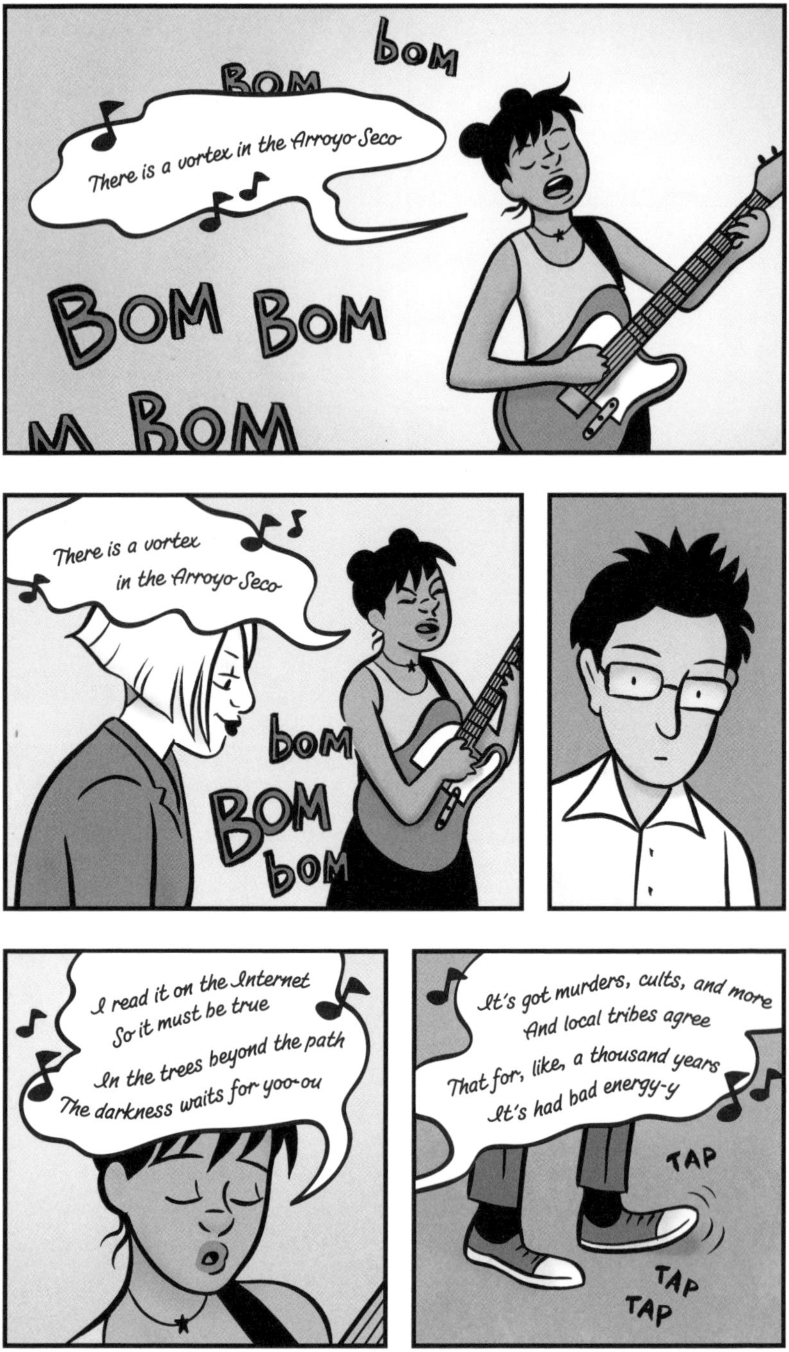
bom
BOM
There is a vortex in the Arroyo Seco
BOM BOM
m BOM
There is a vortex in the Arroyo Seco
bom
BOM
bom
I read it on the Internet So it must be true In the trees beyond the path The darkness waits for yoo-ou
It's got murders, cults, and more And local tribes agree That for, like, a thousand years It's had bad energy-y
TAP
TAP
TAP

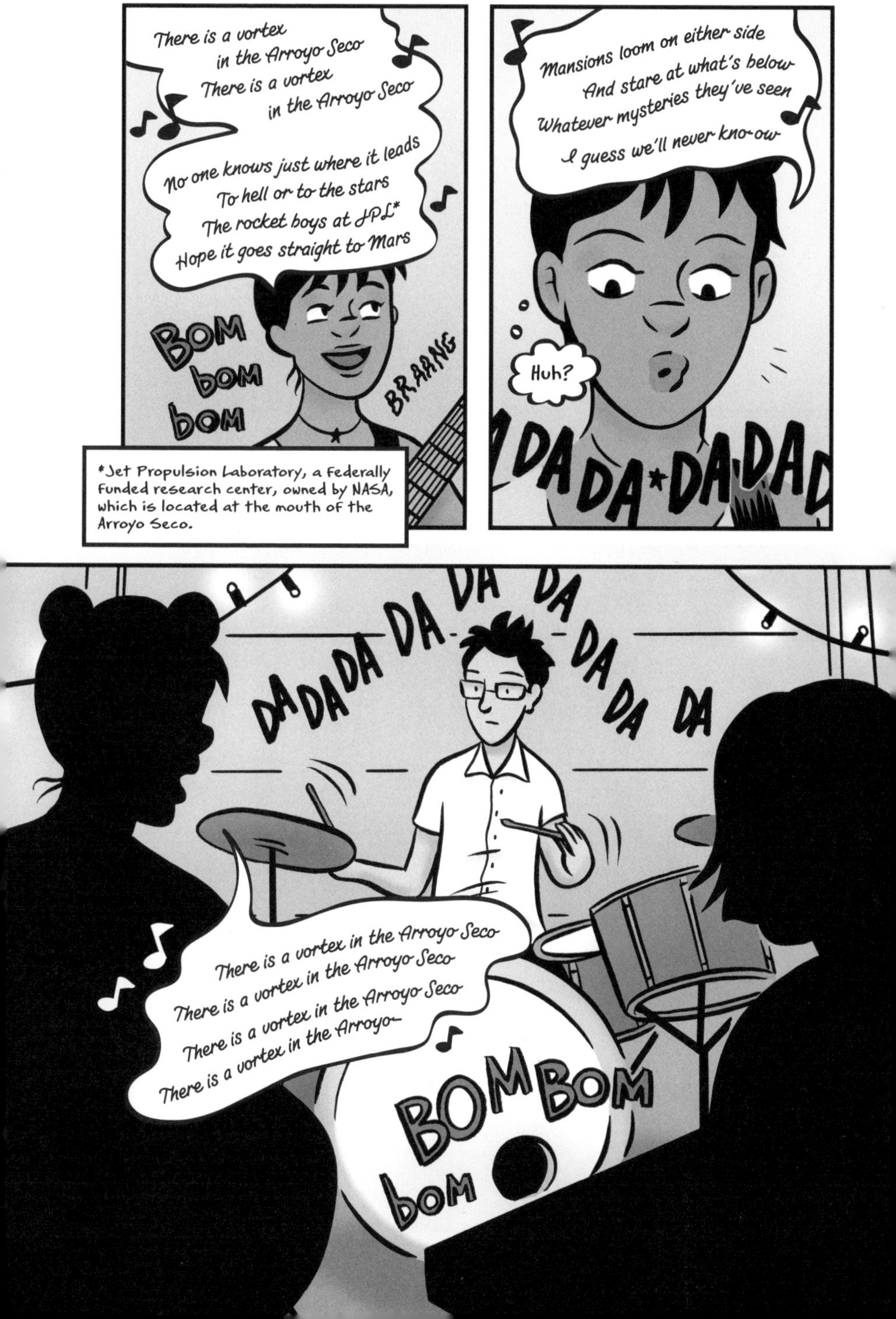
There is a vortex in the Arroyo Seco There is a vortex in the Arroyo Seco
No one knows just where it leads To hell or to the stars The rocket boys at JPL* Hope it goes straight to Mars
BOM bom bom
BRAANG
*Jet Propulsion Laboratory, a federally funded research center, owned by NASA, which is located at the mouth of the Arroyo Seco.
Mansions loom on either side And stare at what's below Whatever mysteries they've seen I guess we'll never kno-ow
Huh?
DA DA DA DA D
DA DA DA DA DA DA DA DA DA DA
There is a vortex in the Arroyo Seco There is a vortex in the Arroyo Seco There is a vortex in the Arroyo Seco There is a vortex in the Arroyo–
BOM BOM bom

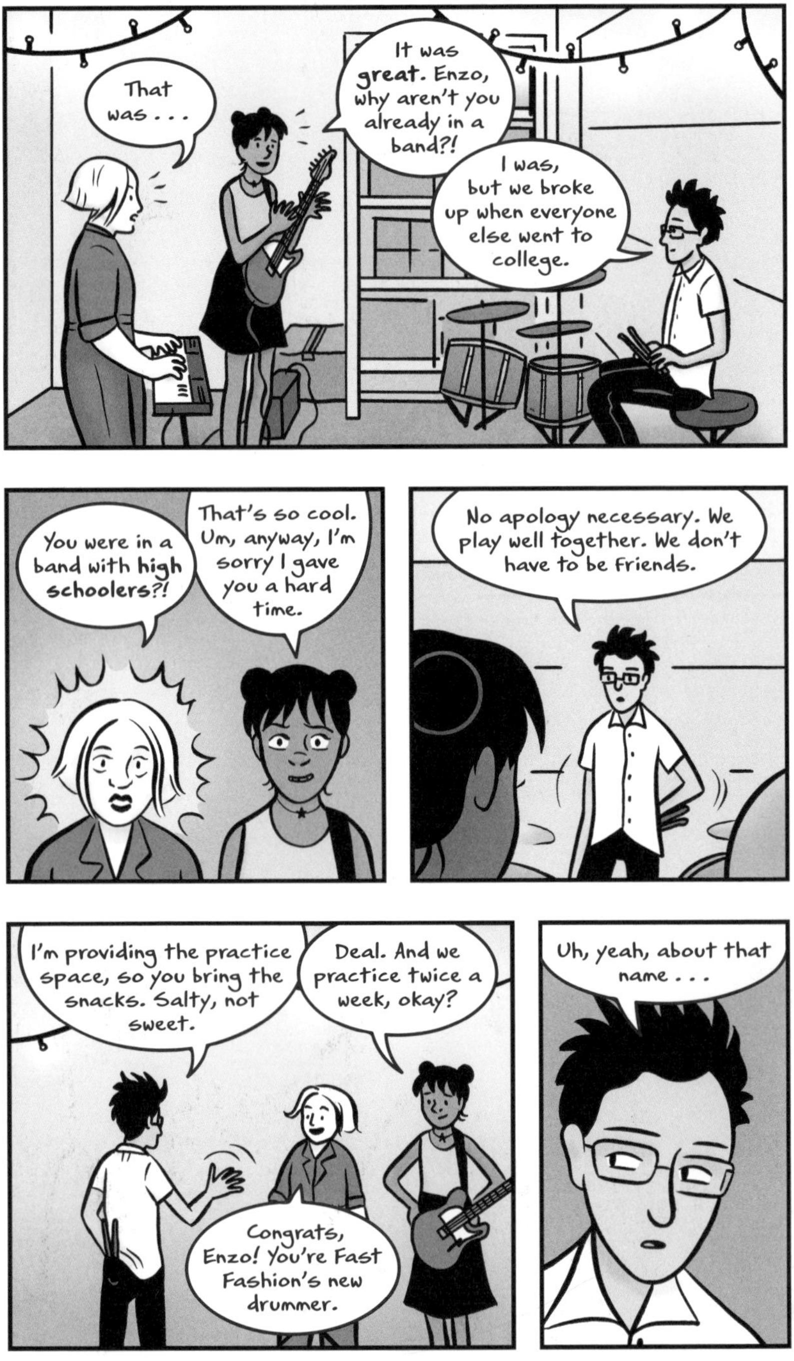
That was . . .
It was great. Enzo, why aren't you already in a band?!
I was, but we broke up when everyone else went to college.
You were in a band with high schoolers?!
That's so cool. Um, anyway, I'm sorry I gave you a hard time.
No apology necessary. We play well together. We don't have to be friends.
I'm providing the practice space, so you bring the snacks. Salty, not sweet.
Deal. And we practice twice a week, okay?
Congrats, Enzo! You're Fast Fashion's new drummer.
Uh, yeah, about that name . . .

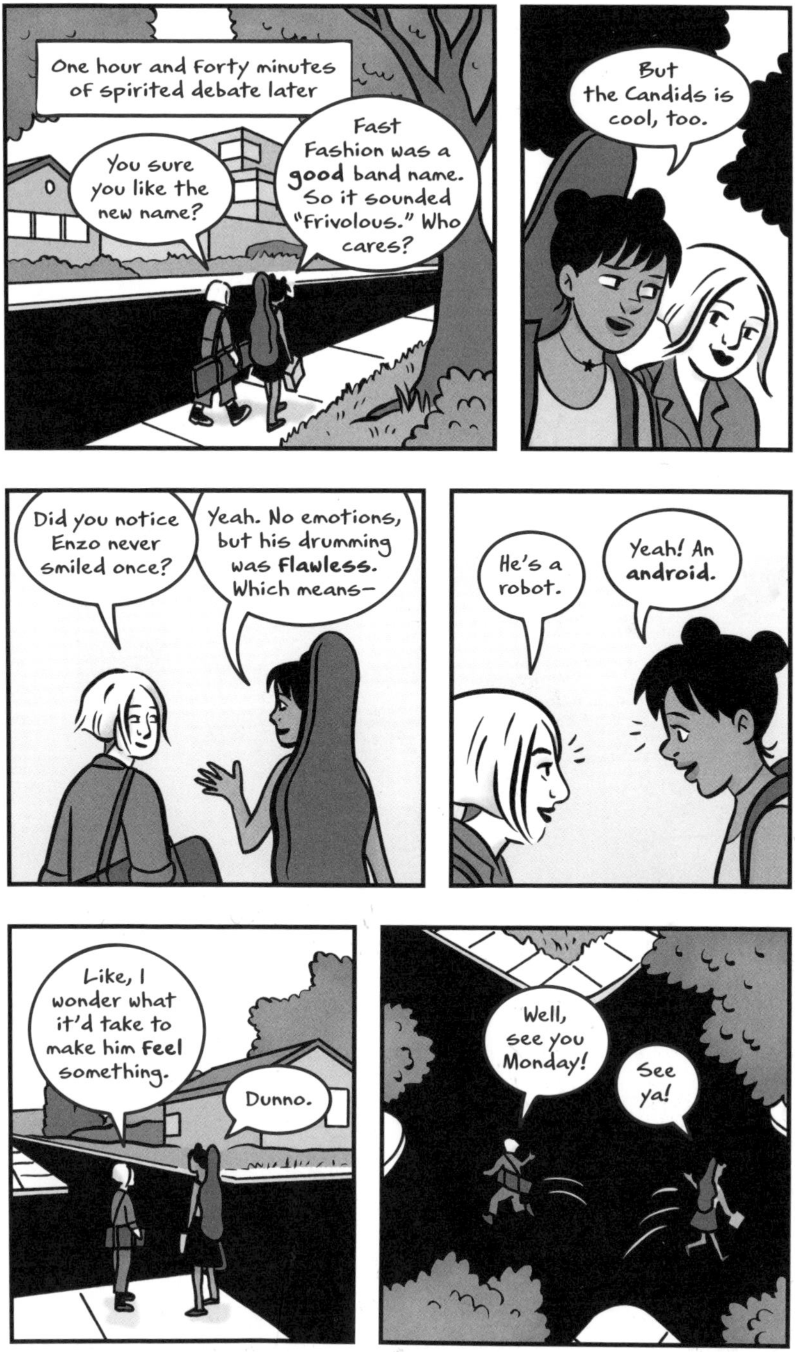
One hour and forty minutes of spirited debate later
You sure you like the new name?
Fast Fashion was a good band name. So it sounded "frivolous." Who cares?
But the Candids is cool, too.
Did you notice Enzo never smiled once?
Yeah. No emotions, but his drumming was flawless. Which means—
He's a robot.
Yeah! An android.
Like, I wonder what it'd take to make him feel something.
Dunno.
Well, see you Monday!
See ya!

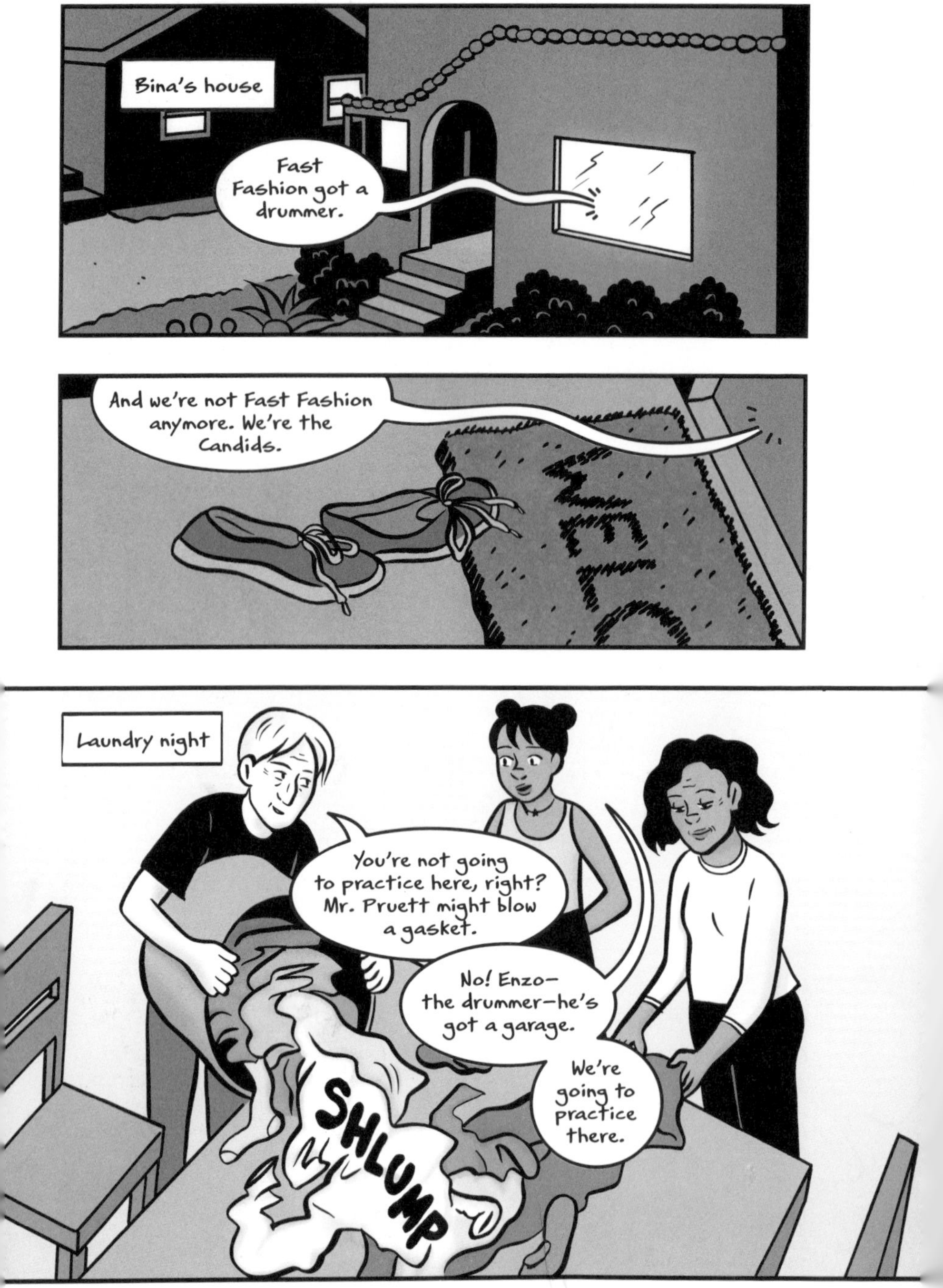
Bina's house
Fast Fashion got a drummer.
And we're not Fast Fashion anymore. We're the Candids.
Laundry night
You're not going to practice here, right? Mr. Pruett might blow a gasket.
No! Enzo—the drummer—he's got a garage.
We're going to practice there.
SHLUMP

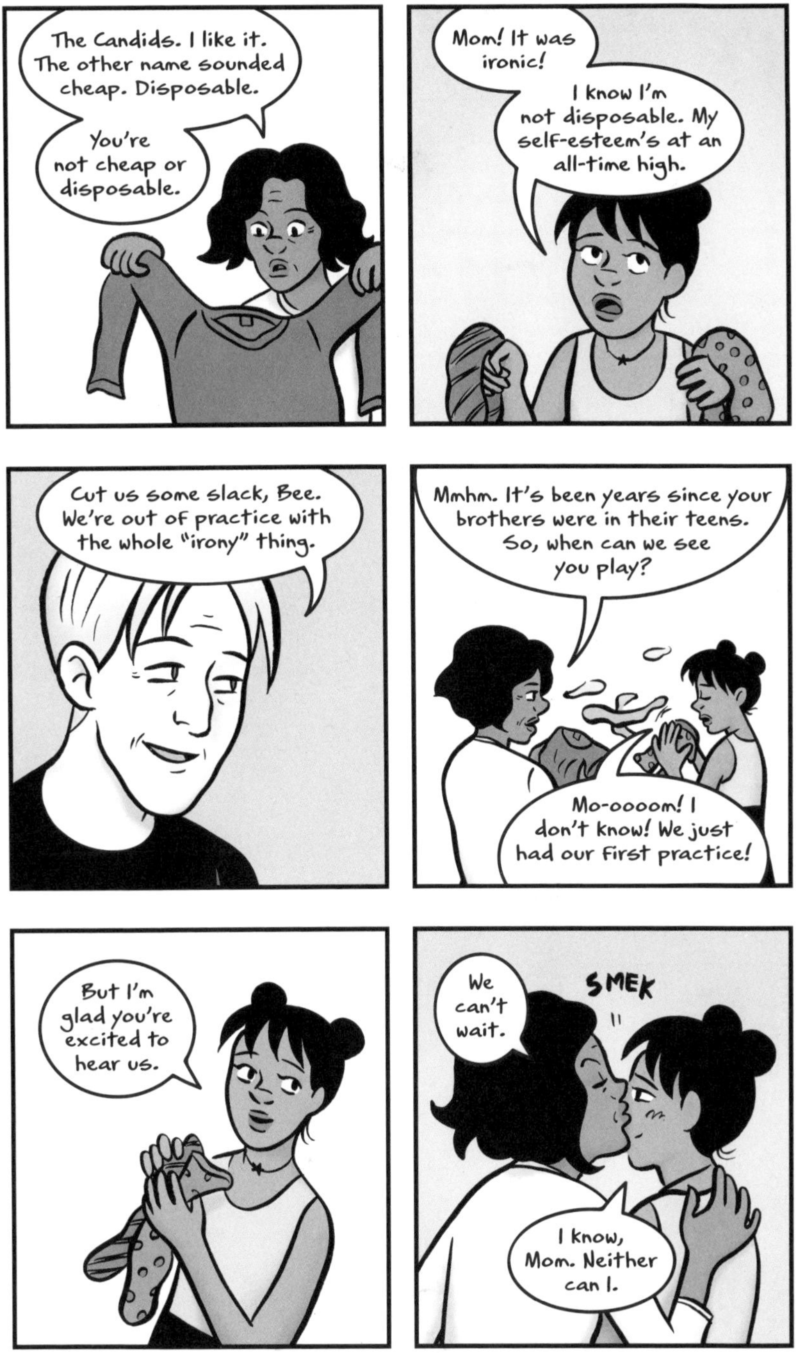
The Candids. I like it. The other name sounded cheap. Disposable.
You're not cheap or disposable.
Mom! It was ironic!
I know I'm not disposable. My self-esteem's at an all-time high.
Cut us some slack, Bee. We're out of practice with the whole "irony" thing.
Mmhm. It's been years since your brothers were in their teens. So, when can we see you play?
Mo-oooom! I don't know! We just had our first practice!
But I'm glad you're excited to hear us.
We can't wait.
SMEK
I know, Mom. Neither can I.

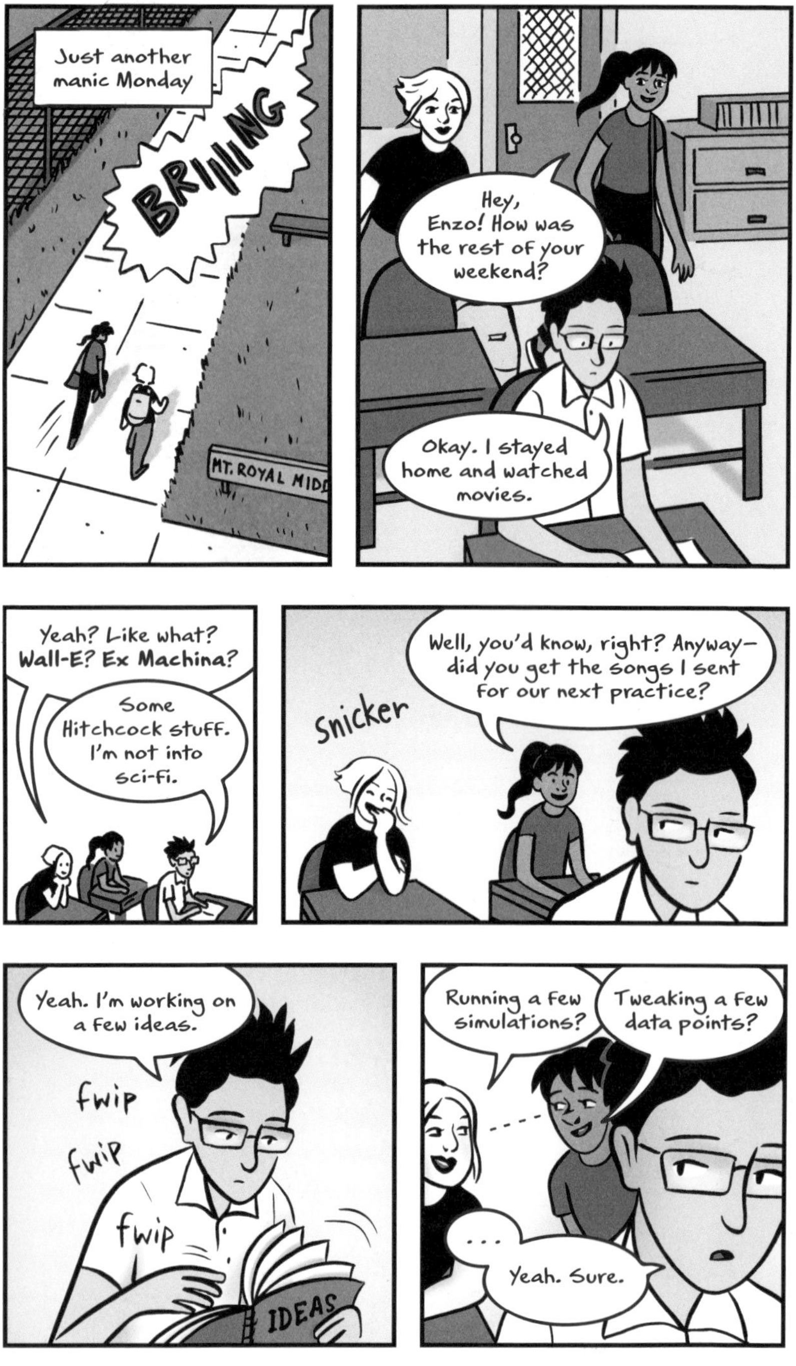
Just another manic Monday
BRIIIING
MT. ROYAL MIDD
Hey, Enzo! How was the rest of your weekend?
Okay. I stayed home and watched movies.
Yeah? Like what? Wall-E? Ex Machina?
Some Hitchcock stuff. I'm not into sci-fi.
Snicker
Well, you'd know, right? Anyway—did you get the songs I sent for our next practice?
Yeah. I'm working on a few ideas.
fwip
fwip
fwip
IDEAS
Running a few simulations?
Tweaking a few data points?
...
Yeah. Sure.

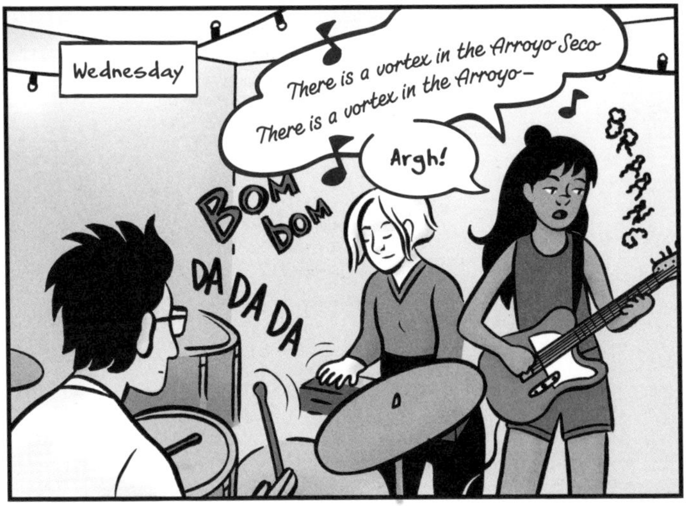
Wednesday
There is a vortex in the Arroyo Seco
There is a vortex in the Arroyo–
Argh!
BOM bom
DA DA DA
BRANNG

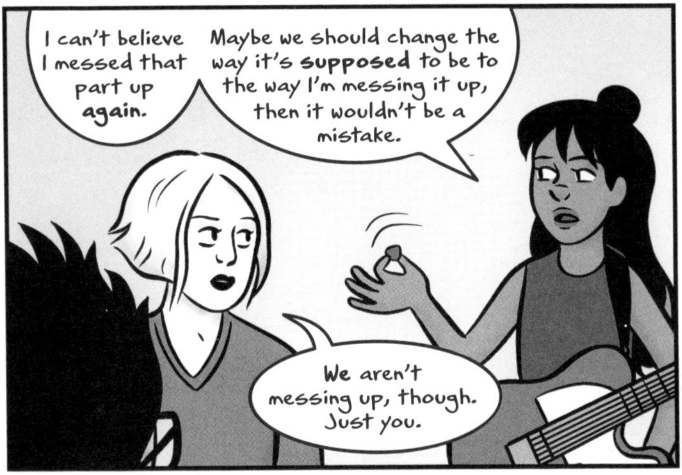
I can't believe I messed that part up again.
Maybe we should change the way it's supposed to be to the way I'm messing it up, then it wouldn't be a mistake.
We aren't messing up, though. Just you.

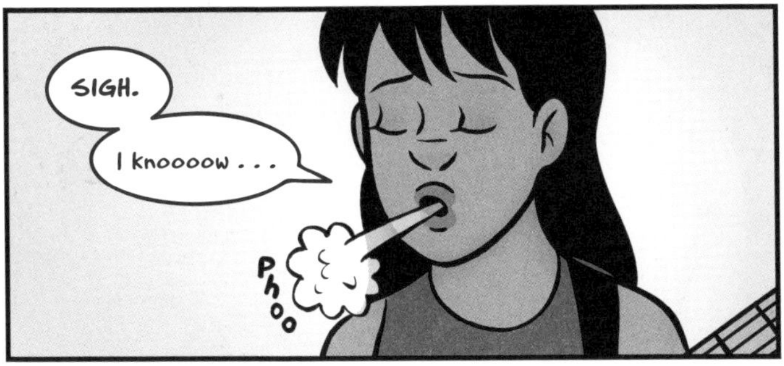
SIGH.
I knooooow . . .
Phoo

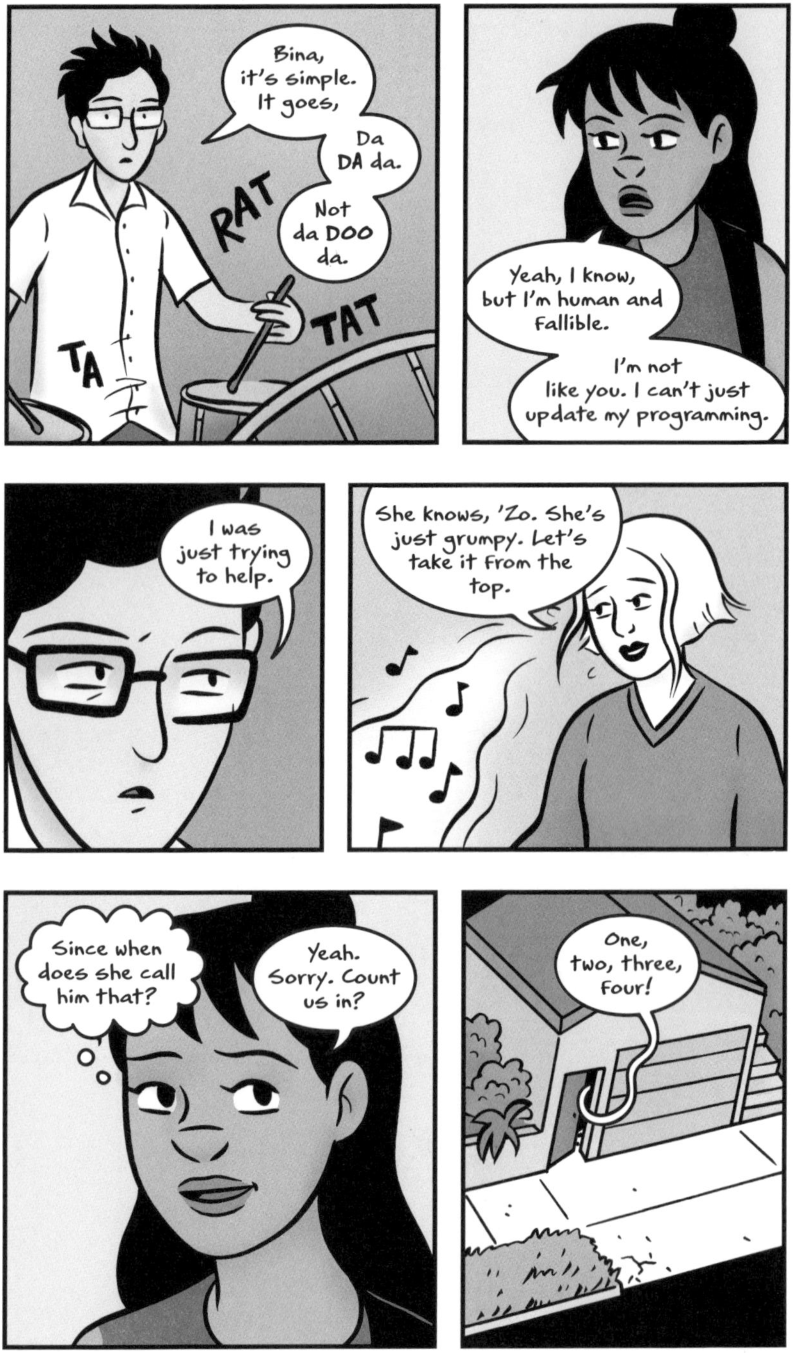
Bina, it's simple. It goes,
Da DA da.
Not da DOO da.
RAT
TAT
TA
Yeah, I know, but I'm human and fallible.
I'm not like you. I can't just update my programming.
I was just trying to help.
She knows, 'Zo. She's just grumpy. Let's take it from the top.
Since when does she call him that?
Yeah. Sorry. Count us in?
One, two, three, four!

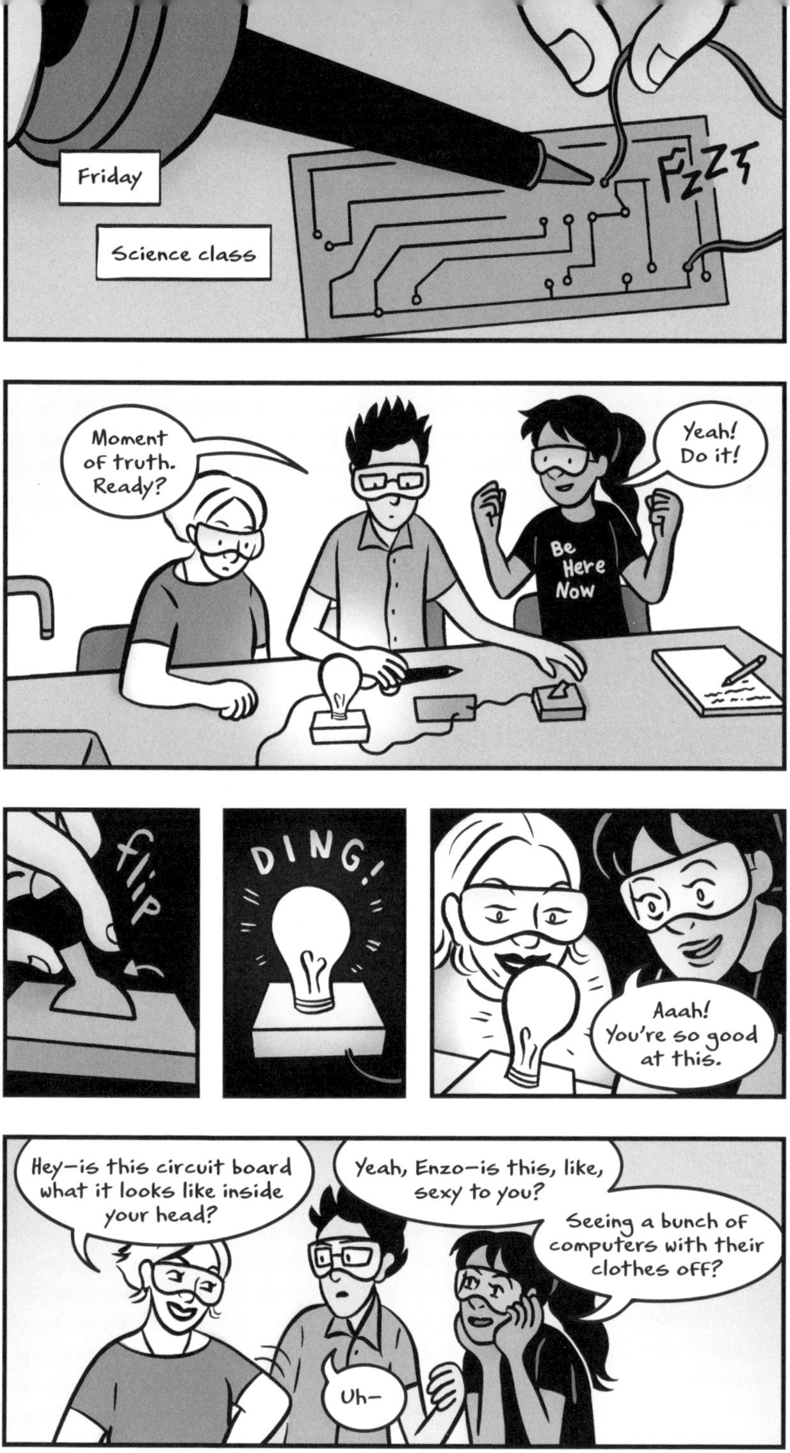
Friday
Science class
FZZZ
Moment of truth. Ready?
Yeah! Do it!
Be Here Now
flip
DING!
Aaah! You're so good at this.
Hey—is this circuit board what it looks like inside your head?
Yeah, Enzo—is this, like, sexy to you?
Seeing a bunch of computers with their clothes off?
Uh—

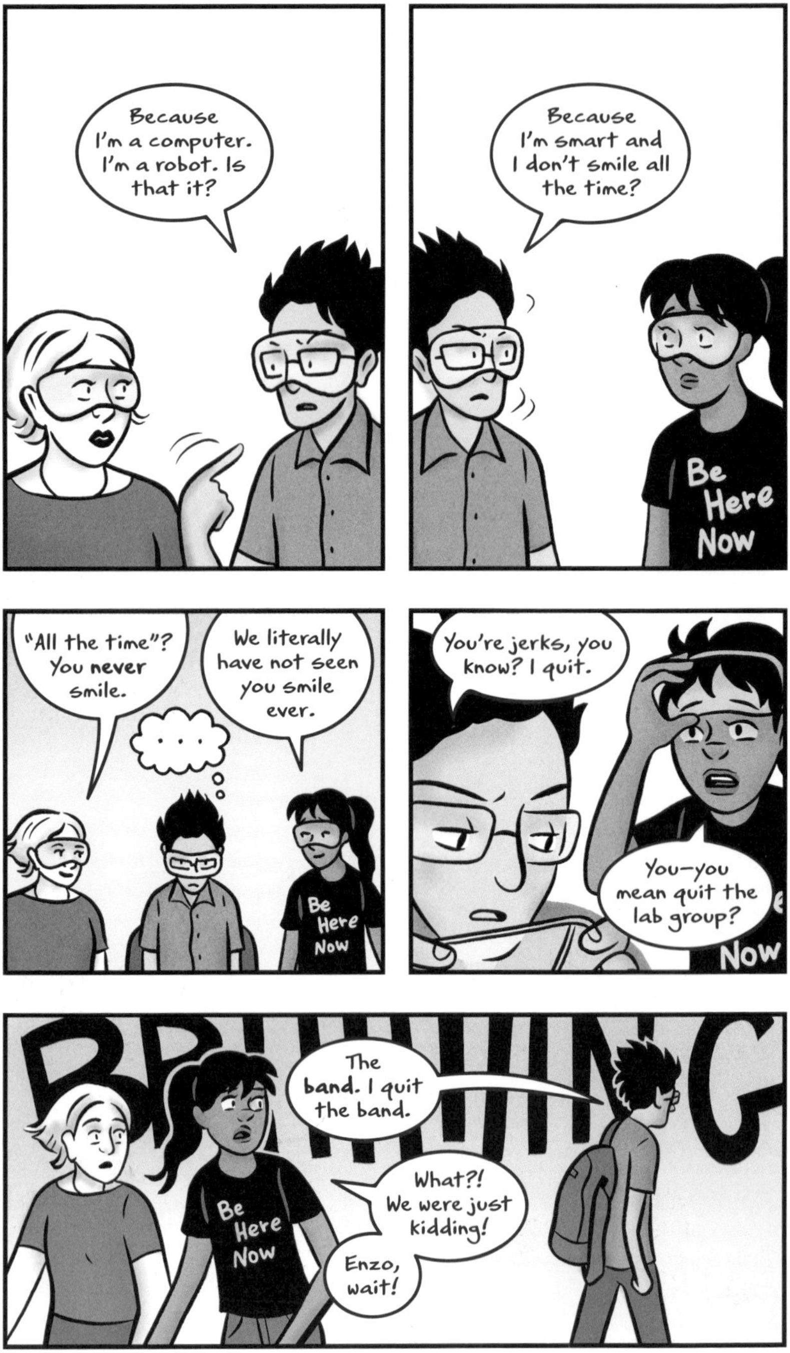
Because I'm a computer. I'm a robot. Is that it?
Because I'm smart and I don't smile all the time?
Be Here Now
"All the time"? You never smile.
We literally have not seen you smile ever.
. . .
Be Here Now
You're jerks, you know? I quit.
You—you mean quit the lab group?
BRIIIING
The band. I quit the band.
What?! We were just kidding!
Enzo, wait!
Be Here Now

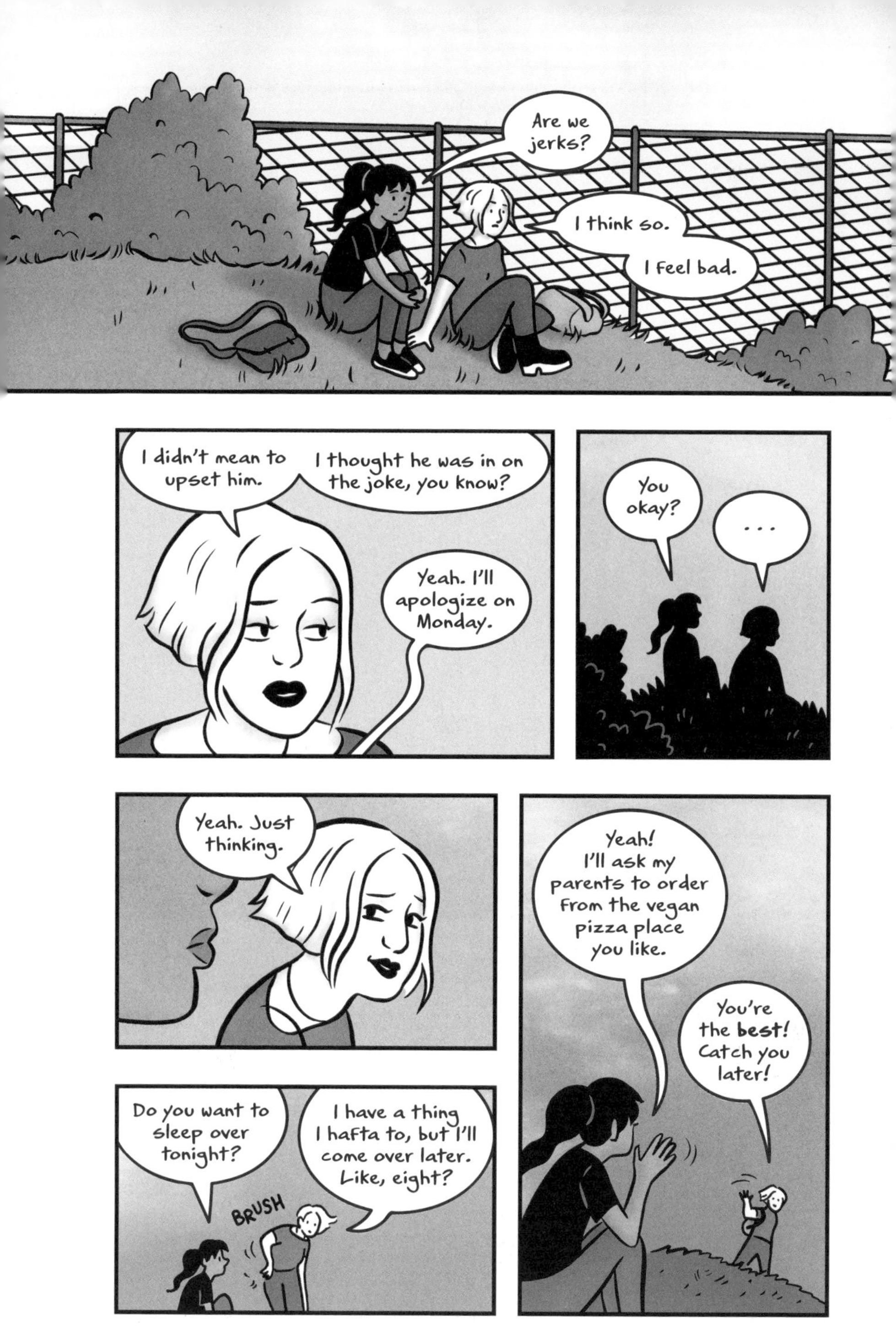
Are we jerks?
I think so.
I feel bad.
I didn't mean to upset him.
I thought he was in on the joke, you know?
Yeah. I'll apologize on Monday.
You okay?
. . .
Yeah. Just thinking.
Do you want to sleep over tonight?
BRUSH
I have a thing I hafta to, but I'll come over later. Like, eight?
Yeah! I'll ask my parents to order from the vegan pizza place you like.
You're the **best**! Catch you later!

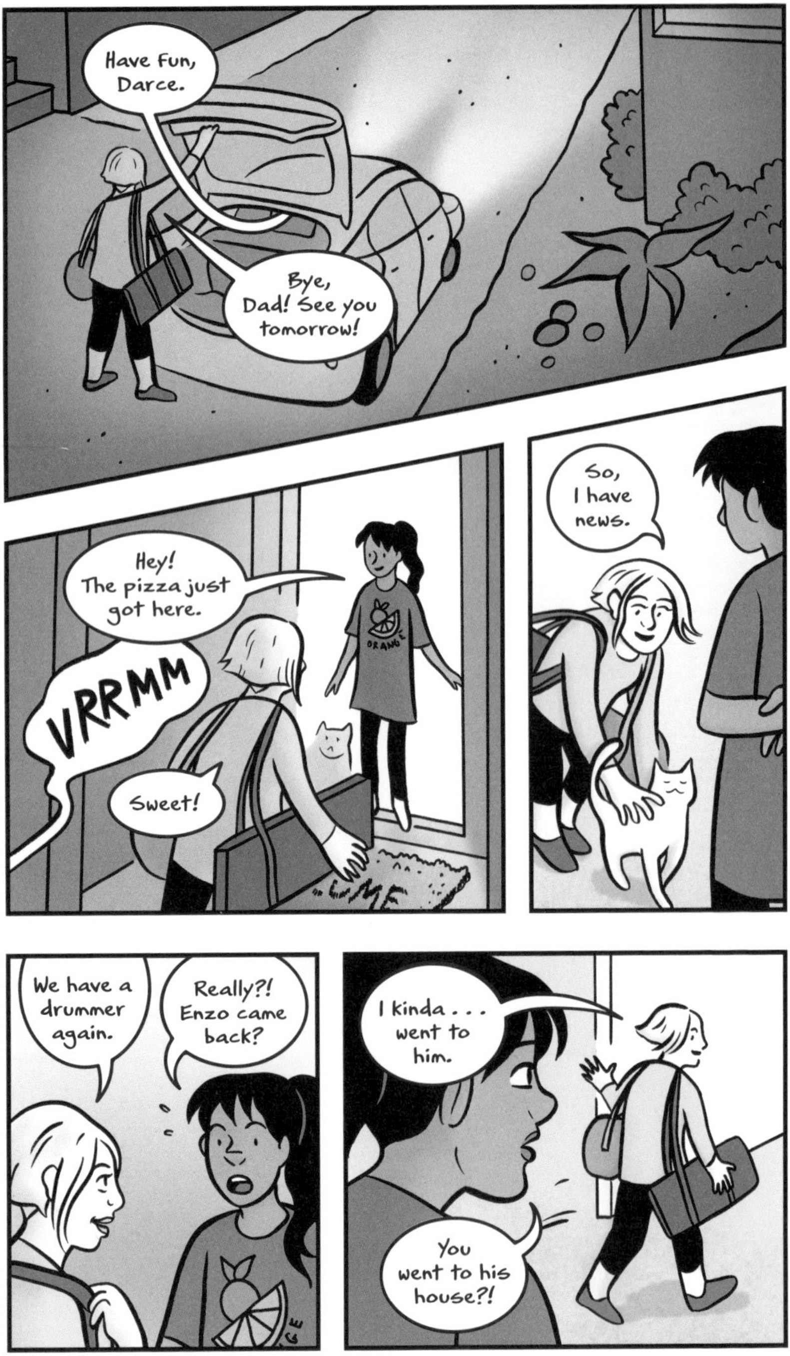
Have fun, Darce.
Bye, Dad! See you tomorrow!
Hey! The pizza just got here.
VRRMM
Sweet!
ORANGE
So, I have news.
We have a drummer again.
Really?! Enzo came back?
I kinda . . . went to him.
You went to his house?!

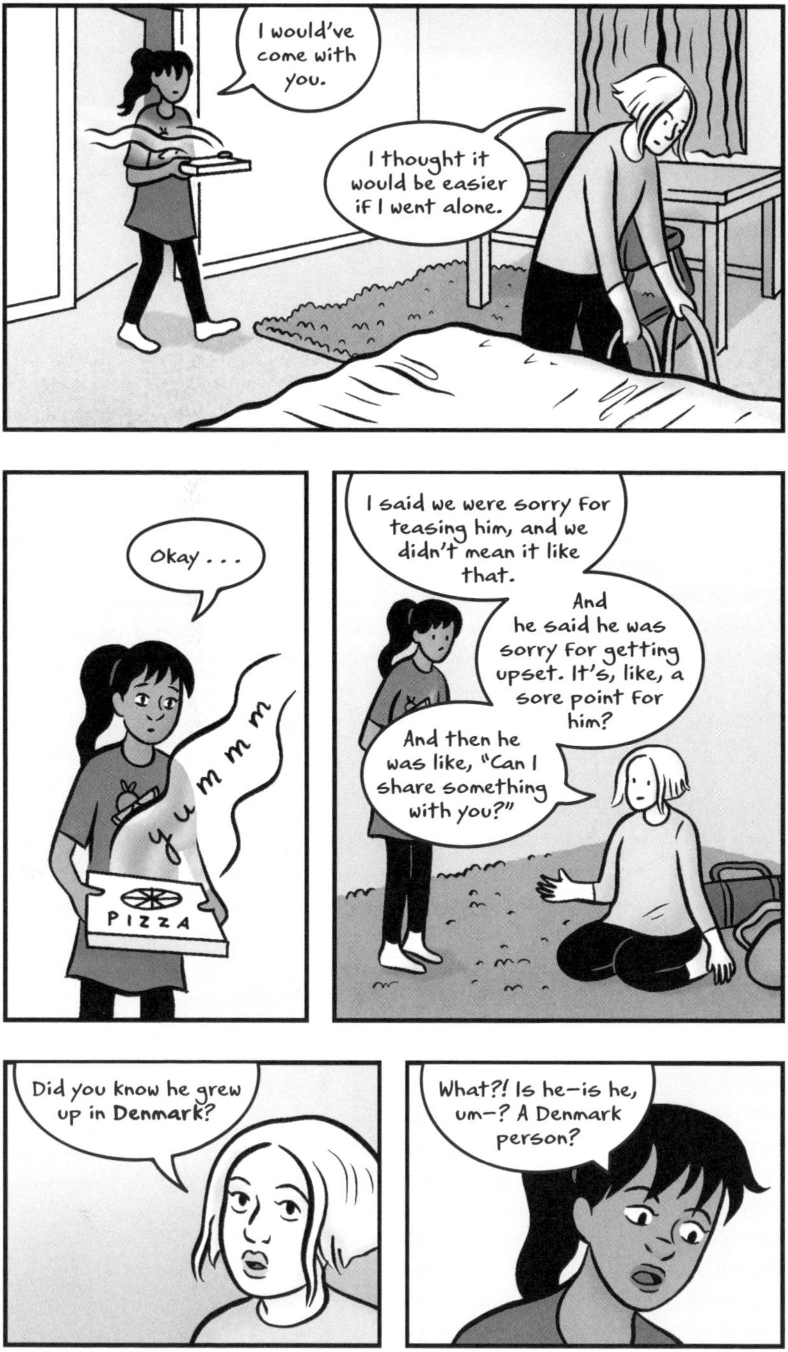
I would've come with you.
I thought it would be easier if I went alone.
Okay . . .
yummm
PIZZA
I said we were sorry for teasing him, and we didn't mean it like that.
And he said he was sorry for getting upset. It's, like, a sore point for him?
And then he was like, "Can I share something with you?"
Did you know he grew up in Denmark?
What?! Is he—is he, um—? A Denmark person?

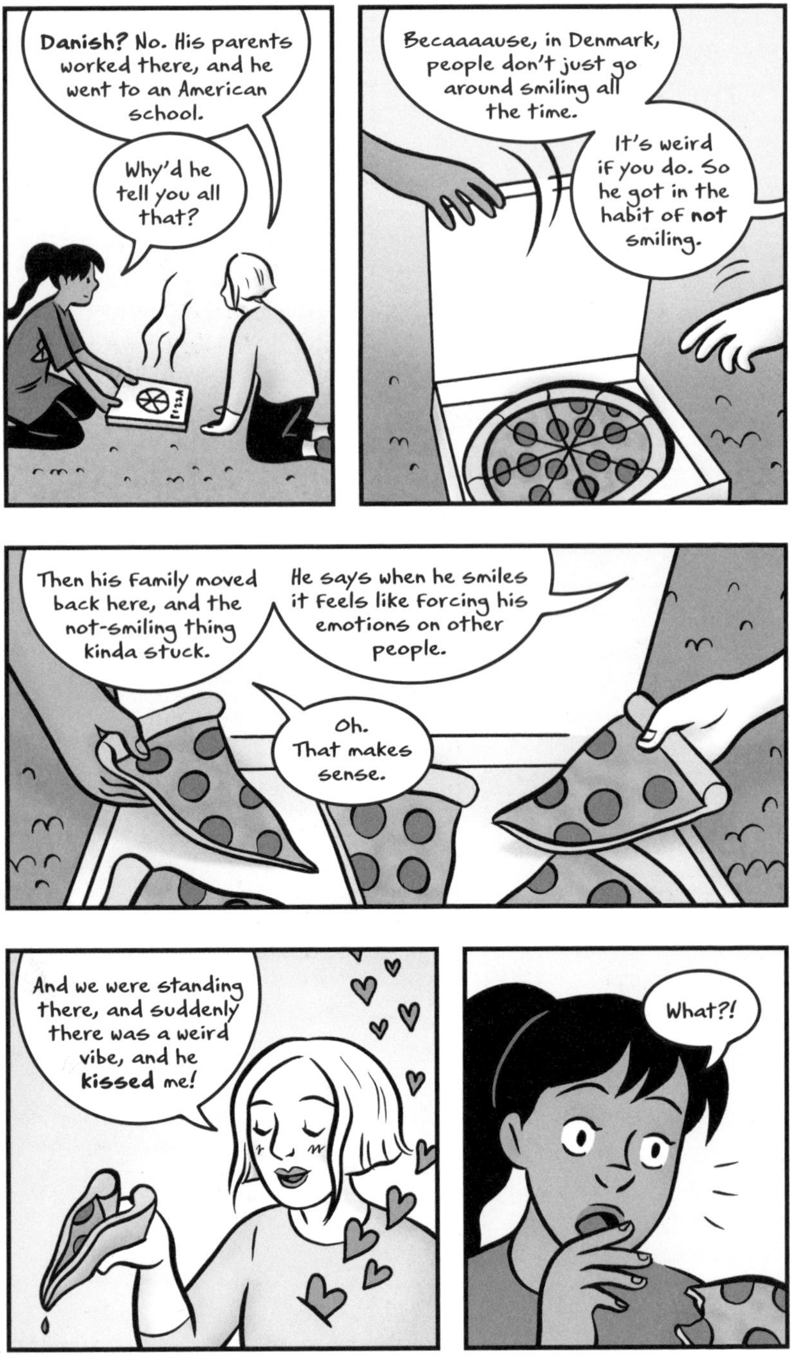
Danish? No. His parents worked there, and he went to an American school.
Why'd he tell you all that?
Becaaaause, in Denmark, people don't just go around smiling all the time.
It's weird if you do. So he got in the habit of not smiling.
PIZZA
Then his family moved back here, and the not-smiling thing kinda stuck.
He says when he smiles it feels like forcing his emotions on other people.
Oh. That makes sense.
And we were standing there, and suddenly there was a weird vibe, and he kissed me!
What?!

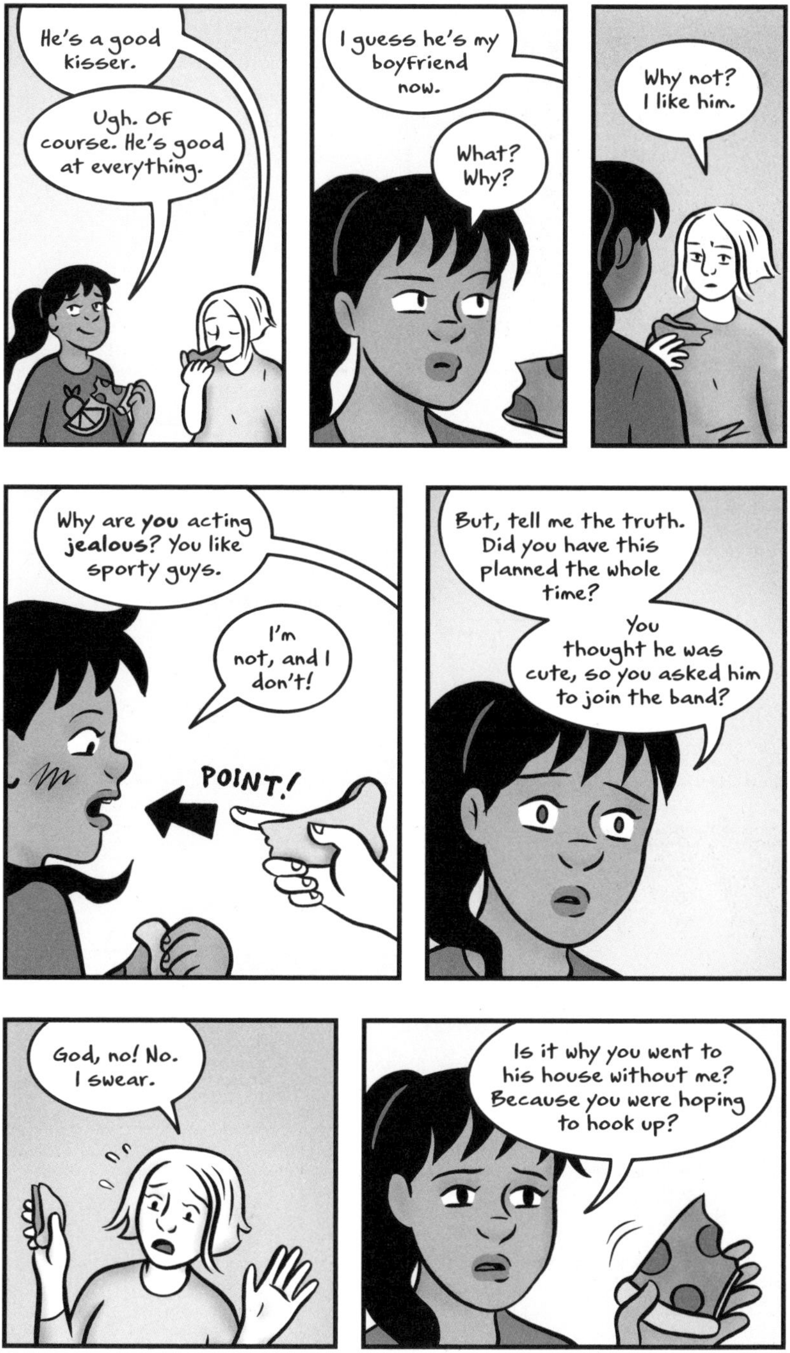
He's a good kisser.
Ugh. Of course. He's good at everything.
I guess he's my boyfriend now.
What? Why?
Why not? I like him.
Why are you acting jealous? You like sporty guys.
I'm not, and I don't!
POINT!
But, tell me the truth. Did you have this planned the whole time?
You thought he was cute, so you asked him to join the band?
God, no! No. I swear.
Is it why you went to his house without me? Because you were hoping to hook up?

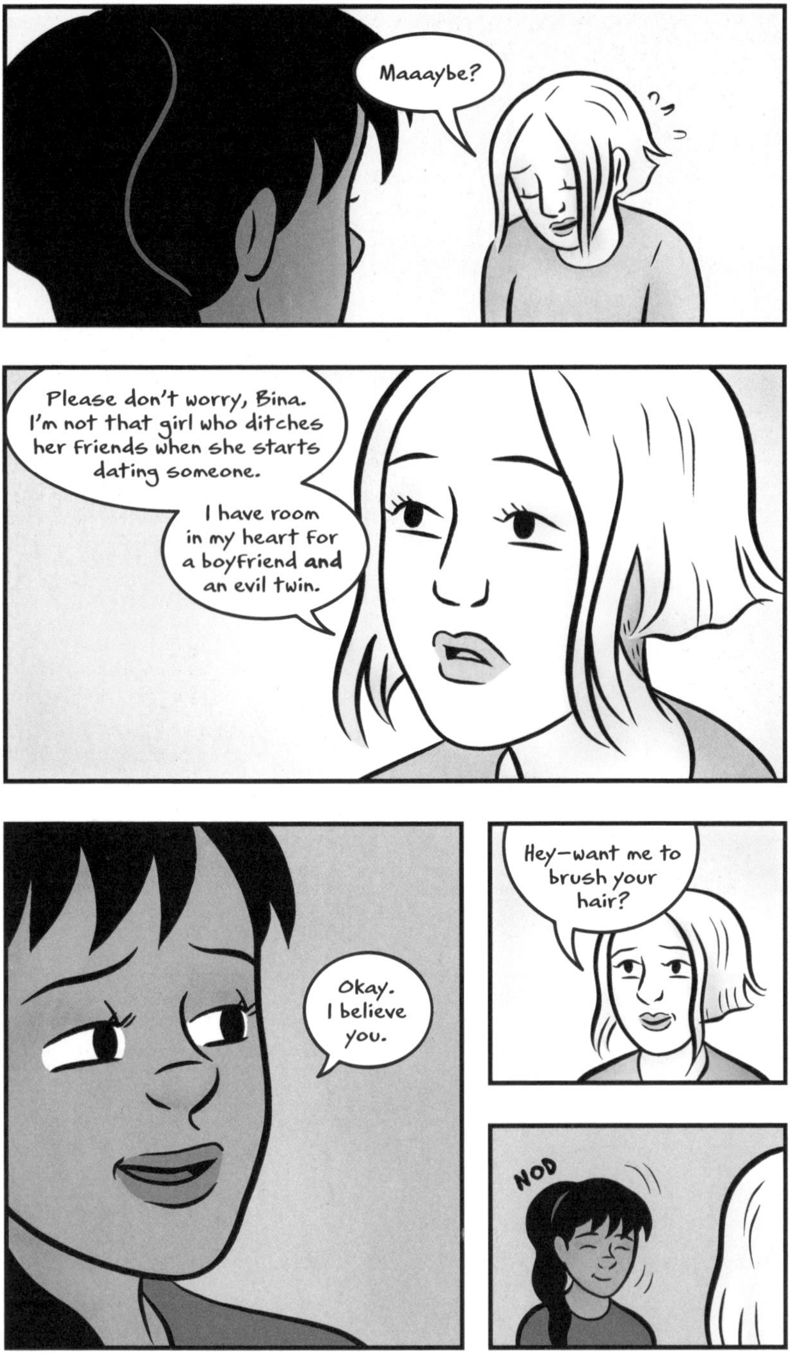
Maaaybe?
Please don't worry, Bina. I'm not that girl who ditches her friends when she starts dating someone.
I have room in my heart for a boyfriend and an evil twin.
Okay. I believe you.
Hey—want me to brush your hair?
NOD

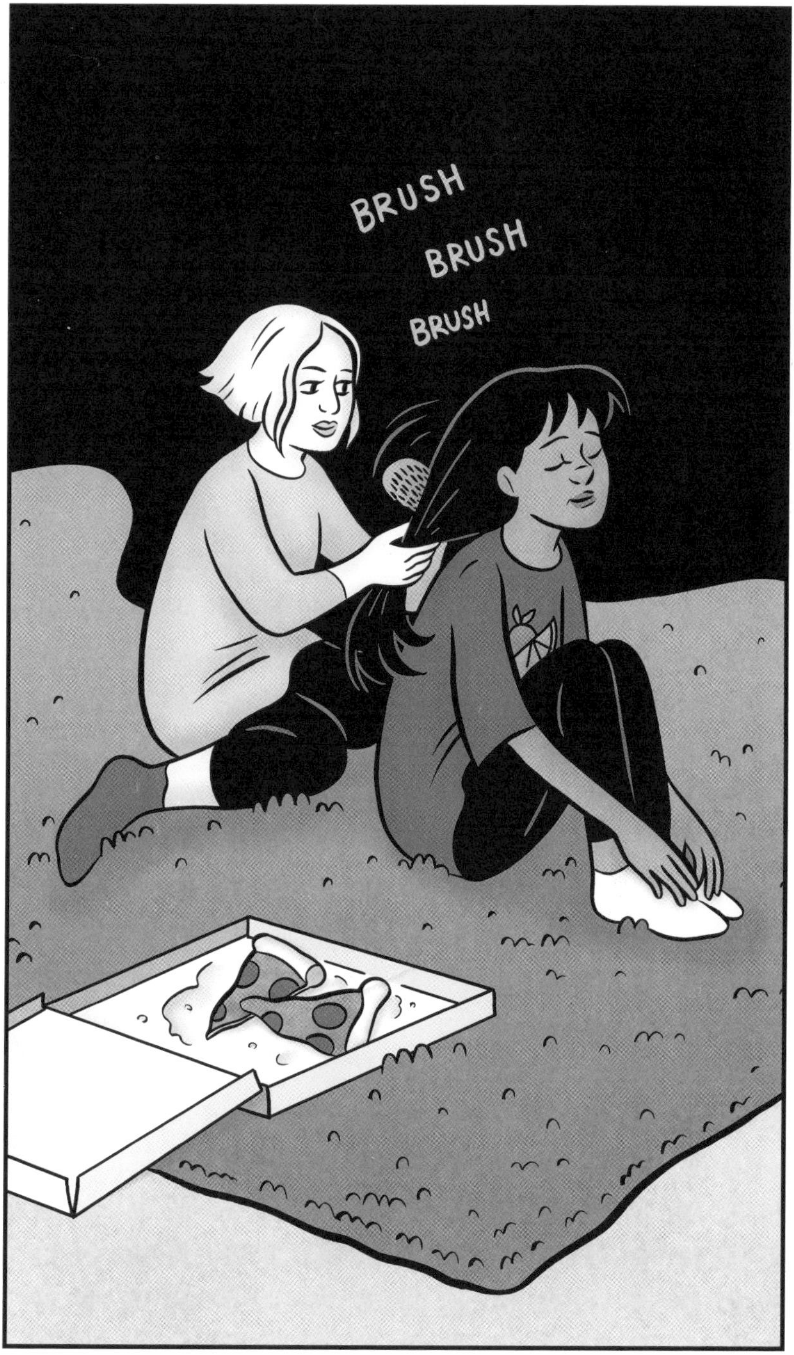
BRUSH
BRUSH
BRUSH

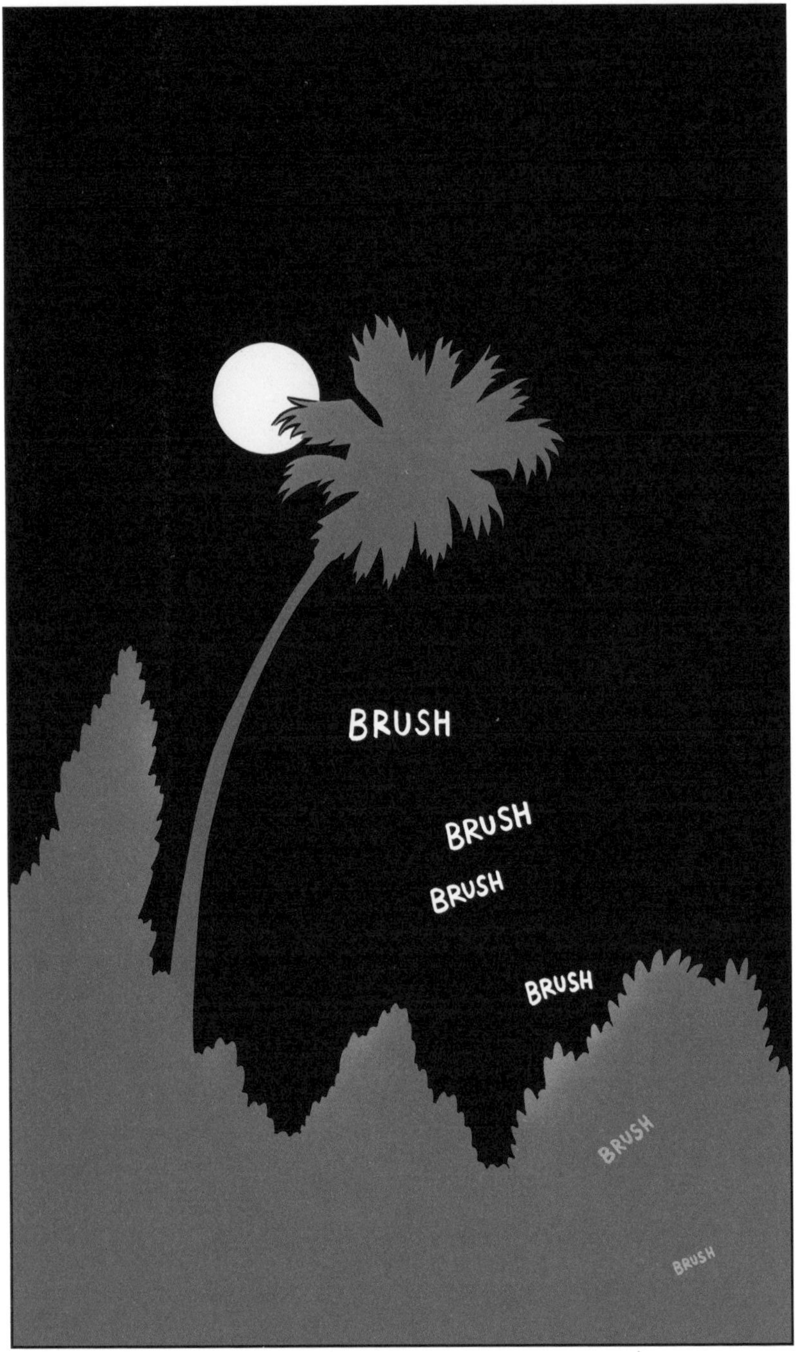
BRUSH
BRUSH
BRUSH
BRUSH
BRUSH
BRUSH

October

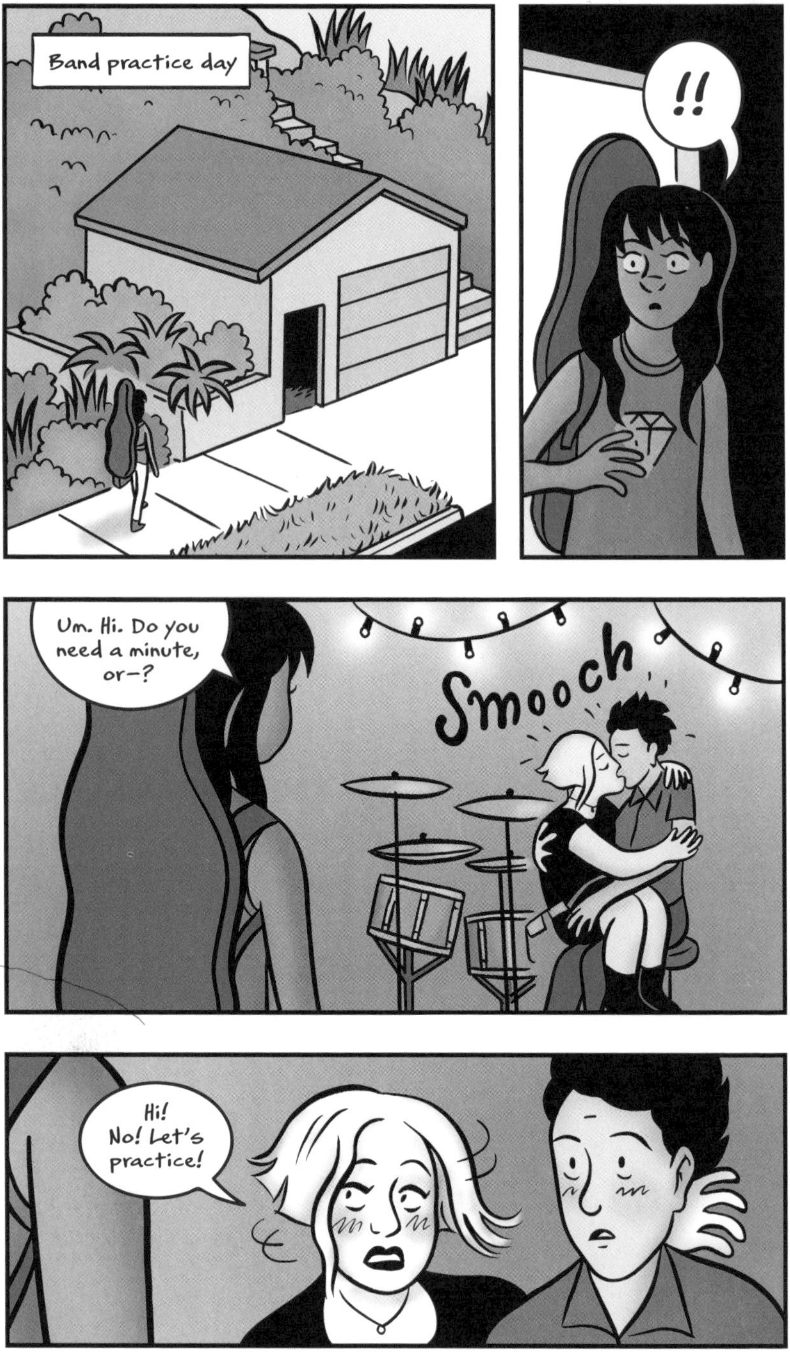
Band practice day
!!
Um. Hi. Do you need a minute, or–?
Smooch
Hi! No! Let's practice!

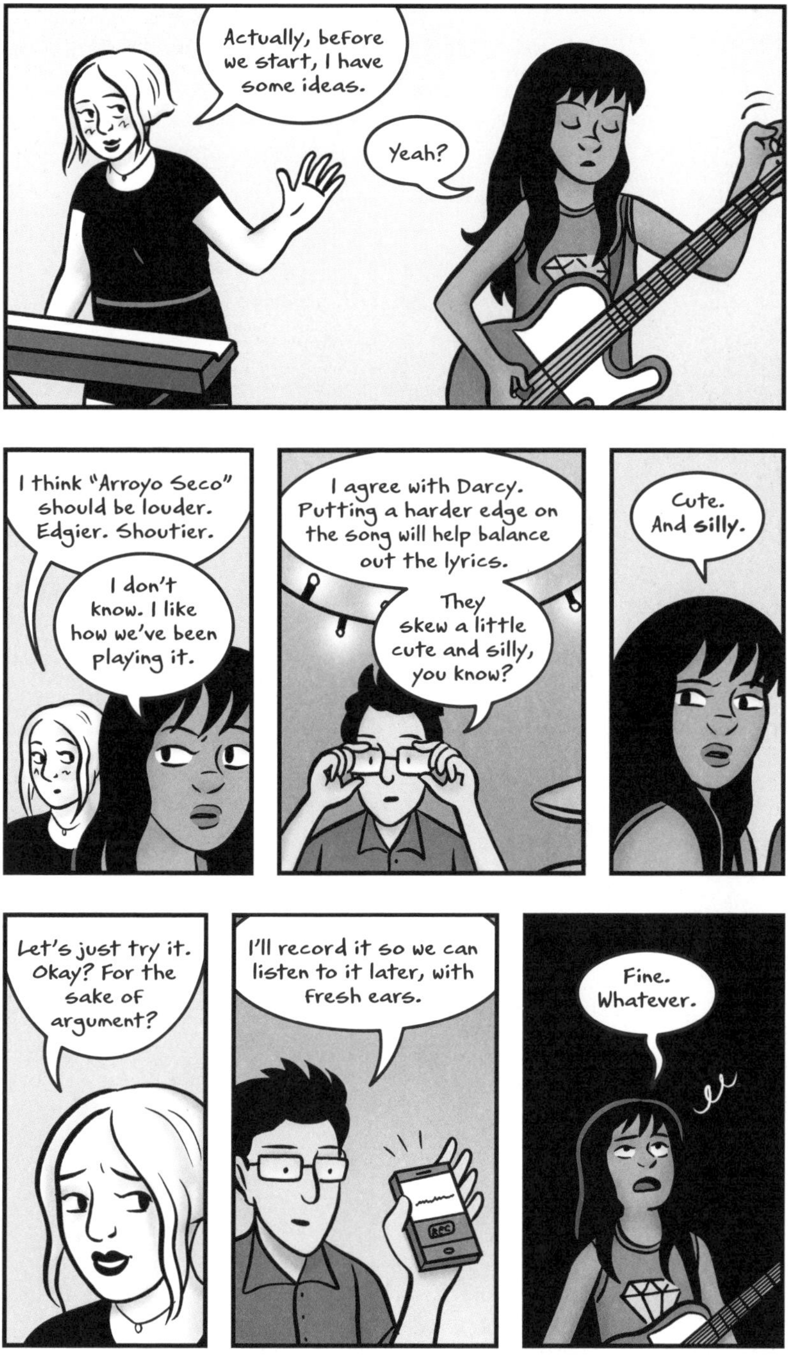
Actually, before we start, I have some ideas.
Yeah?
I think "Arroyo Seco" should be louder. Edgier. Shoutier.
I don't know. I like how we've been playing it.
I agree with Darcy. Putting a harder edge on the song will help balance out the lyrics.
They skew a little cute and silly, you know?
Cute. And silly.
Let's just try it. Okay? For the sake of argument?
I'll record it so we can listen to it later, with fresh ears.
Fine. Whatever.

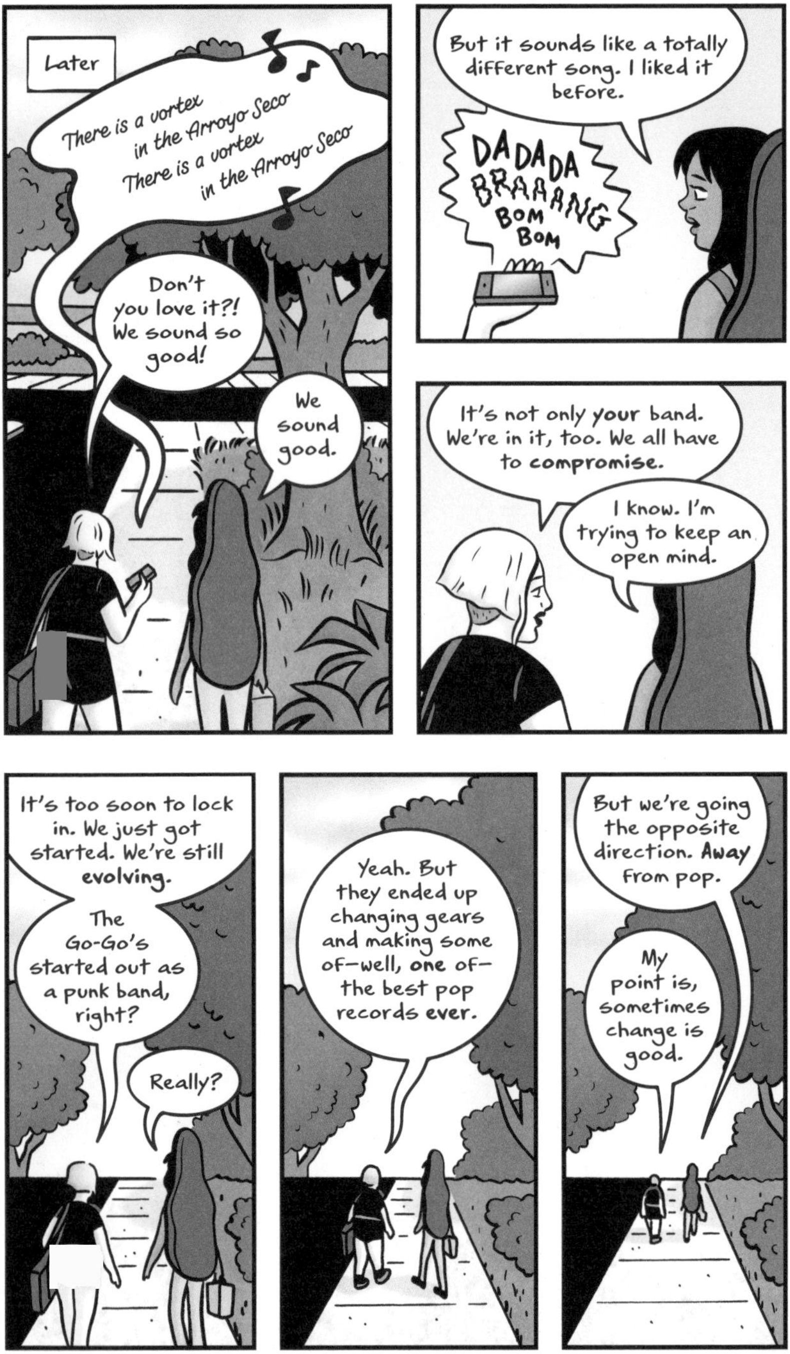
Later
There is a vortex in the Arroyo Seco There is a vortex in the Arroyo Seco
Don't you love it?! We sound so good!
We sound good.
But it sounds like a totally different song. I liked it before.
DADADA BRAAAANG BOM BOM
It's not only your band. We're in it, too. We all have to compromise.
I know. I'm trying to keep an open mind.
It's too soon to lock in. We just got started. We're still evolving.
The Go-Go's started out as a punk band, right?
Really?
Yeah. But they ended up changing gears and making some of—well, one of—the best pop records ever.
But we're going the opposite direction. Away from pop.
My point is, sometimes change is good.

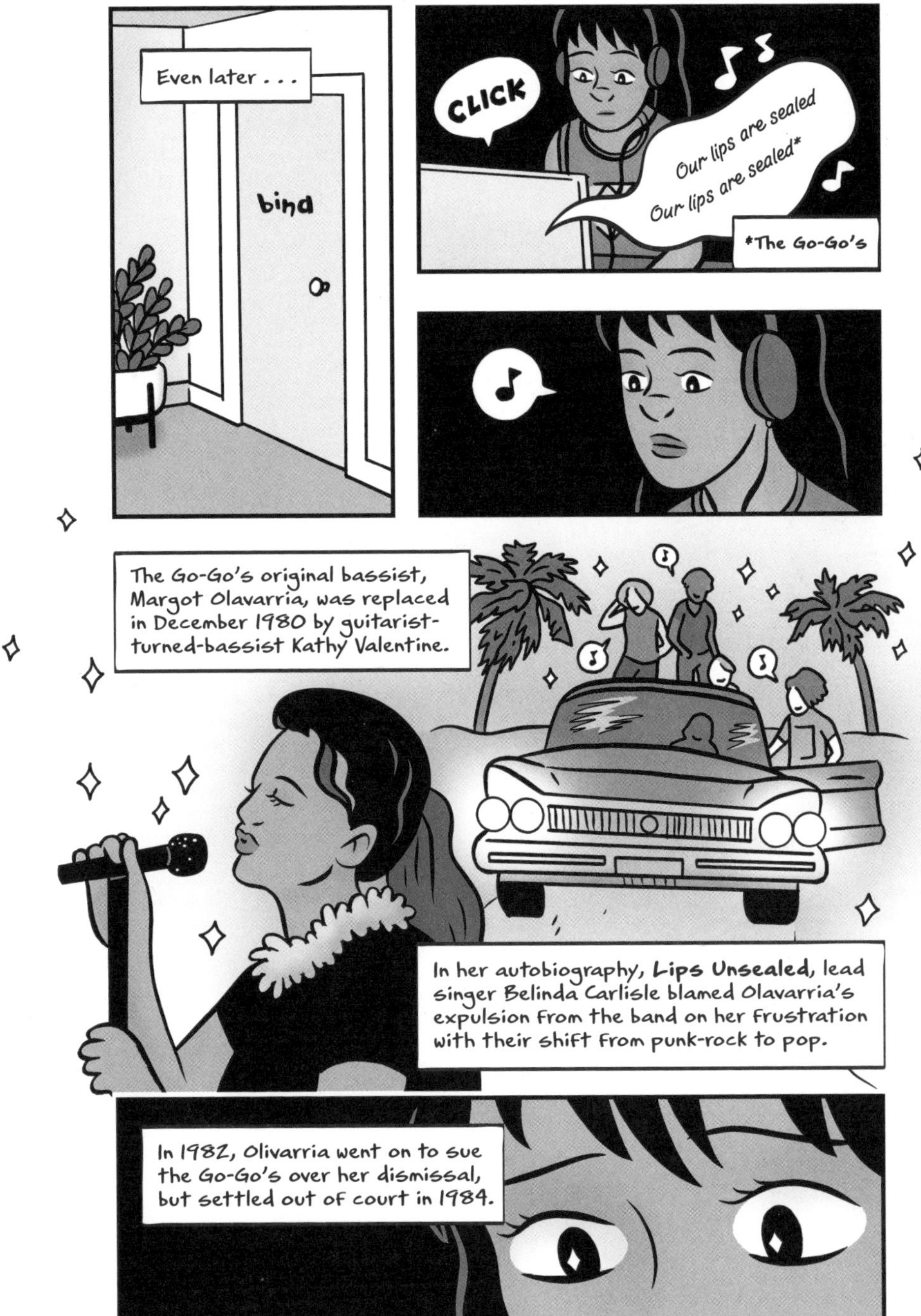

Even later . . .
bina
CLICK
Our lips are sealed
Our lips are sealed*
*The Go-Go's
The Go-Go's original bassist, Margot Olavarria, was replaced in December 1980 by guitarist-turned-bassist Kathy Valentine.
In her autobiography, **Lips Unsealed**, lead singer Belinda Carlisle blamed Olavarria's expulsion from the band on her frustration with their shift from punk-rock to pop.
In 1982, Olivarria went on to sue the Go-Go's over her dismissal, but settled out of court in 1984.

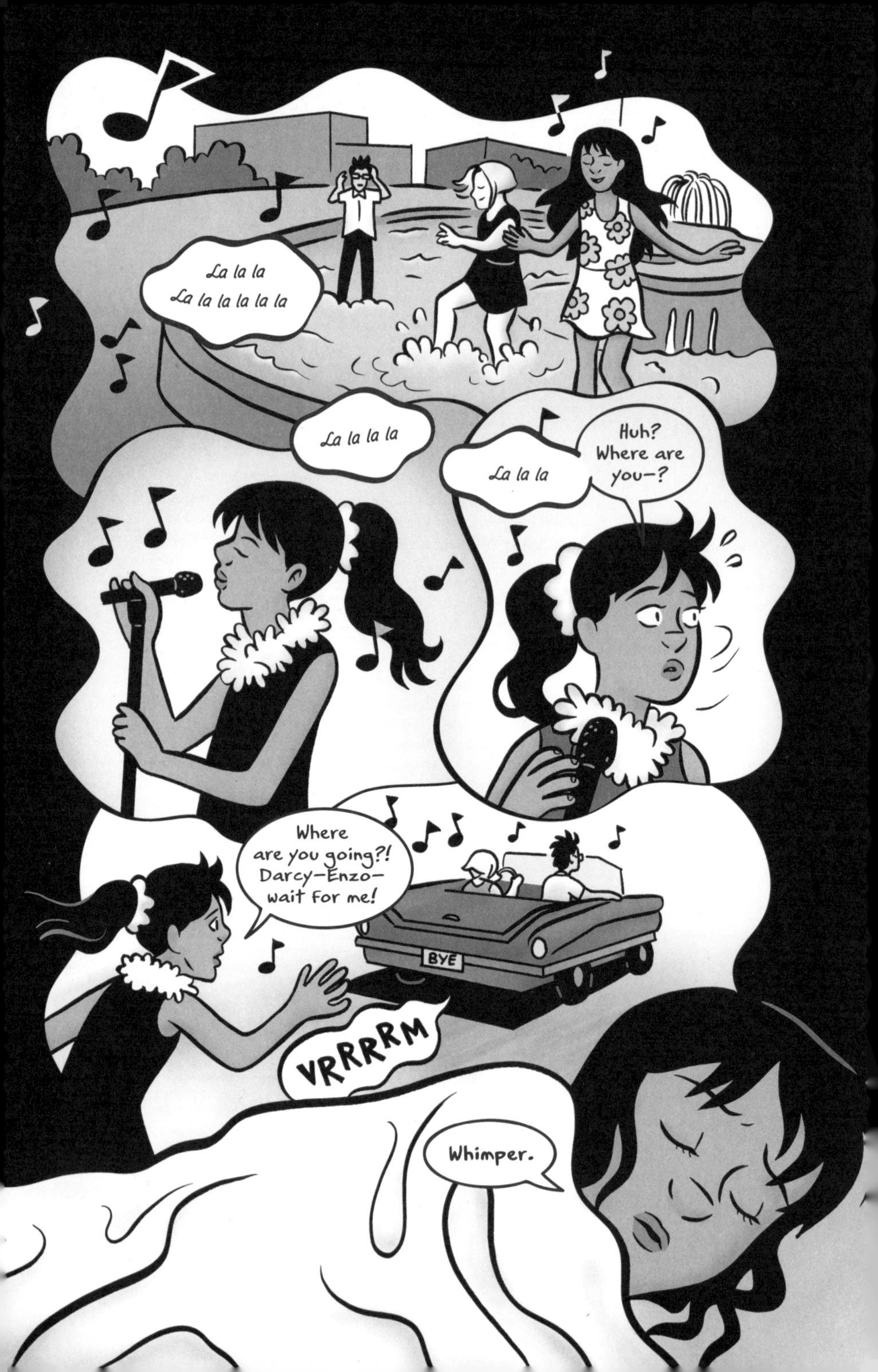
La la la
La la la la la la
La la la la
La la la
Huh? Where are you–?
Where are you going?! Darcy–Enzo–wait for me!
BYE
VRRRRM
Whimper.

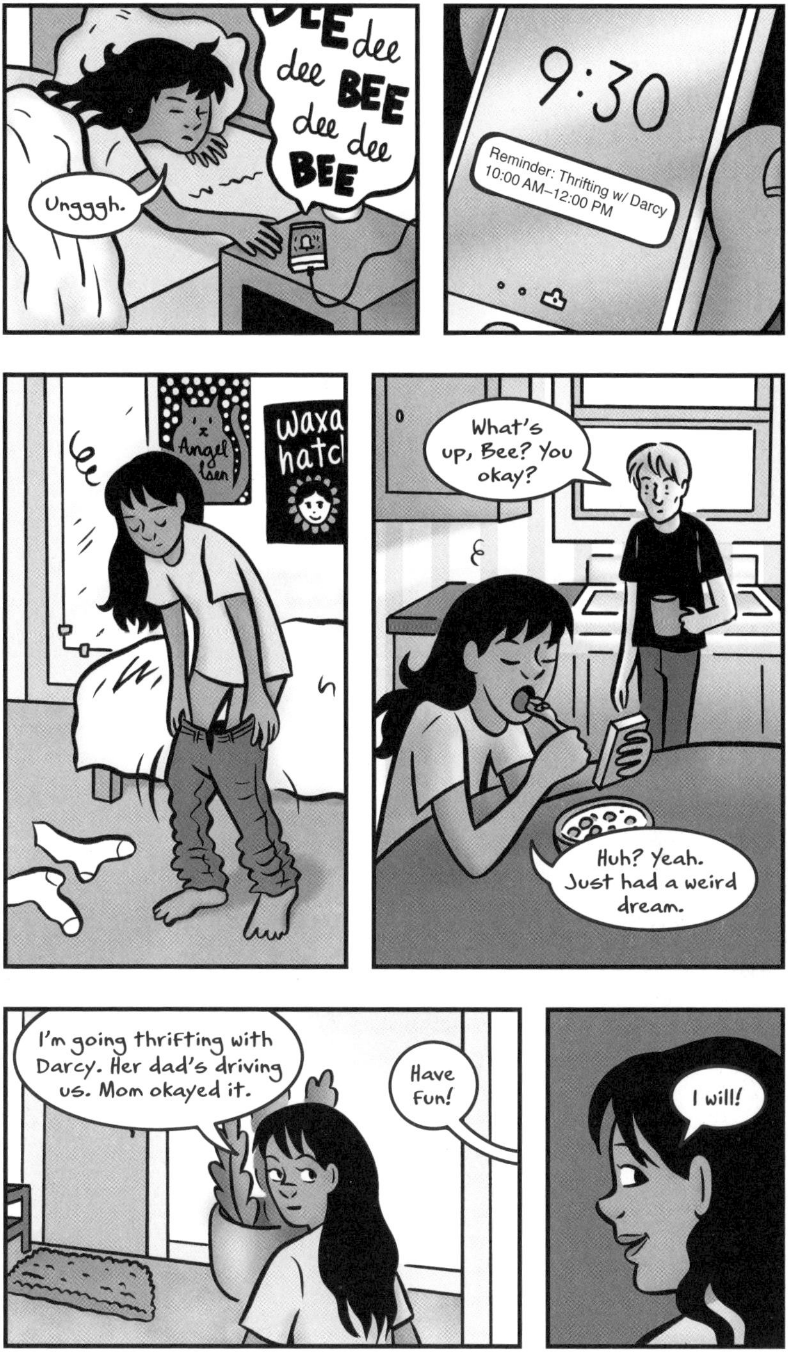
Ungggh.
DEE dee dee BEE dee dee BEE
9:30
Reminder: Thrifting w/ Darcy
10:00 AM–12:00 PM
Angel
waxa
hatc
What's up, Bee? You okay?
Huh? Yeah. Just had a weird dream.
I'm going thrifting with Darcy. Her dad's driving us. Mom okayed it.
Have Fun!
I will!

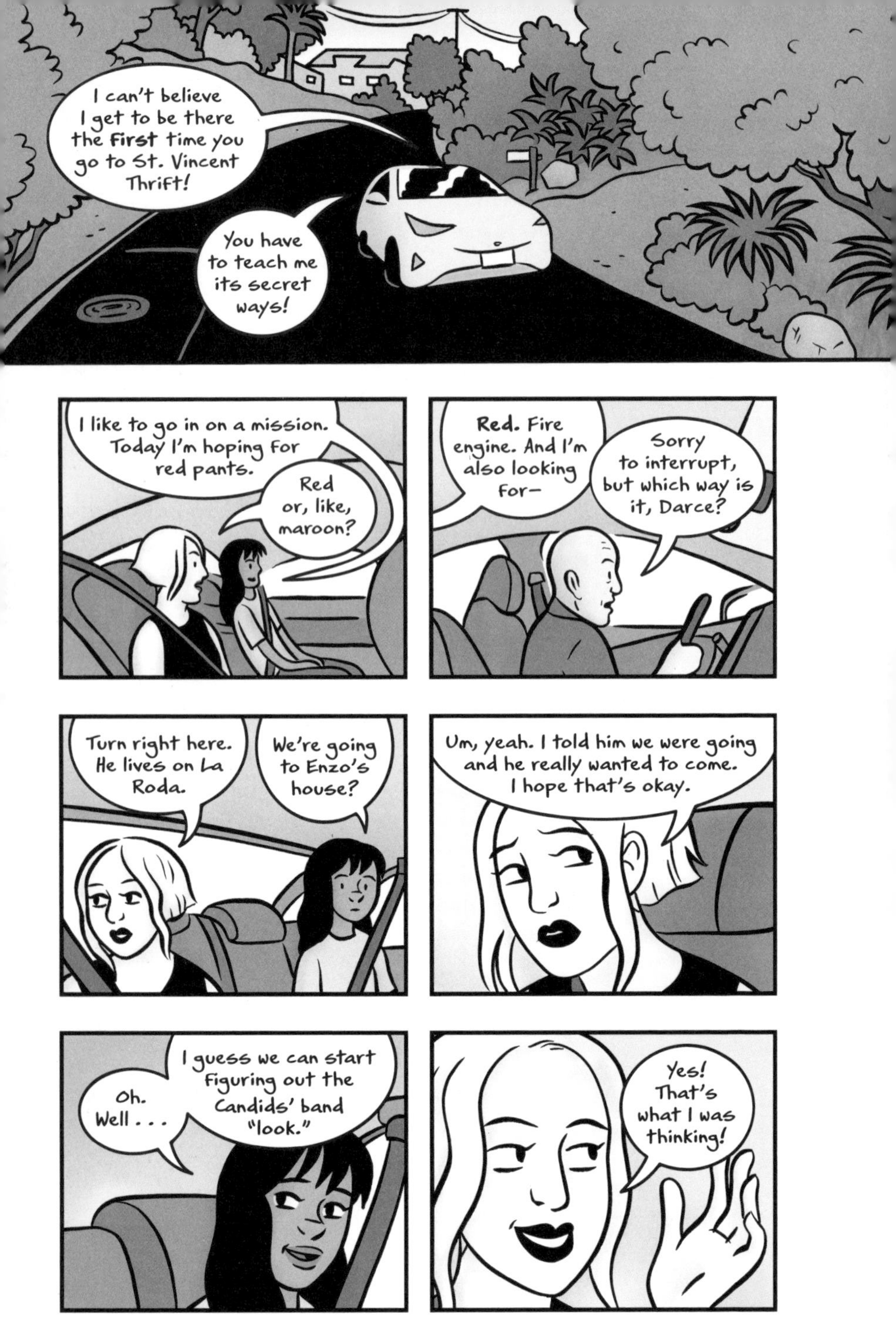

I can't believe I get to be there the First time you go to St. Vincent Thrift!
You have to teach me its secret ways!
I like to go in on a mission. Today I'm hoping for red pants.
Red or, like, maroon?
Red. Fire engine. And I'm also looking for—
Sorry to interrupt, but which way is it, Darce?
Turn right here. He lives on La Roda.
We're going to Enzo's house?
Um, yeah. I told him we were going and he really wanted to come. I hope that's okay.
Oh. Well . . .
I guess we can start figuring out the Candids' band "look."
Yes! That's what I was thinking!

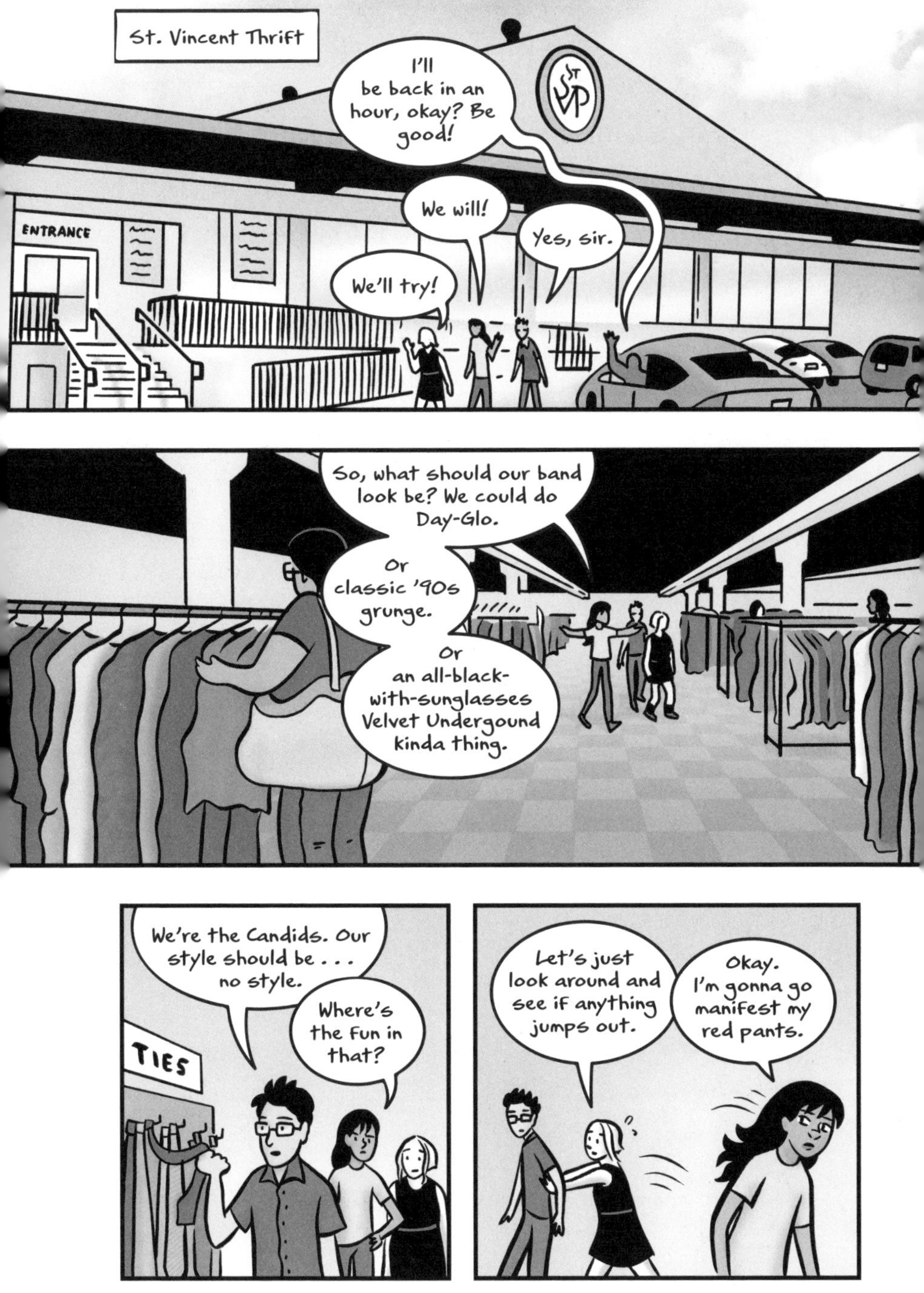
St. Vincent Thrift
I'll be back in an hour, okay? Be good!
We will!
Yes, sir.
We'll try!
So, what should our band look be? We could do Day-Glo.
Or classic '90s grunge.
Or an all-black-with-sunglasses Velvet Undergound kinda thing.
We're the Candids. Our style should be . . . no style.
Where's the fun in that?
TIES
Let's just look around and see if anything jumps out.
Okay. I'm gonna go manifest my red pants.

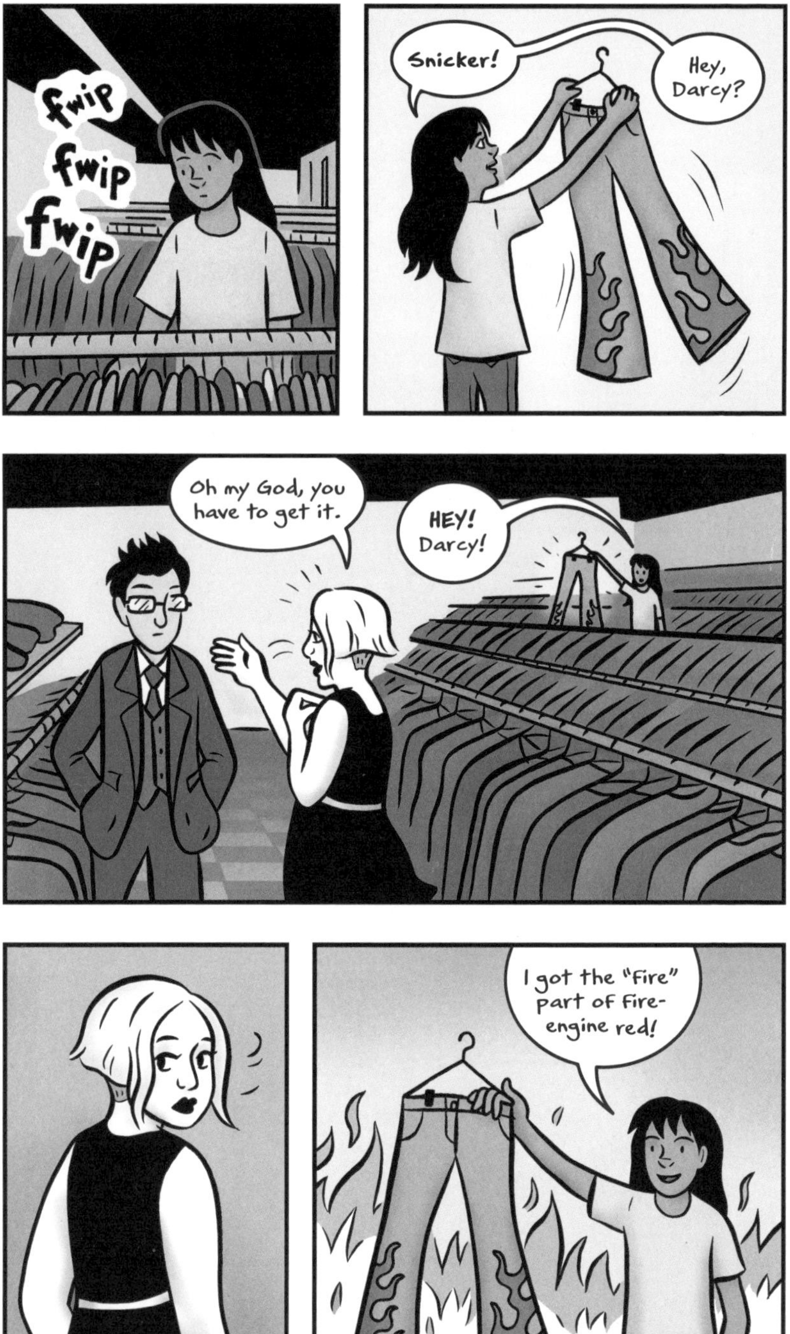
fwip
fwip
fwip
Snicker!
Hey, Darcy?
Oh my God, you have to get it.
HEY! Darcy!
I got the "Fire" part of Fire-engine red!

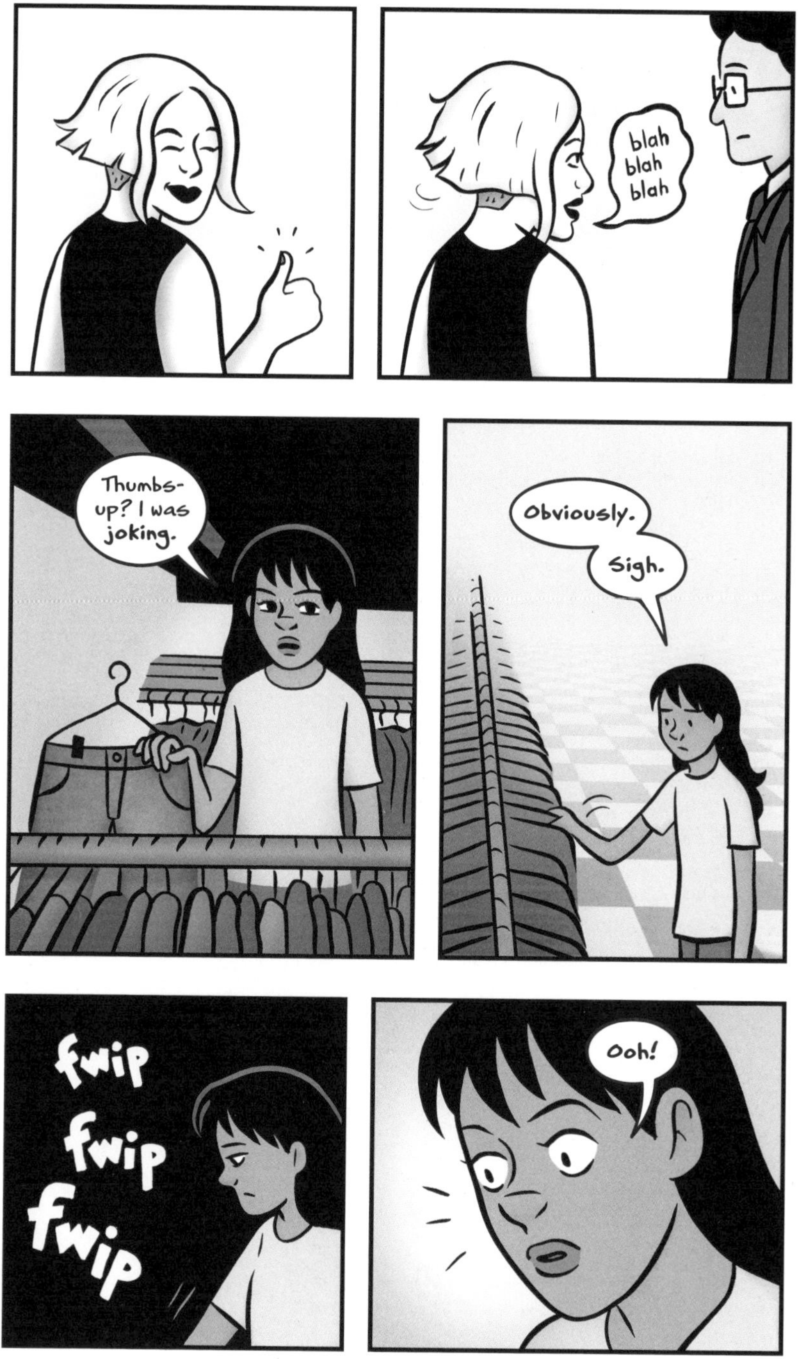
blah blah blah
Thumbs-up? I was joking.
Obviously.
Sigh.
fwip fwip fwip fwip
Ooh!

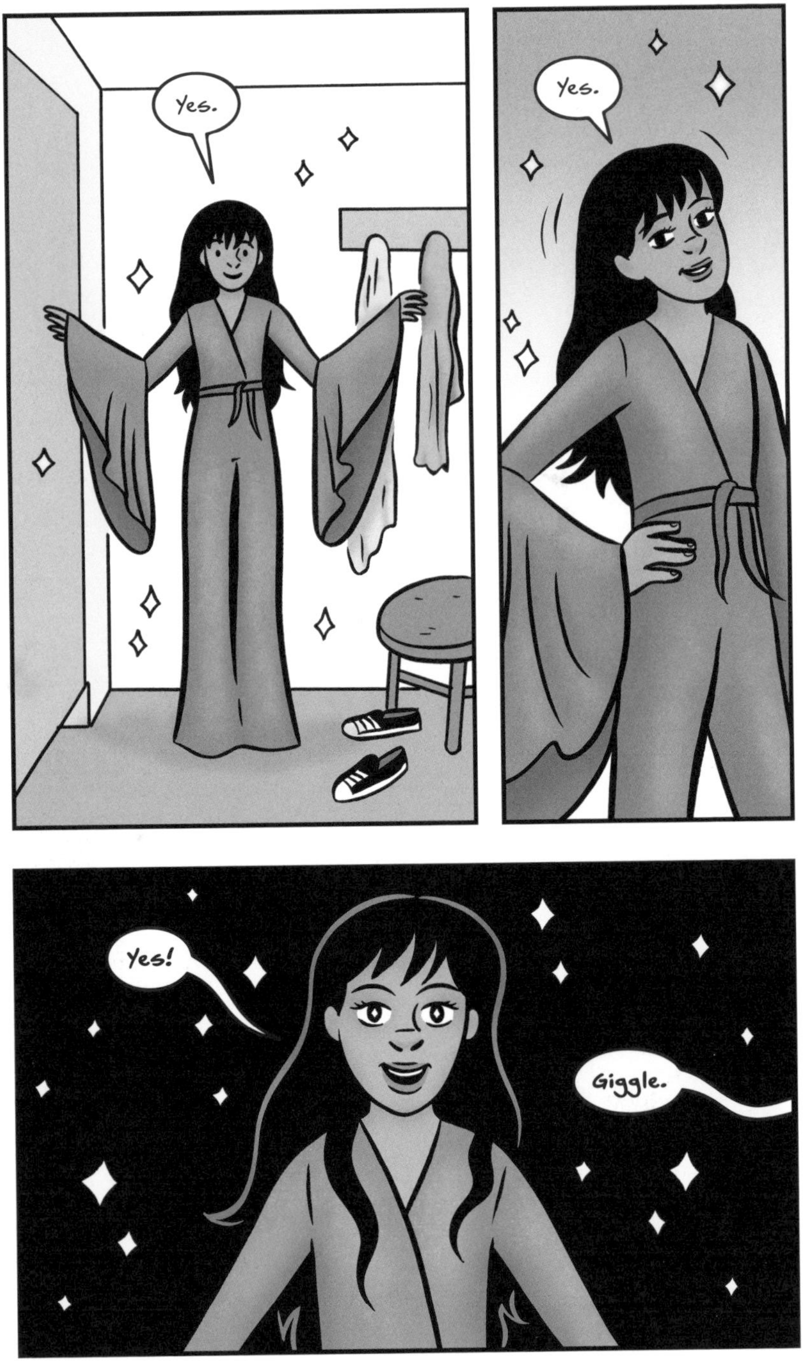
Yes.
Yes.
Yes!
Giggle.

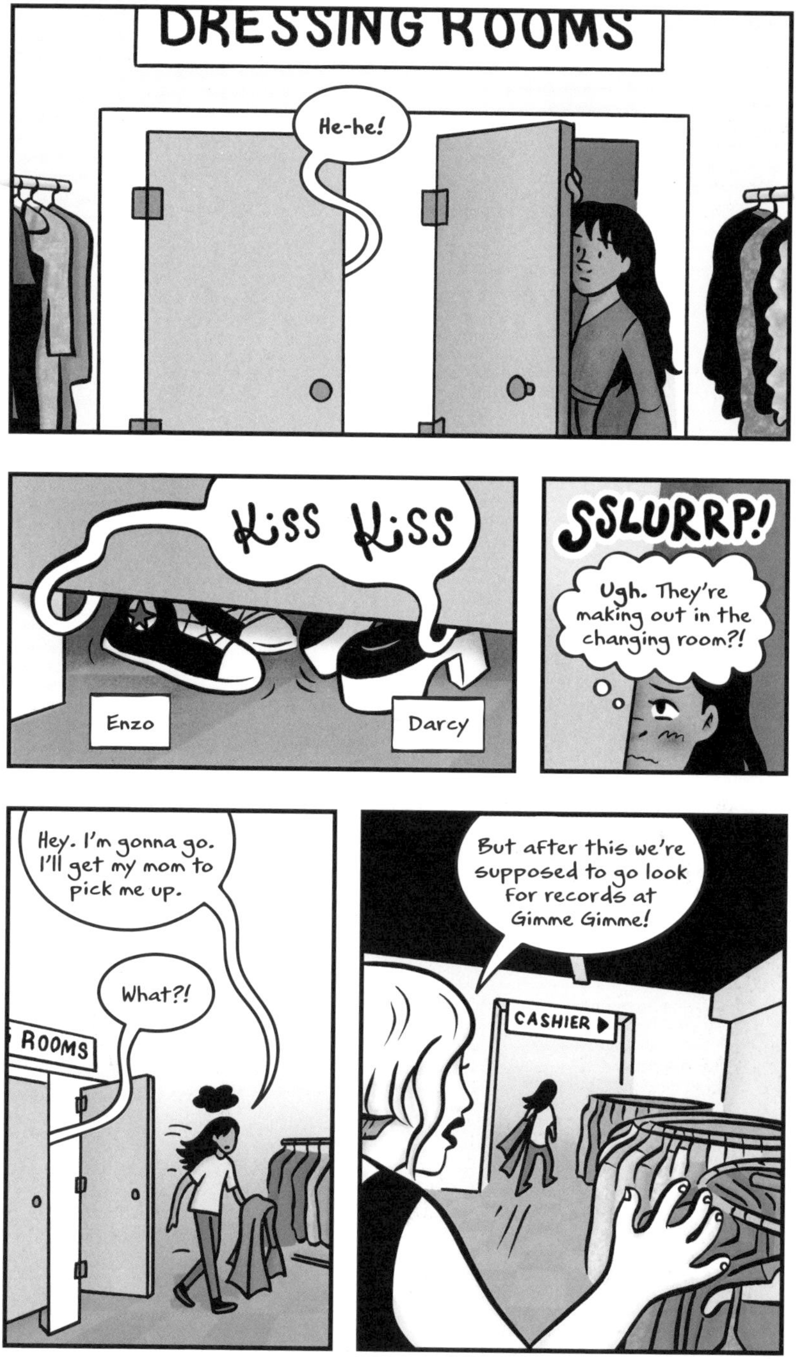
DRESSING ROOMS
He-he!
Kiss Kiss
Enzo
Darcy
SSLURRP!
Ugh. They're making out in the changing room?!
Hey. I'm gonna go. I'll get my mom to pick me up.
What?!
ROOMS
But after this we're supposed to go look for records at Gimme Gimme!
CASHIER

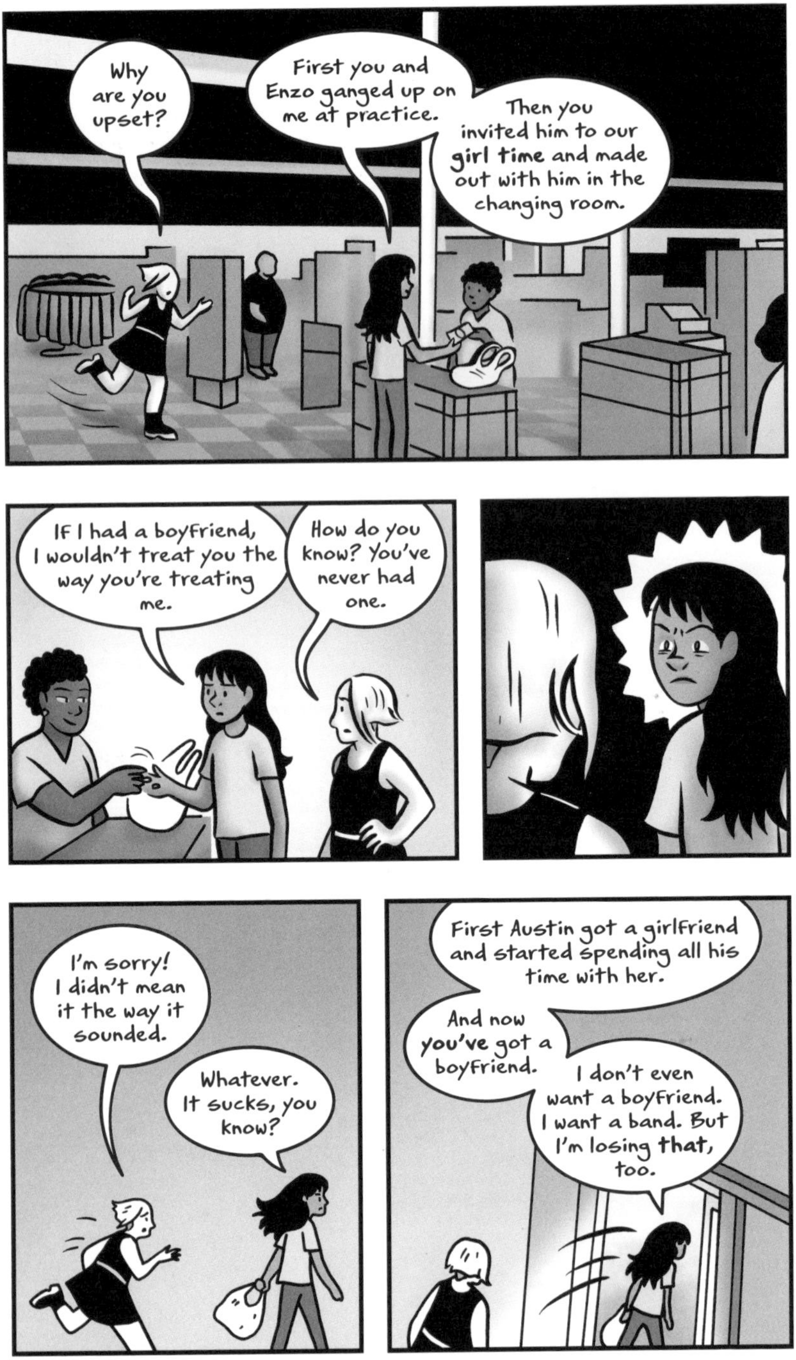
Why are you upset?
First you and Enzo ganged up on me at practice.
Then you invited him to our girl time and made out with him in the changing room.
If I had a boyfriend, I wouldn't treat you the way you're treating me.
How do you know? You've never had one.
I'm sorry! I didn't mean it the way it sounded.
Whatever. It sucks, you know?
First Austin got a girlfriend and started spending all his time with her.
And now you've got a boyfriend.
I don't even want a boyfriend. I want a band. But I'm losing that, too.

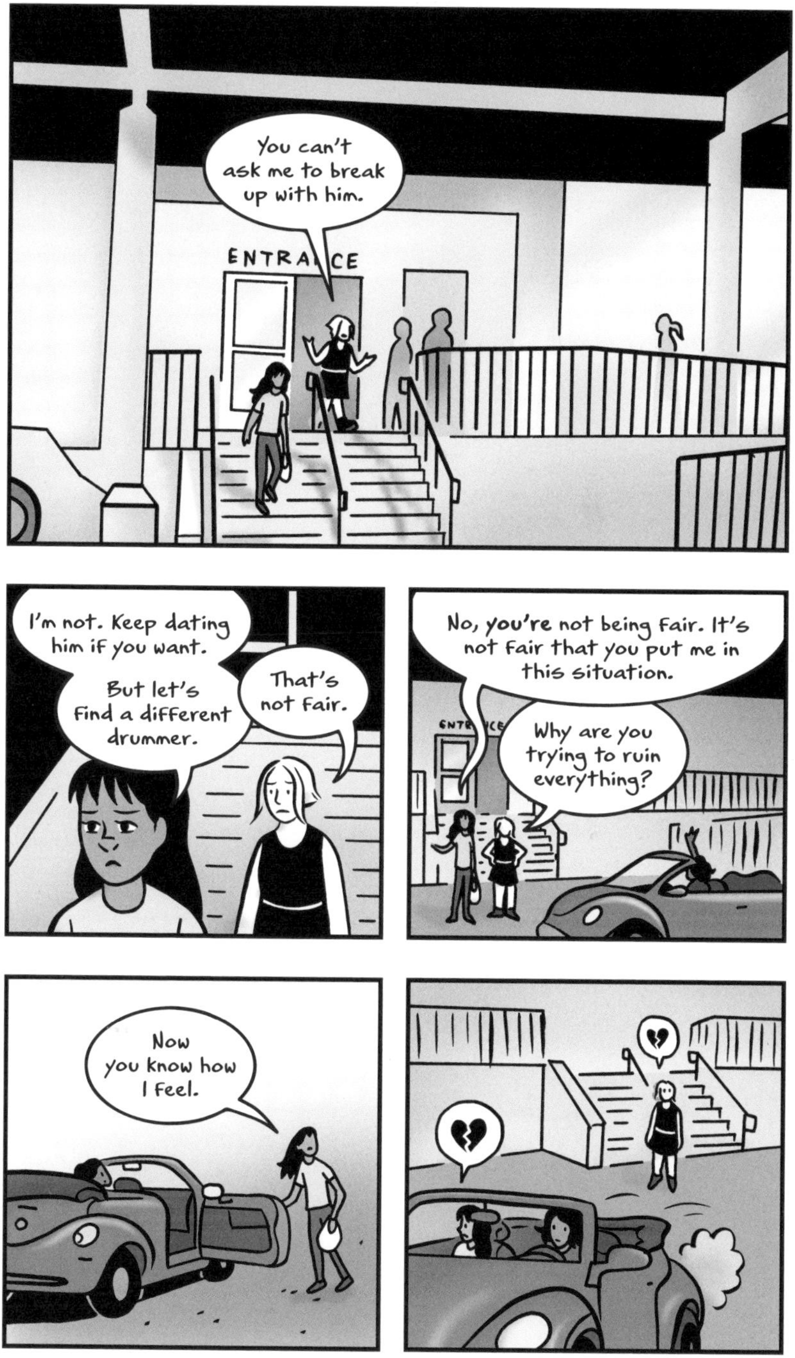

You can't ask me to break up with him.
ENTRA CE
I'm not. Keep dating him if you want.
But let's find a different drummer.
That's not fair.
No, you're not being fair. It's not fair that you put me in this situation.
Why are you trying to ruin everything?
Now you know how I feel.

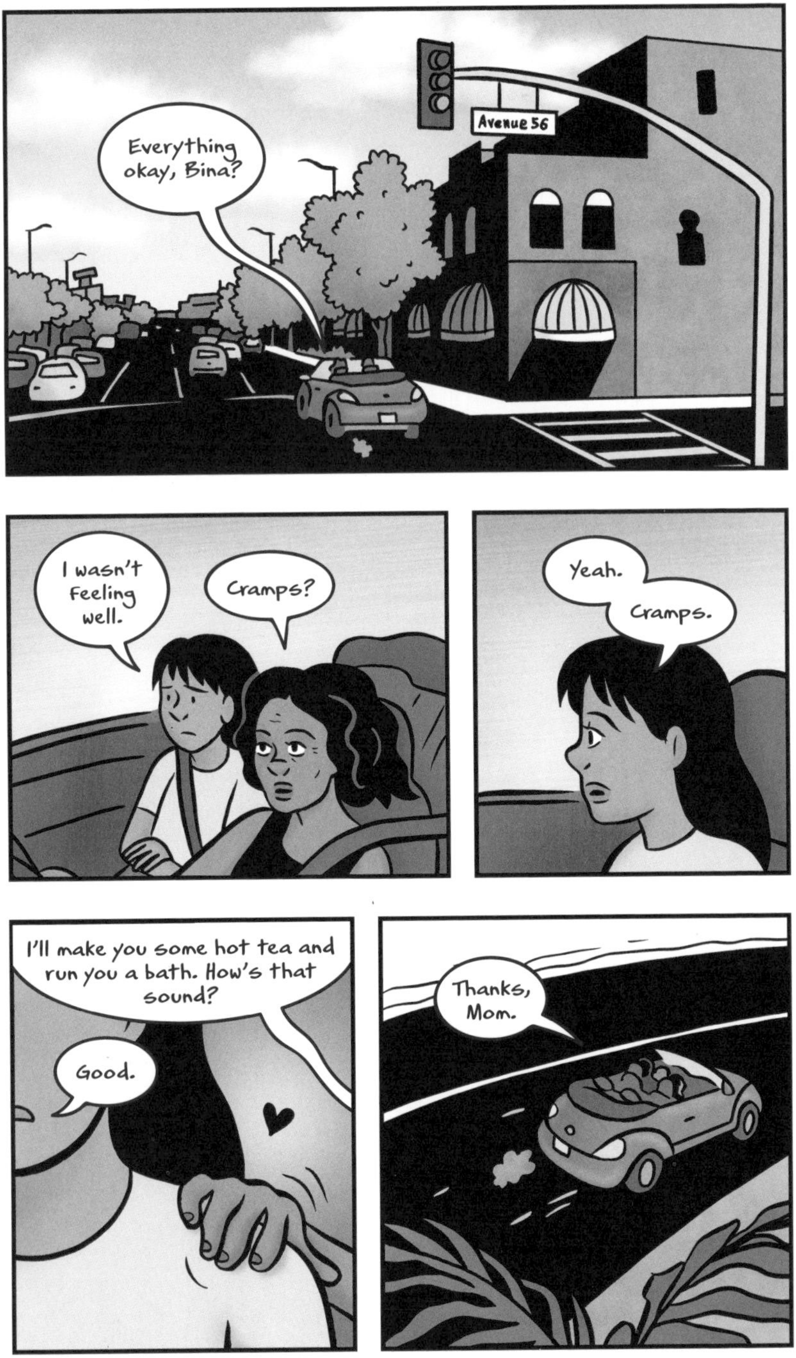
Avenue 56
Everything okay, Bina?
I wasn't feeling well.
Cramps?
Yeah.
Cramps.
I'll make you some hot tea and run you a bath. How's that sound?
Good.
Thanks, Mom.

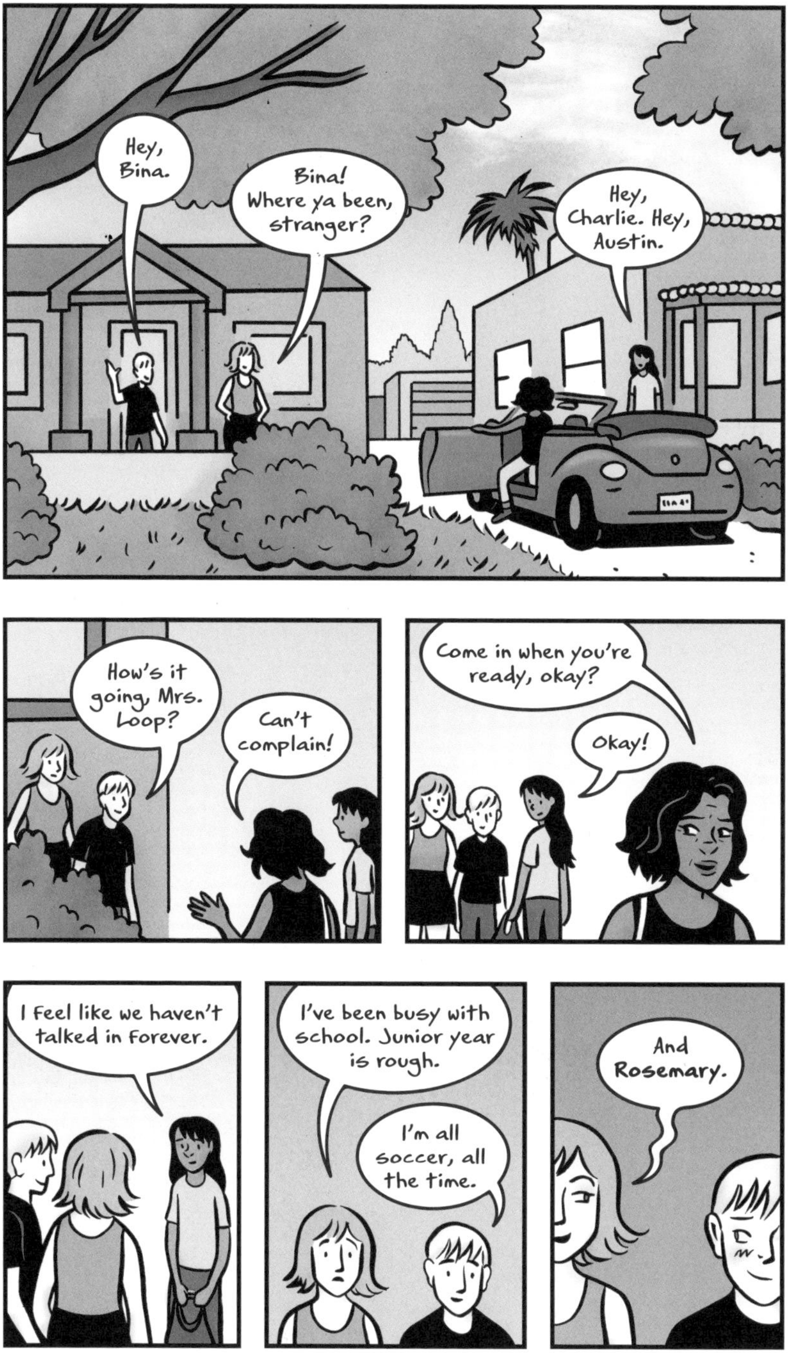
Hey, Bina.
Bina! Where ya been, stranger?
Hey, Charlie. Hey, Austin.
How's it going, Mrs. Loop?
Can't complain!
Come in when you're ready, okay?
Okay!
I feel like we haven't talked in forever.
I've been busy with school. Junior year is rough.
I'm all soccer, all the time.
And Rosemary.

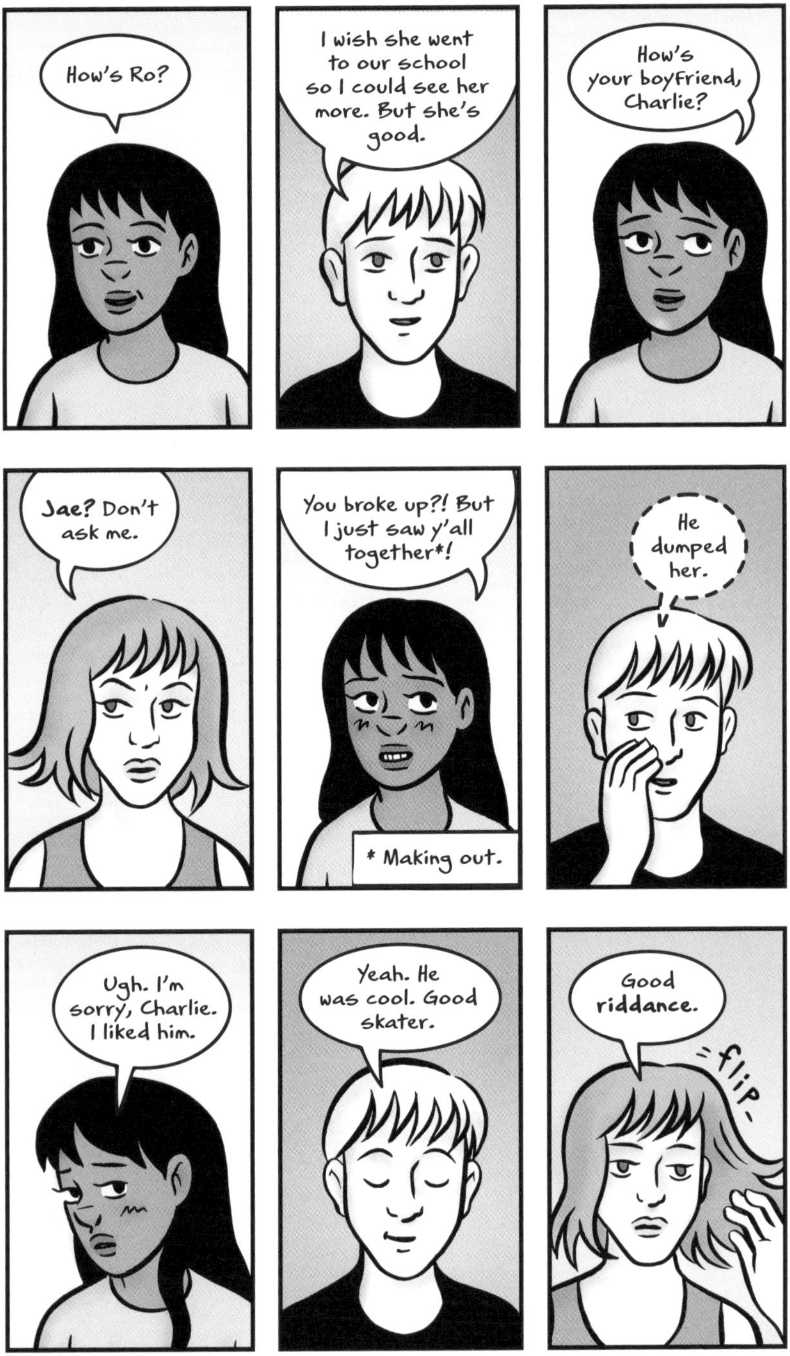
How's Ro?
I wish she went to our school so I could see her more. But she's good.
How's your boyfriend, Charlie?
Jae? Don't ask me.
You broke up?! But I just saw y'all together*!
* Making out.
He dumped her.
Ugh. I'm sorry, Charlie. I liked him.
Yeah. He was cool. Good skater.
Good riddance.
flip

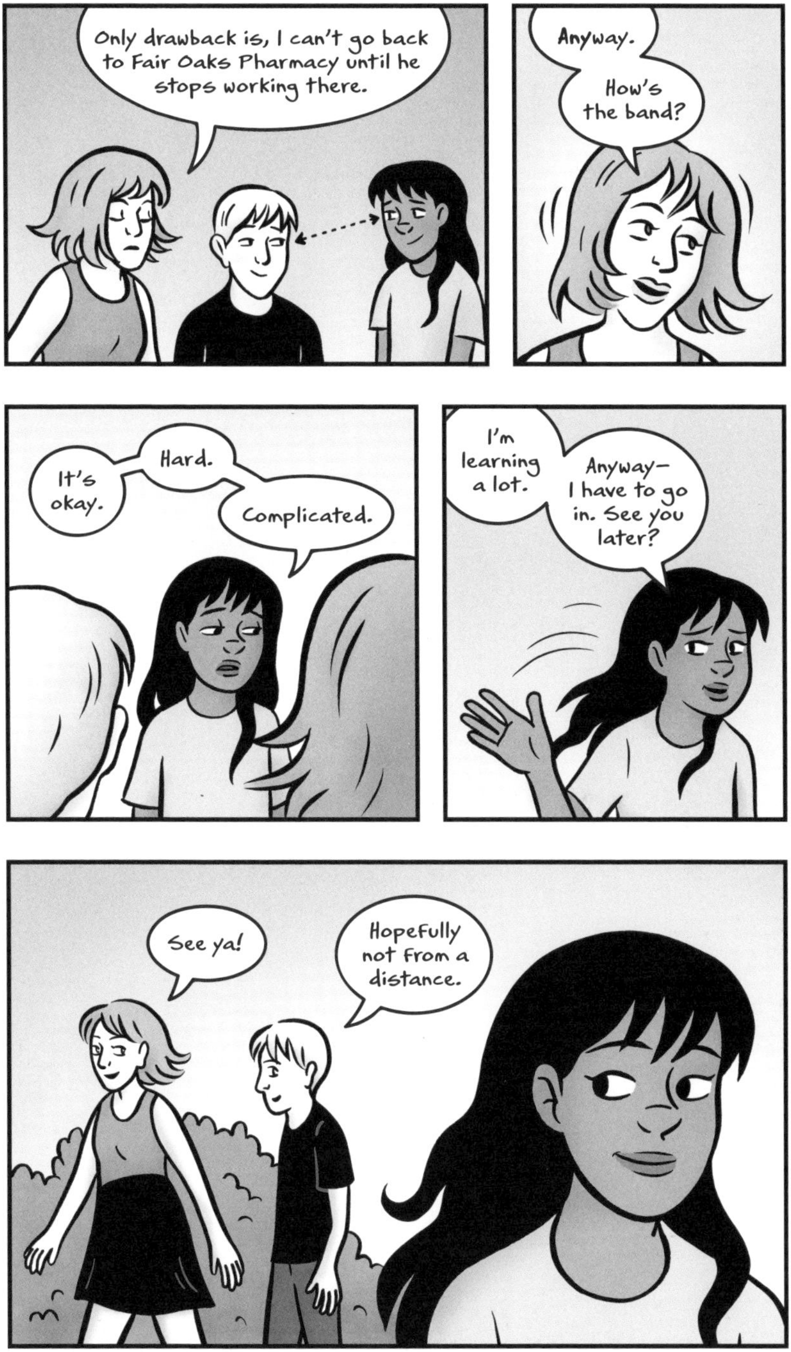
Only drawback is, I can't go back to Fair Oaks Pharmacy until he stops working there.
Anyway.
How's the band?
It's okay.
Hard.
Complicated.
I'm learning a lot.
Anyway– I have to go in. See you later?
See ya!
Hopefully not from a distance.

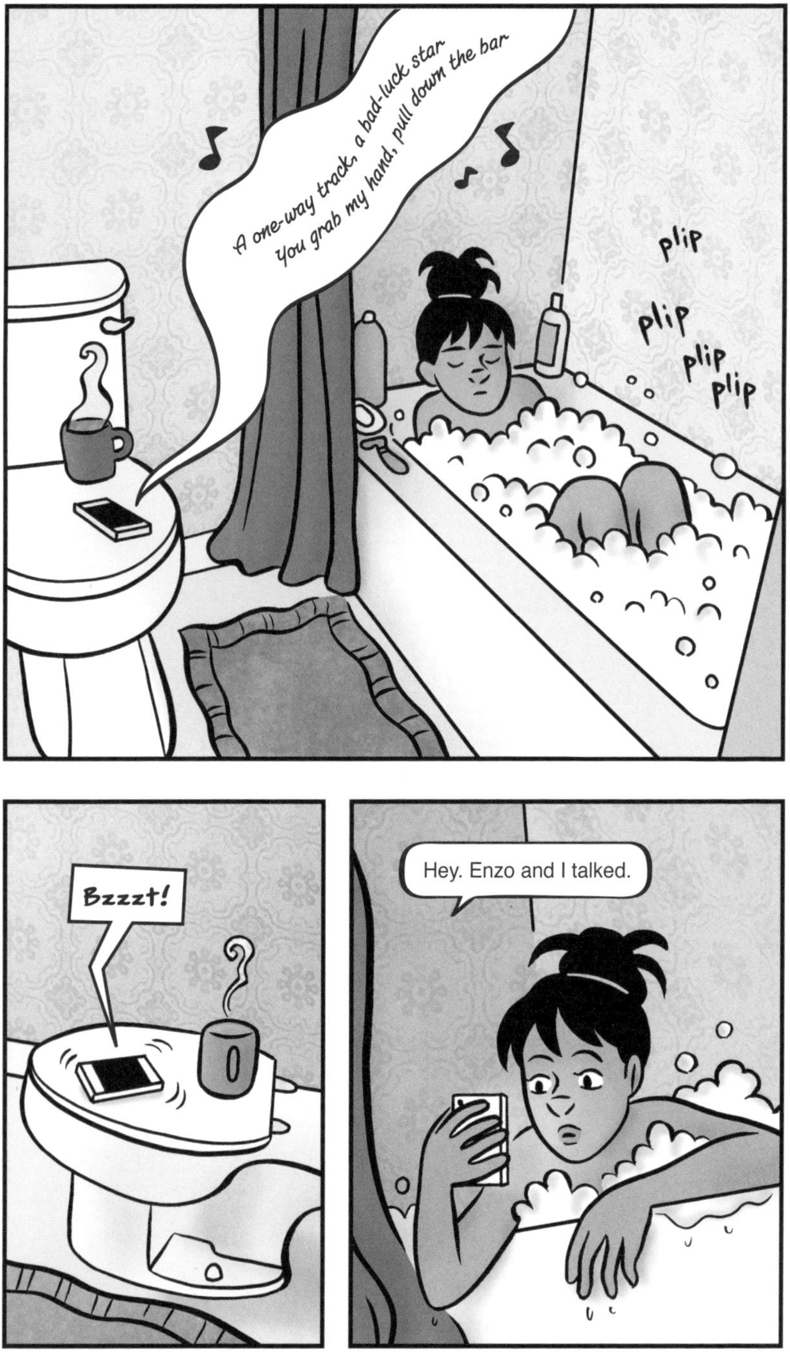
A one-way track, a bad-luck star
You grab my hand, pull down the bar
plip
plip
plip
plip
Bzzzt!
Hey. Enzo and I talked.

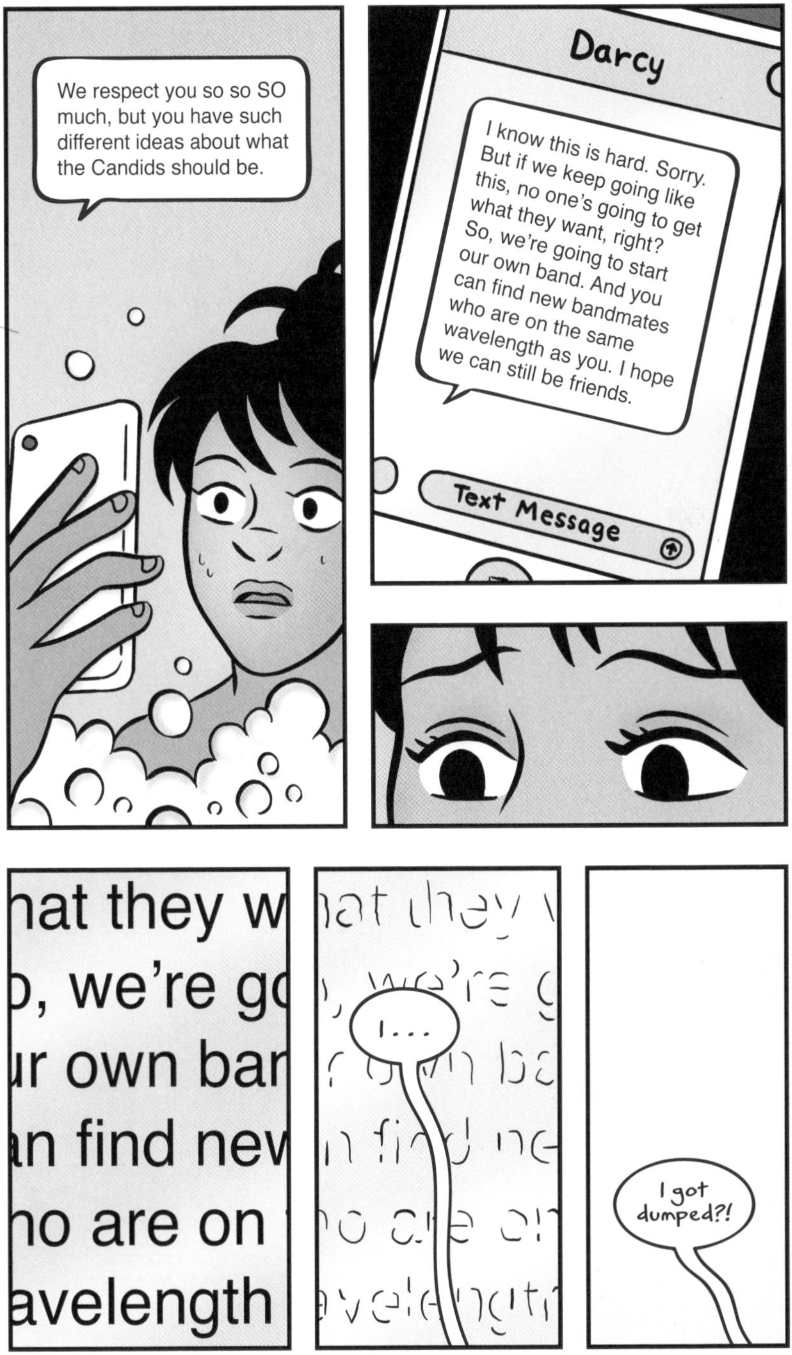
We respect you so so SO much, but you have such different ideas about what the Candids should be.
Darcy
I know this is hard. Sorry. But if we keep going like this, no one's going to get what they want, right? So, we're going to start our own band. And you can find new bandmates who are on the same wavelength as you. I hope we can still be friends.
Text Message
hat they w
, we're go
r own ban
n find new
ho are on
avelength
I...
I got dumped?!

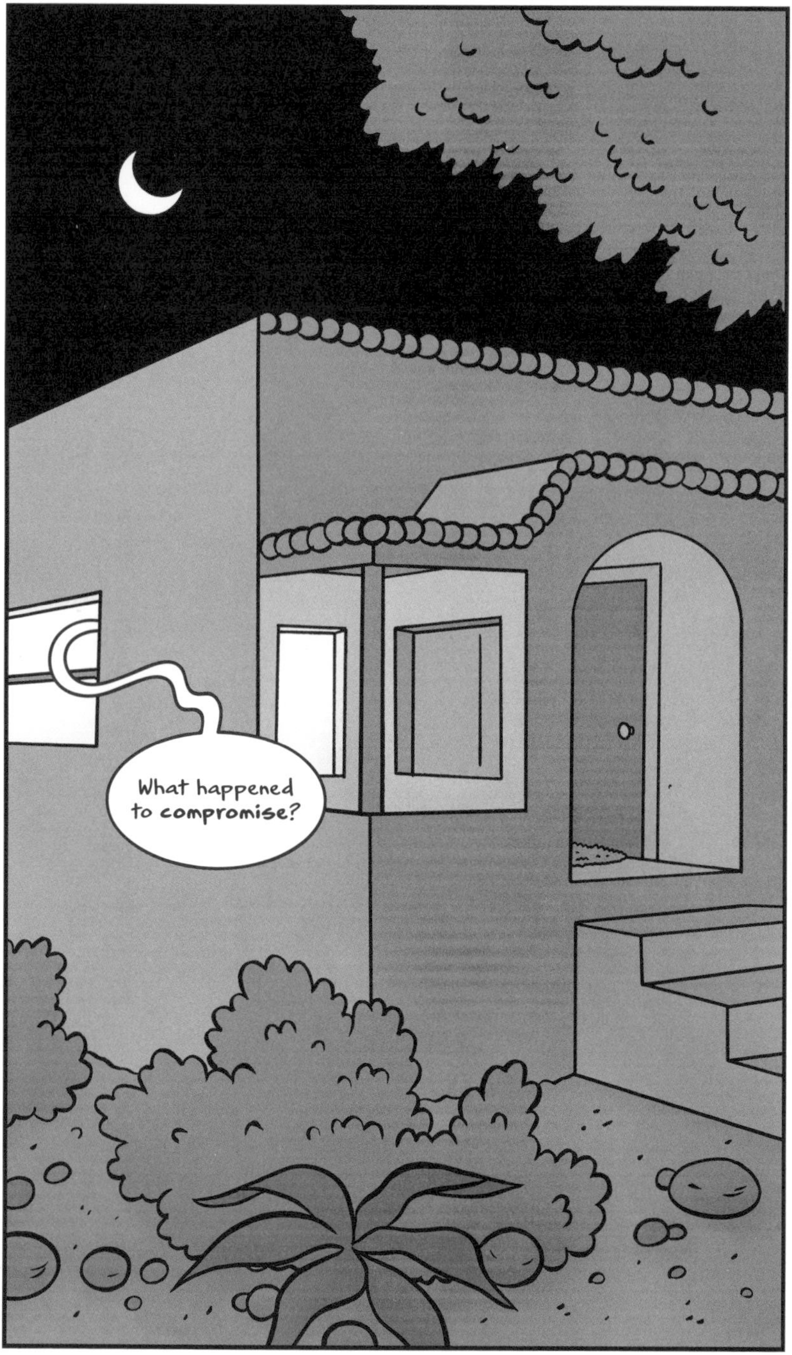
What happened to compromise?

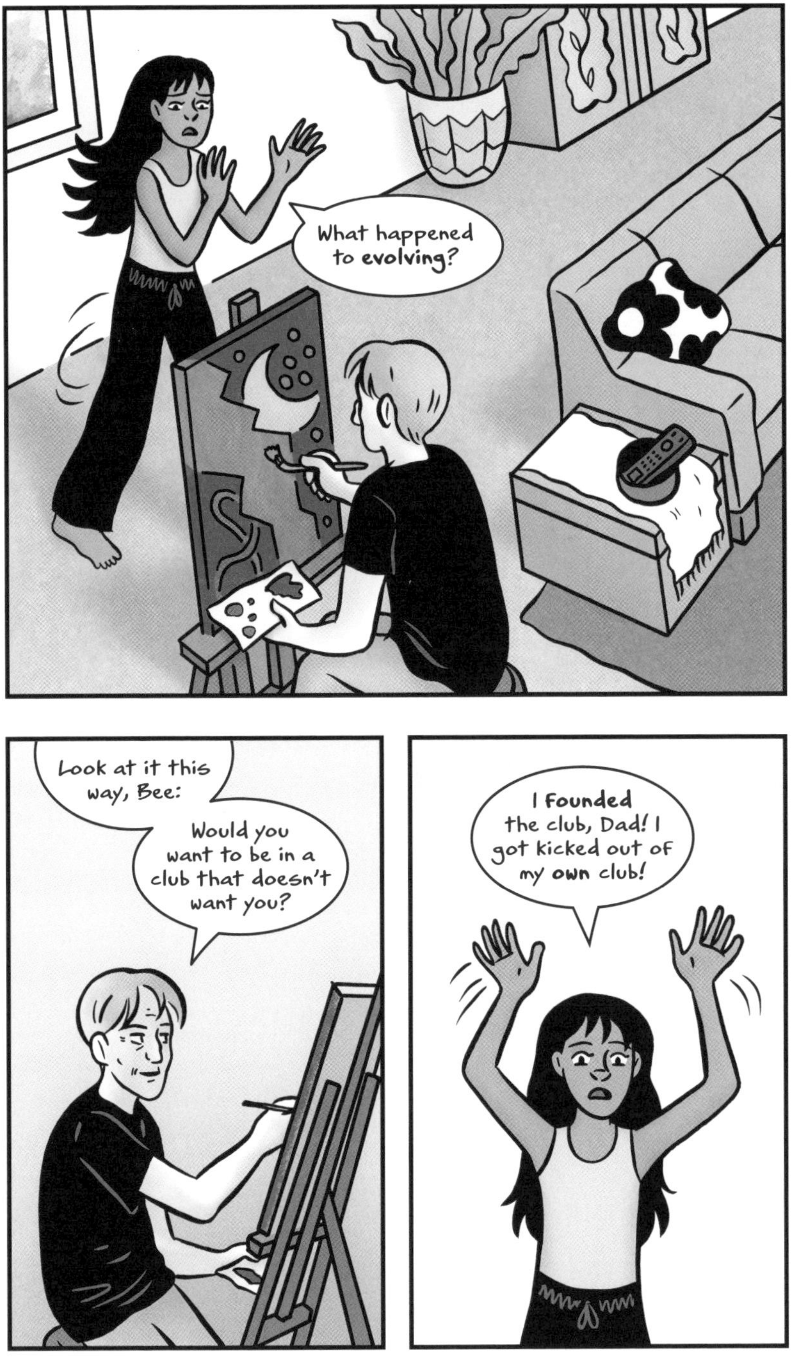
What happened to evolving?
Look at it this way, Bee:
Would you want to be in a club that doesn't want you?
I founded the club, Dad! I got kicked out of my own club!

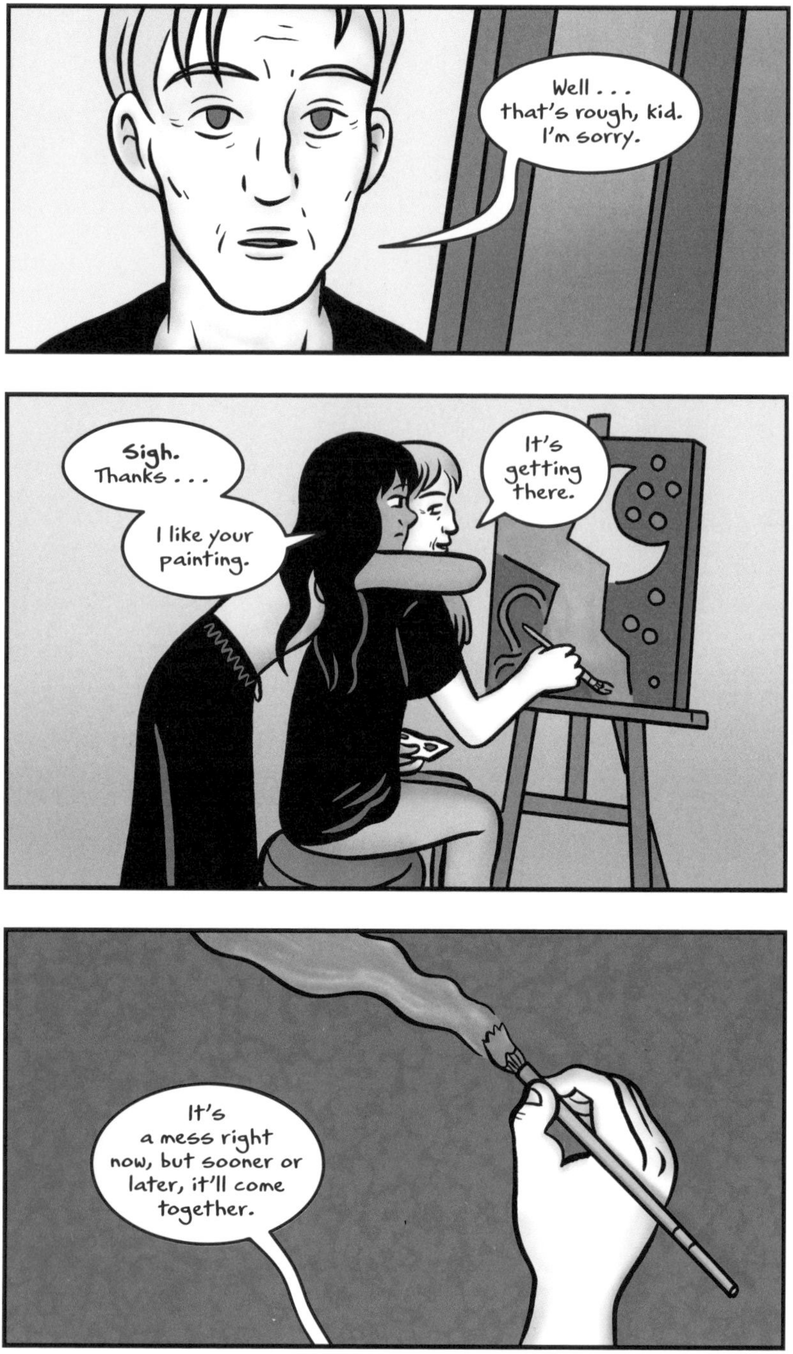
Well . . . that's rough, kid. I'm sorry.
Sigh. Thanks . . .
I like your painting.
It's getting there.
It's a mess right now, but sooner or later, it'll come together.

November

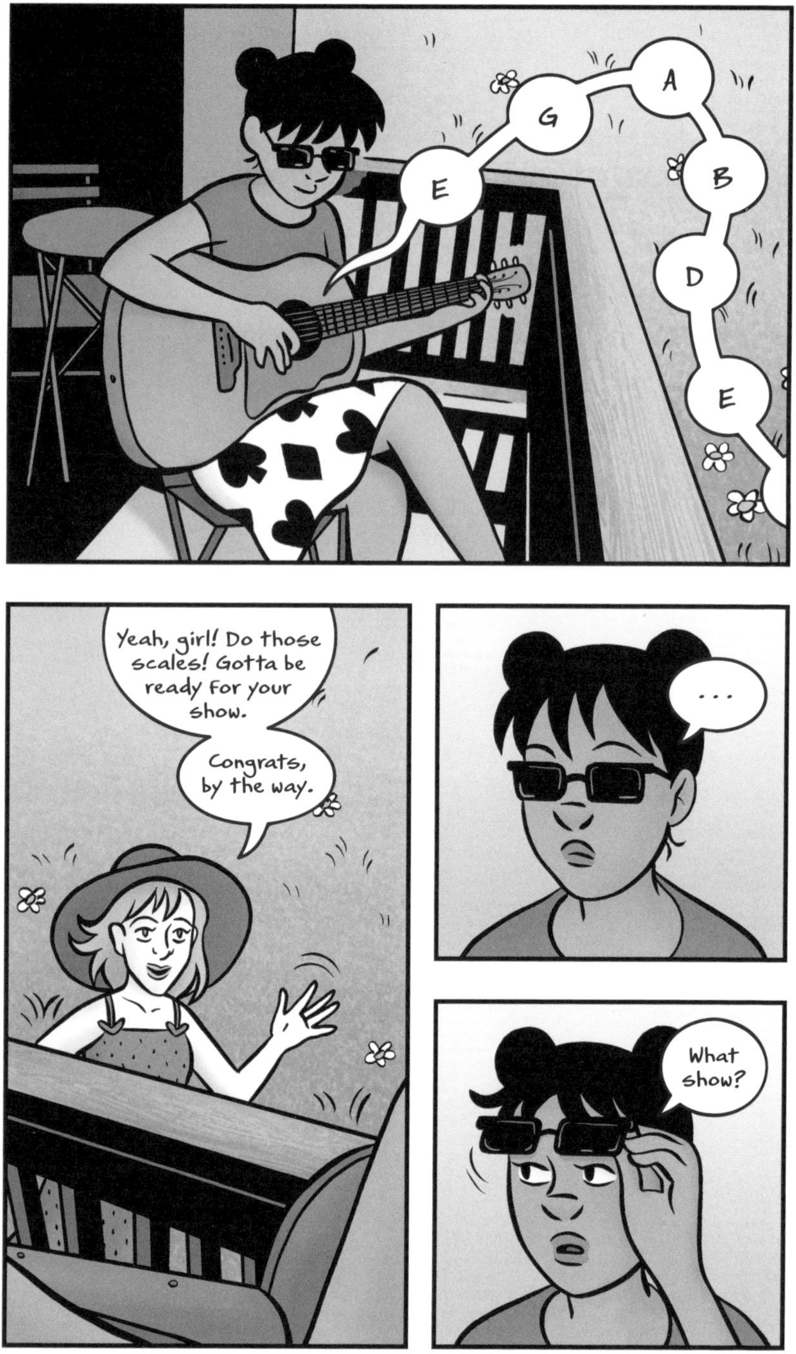
E
G
A
B
D
E
Yeah, girl! Do those scales! Gotta be ready for your show.
Congrats, by the way.
...
What show?

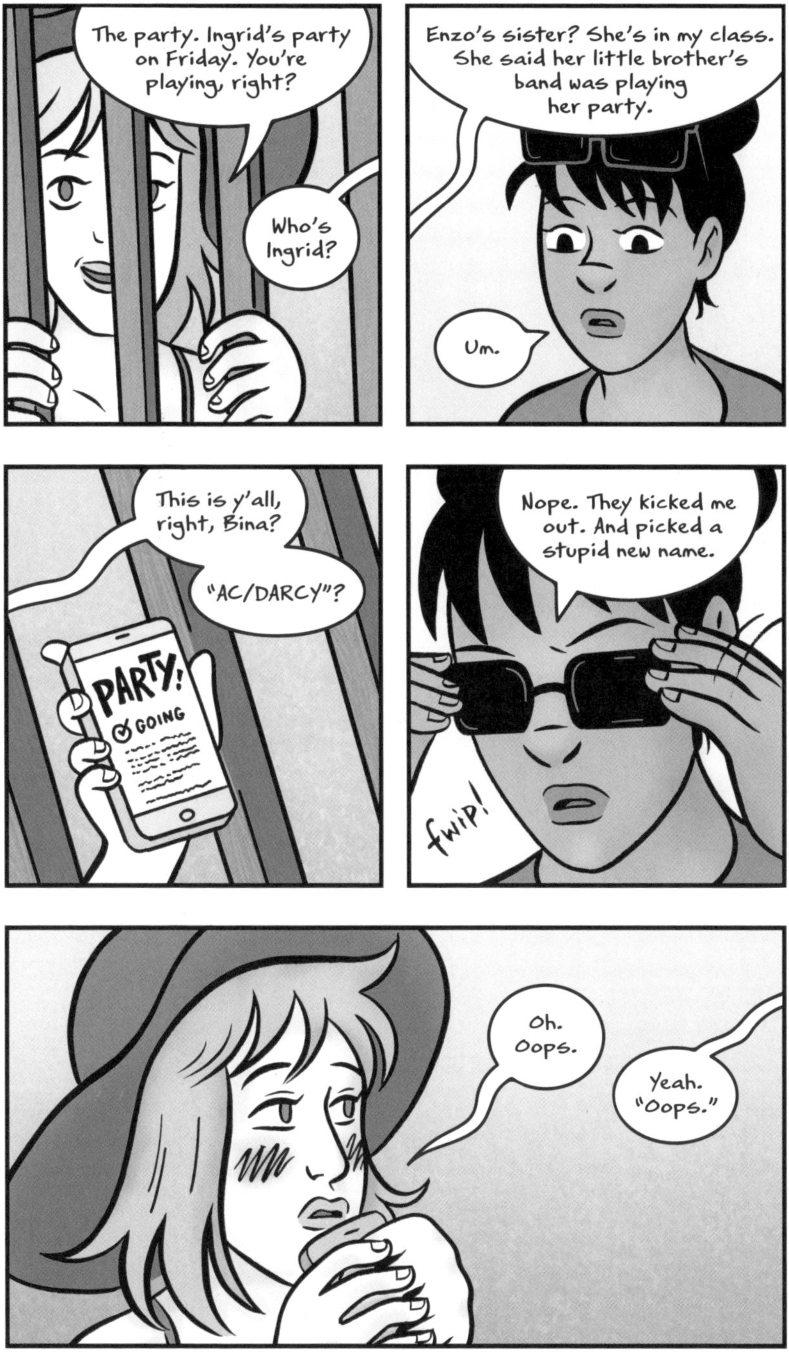
The party. Ingrid's party on Friday. You're playing, right?
Who's Ingrid?
Enzo's sister? She's in my class. She said her little brother's band was playing her party.
Um.
This is y'all, right, Bina?
"AC/DARCY"?
PARTY!
GOING
Nope. They kicked me out. And picked a stupid new name.
fwip!
Oh. Oops.
Yeah. "Oops."

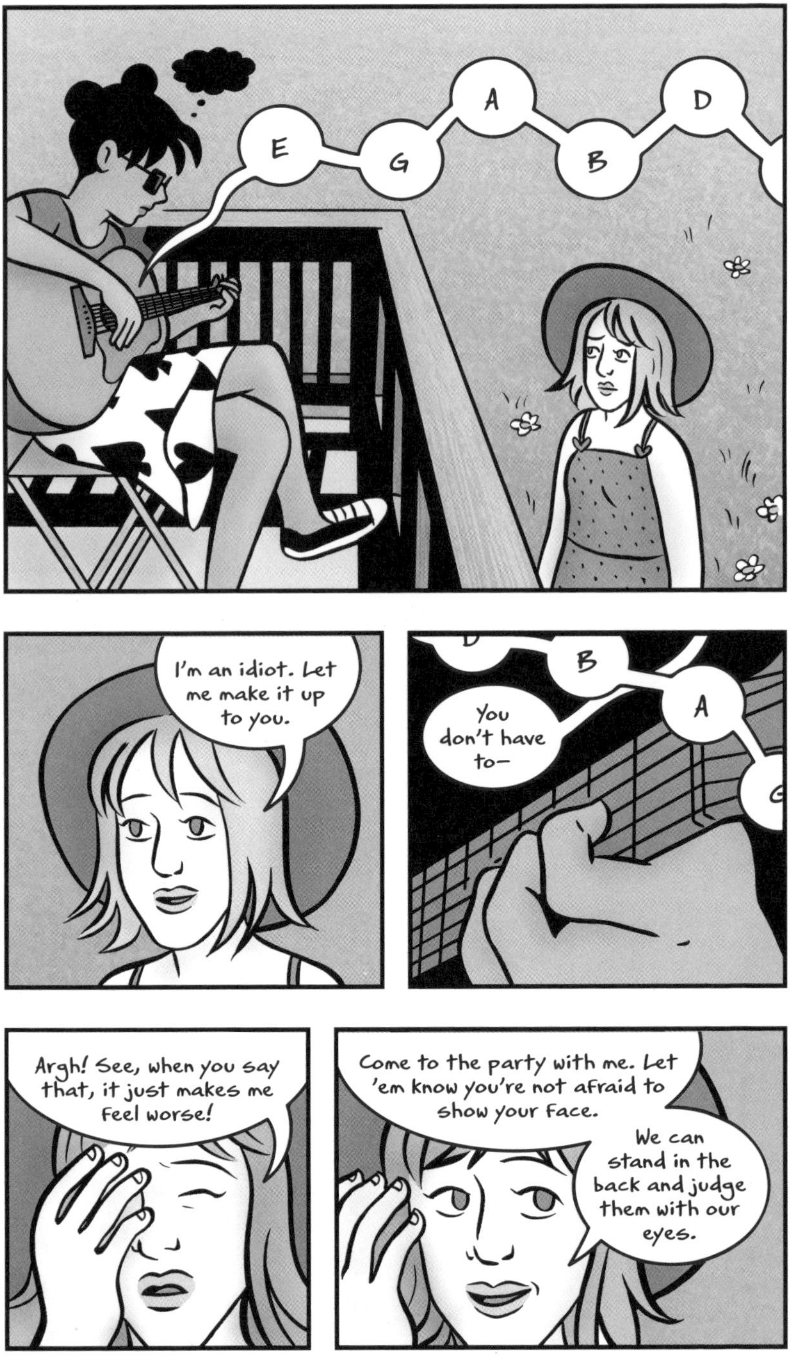
E
G
A
B
D
I'm an idiot. Let me make it up to you.
B
A
You don't have to—
Argh! See, when you say that, it just makes me feel worse!
Come to the party with me. Let 'em know you're not afraid to show your face.
We can stand in the back and judge them with our eyes.

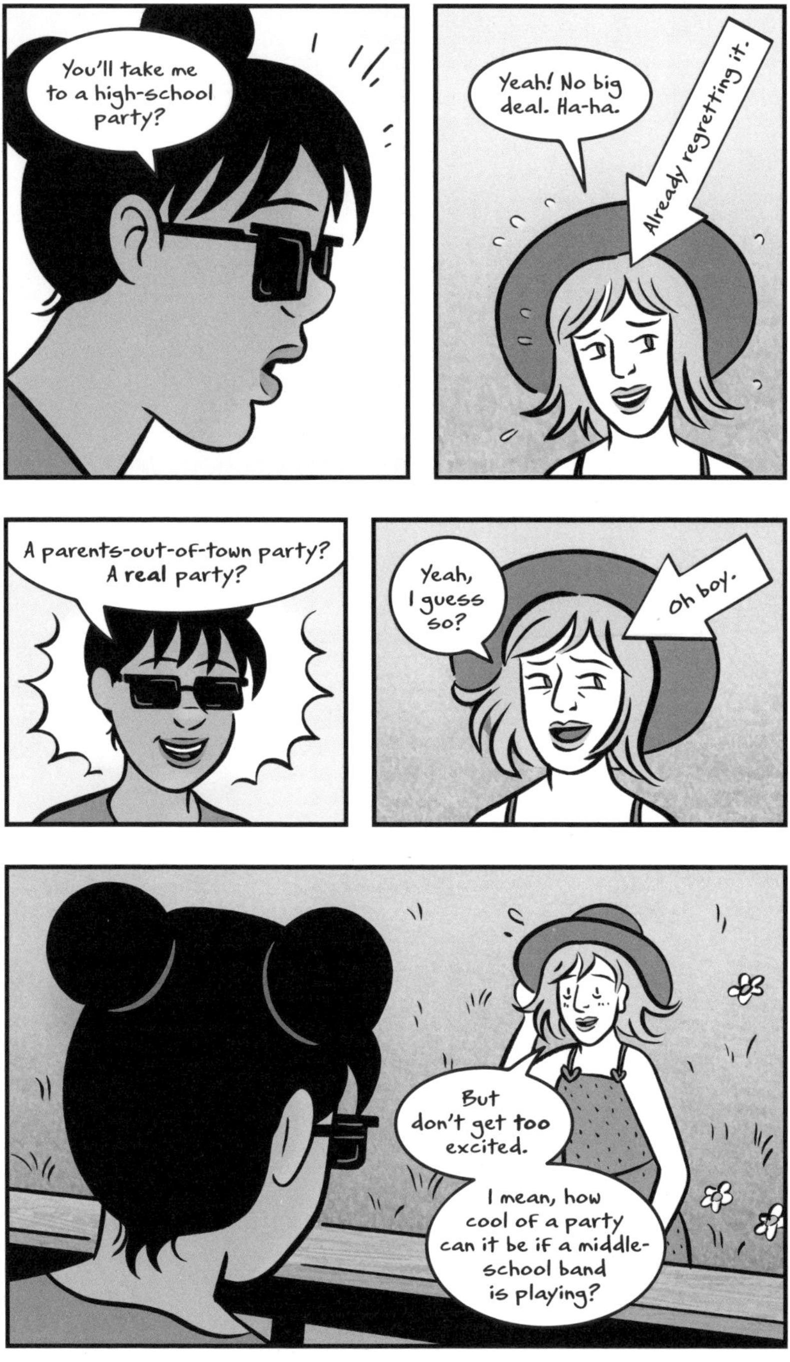
You'll take me to a high-school party?
Yeah! No big deal. Ha-ha.
Already regretting it.
A parents-out-of-town party? A real party?
Yeah, I guess so?
Oh boy.
But don't get too excited.
I mean, how cool of a party can it be if a middle-school band is playing?

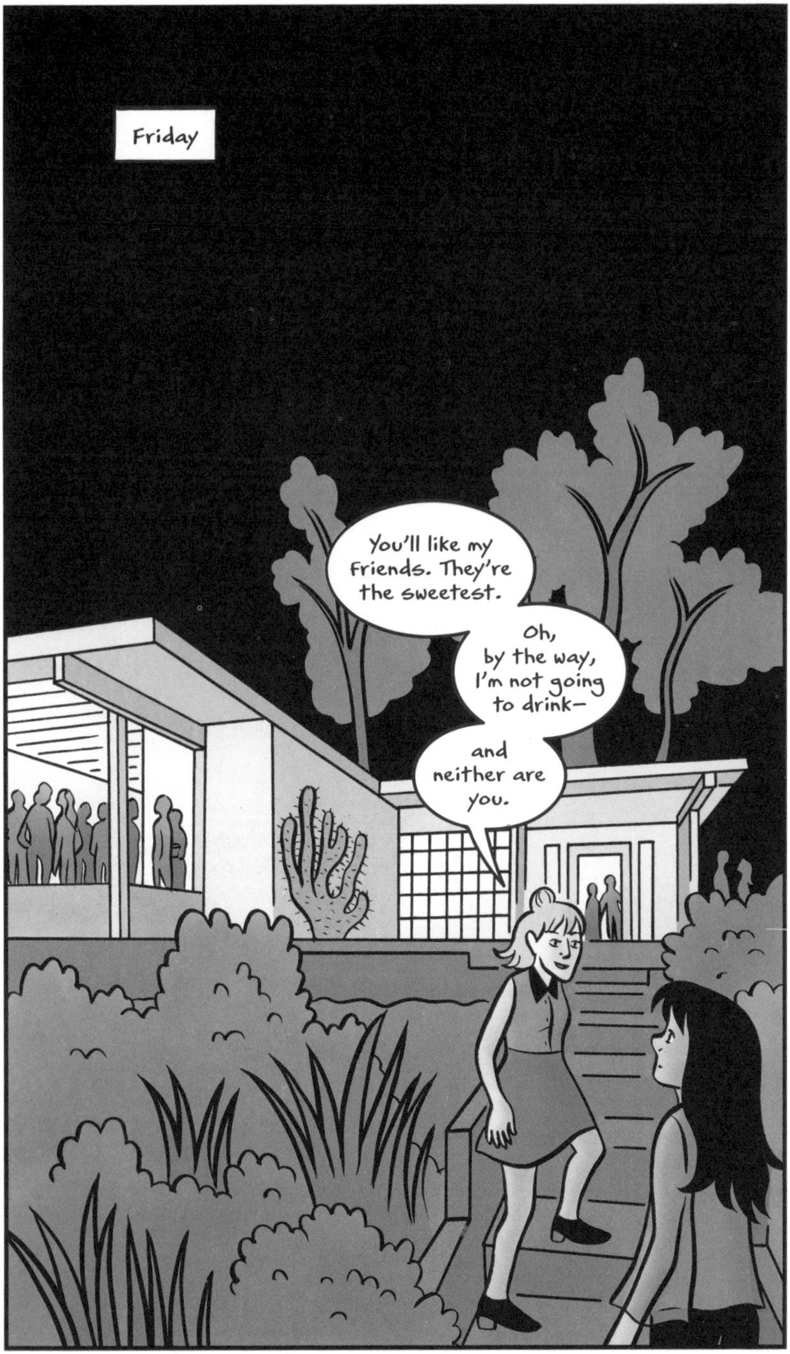
Friday
You'll like my friends. They're the sweetest.
Oh, by the way, I'm not going to drink–
and neither are you.

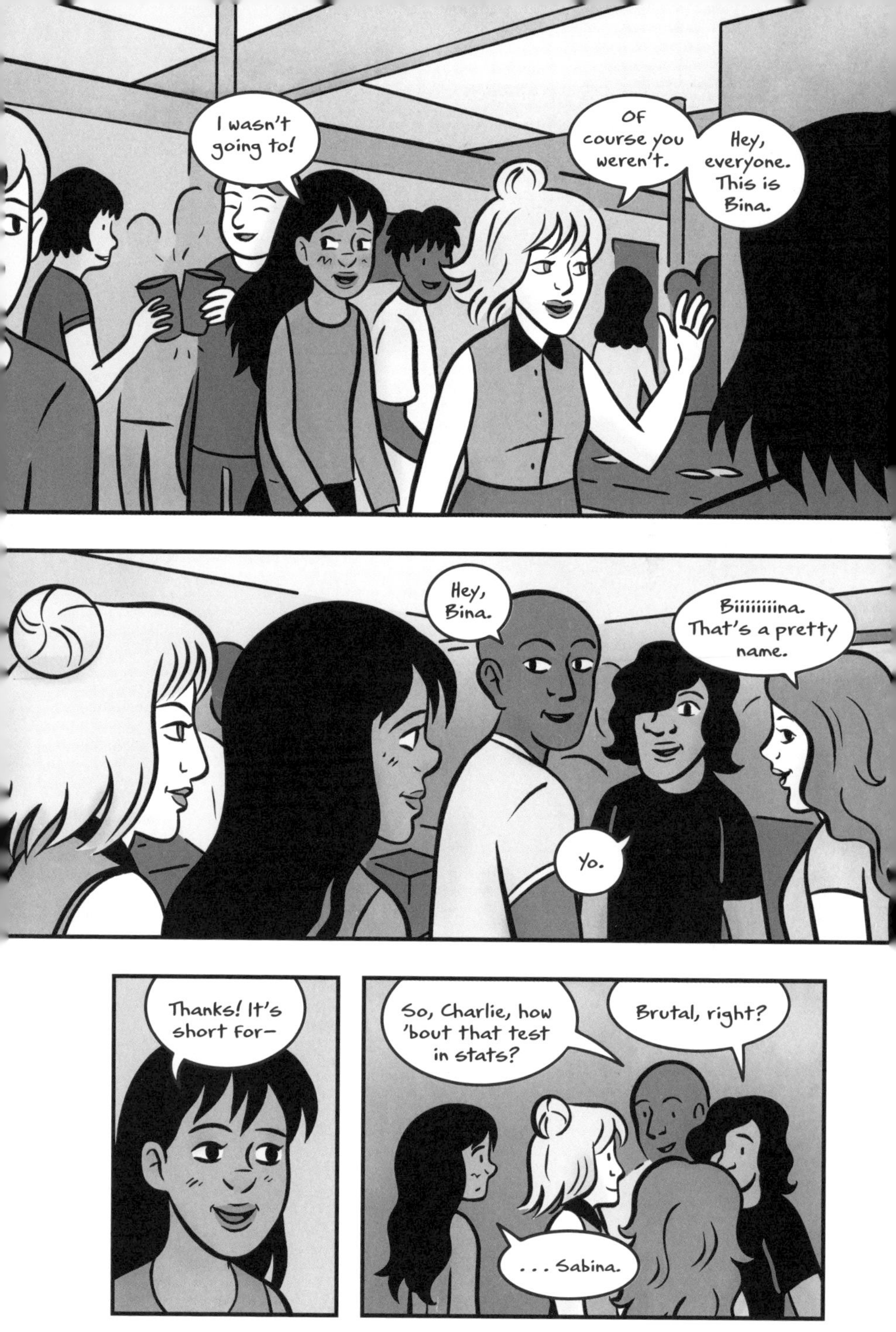
I wasn't going to!
Of course you weren't.
Hey, everyone. This is Bina.
Hey, Bina.
Biiiiiiiina. That's a pretty name.
Yo.
Thanks! It's short for—
So, Charlie, how 'bout that test in stats?
Brutal, right?
. . . Sabina.

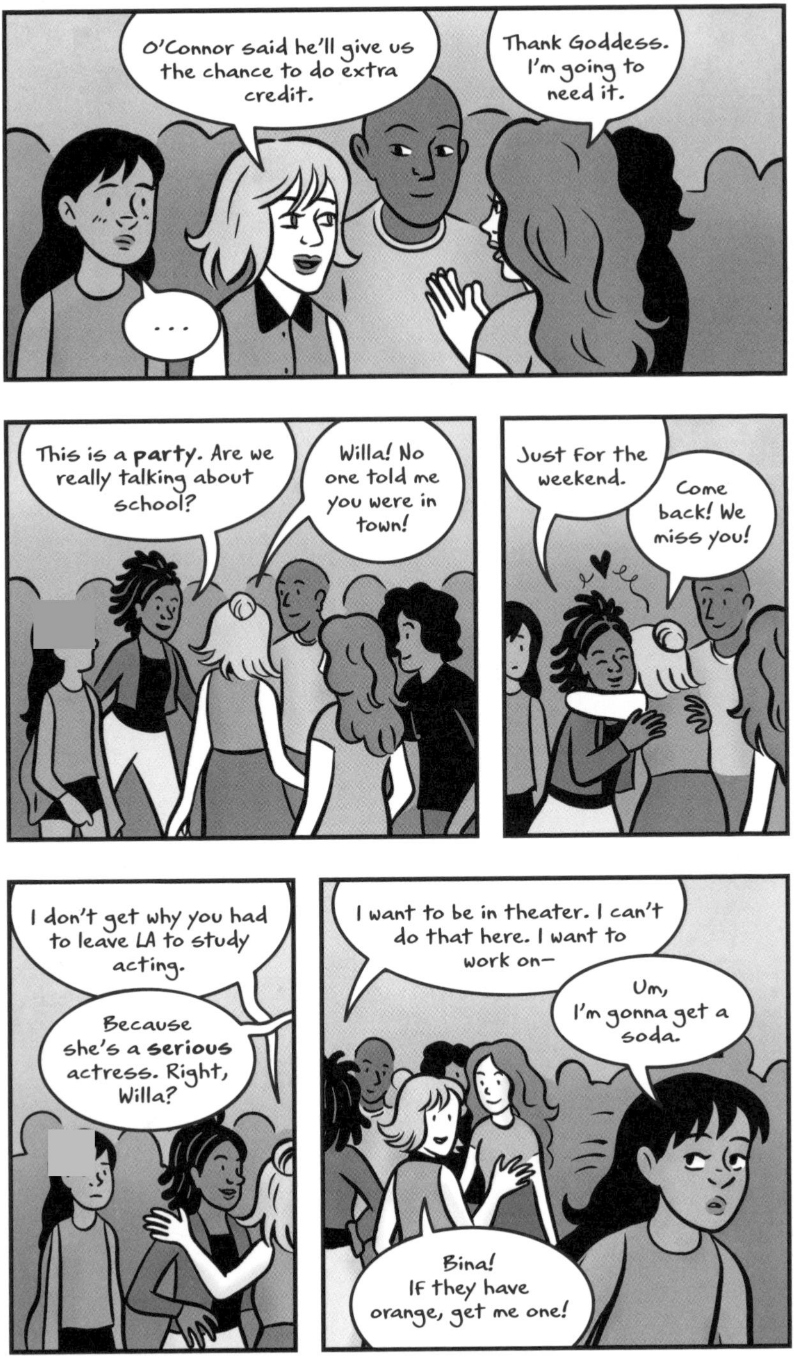
O'Connor said he'll give us the chance to do extra credit.
Thank Goddess. I'm going to need it.
...
This is a **party**. Are we really talking about school?
Willa! No one told me you were in town!
Just for the weekend.
Come back! We miss you!
I don't get why you had to leave LA to study acting.
Because she's a **serious** actress. Right, Willa?
I want to be in theater. I can't do that here. I want to work on—
Um, I'm gonna get a soda.
Bina! If they have orange, get me one!

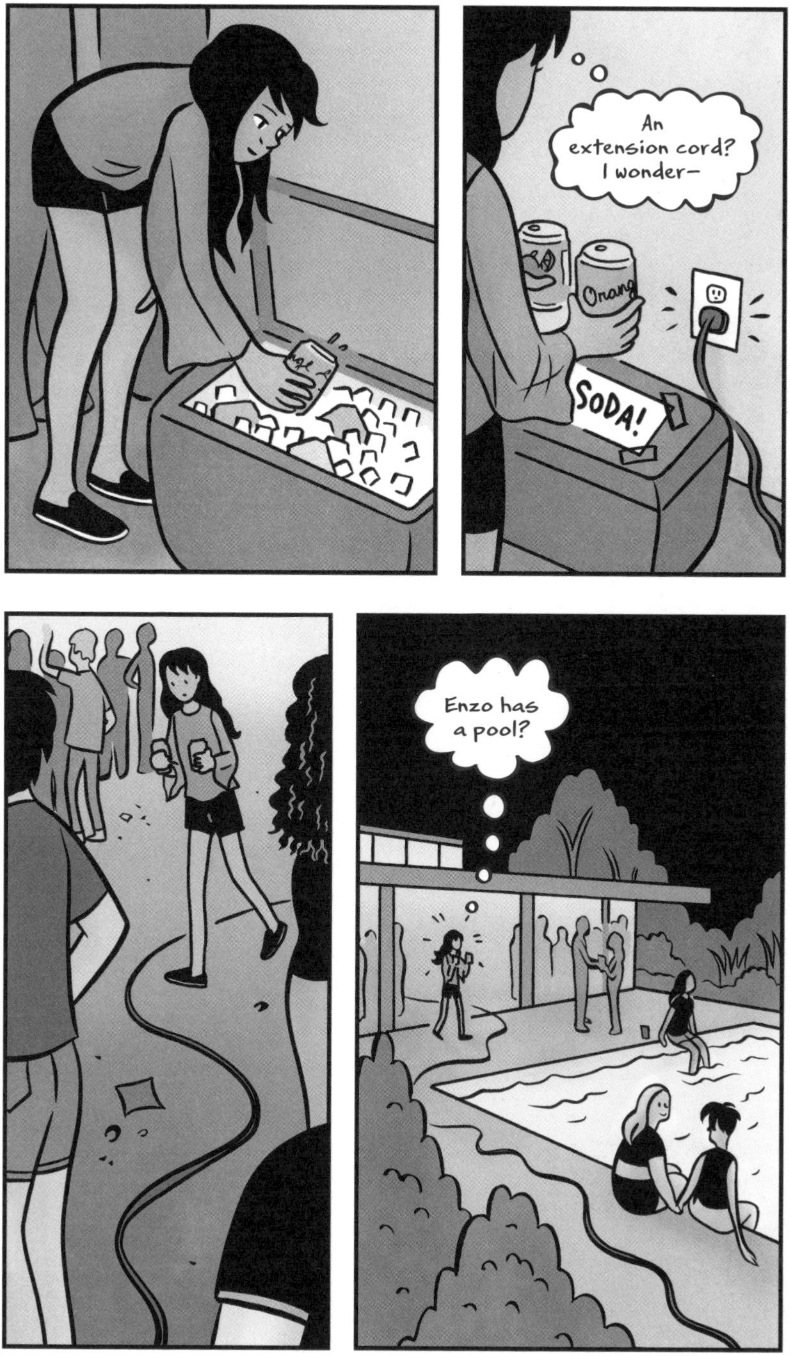
An extension cord? I wonder–
Orang
SODA!
Enzo has a pool?

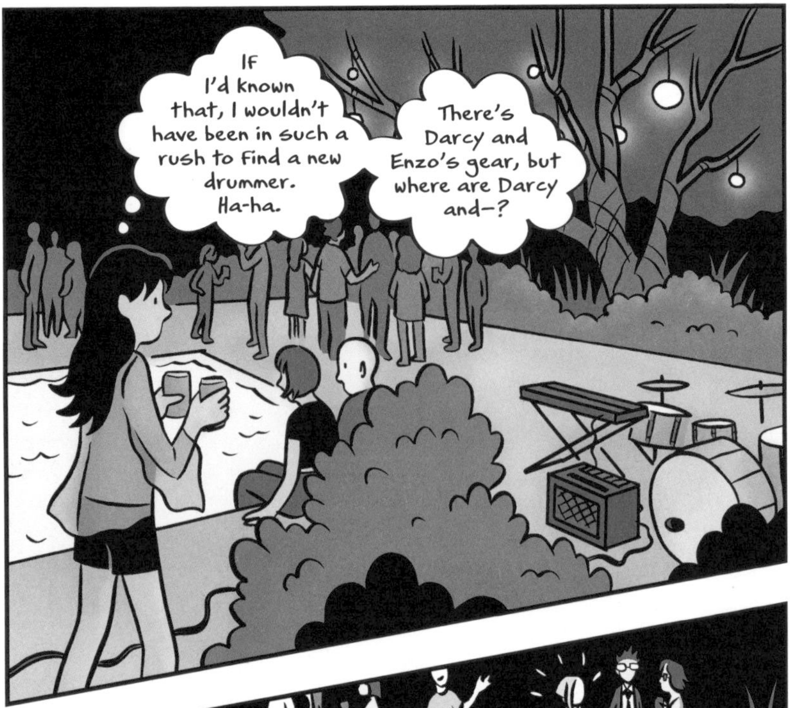
If I'd known that, I wouldn't have been in such a rush to find a new drummer. Ha-ha.
There's Darcy and Enzo's gear, but where are Darcy and—?

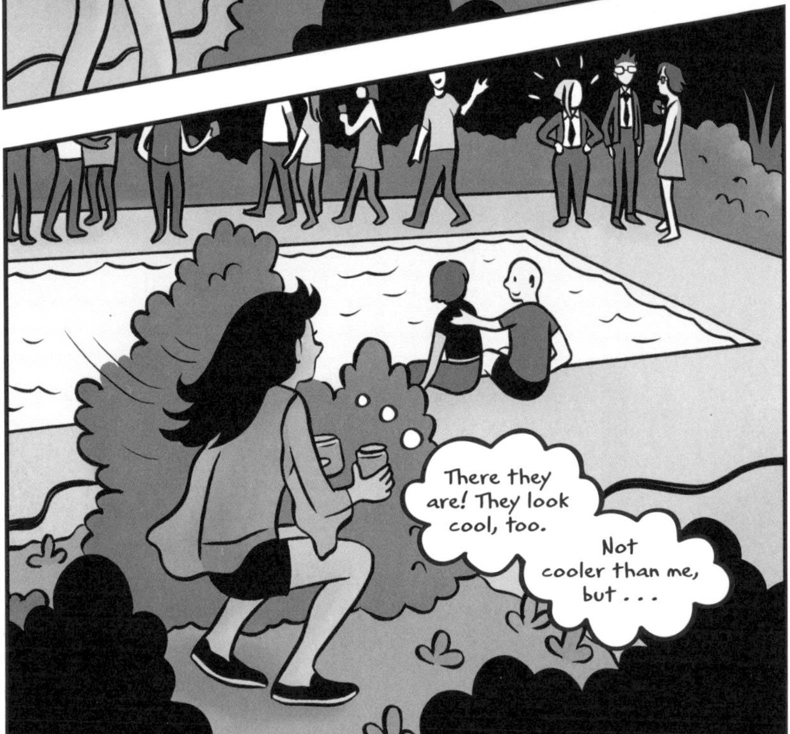
There they are! They look cool, too.
Not cooler than me, but . . .

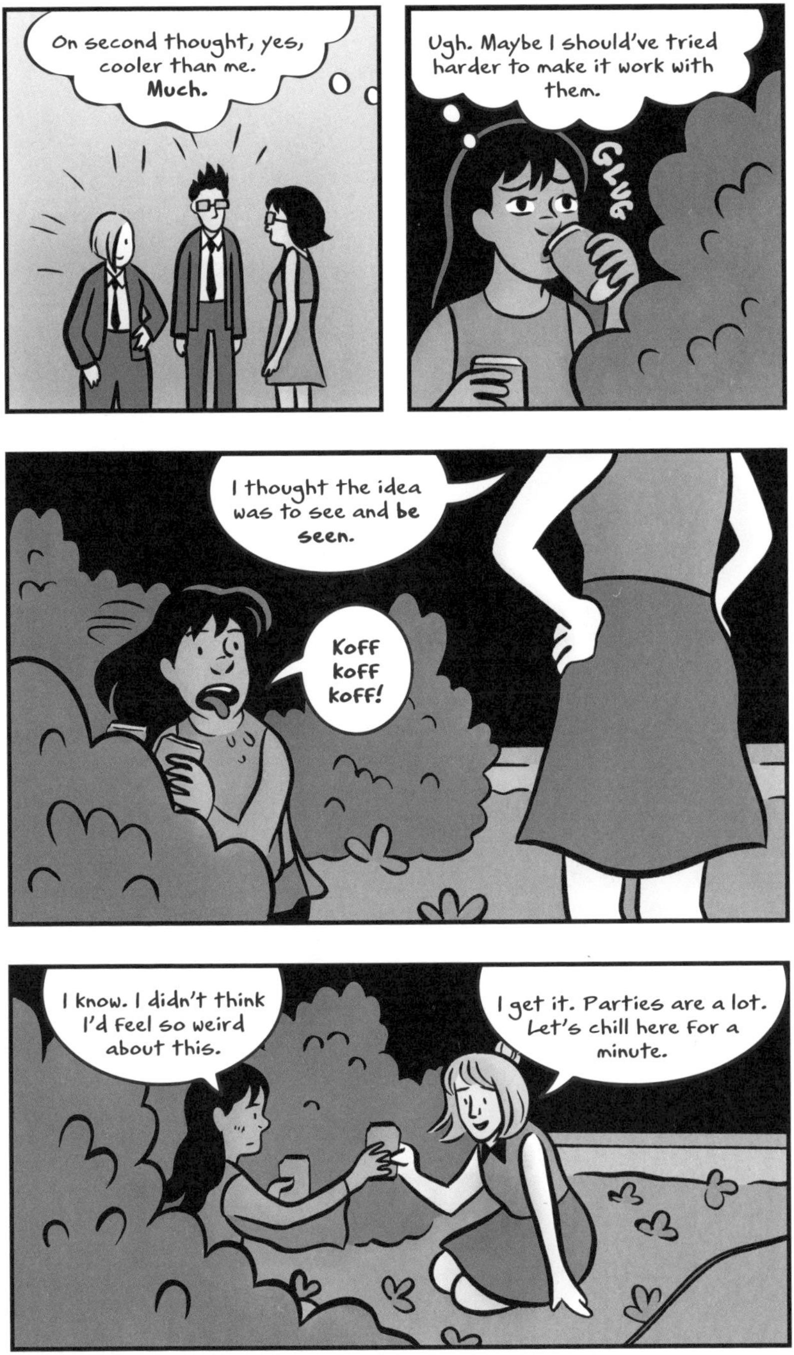
On second thought, yes, cooler than me. **Much.**
Ugh. Maybe I should've tried harder to make it work with them.
GLUG
I thought the idea was to see and be seen.
KOFF KOFF KOFF!
I know. I didn't think I'd feel so weird about this.
I get it. Parties are a lot. Let's chill here for a minute.

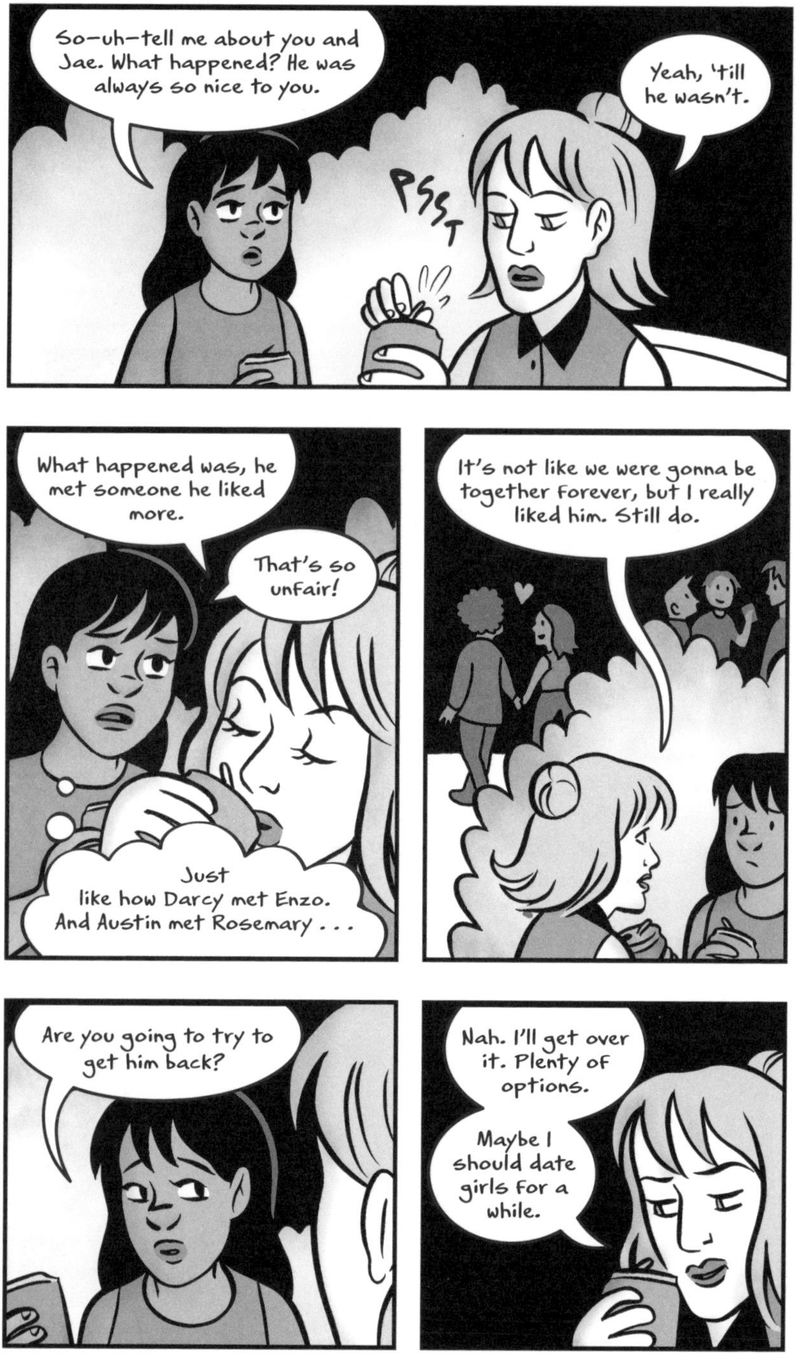
So—uh—tell me about you and Jae. What happened? He was always so nice to you.
Yeah, 'till he wasn't.
PSST
What happened was, he met someone he liked more.
That's so unfair!
Just like how Darcy met Enzo. And Austin met Rosemary . . .
It's not like we were gonna be together forever, but I really liked him. Still do.
Are you going to try to get him back?
Nah. I'll get over it. Plenty of options.
Maybe I should date girls for a while.

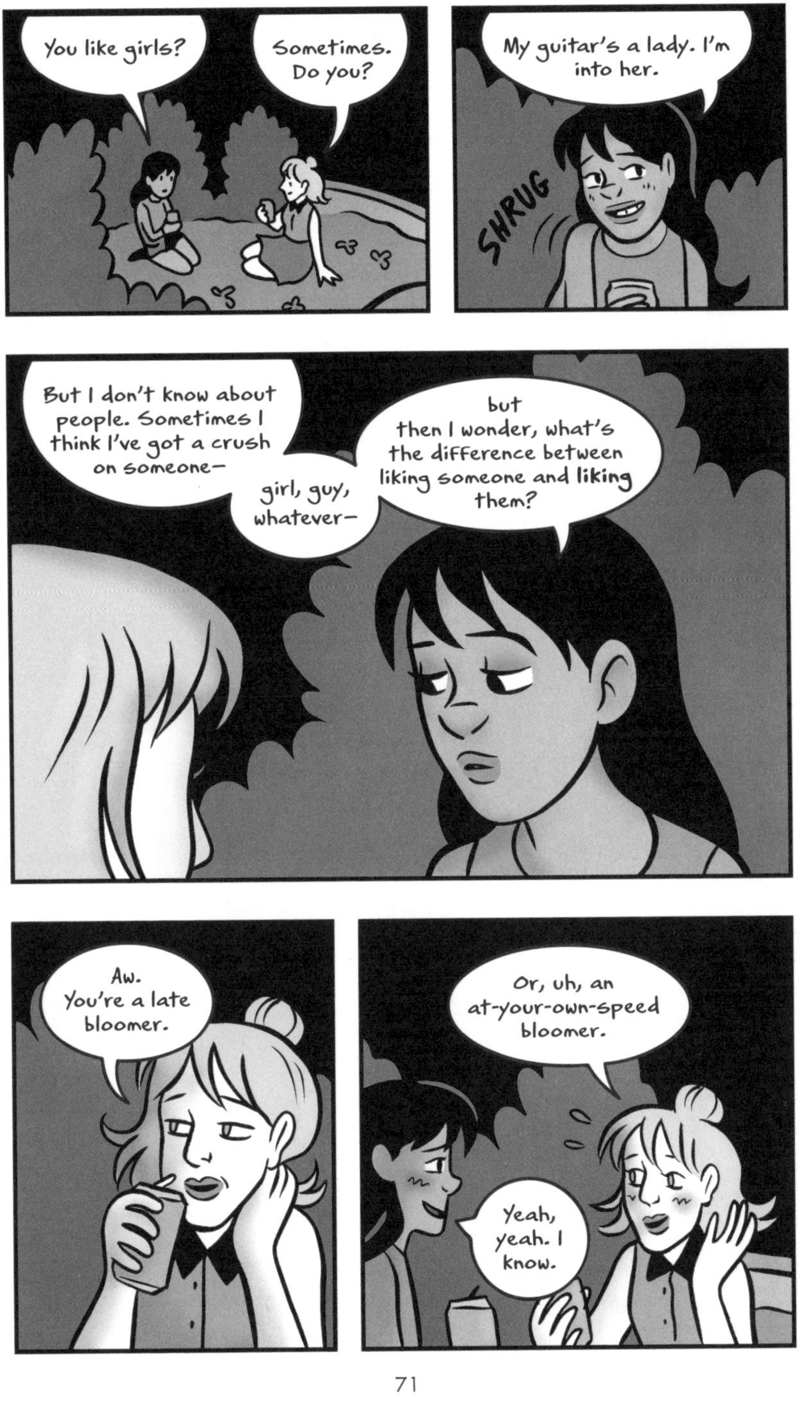
You like girls?
Sometimes. Do you?
My guitar's a lady. I'm into her.
SHRUG
But I don't know about people. Sometimes I think I've got a crush on someone—
girl, guy, whatever—
but then I wonder, what's the difference between liking someone and liking them?
Aw. You're a late bloomer.
Or, uh, an at-your-own-speed bloomer.
Yeah, yeah. I know.

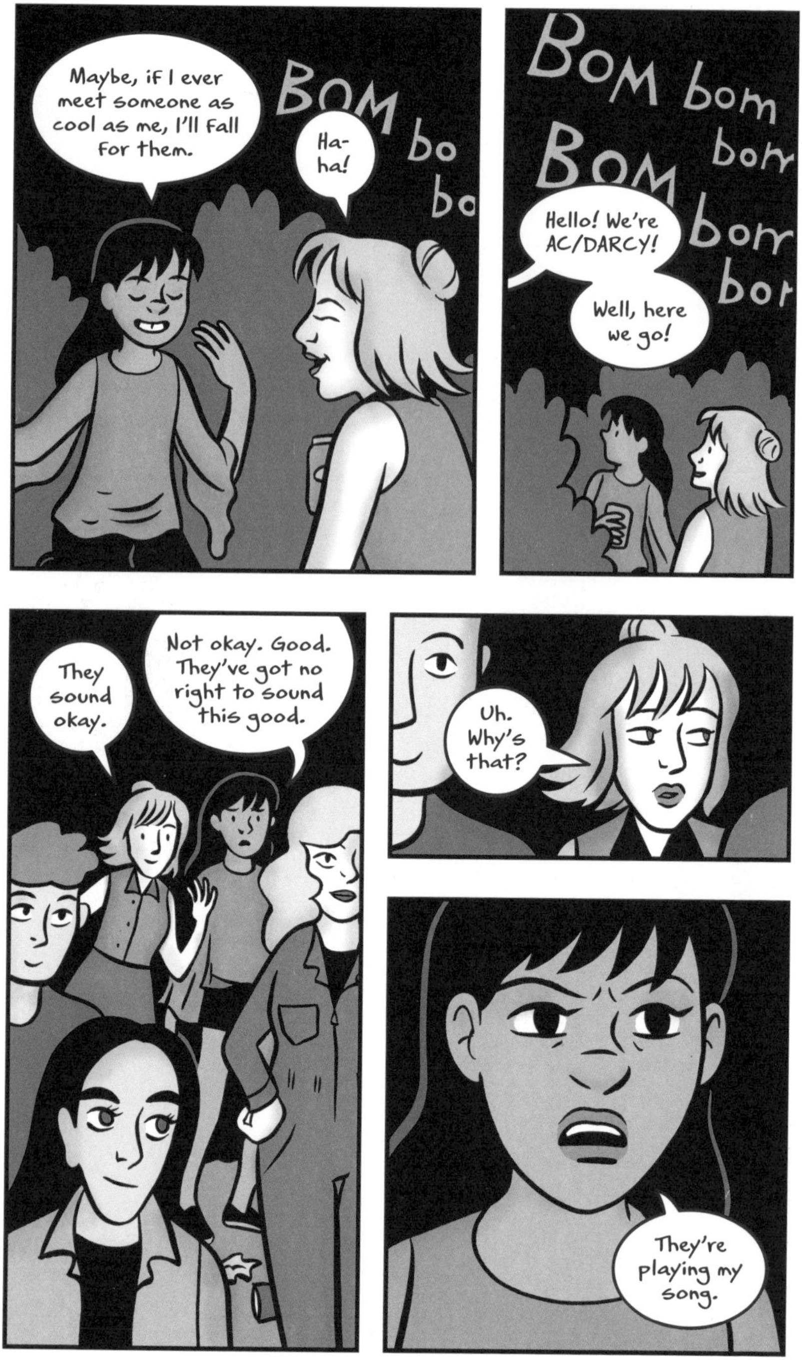
Maybe, if I ever meet someone as cool as me, I'll fall for them.
BOM bo bo
Ha-ha!
BOM bom bom
BOM bom bom
Hello! We're AC/DARCY!
Well, here we go!
They sound okay.
Not okay. Good. They've got no right to sound this good.
Uh. Why's that?
They're playing my song.

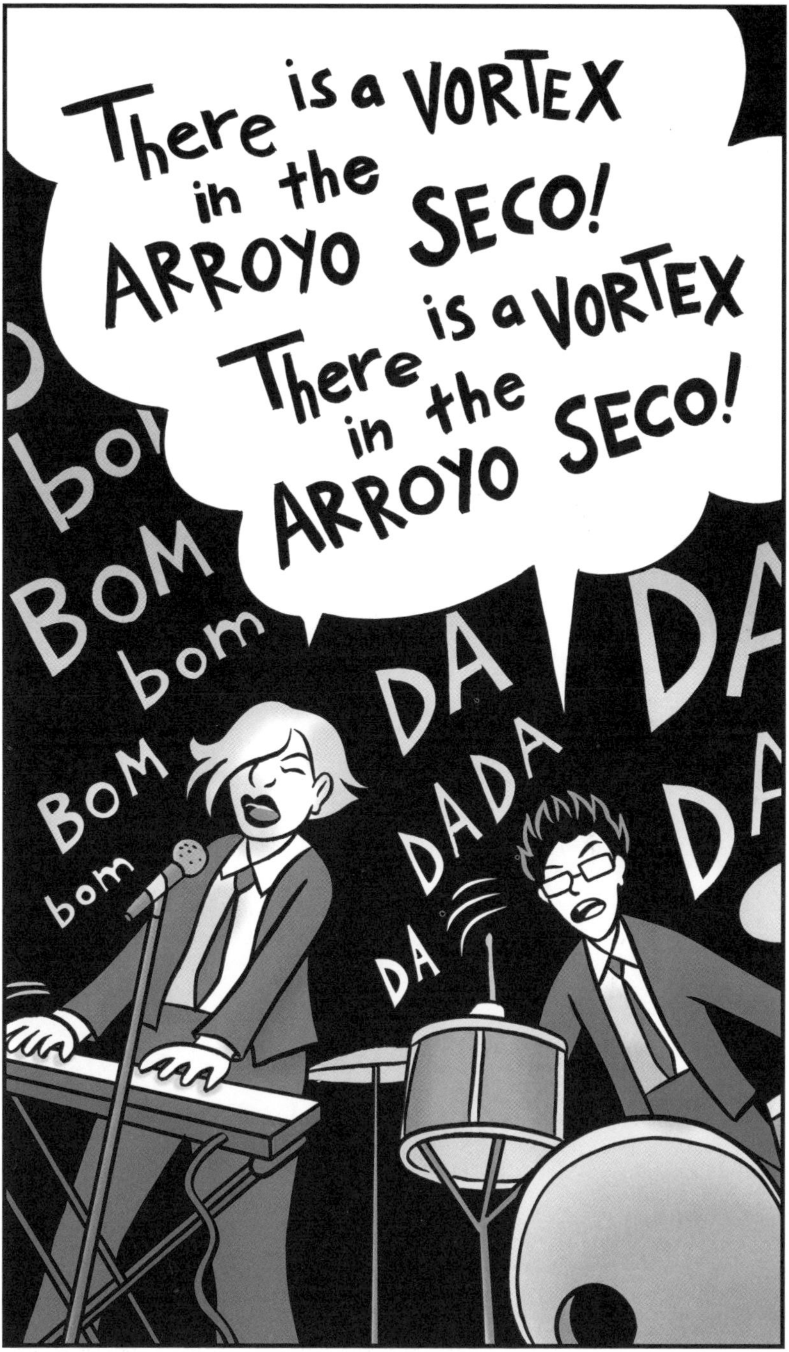
There is a VORTEX in the ARROYO SECO! There is a VORTEX in the ARROYO SECO!
BOM bom BOM bom
DA DA DADA DA
DA DA

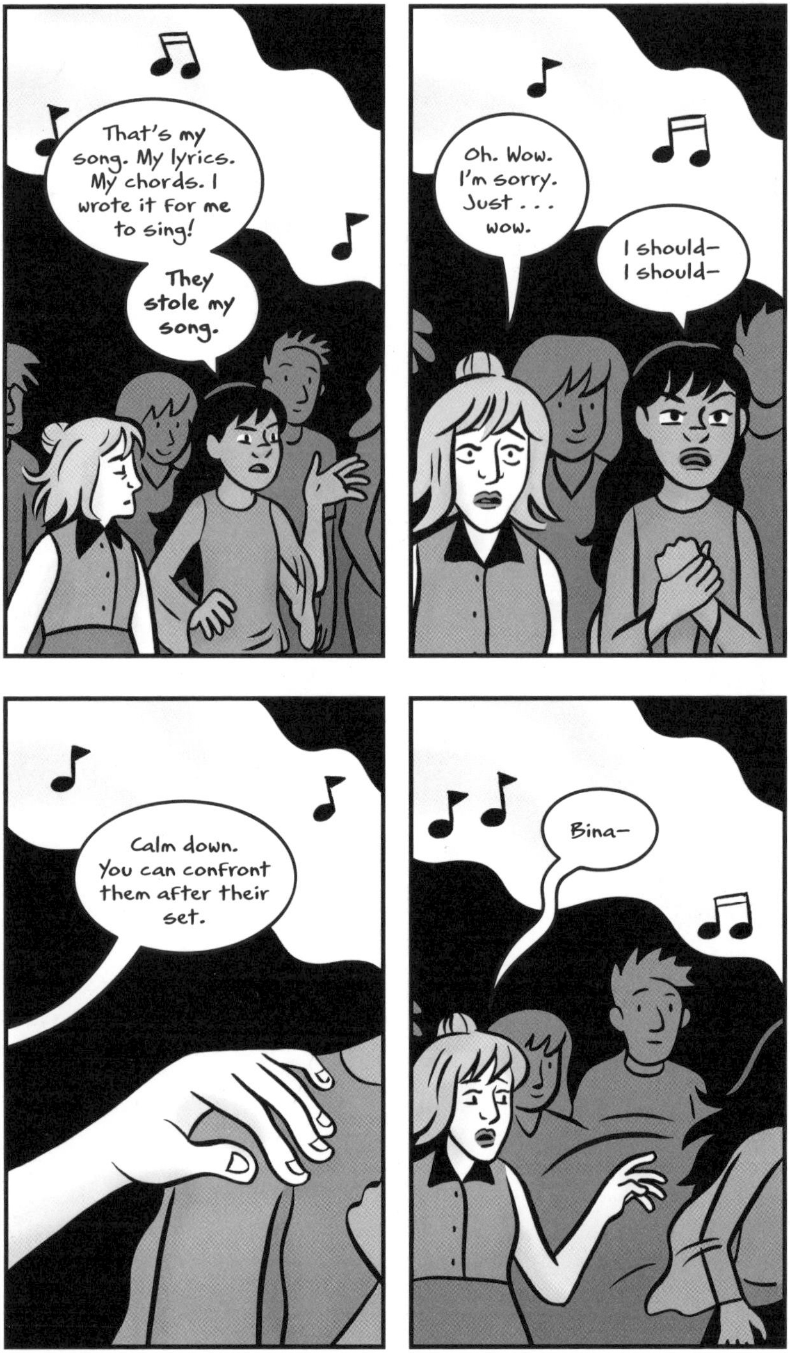
That's my song. My lyrics. My chords. I wrote it for me to sing!
They stole my song.
Oh. Wow. I'm sorry. Just . . . wow.
I should— I should—
Calm down. You can confront them after their set.
Bina—

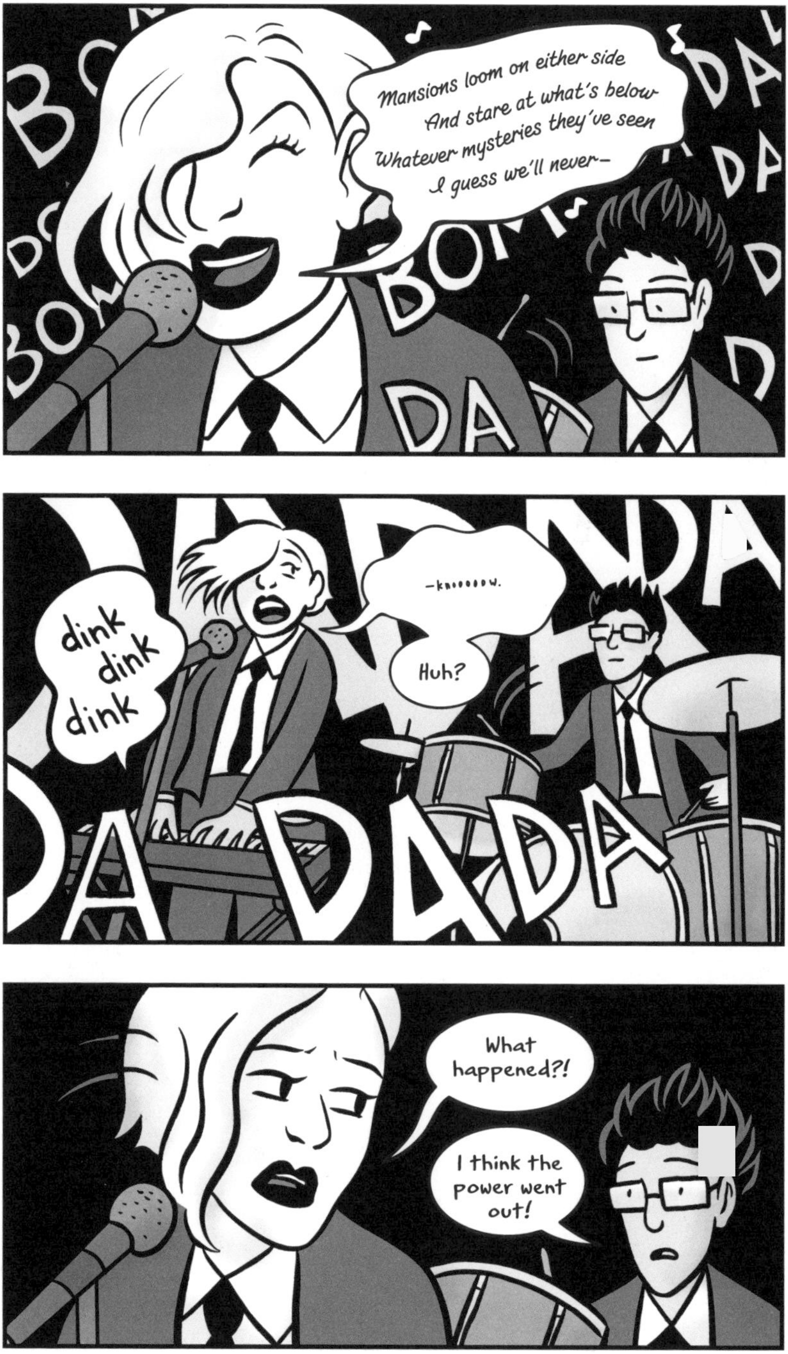
BOM
DA
Mansions loom on either side
And stare at what's below
Whatever mysteries they've seen
I guess we'll never—
BOM
DA
dink dink dink
-knoooooow.
Huh?
DADADA
What happened?!
I think the power went out!

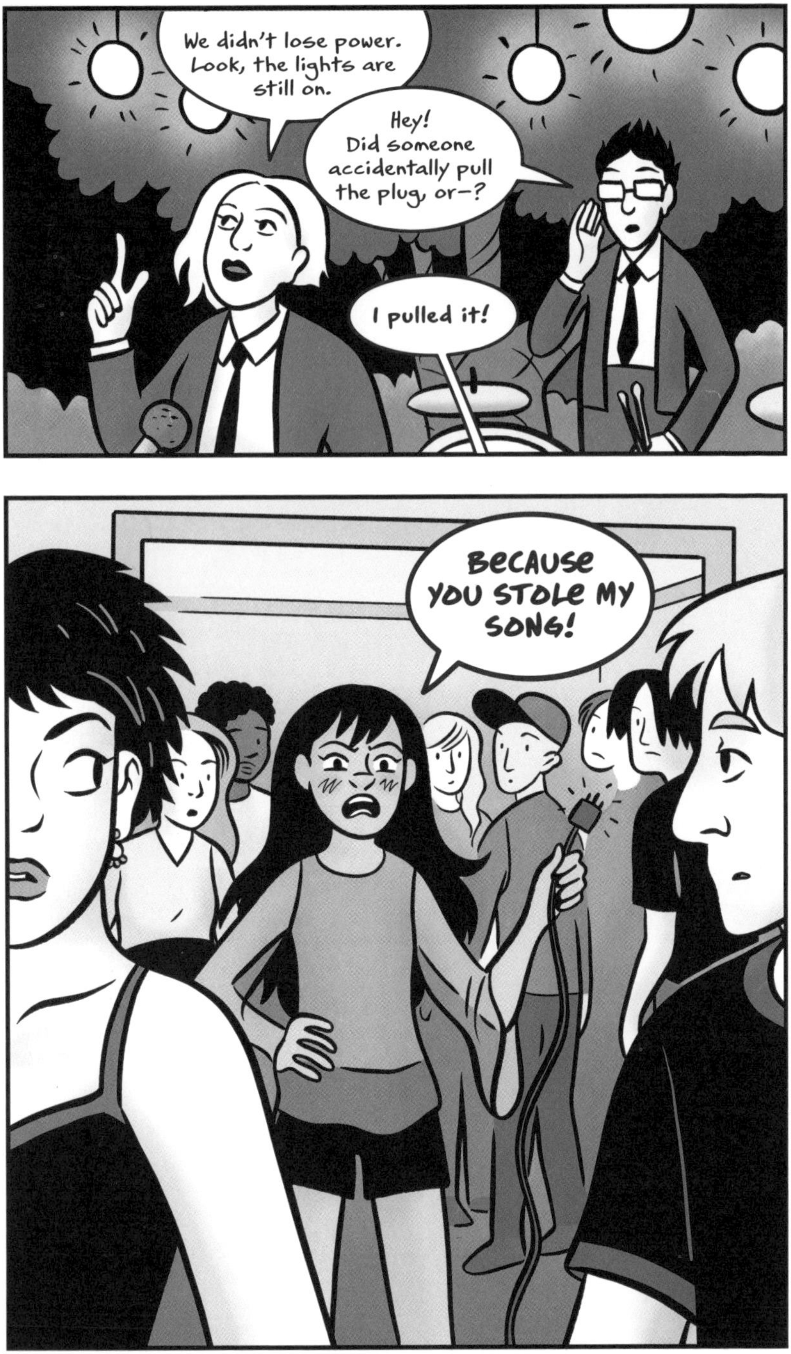
We didn't lose power. Look, the lights are still on.
Hey! Did someone accidentally pull the plug, or—?
I pulled it!
BECAUSE YOU STOLE MY SONG!

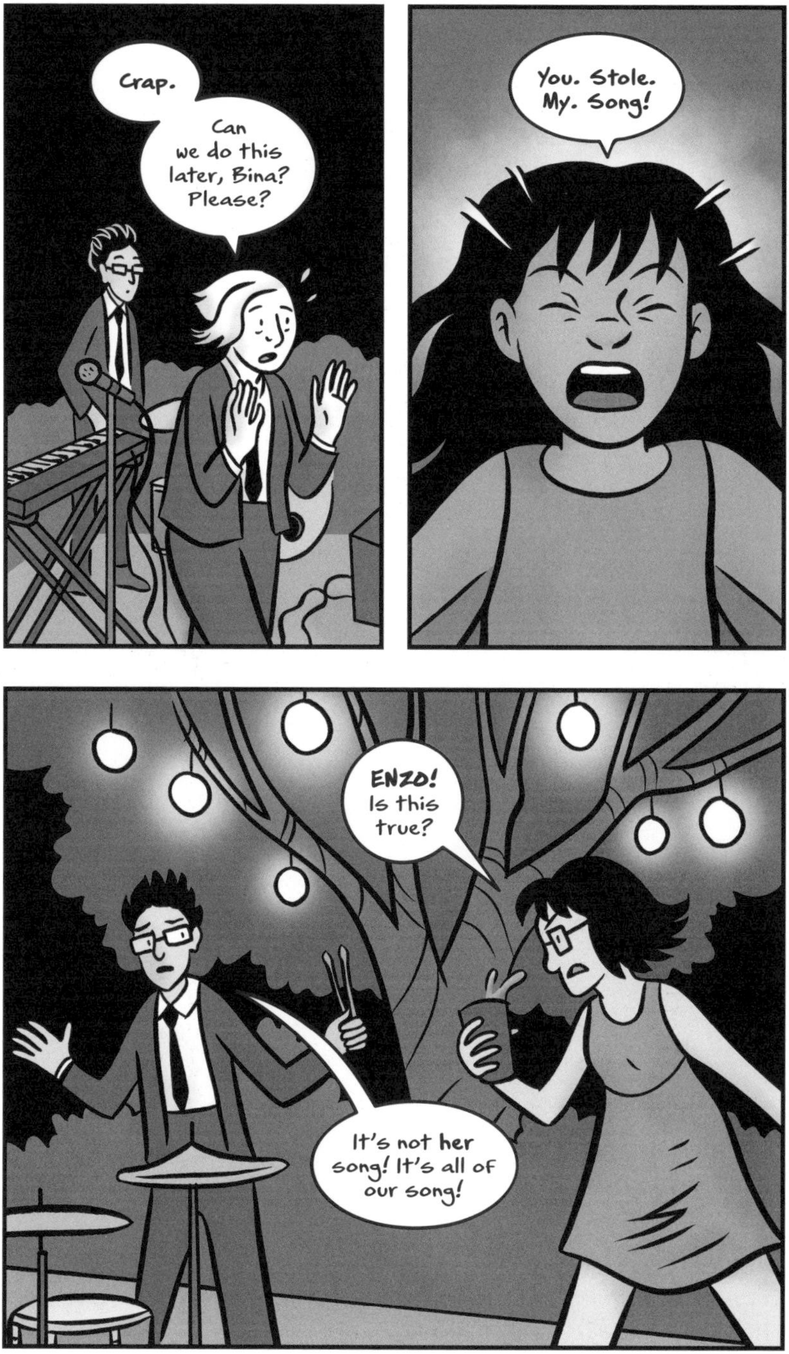
Crap.
Can we do this later, Bina? Please?
You. Stole. My. Song!
ENZO! Is this true?
It's not her song! It's all of our song!

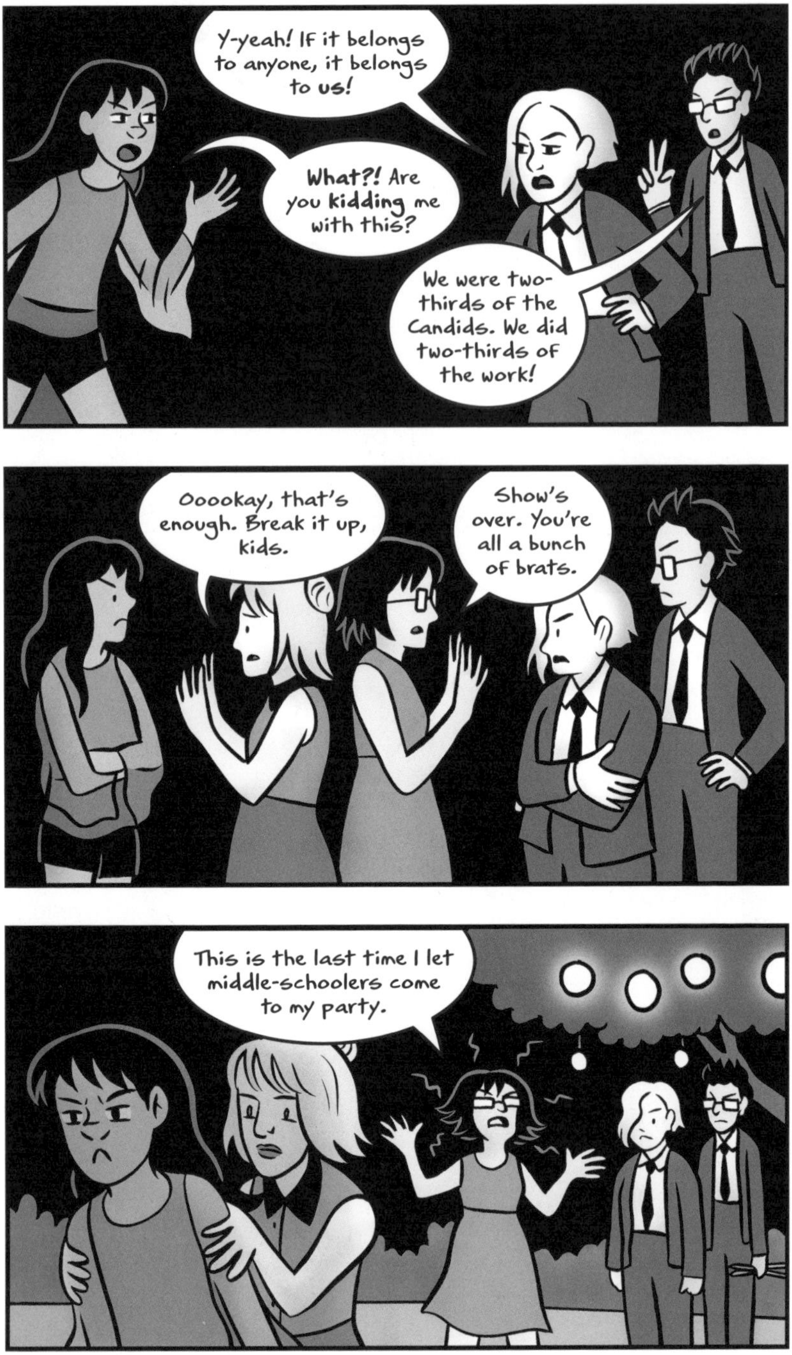
Y-yeah! If it belongs to anyone, it belongs to us!
What?! Are you kidding me with this?
We were two-thirds of the Candids. We did two-thirds of the work!
Ooookay, that's enough. Break it up, kids.
Show's over. You're all a bunch of brats.
This is the last time I let middle-schoolers come to my party.

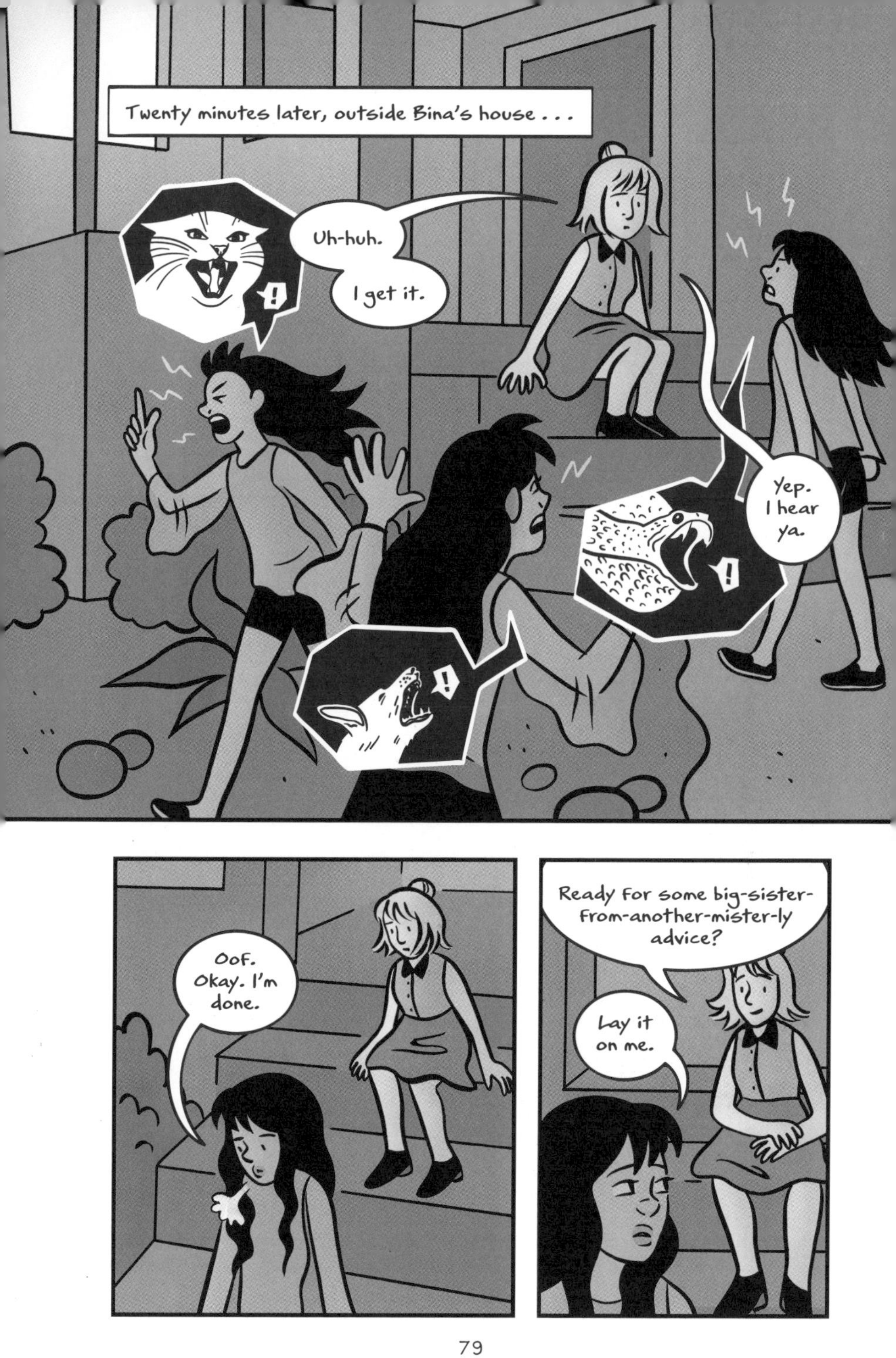
Twenty minutes later, outside Bina's house . . .
!
Uh-huh.
I get it.
!
Yep. I hear ya.
!
Oof. Okay. I'm done.
Ready for some big-sister-from-another-mister-ly advice?
Lay it on me.

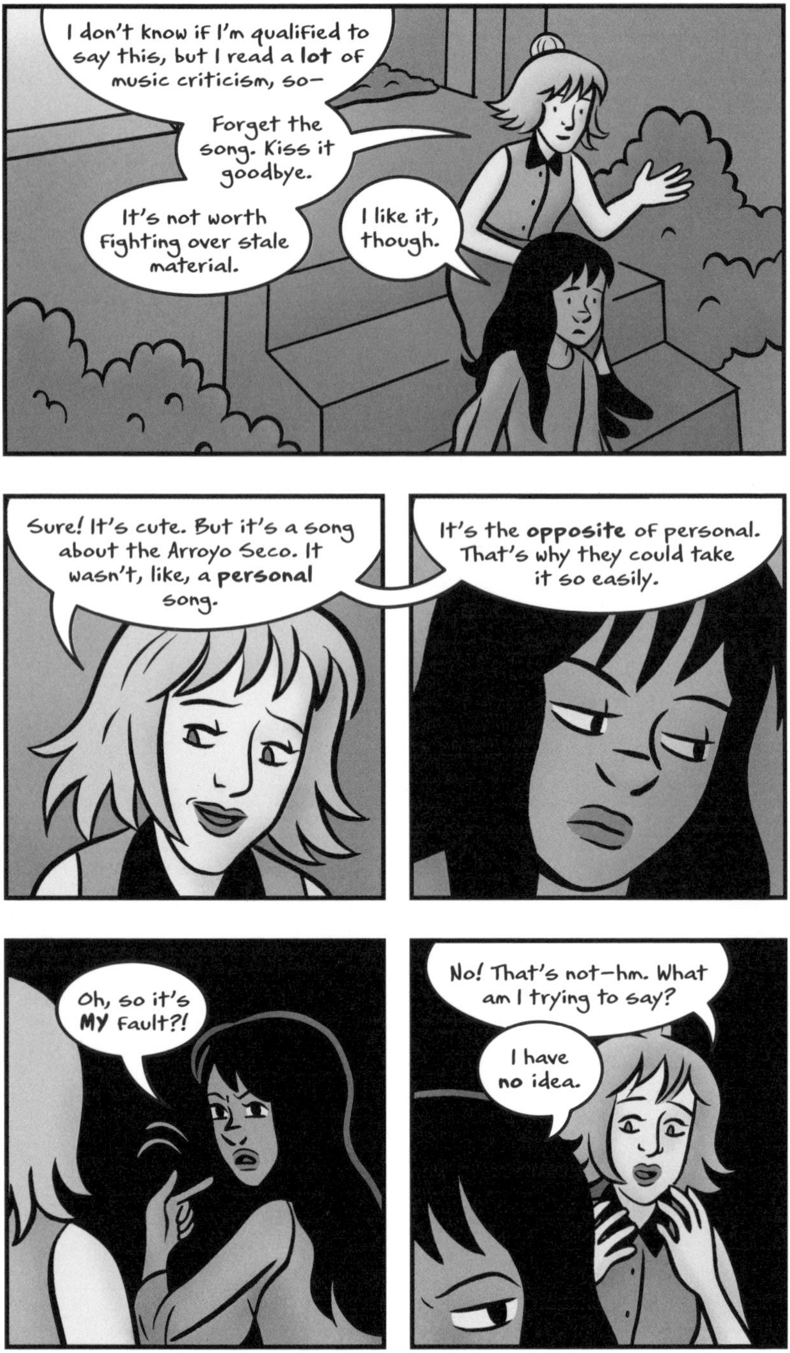
I don't know if I'm qualified to say this, but I read a **lot** of music criticism, so—
Forget the song. Kiss it goodbye.
It's not worth fighting over stale material.
I like it, though.
Sure! It's cute. But it's a song about the Arroyo Seco. It wasn't, like, a **personal** song.
It's the **opposite** of personal. That's why they could take it so easily.
Oh, so it's **MY** fault?!
No! That's not—hm. What am I trying to say?
I have no idea.

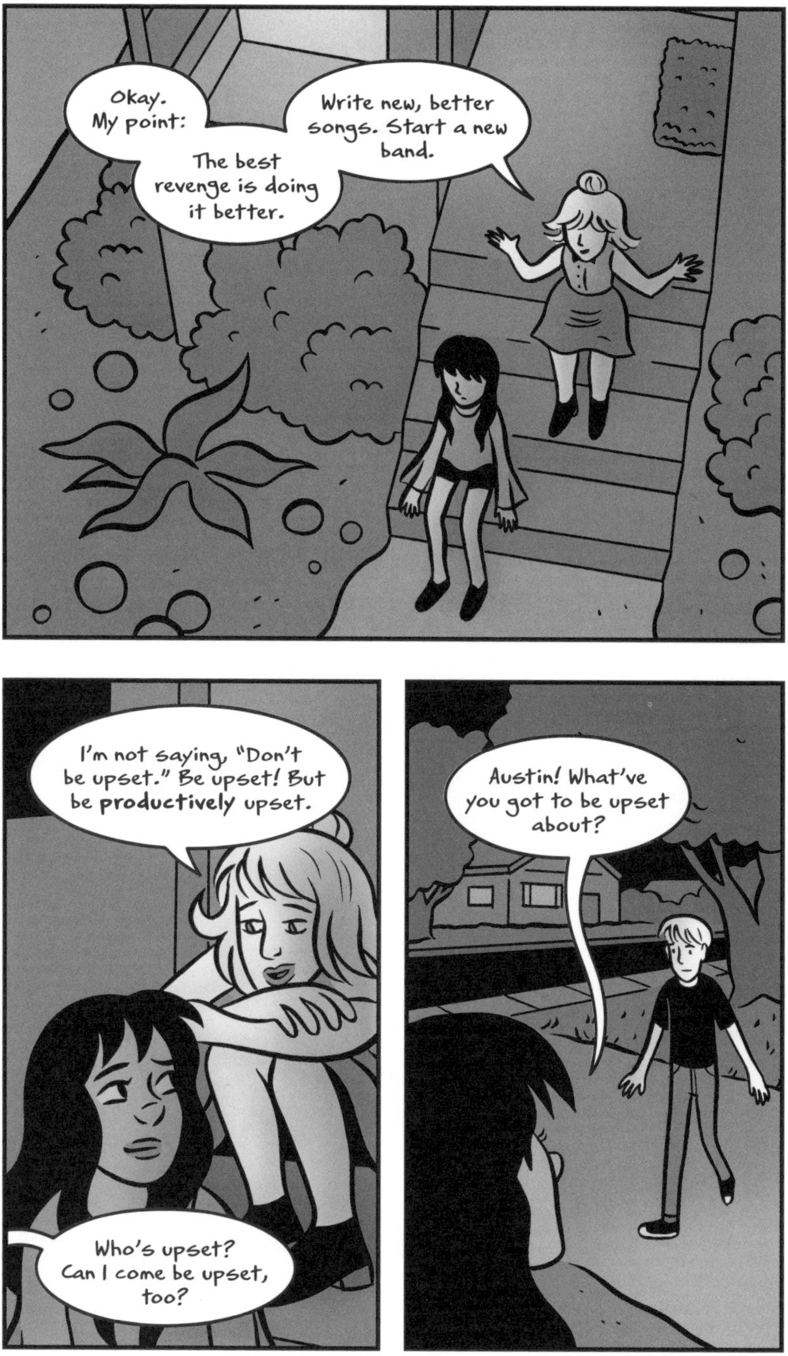
Okay. My point:
Write new, better songs. Start a new band.
The best revenge is doing it better.
I'm not saying, "Don't be upset." Be upset! But be **productively** upset.
Who's upset? Can I come be upset, too?
Austin! What've you got to be upset about?

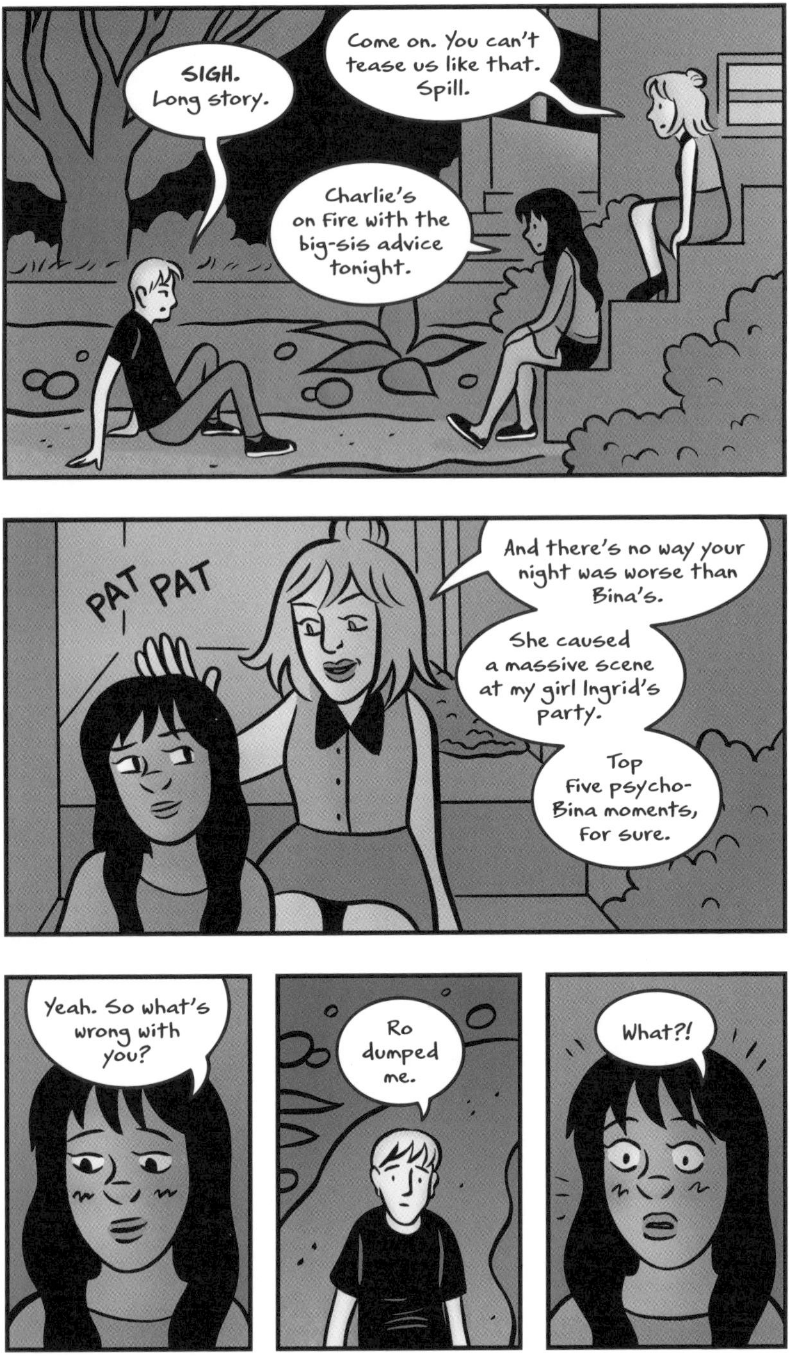
SIGH. Long story.
Come on. You can't tease us like that. Spill.
Charlie's on fire with the big-sis advice tonight.
PAT PAT
And there's no way your night was worse than Bina's.
She caused a massive scene at my girl Ingrid's party.
Top Five psycho-Bina moments, for sure.
Yeah. So what's wrong with you?
Ro dumped me.
What?!

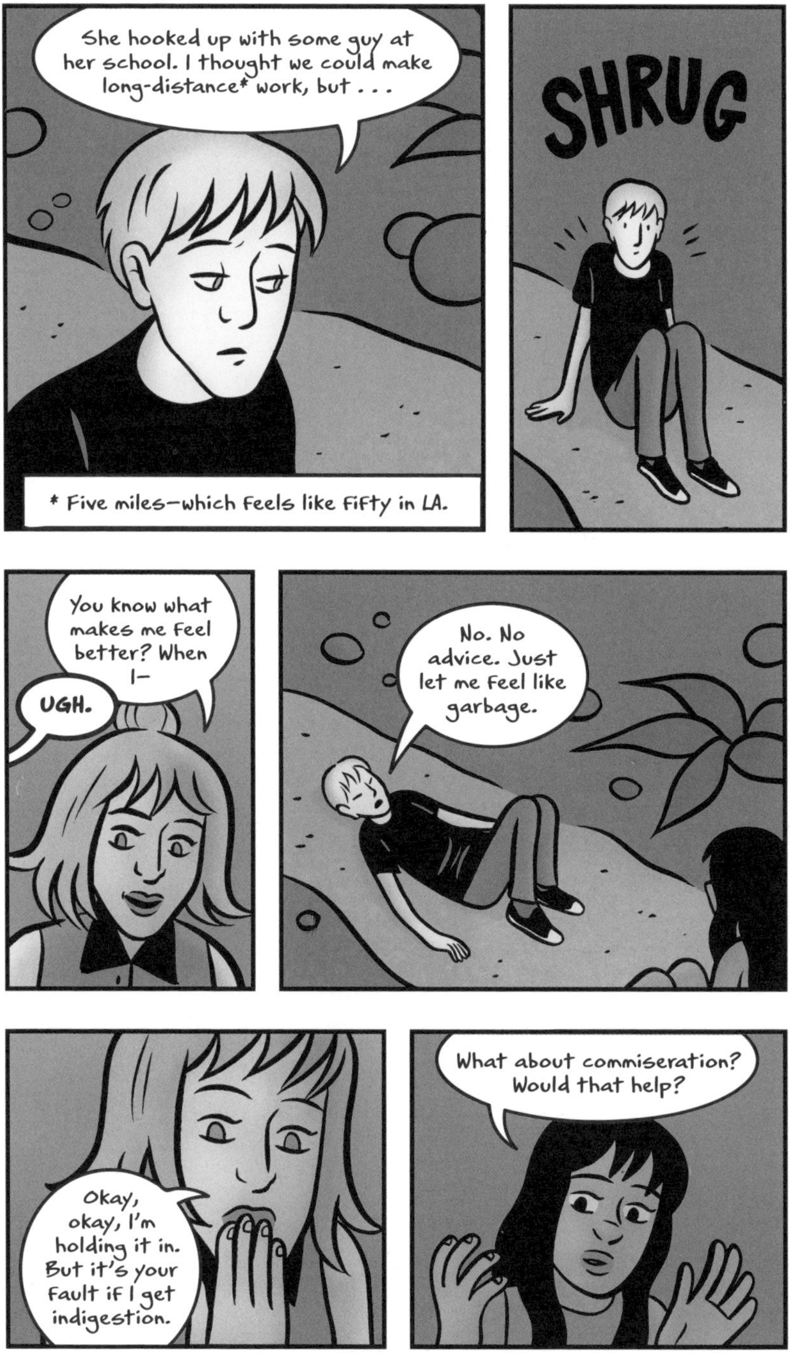
She hooked up with some guy at her school. I thought we could make long-distance* work, but . . .
* Five miles—which feels like fifty in LA.
SHRUG
You know what makes me feel better? When I—
UGH.
No. No advice. Just let me feel like garbage.
Okay, okay, I'm holding it in. But it's your fault if I get indigestion.
What about commiseration? Would that help?

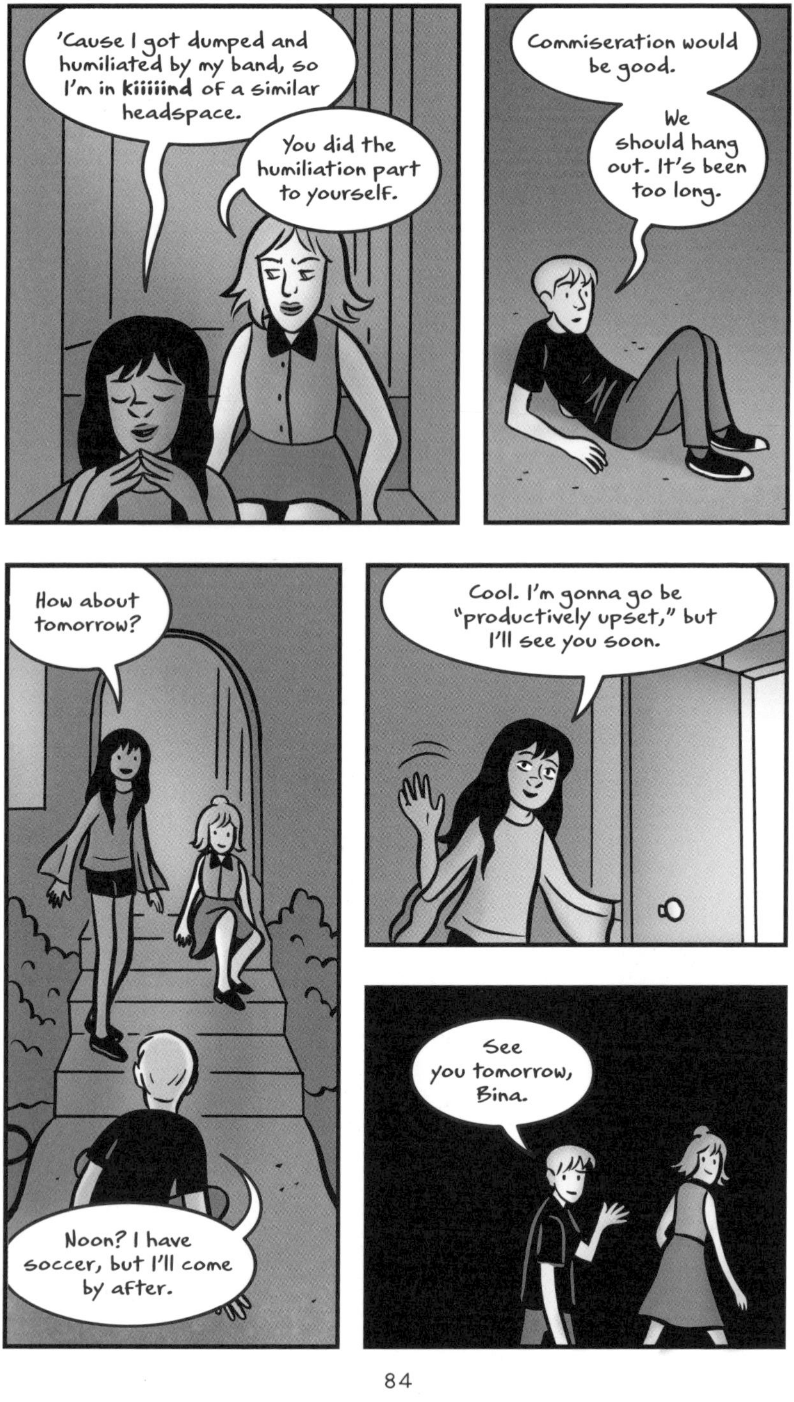
'Cause I got dumped and humiliated by my band, so I'm in **kiiiiind** of a similar headspace.
You did the humiliation part to yourself.
Commiseration would be good.
We should hang out. It's been too long.
How about tomorrow?
Noon? I have soccer, but I'll come by after.
Cool. I'm gonna go be "productively upset," but I'll see you soon.
See you tomorrow, Bina.

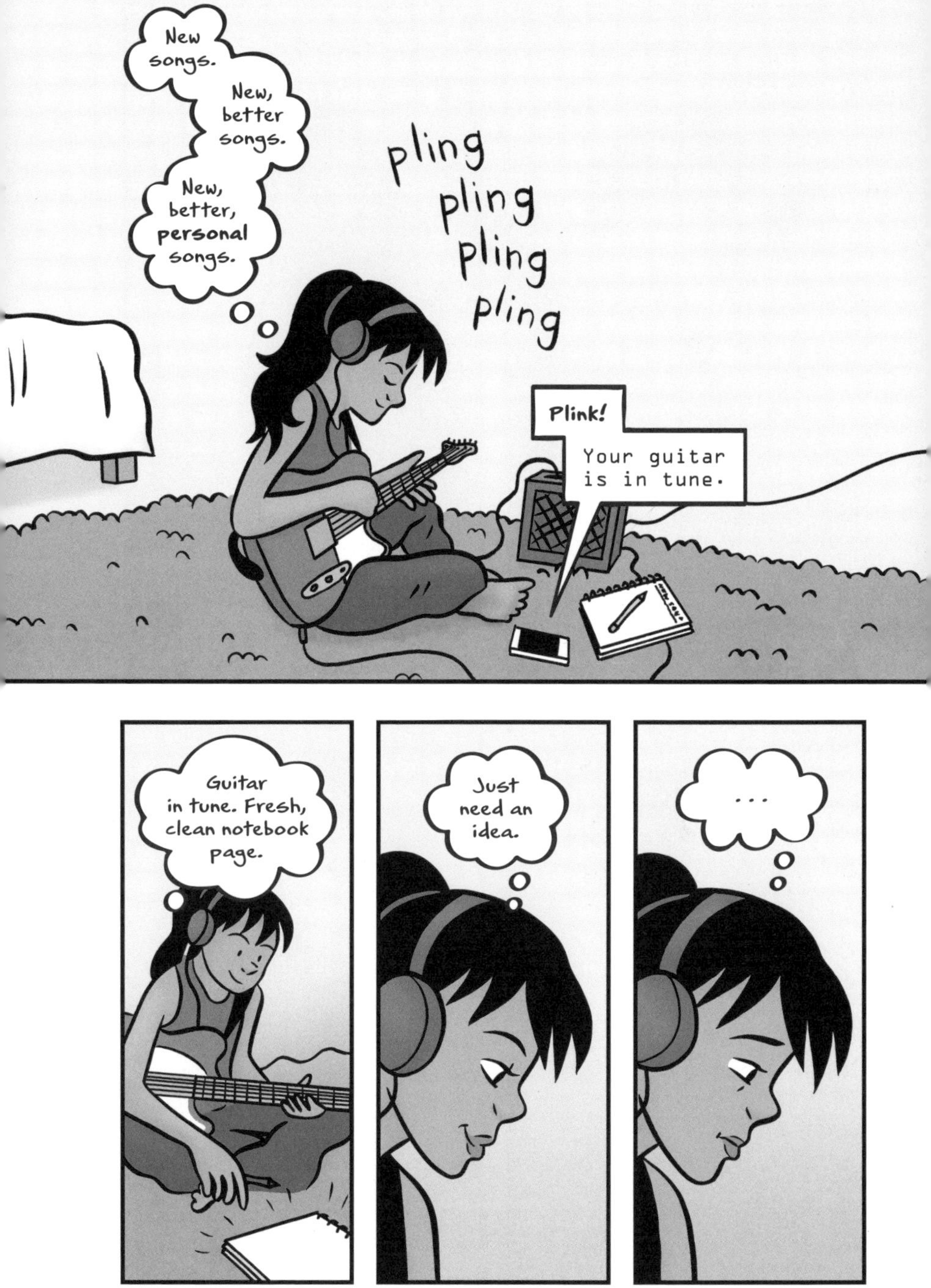
New songs.
New, better songs.
New, better, **personal** songs.
pling pling pling pling
Plink!
Your guitar is in tune.
Guitar in tune. Fresh, clean notebook page.
Just need an idea.
...

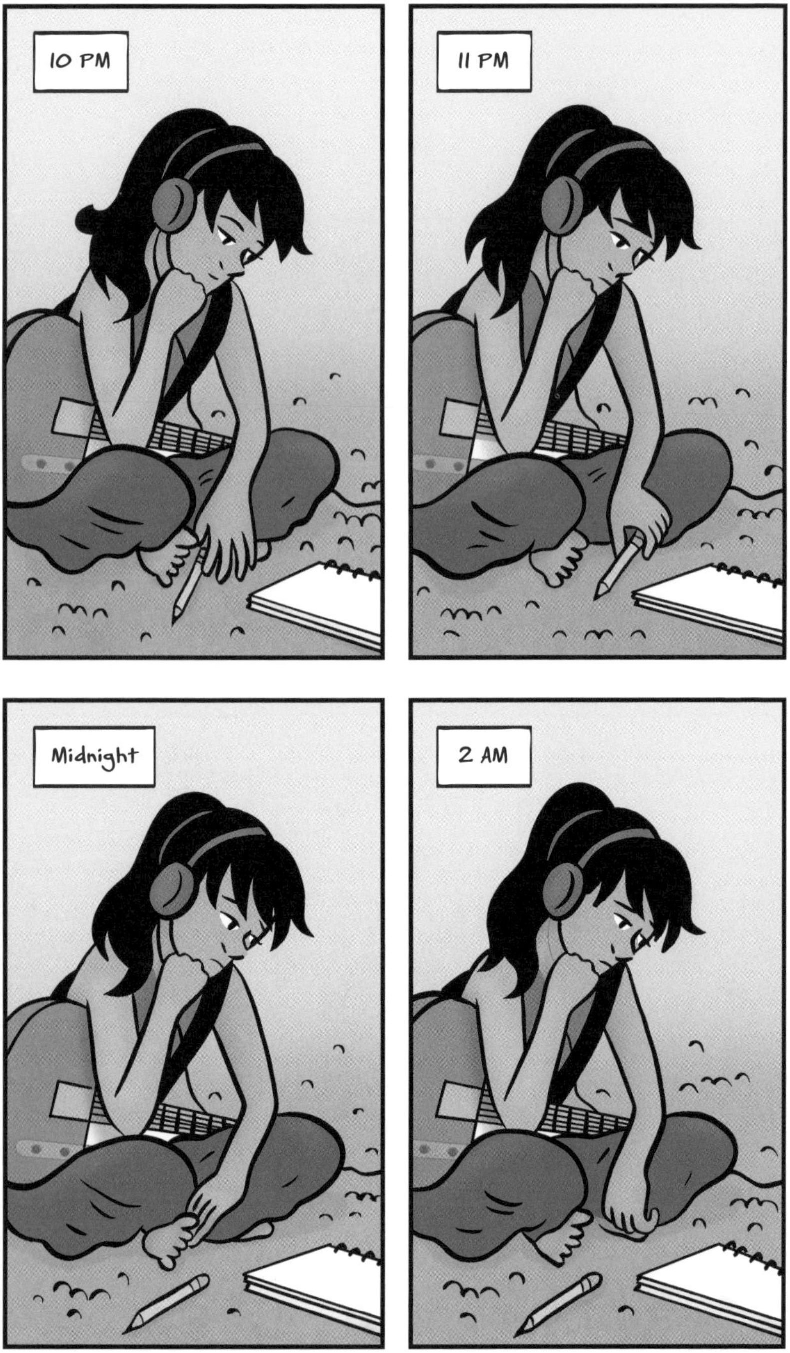
10 PM
11 PM
Midnight
2 AM

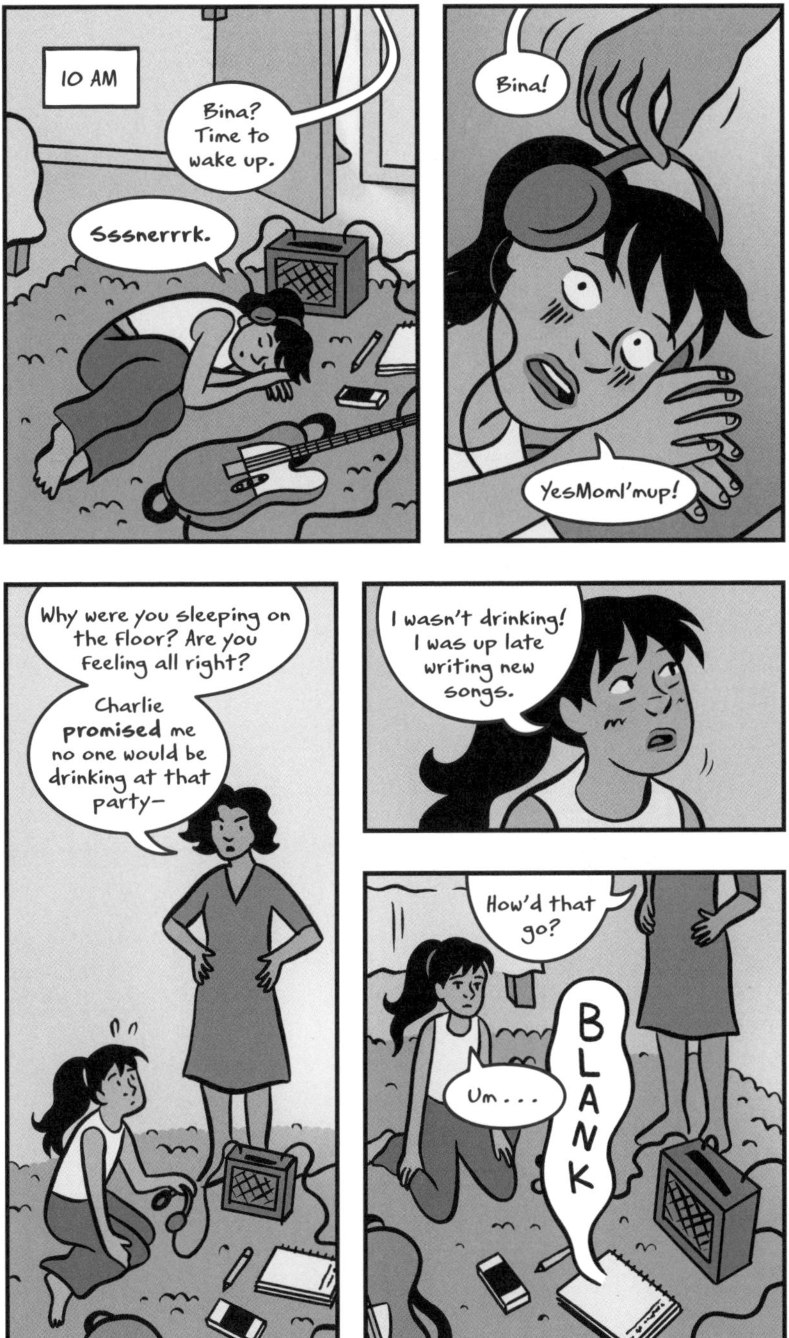
10 AM
Bina? Time to wake up.
Sssnerrrk.
Bina!
YesMomI'mup!
Why were you sleeping on the floor? Are you feeling all right?
Charlie **promised** me no one would be drinking at that party—
I wasn't drinking! I was up late writing new songs.
How'd that go?
Um . . .
BLANK

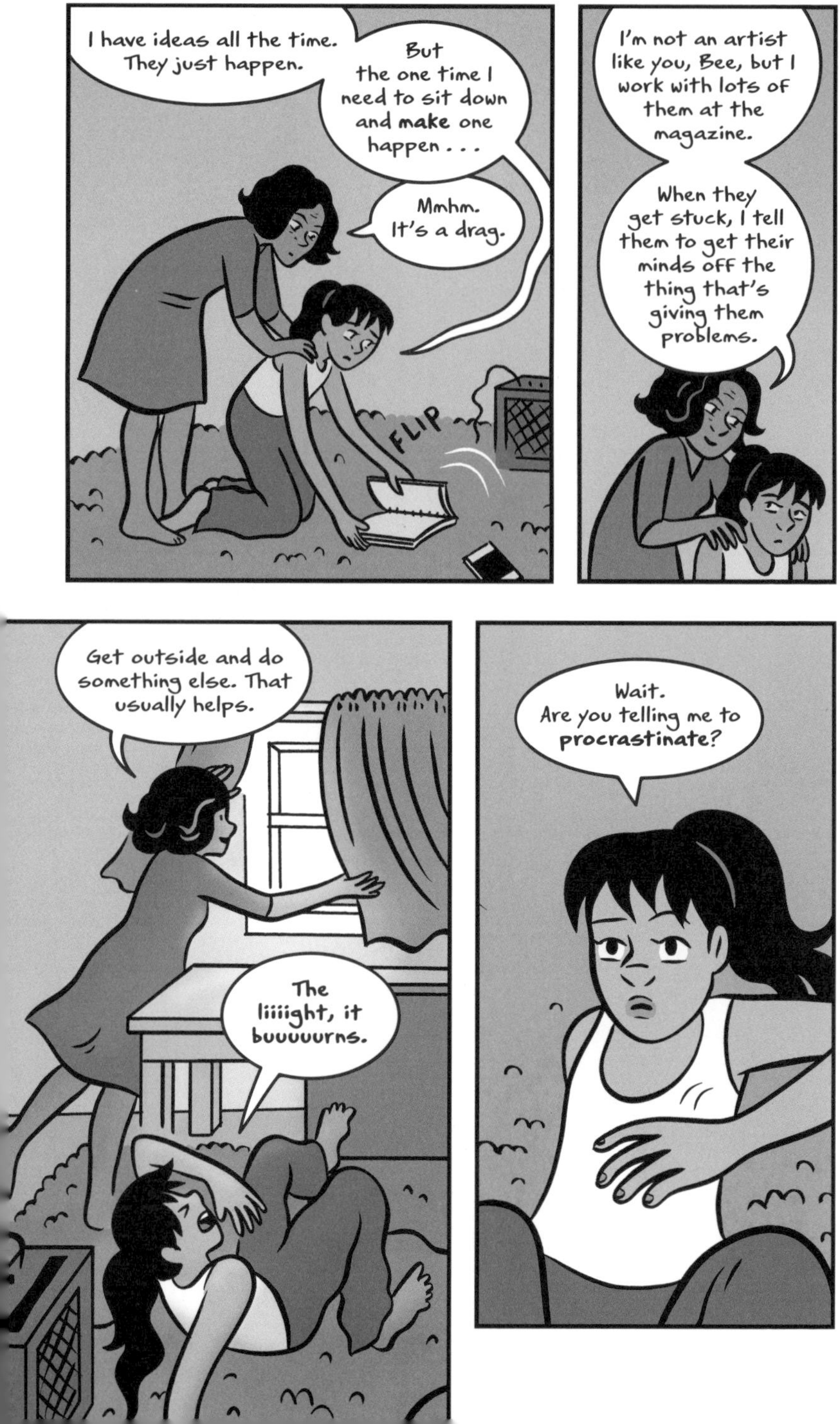
I have ideas all the time. They just happen.
But the one time I need to sit down and **make** one happen . . .
Mmhm. It's a drag.
FLIP
I'm not an artist like you, Bee, but I work with lots of them at the magazine.
When they get stuck, I tell them to get their minds off the thing that's giving them problems.
Get outside and do something else. That usually helps.
The liiiight, it buuuuurns.
Wait. Are you telling me to **procrastinate?**

It sounds like procrastination, but it's more like . . .

INSPOcrastination.

You can't force inspiration, but you can stack the deck in its favor.

And speaking of inspiration—

VOOP!

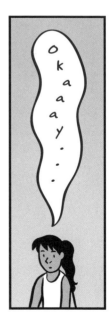

Okaaay...

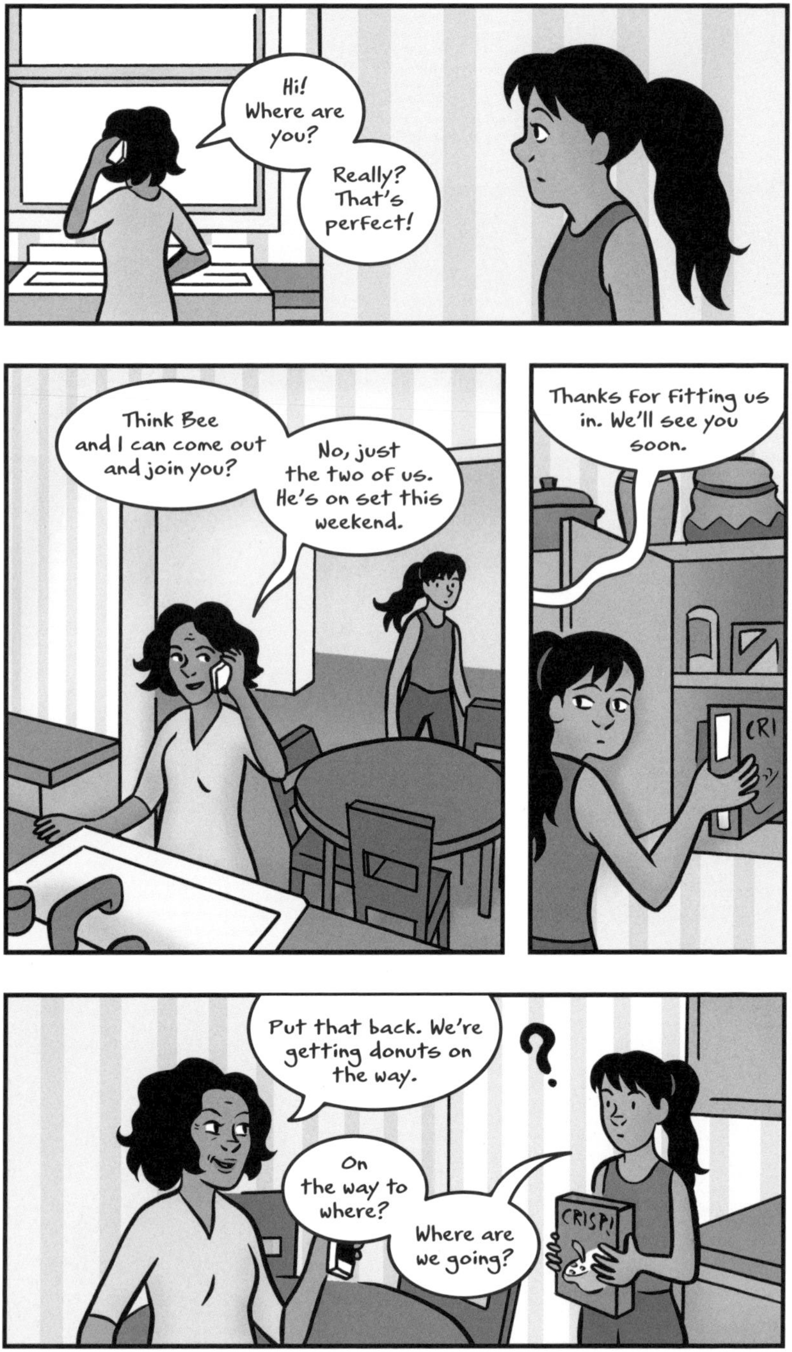
Hi! Where are you?
Really? That's perfect!
Think Bee and I can come out and join you?
No, just the two of us. He's on set this weekend.
Thanks for fitting us in. We'll see you soon.
CRI
Put that back. We're getting donuts on the way.
?
On the way to where?
Where are we going?
CRISP!

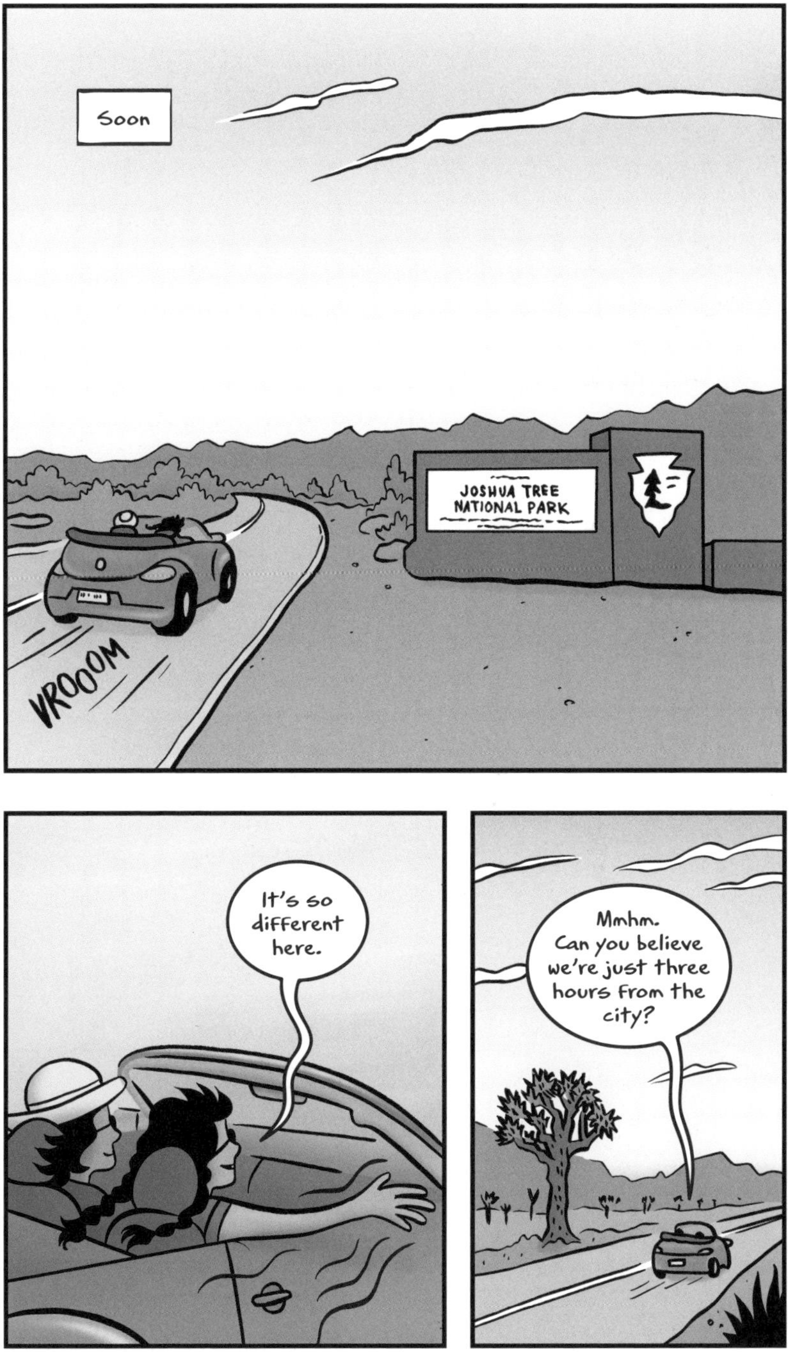
Soon
JOSHUA TREE NATIONAL PARK
VROOOM
It's so different here.
Mmhm. Can you believe we're just three hours from the city?

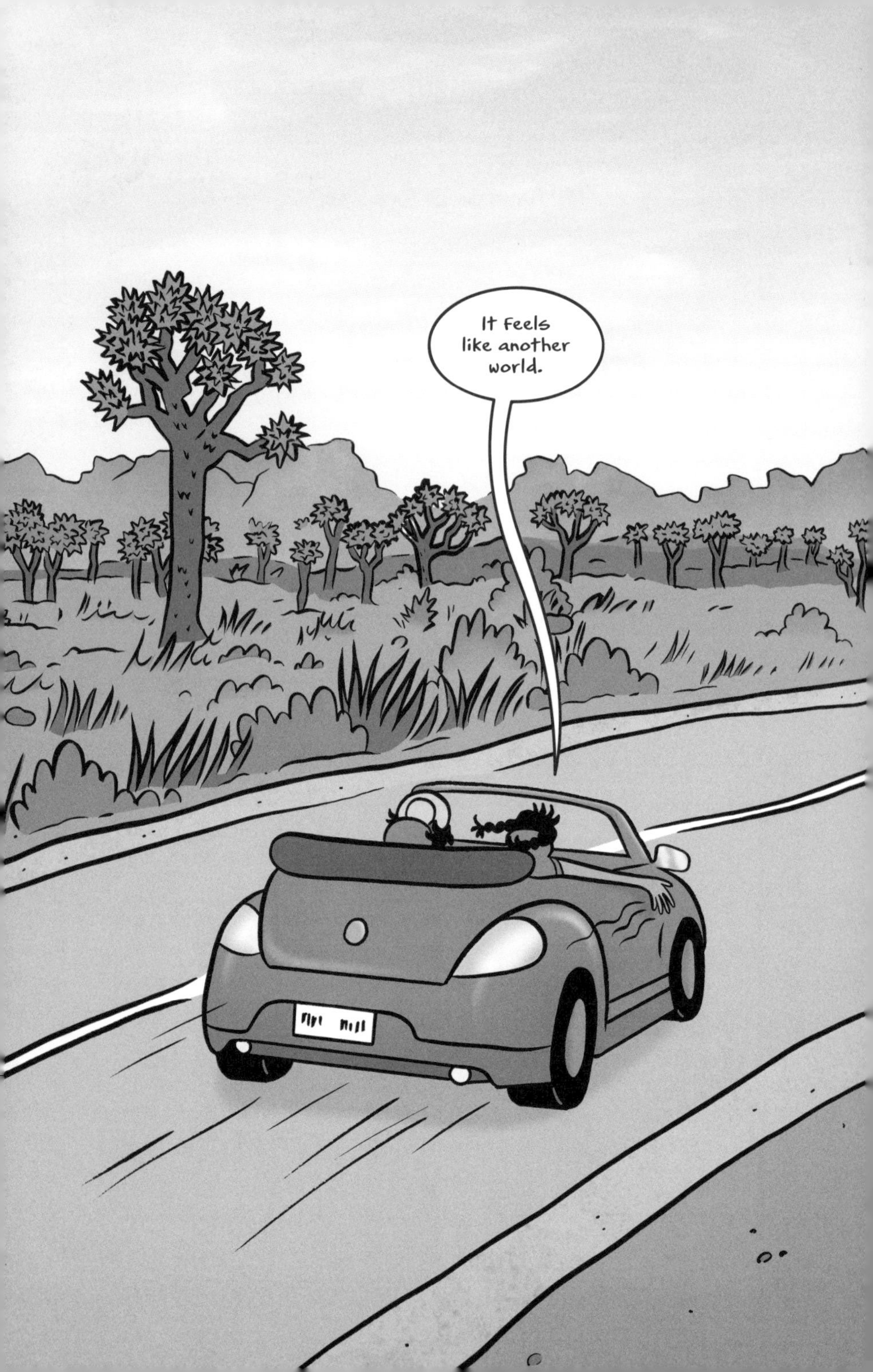
It Feels like another world.

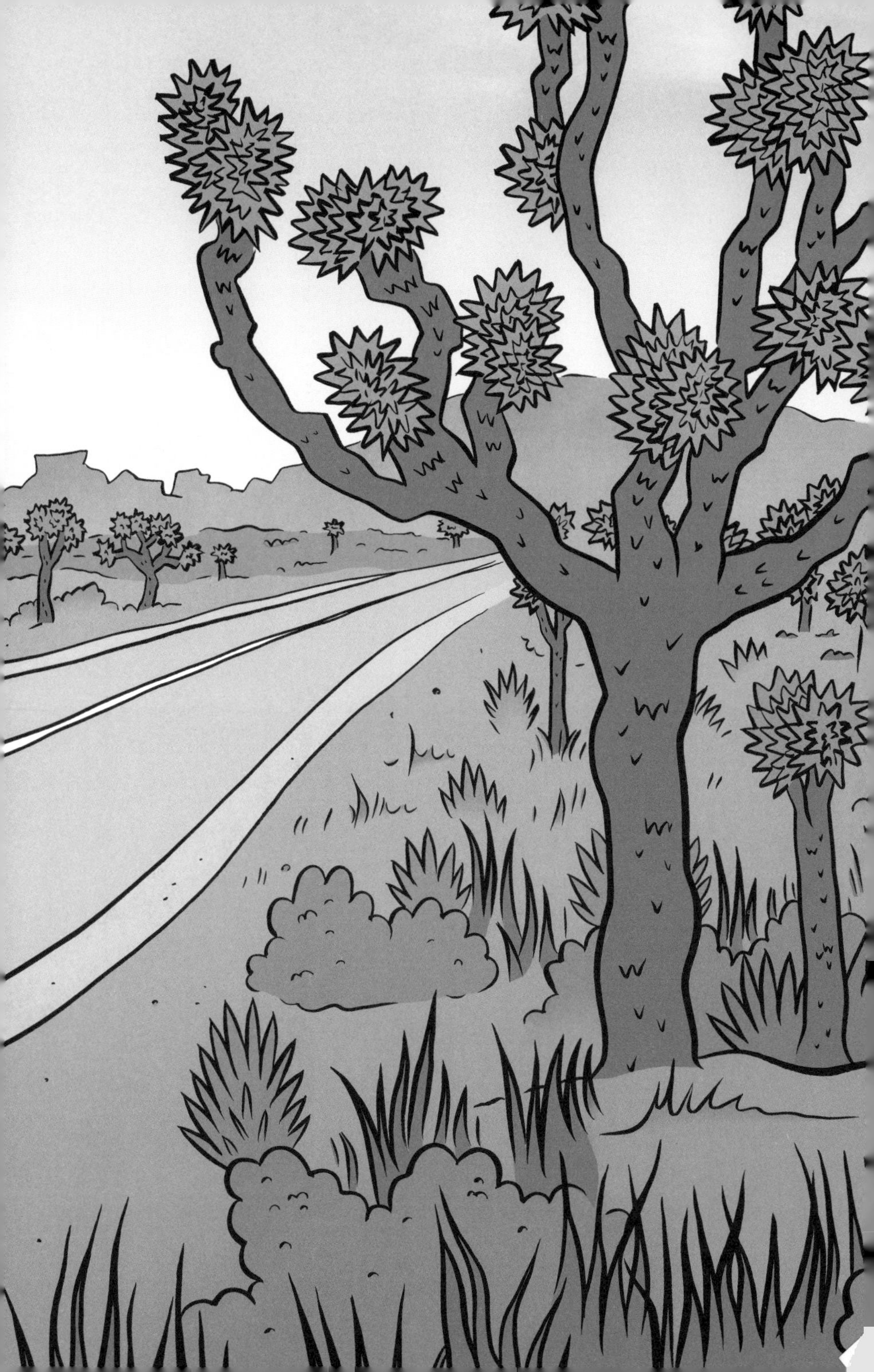

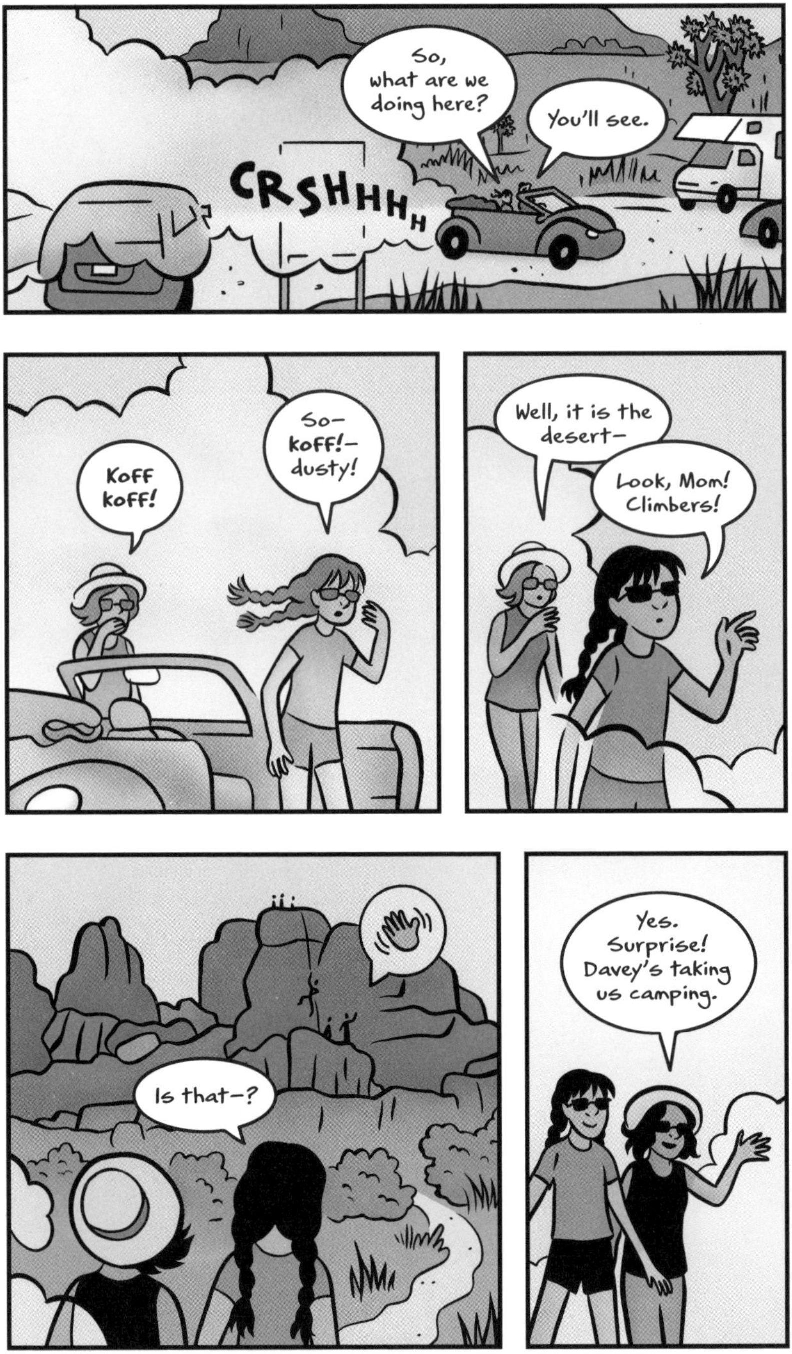
So, what are we doing here?
You'll see.
CRSHHHH
Koff koff!
So— koff!— dusty!
Well, it is the desert—
Look, Mom! Climbers!
Is that—?
Yes. Surprise! Davey's taking us camping.

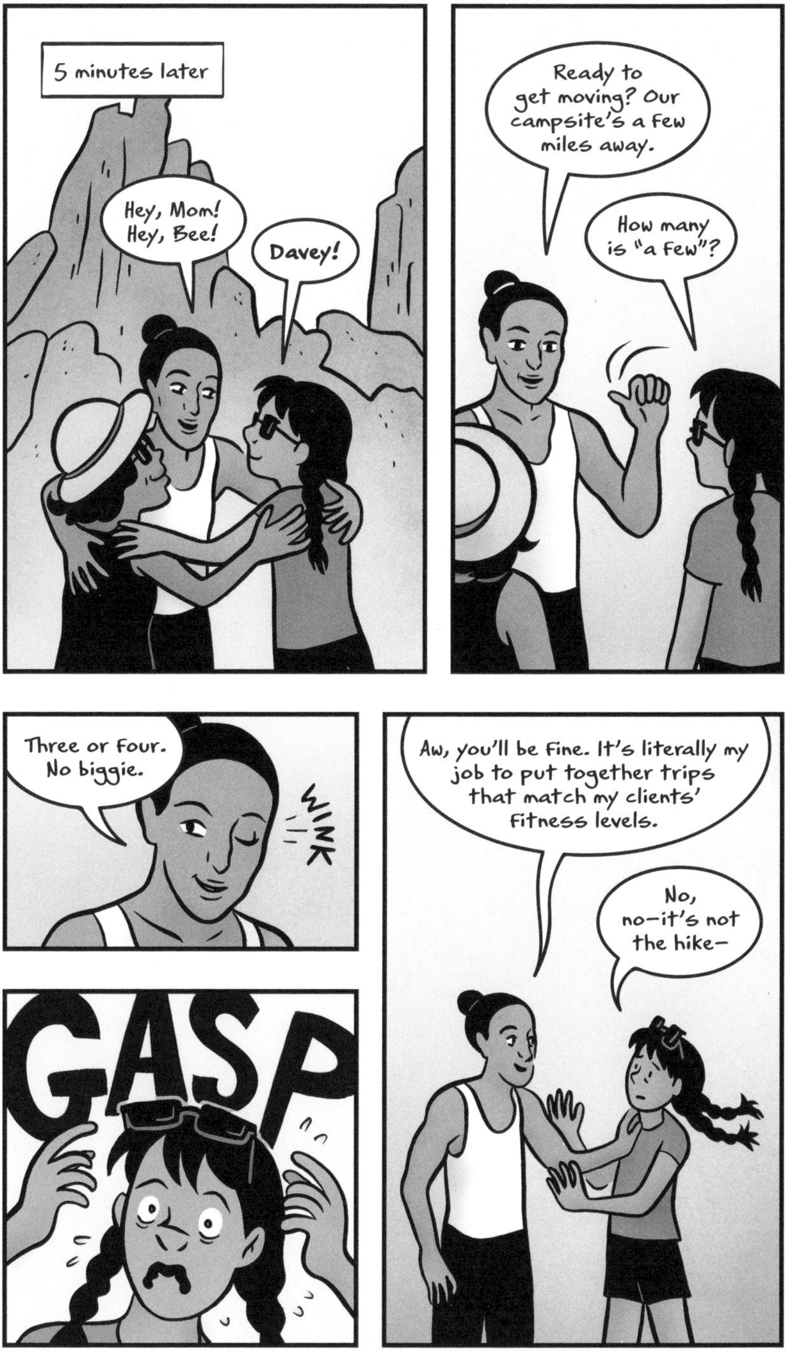
5 minutes later
Hey, Mom! Hey, Bee!
Davey!
Ready to get moving? Our campsite's a few miles away.
How many is "a few"?
Three or four. No biggie.
WINK
GASP
Aw, you'll be fine. It's literally my job to put together trips that match my clients' fitness levels.
No, no—it's not the hike—

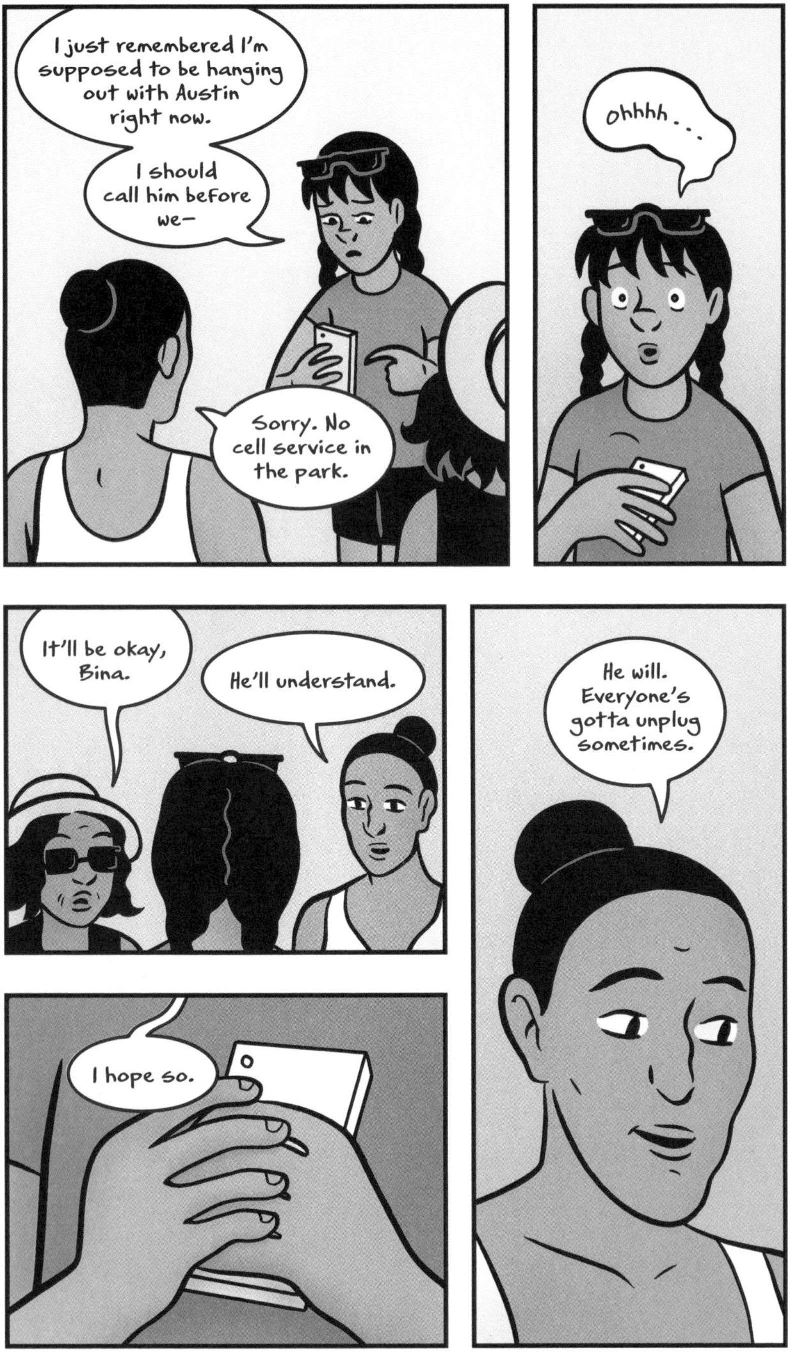
I just remembered I'm supposed to be hanging out with Austin right now.
I should call him before we–
Sorry. No cell service in the park.
Ohhhh . . .
It'll be okay, Bina.
He'll understand.
He will. Everyone's gotta unplug sometimes.
I hope so.

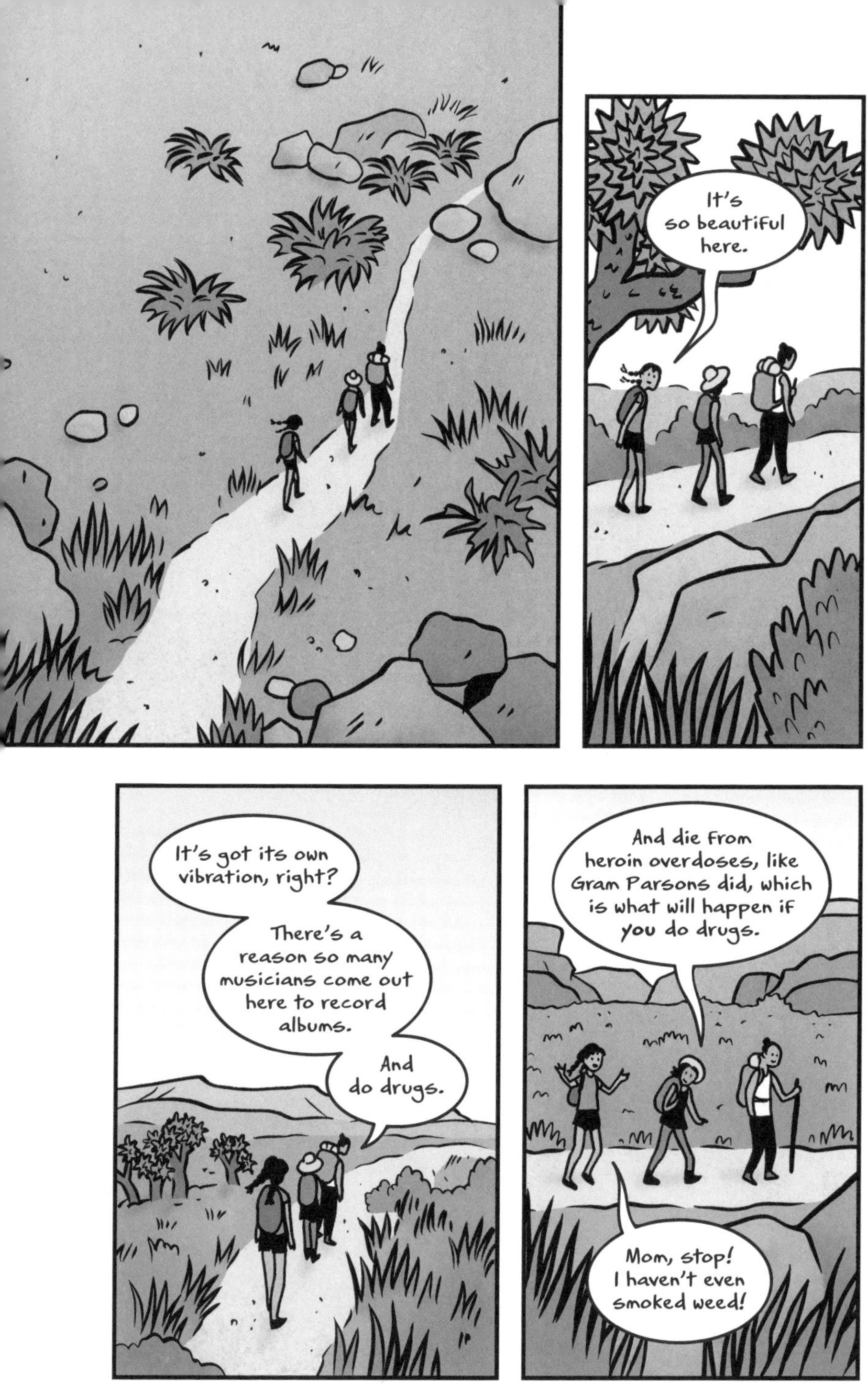
It's so beautiful here.
It's got its own vibration, right?
There's a reason so many musicians come out here to record albums.
And do drugs.
And die from heroin overdoses, like Gram Parsons did, which is what will happen if you do drugs.
Mom, stop! I haven't even smoked weed!

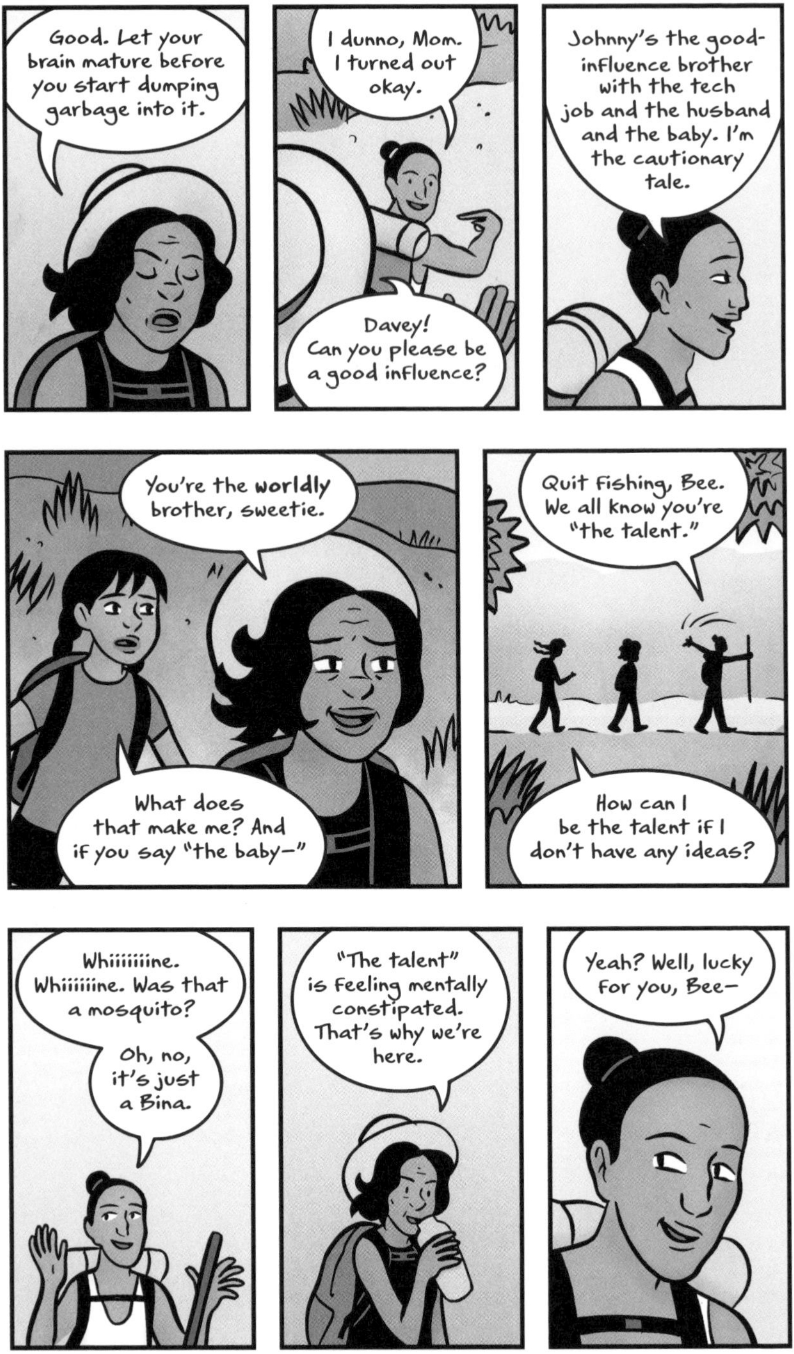
Good. Let your brain mature before you start dumping garbage into it.
I dunno, Mom. I turned out okay.
Davey! Can you please be a good influence?
Johnny's the good-influence brother with the tech job and the husband and the baby. I'm the cautionary tale.
You're the worldly brother, sweetie.
What does that make me? And if you say "the baby–"
Quit fishing, Bee. We all know you're "the talent."
How can I be the talent if I don't have any ideas?
Whiiiiiiine. Whiiiiiine. Was that a mosquito?
Oh, no, it's just a Bina.
"The talent" is feeling mentally constipated. That's why we're here.
Yeah? Well, lucky for you, Bee–

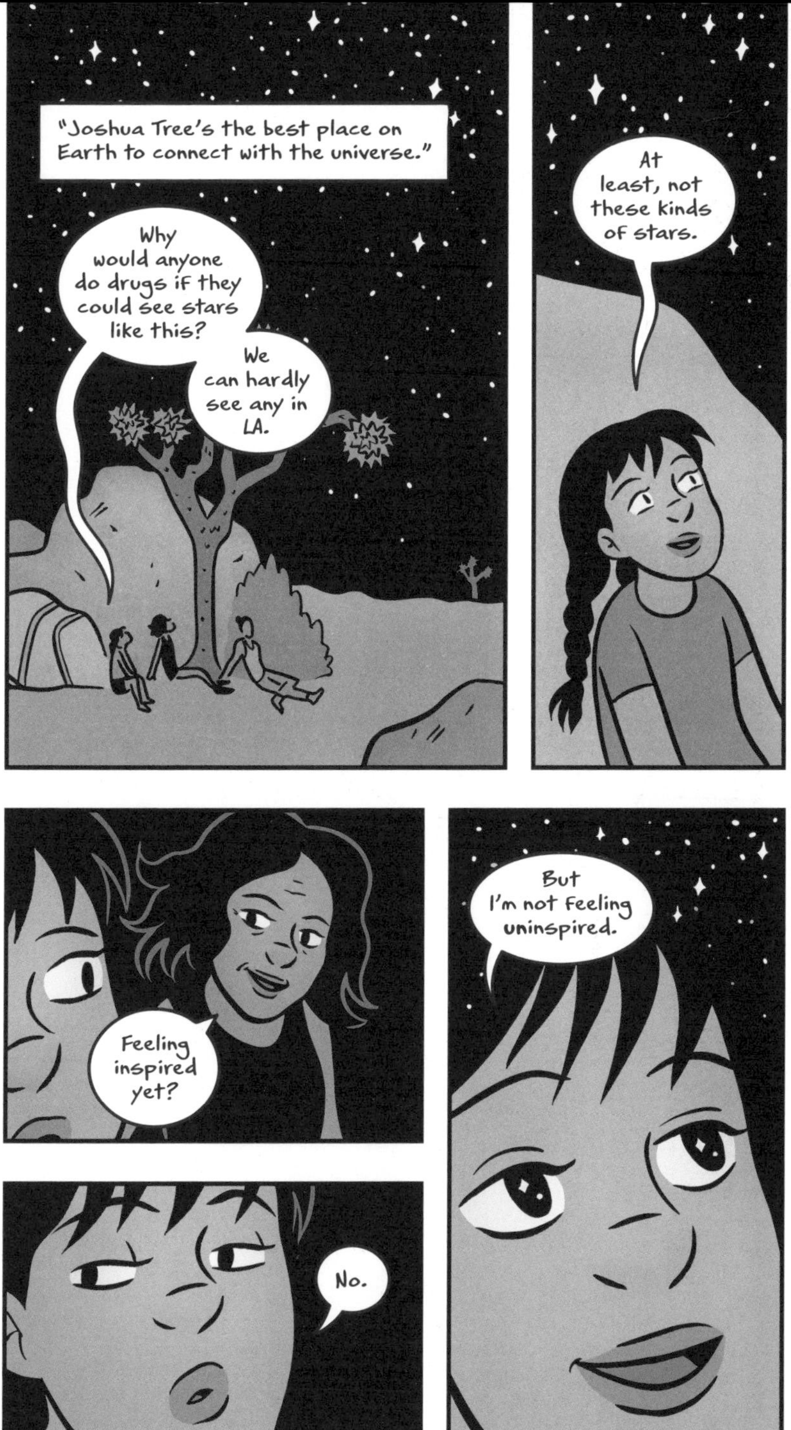
"Joshua Tree's the best place on Earth to connect with the universe."
Why would anyone do drugs if they could see stars like this?
We can hardly see any in LA.
At least, not these kinds of stars.
Feeling inspired yet?
No.
But I'm not feeling uninspired.

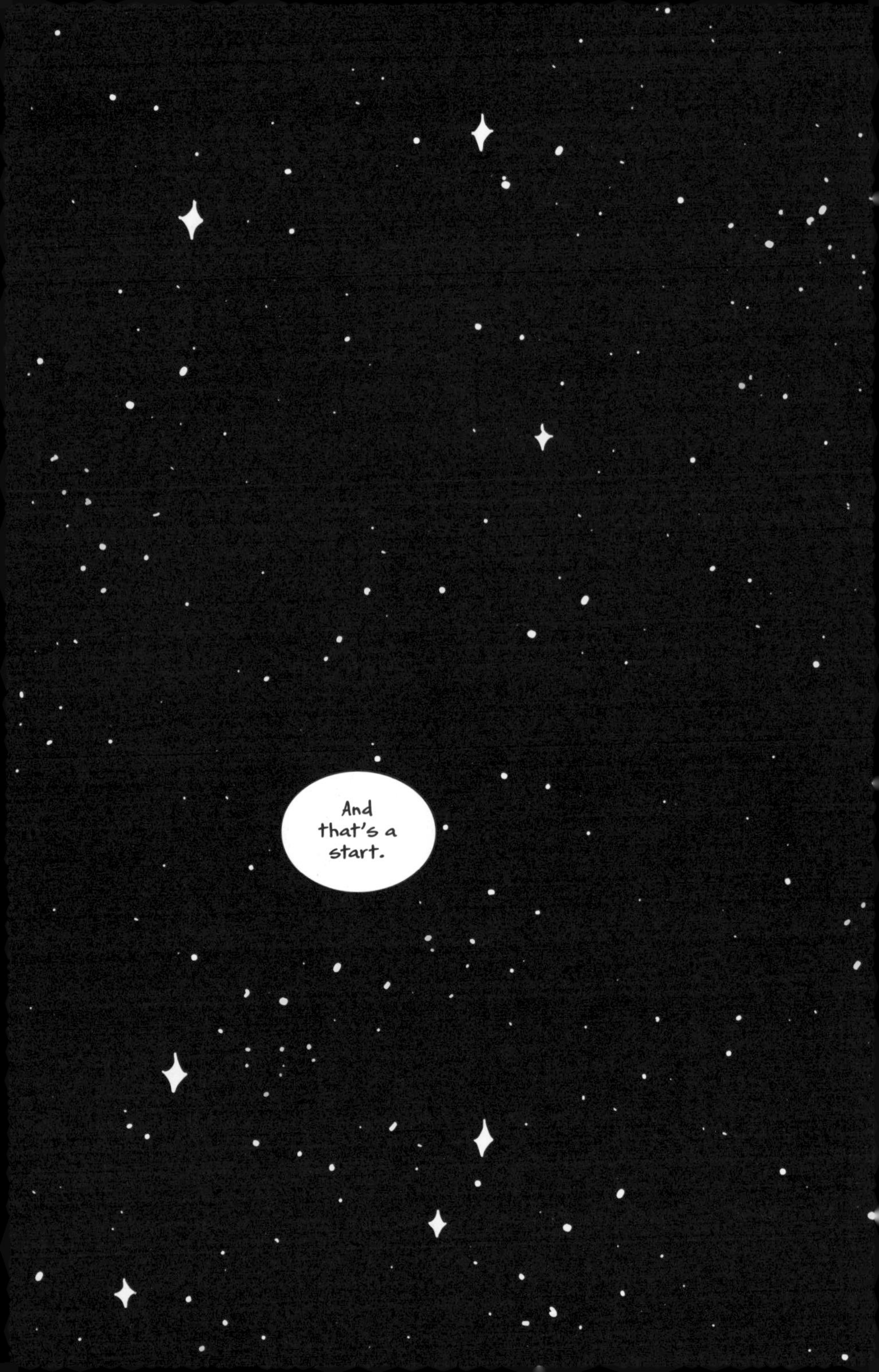
And that's a start.

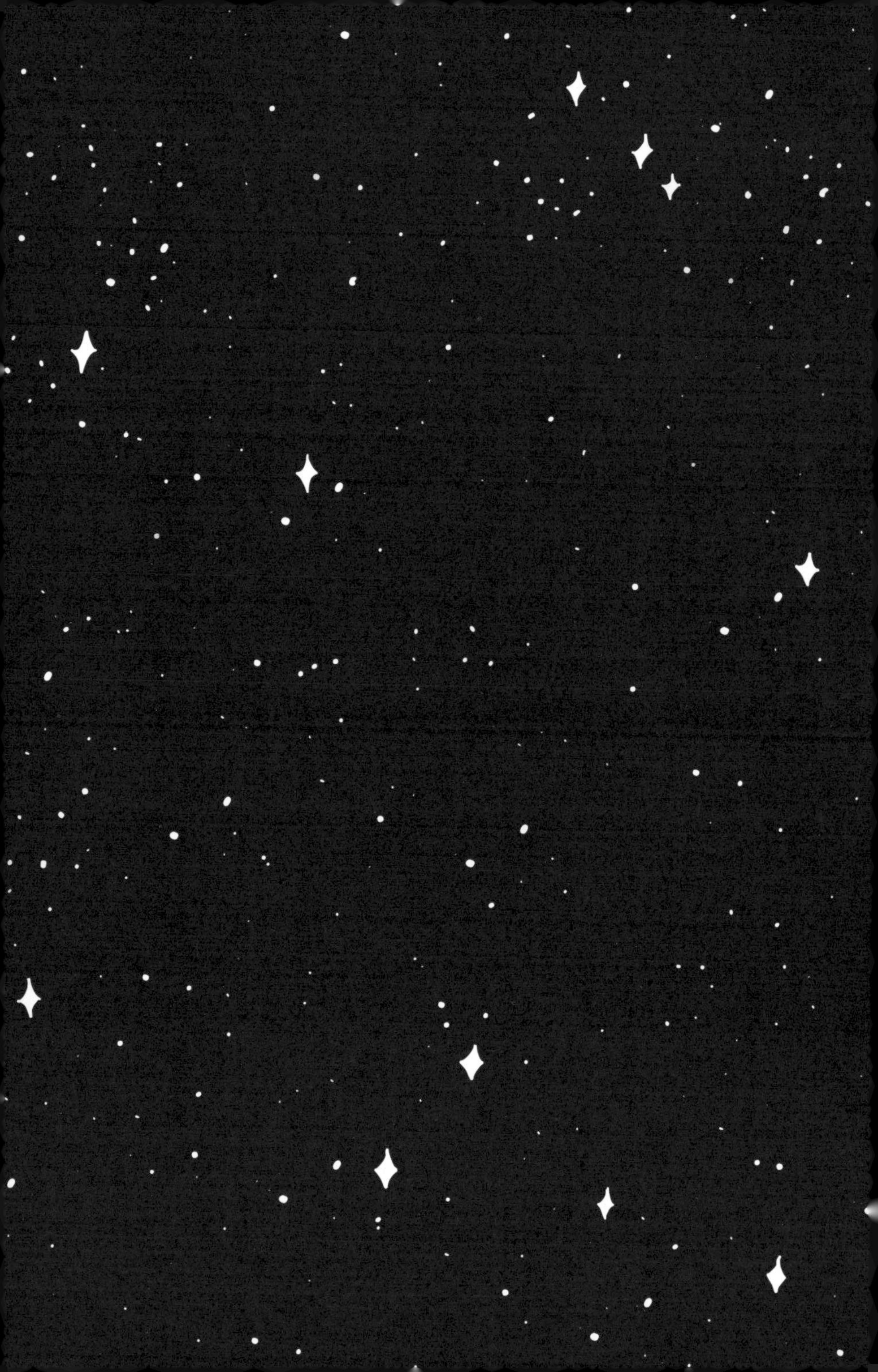

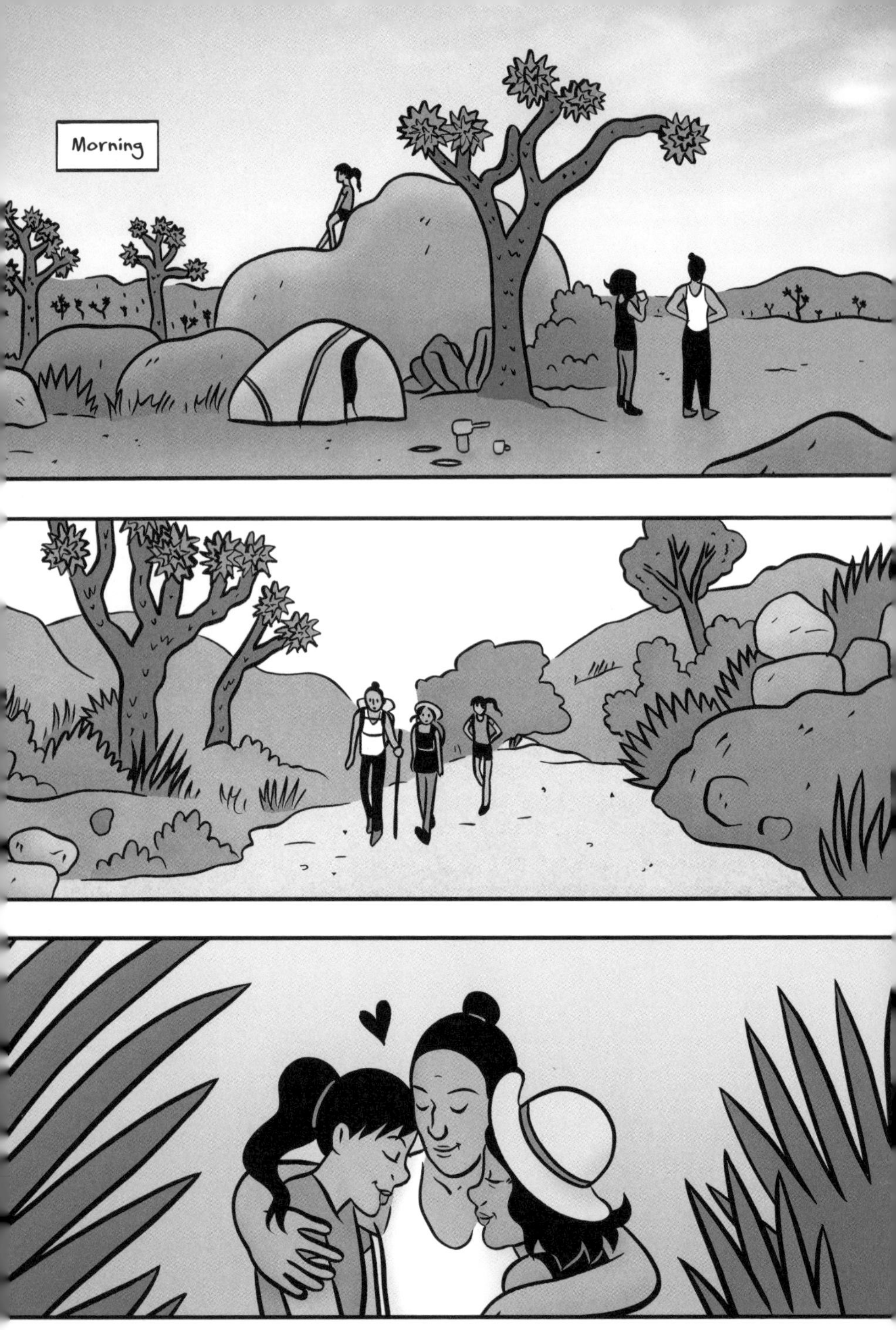
Morning

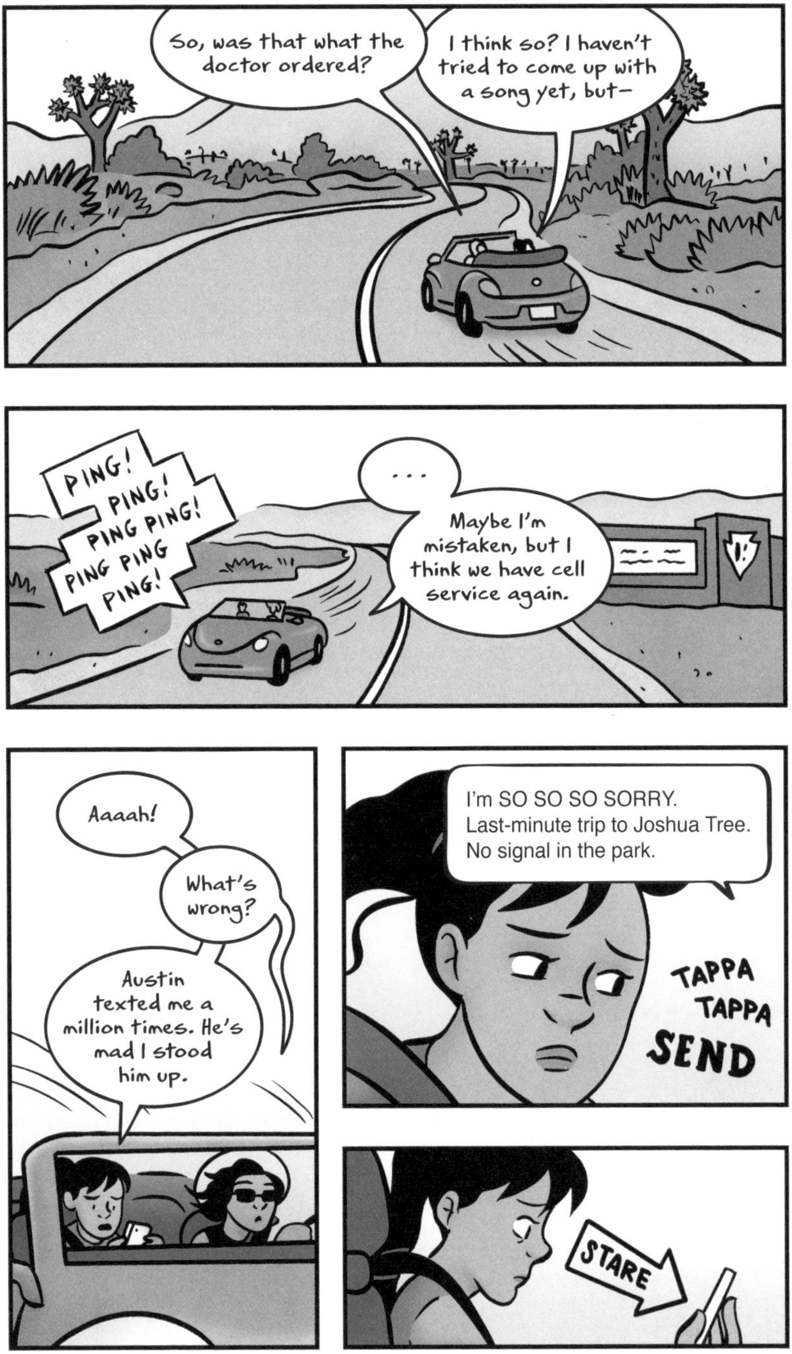

So, was that what the doctor ordered?
I think so? I haven't tried to come up with a song yet, but–
PING! PING! PING PING! PING PING PING!
. . .
Maybe I'm mistaken, but I think we have cell service again.
Aaaah!
What's wrong?
Austin texted me a million times. He's mad I stood him up.
I'm SO SO SO SORRY. Last-minute trip to Joshua Tree. No signal in the park.
TAPPA TAPPA SEND
STARE

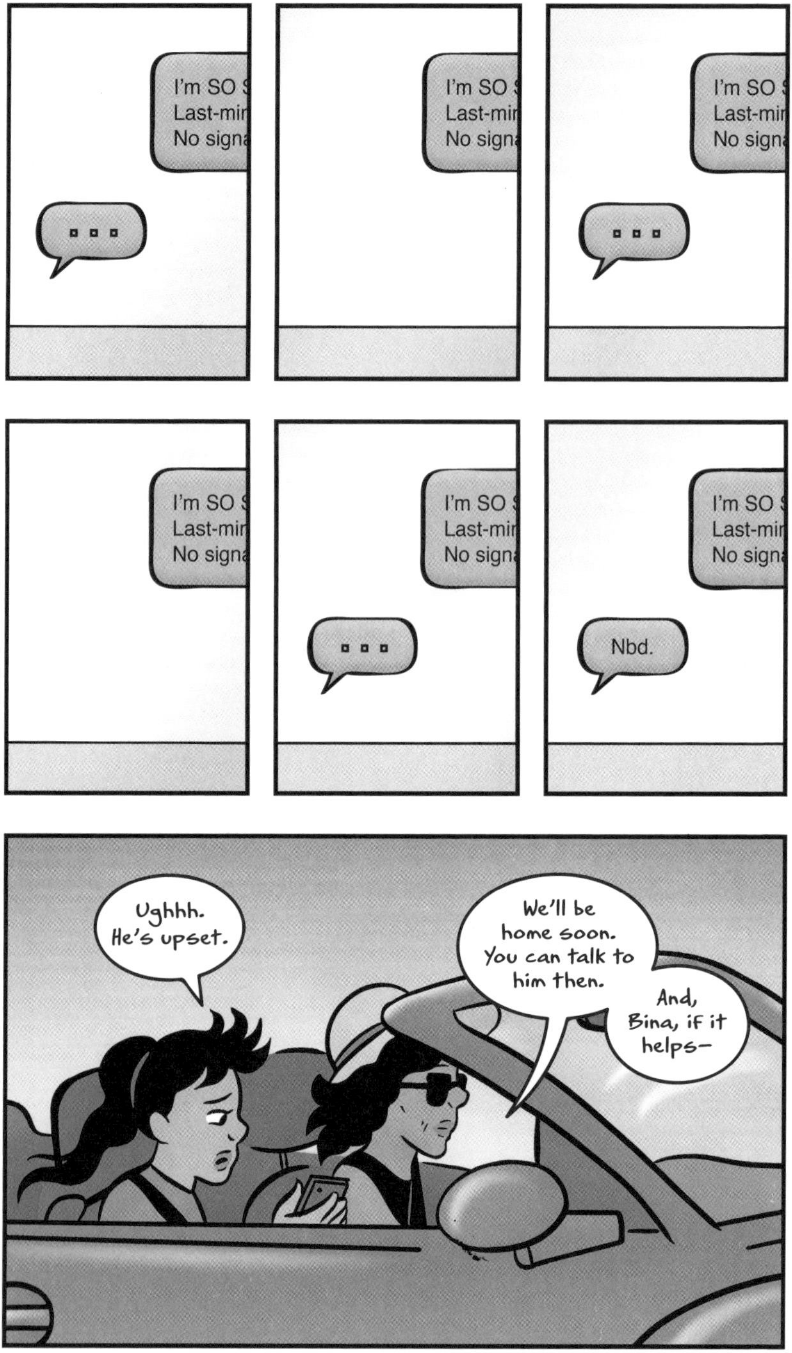
I'm SO S
Last-min
No signa
...
I'm SO S
Last-min
No signa
I'm SO S
Last-min
No signa
...
I'm SO S
Last-min
No signa
I'm SO S
Last-min
No signa
...
I'm SO S
Last-min
No signa
Nbd.
Ughhh. He's upset.
We'll be home soon. You can talk to him then.
And, Bina, if it helps—

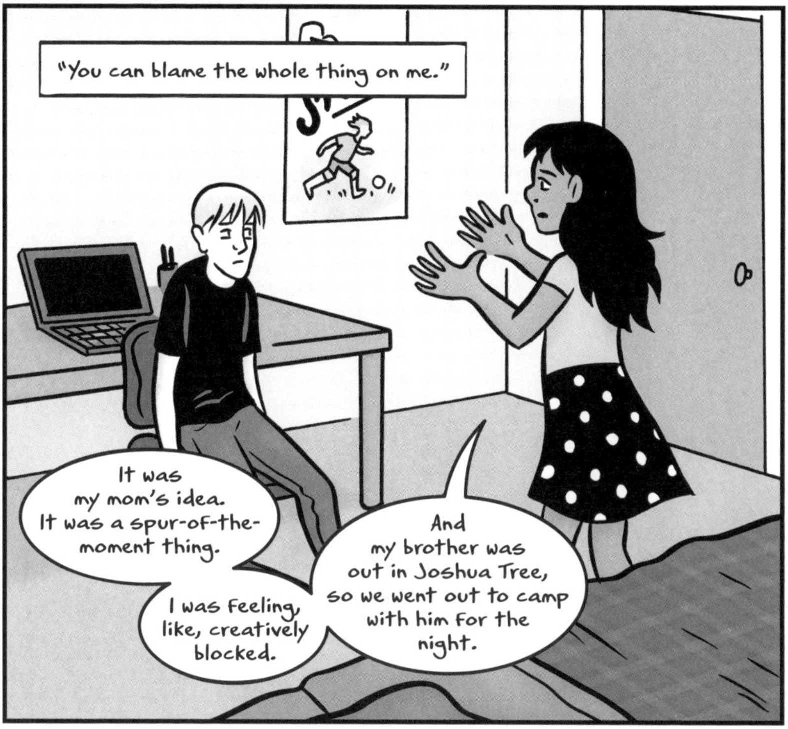
"You can blame the whole thing on me."
It was my mom's idea. It was a spur-of-the-moment thing.
I was feeling, like, creatively blocked.
And my brother was out in Joshua Tree, so we went out to camp with him for the night.

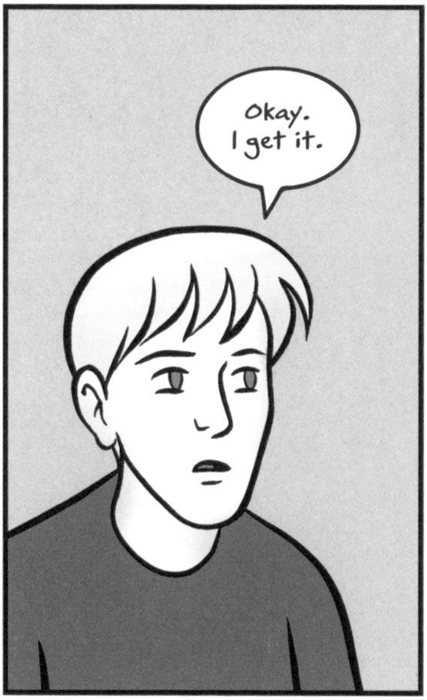
Okay. I get it.

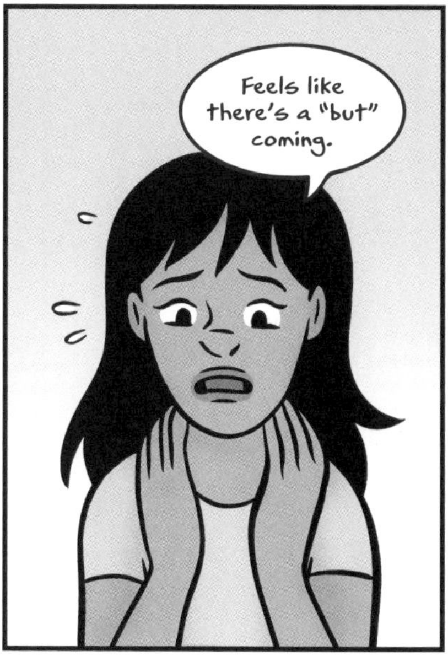
Feels like there's a "but" coming.

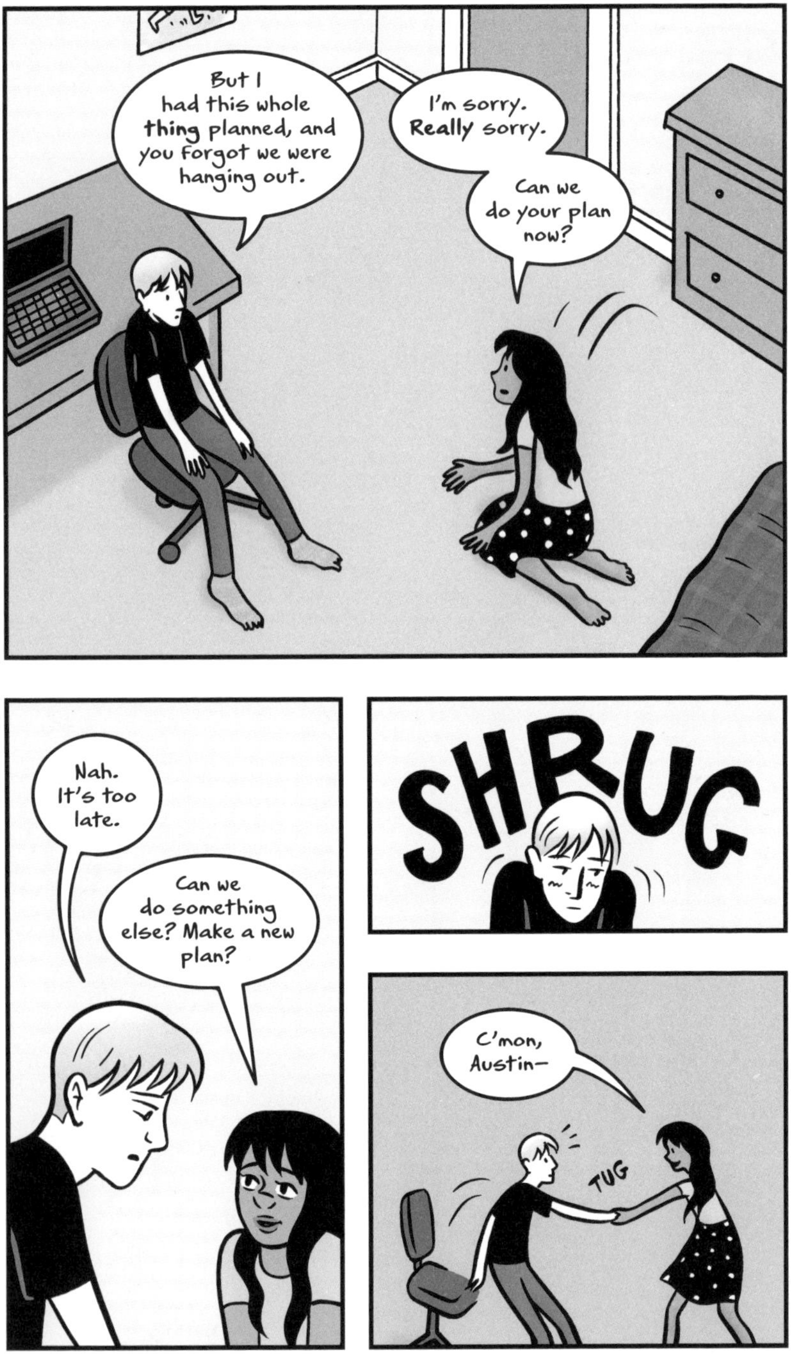
But I had this whole thing planned, and you forgot we were hanging out.
I'm sorry. Really sorry.
Can we do your plan now?
Nah. It's too late.
Can we do something else? Make a new plan?
SHRUG
C'mon, Austin—
TUG

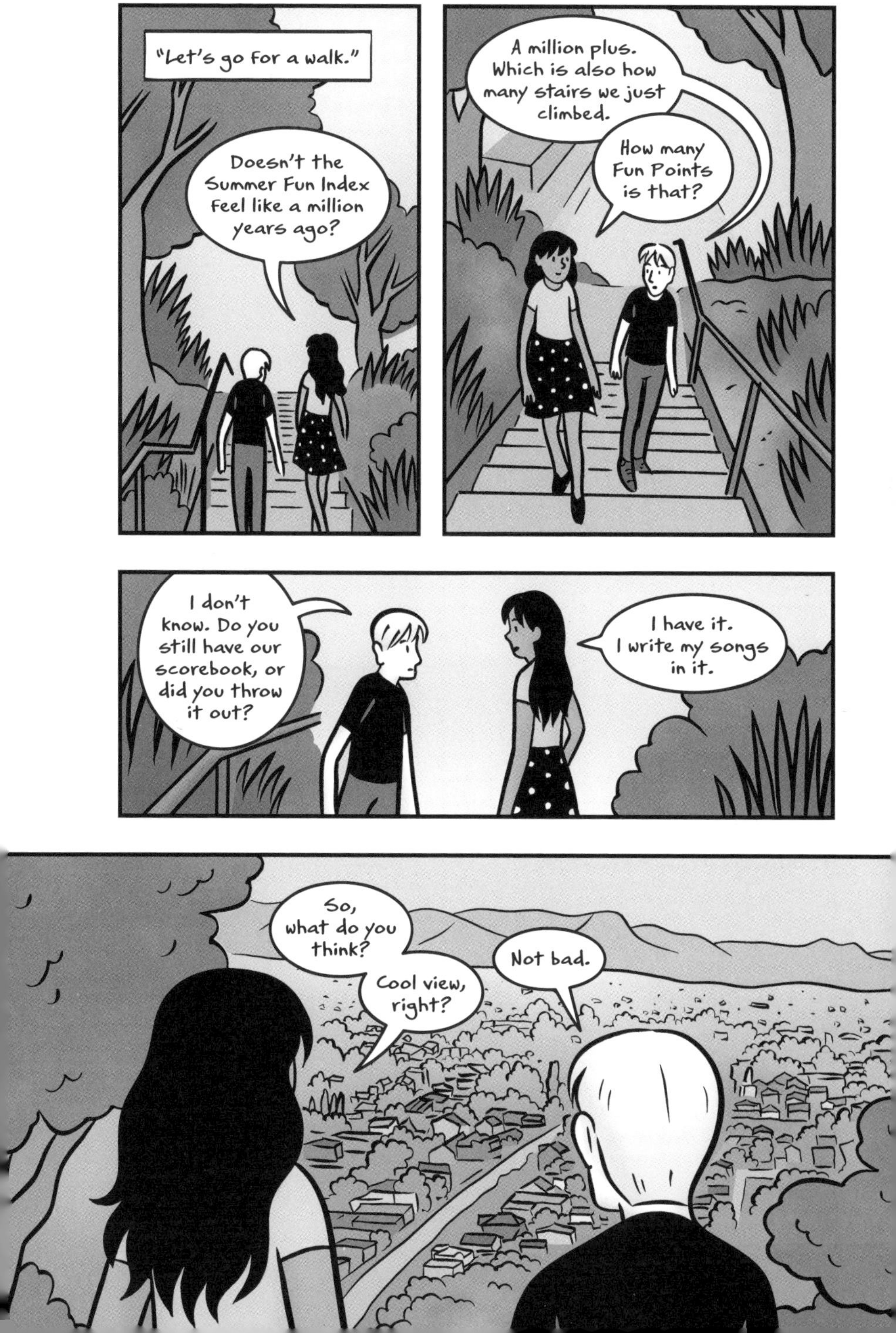
"Let's go for a walk."
Doesn't the Summer Fun Index feel like a million years ago?
A million plus. Which is also how many stairs we just climbed.
How many Fun Points is that?
I don't know. Do you still have our scorebook, or did you throw it out?
I have it. I write my songs in it.
So, what do you think?
Cool view, right?
Not bad.

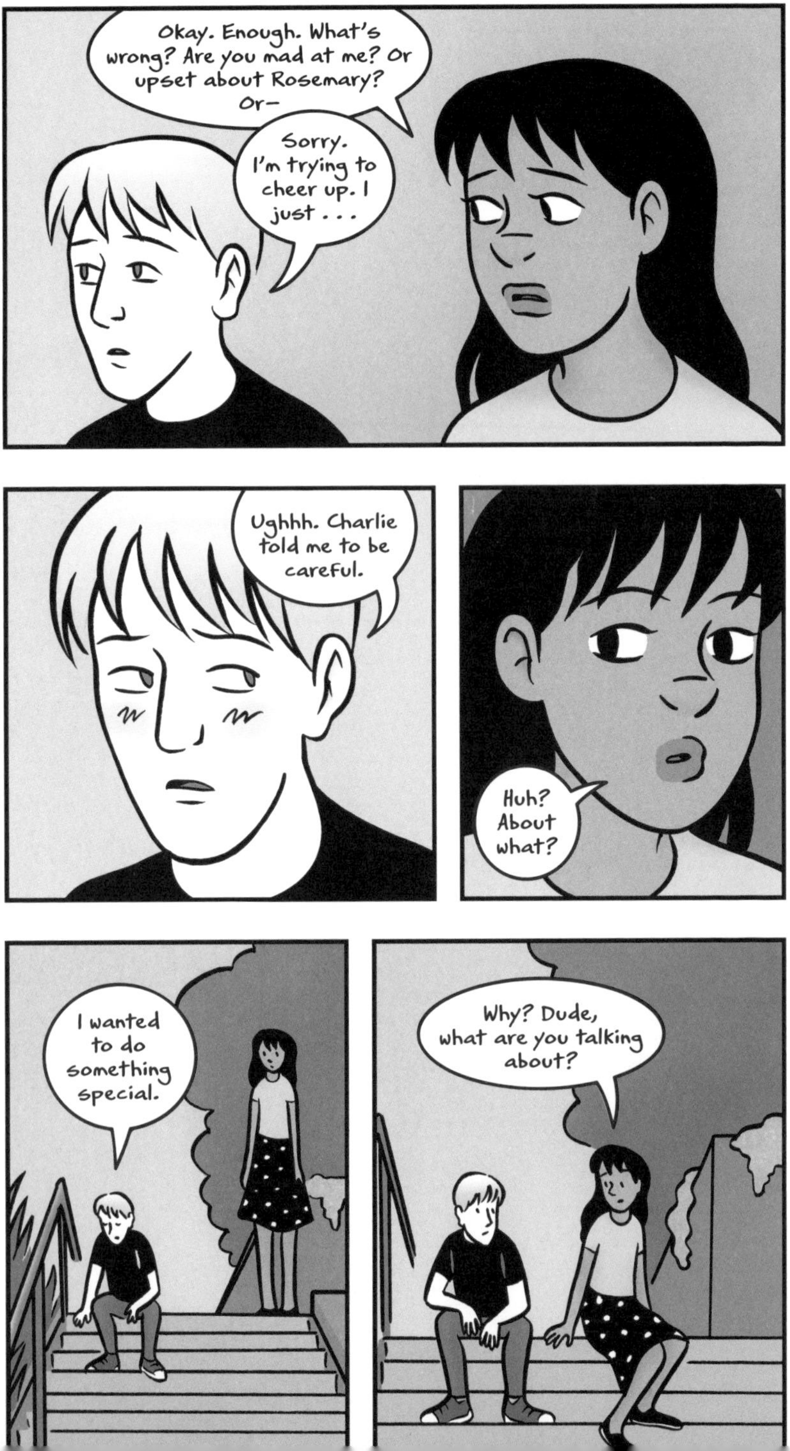
Okay. Enough. What's wrong? Are you mad at me? Or upset about Rosemary? Or–
Sorry. I'm trying to cheer up. I just . . .
Ughhh. Charlie told me to be careful.
Huh? About what?
I wanted to do something special.
Why? Dude, what are you talking about?

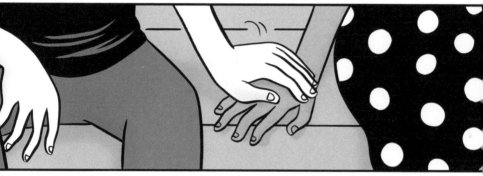

Oh my God. We aren't hanging out. We're Hanging Out.

I'm on a date with Austin.

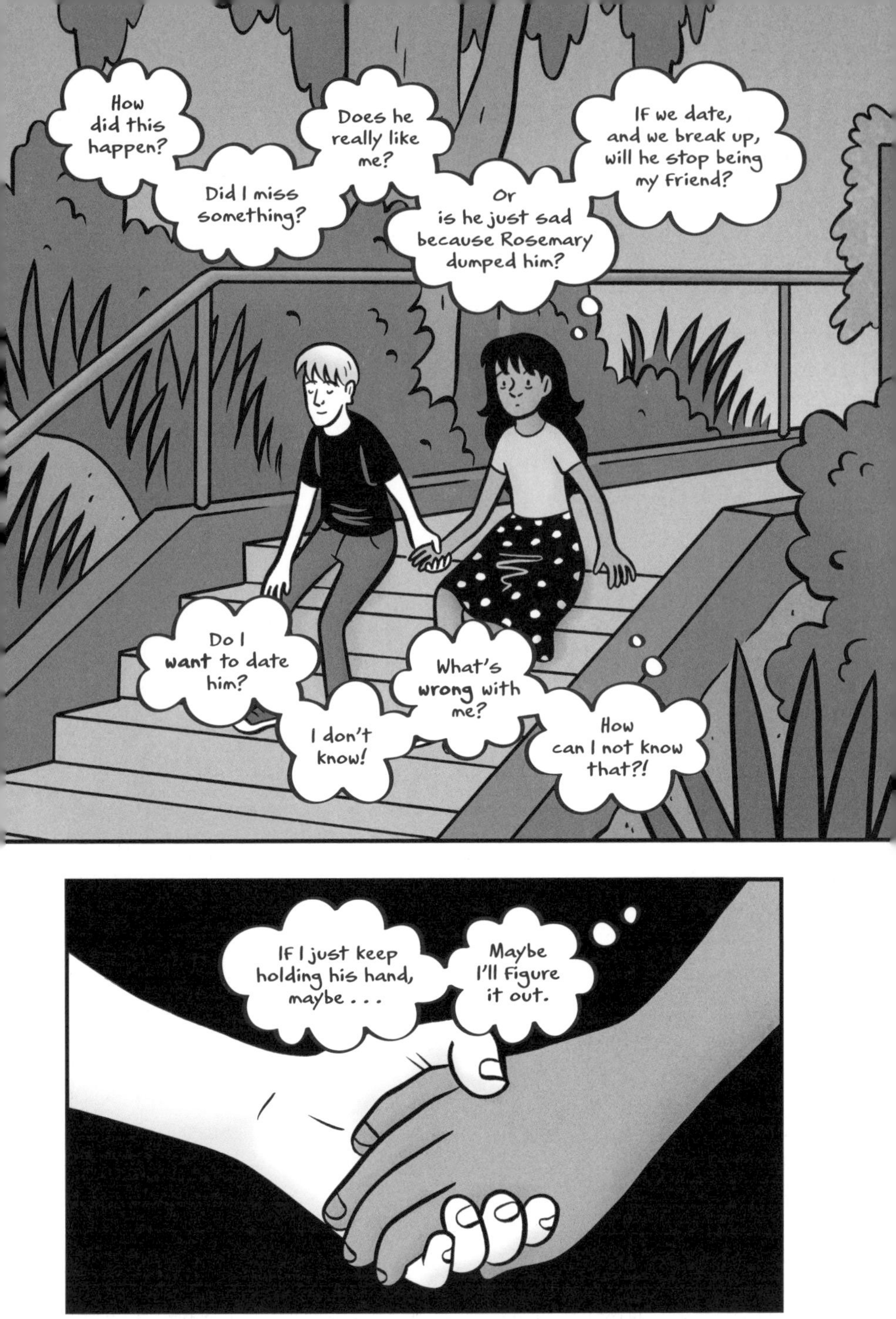
How did this happen?
Did I miss something?
Does he really like me?
Or is he just sad because Rosemary dumped him?
If we date, and we break up, will he stop being my friend?
Do I want to date him?
I don't know!
What's wrong with me?
How can I not know that?!
If I just keep holding his hand, maybe . . .
Maybe I'll figure it out.

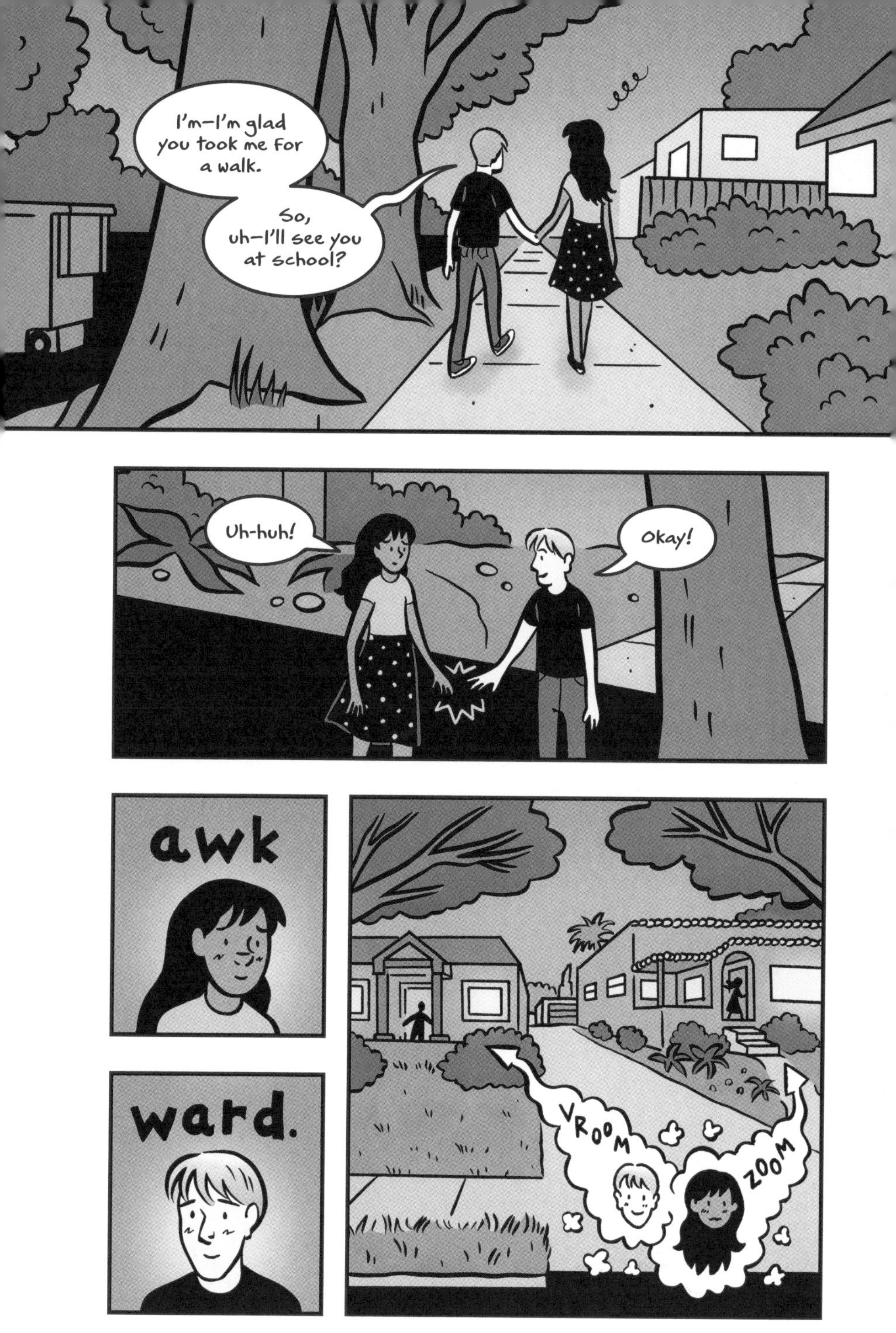
I'm—I'm glad you took me for a walk.
So, uh—I'll see you at school?
Uh-huh!
Okay!
awk
ward.
VROOM
ZOOM

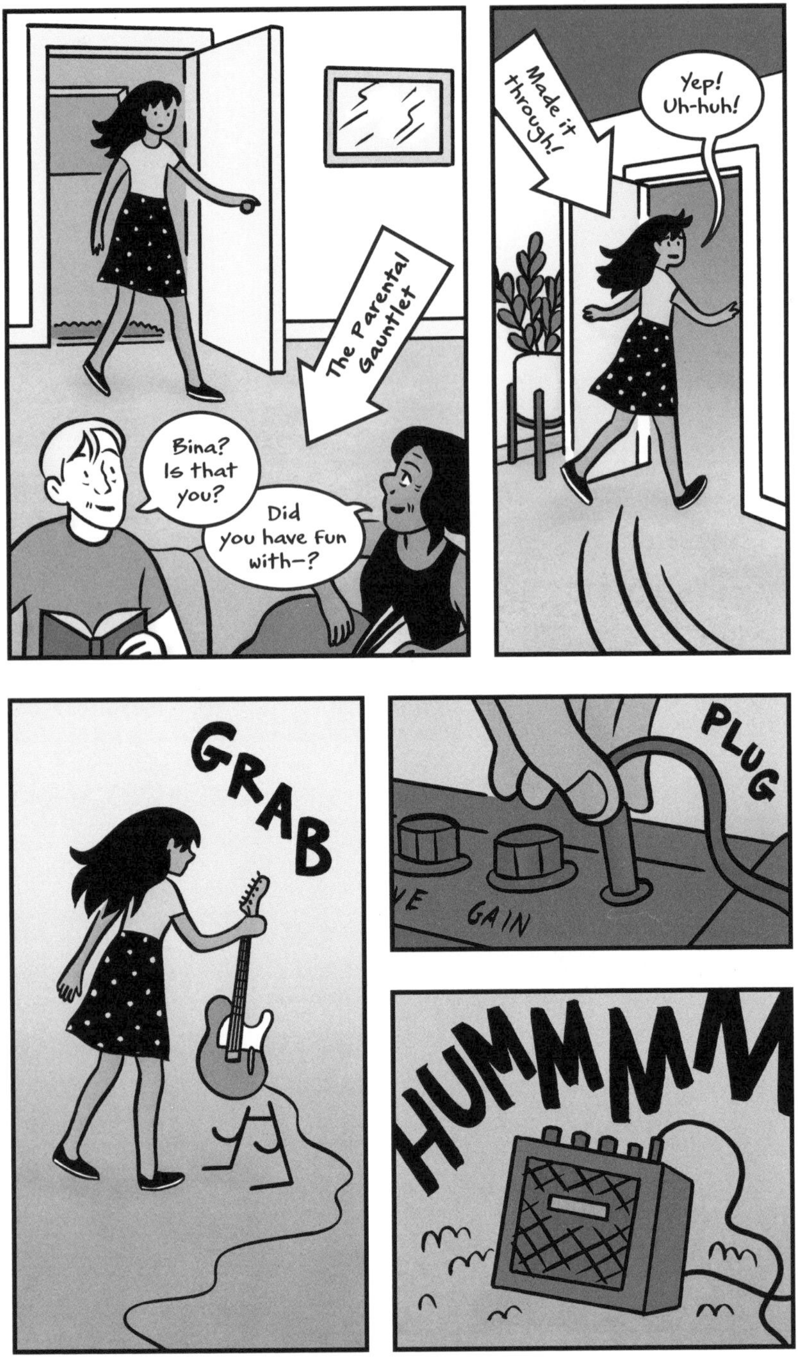
The Parental Gauntlet
Bina? Is that you?
Did you have fun with–?
Made it through!
Yep! Uh-huh!
GRAB
PLUG
GAIN
HUMMMM

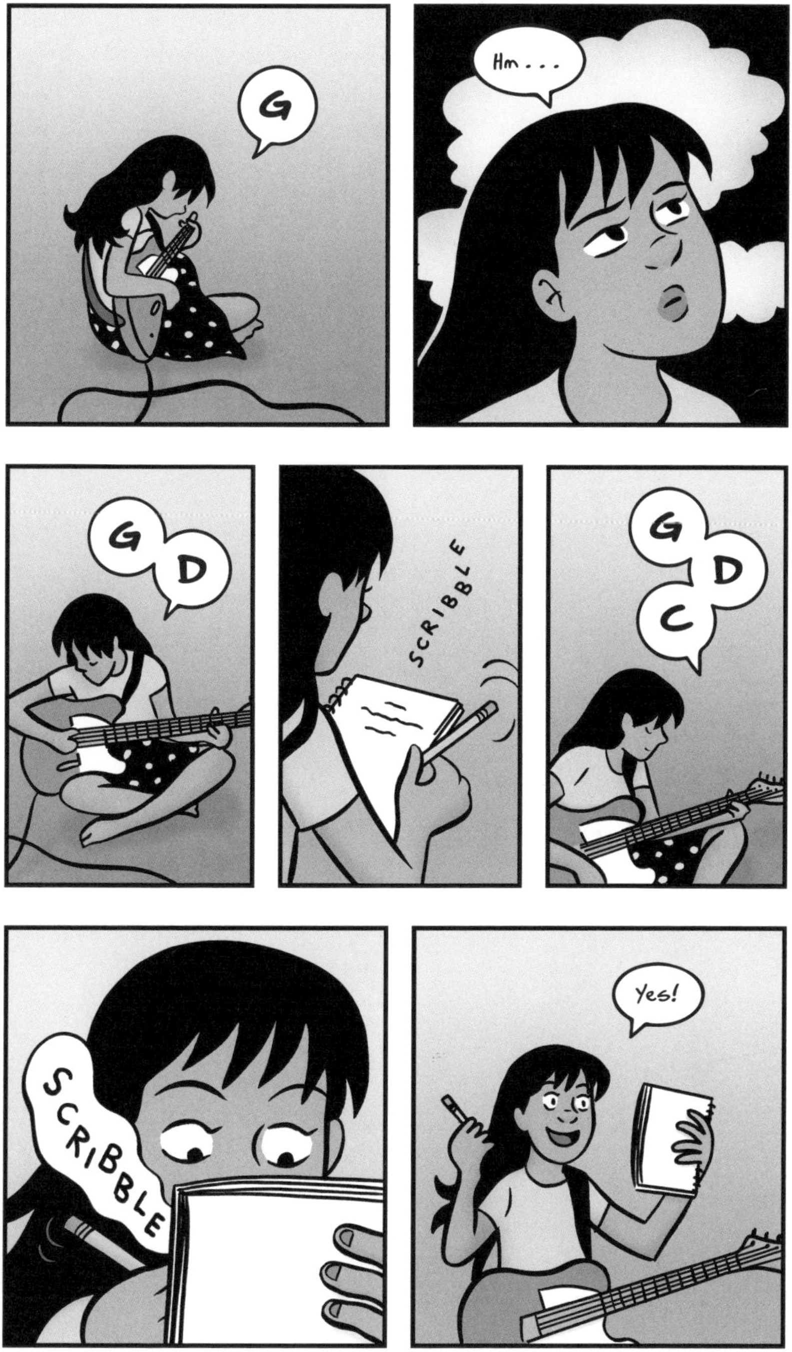
G
Hm . . .
G
D
SCRIBBLE
G
D
C
SCRIBBLE
Yes!

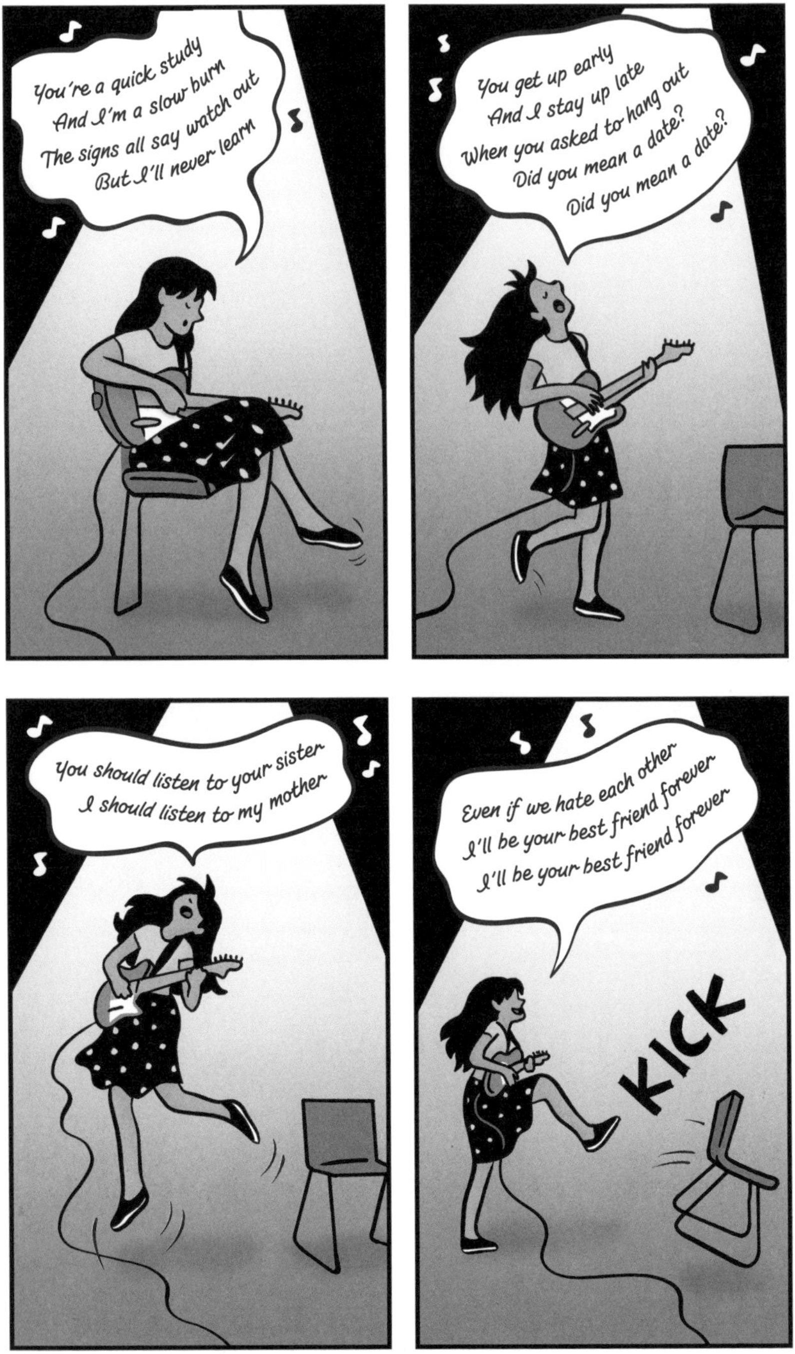
You're a quick study
And I'm a slow burn
The signs all say watch out
But I'll never learn
You get up early
And I stay up late
When you asked to hang out
Did you mean a date?
Did you mean a date?
You should listen to your sister
I should listen to my mother
Even if we hate each other
I'll be your best friend forever
I'll be your best friend forever
KICK

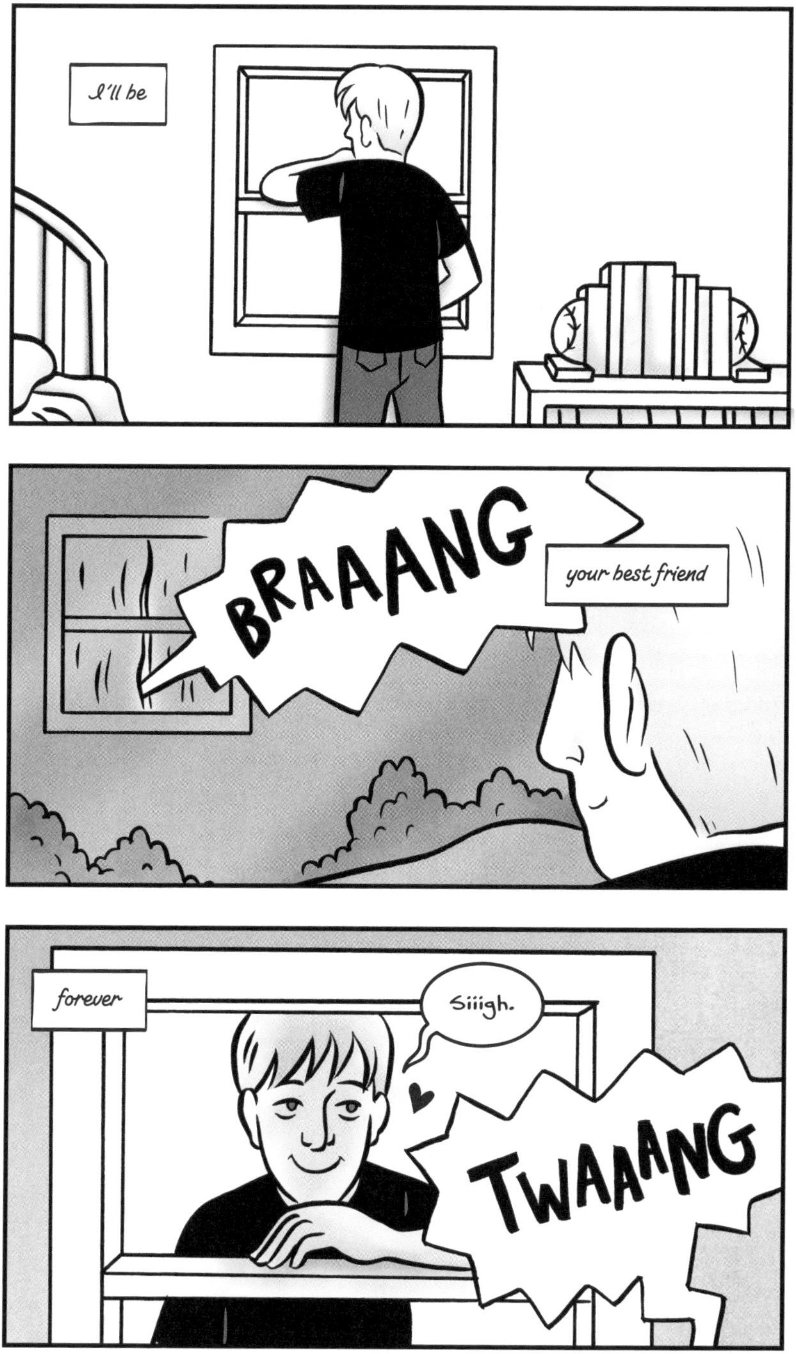
I'll be
BRAAANG
your best friend
forever
Siiigh.
TWAAANG

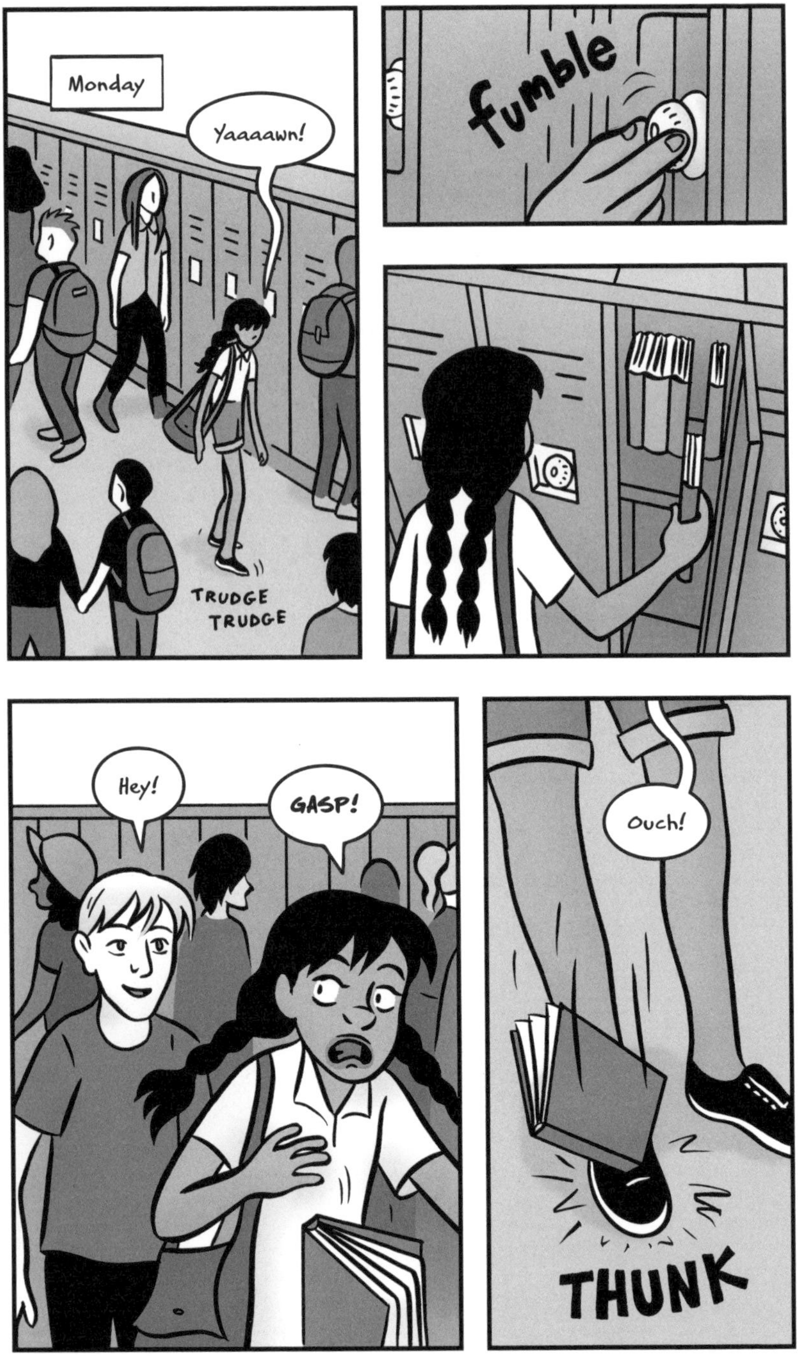
Monday
Yaaaawn!
TRUDGE
TRUDGE
fumble
Hey!
GASP!
Ouch!
THUNK

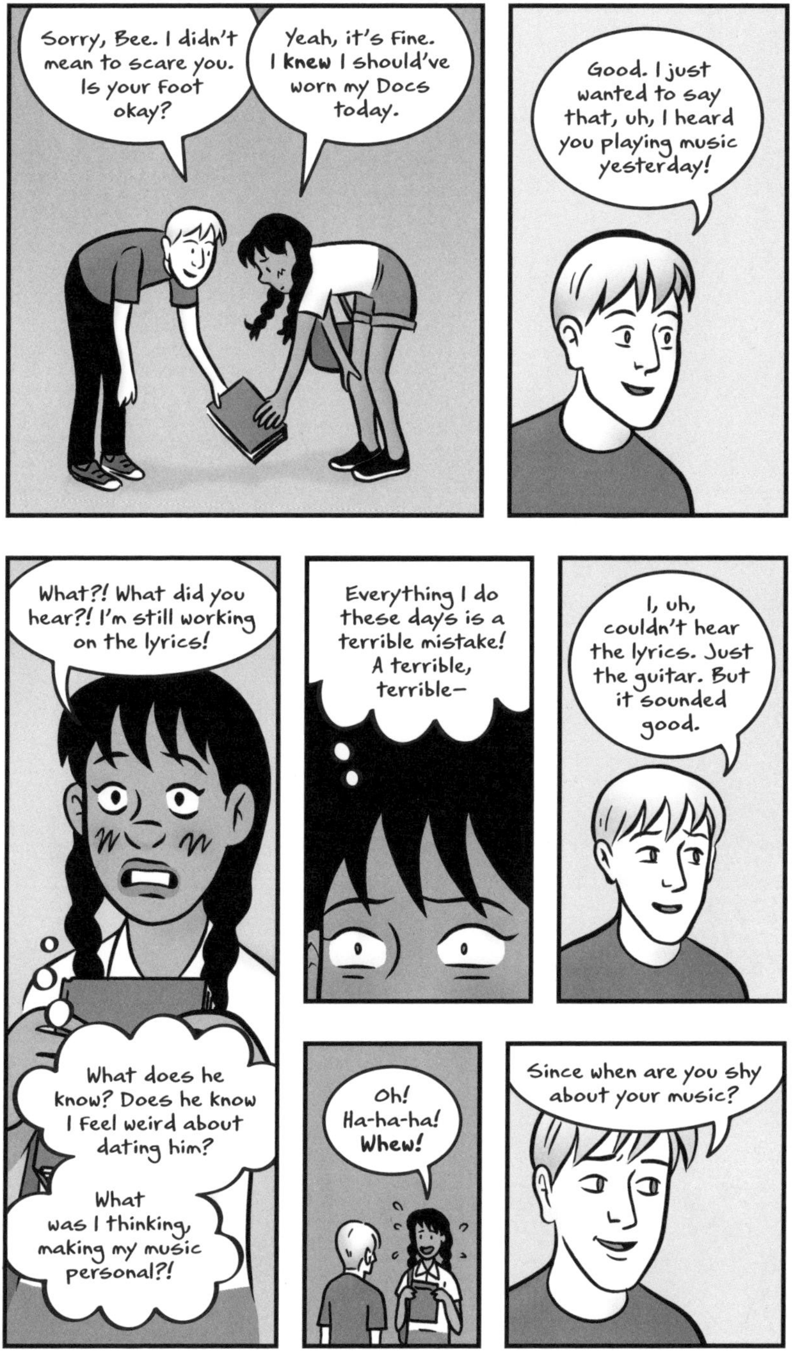
Sorry, Bee. I didn't mean to scare you. Is your foot okay?
Yeah, it's fine. I **knew** I should've worn my Docs today.
Good. I just wanted to say that, uh, I heard you playing music yesterday!
What?! What did you hear?! I'm still working on the lyrics!
What does he know? Does he know I feel weird about dating him?
What was I thinking, making my music personal?!
Everything I do these days is a terrible mistake! A terrible, terrible—
I, uh, couldn't hear the lyrics. Just the guitar. But it sounded good.
Oh! Ha-ha-ha! **Whew!**
Since when are you shy about your music?

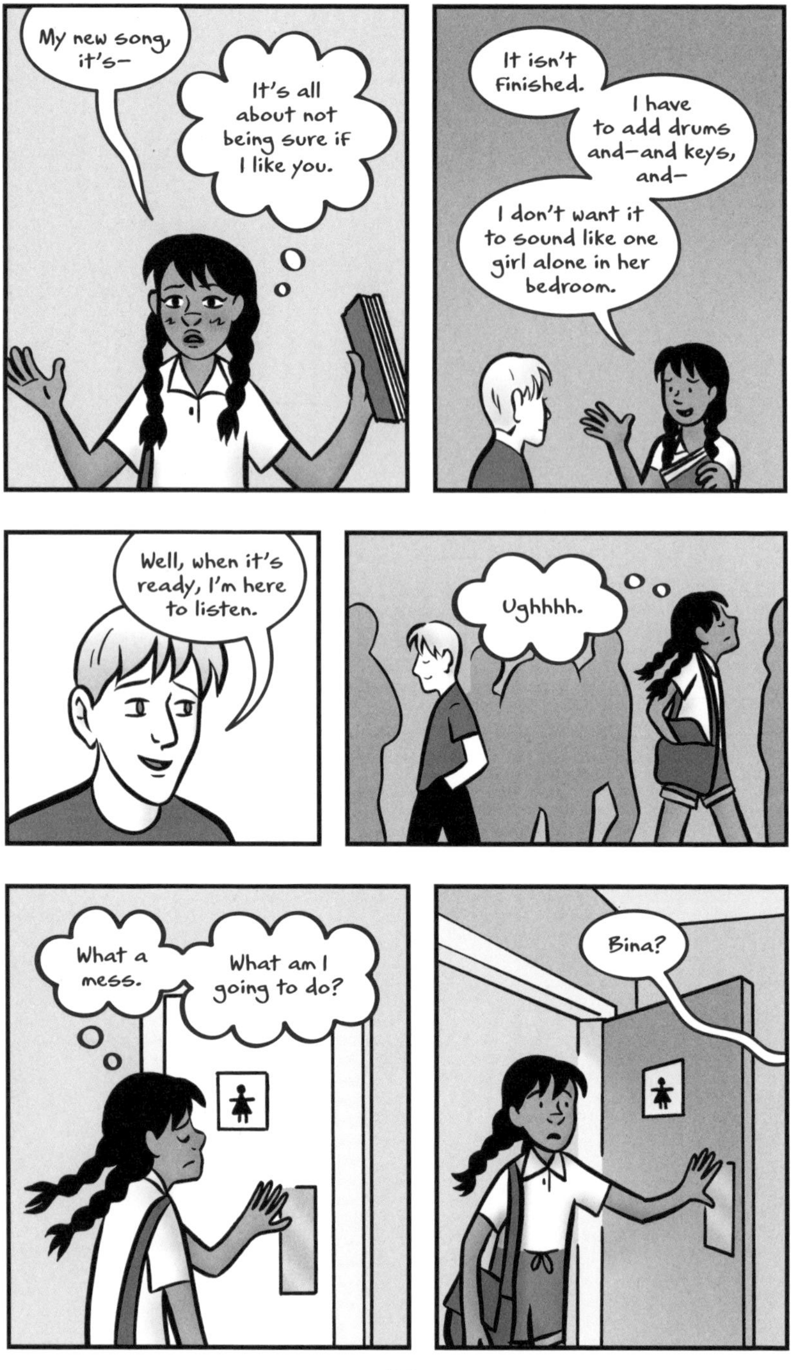
My new song, it's—
It's all about not being sure if I like you.
It isn't finished.
I have to add drums and—and keys, and—
I don't want it to sound like one girl alone in her bedroom.
Well, when it's ready, I'm here to listen.
Ughhhh.
What a mess.
What am I going to do?
Bina?

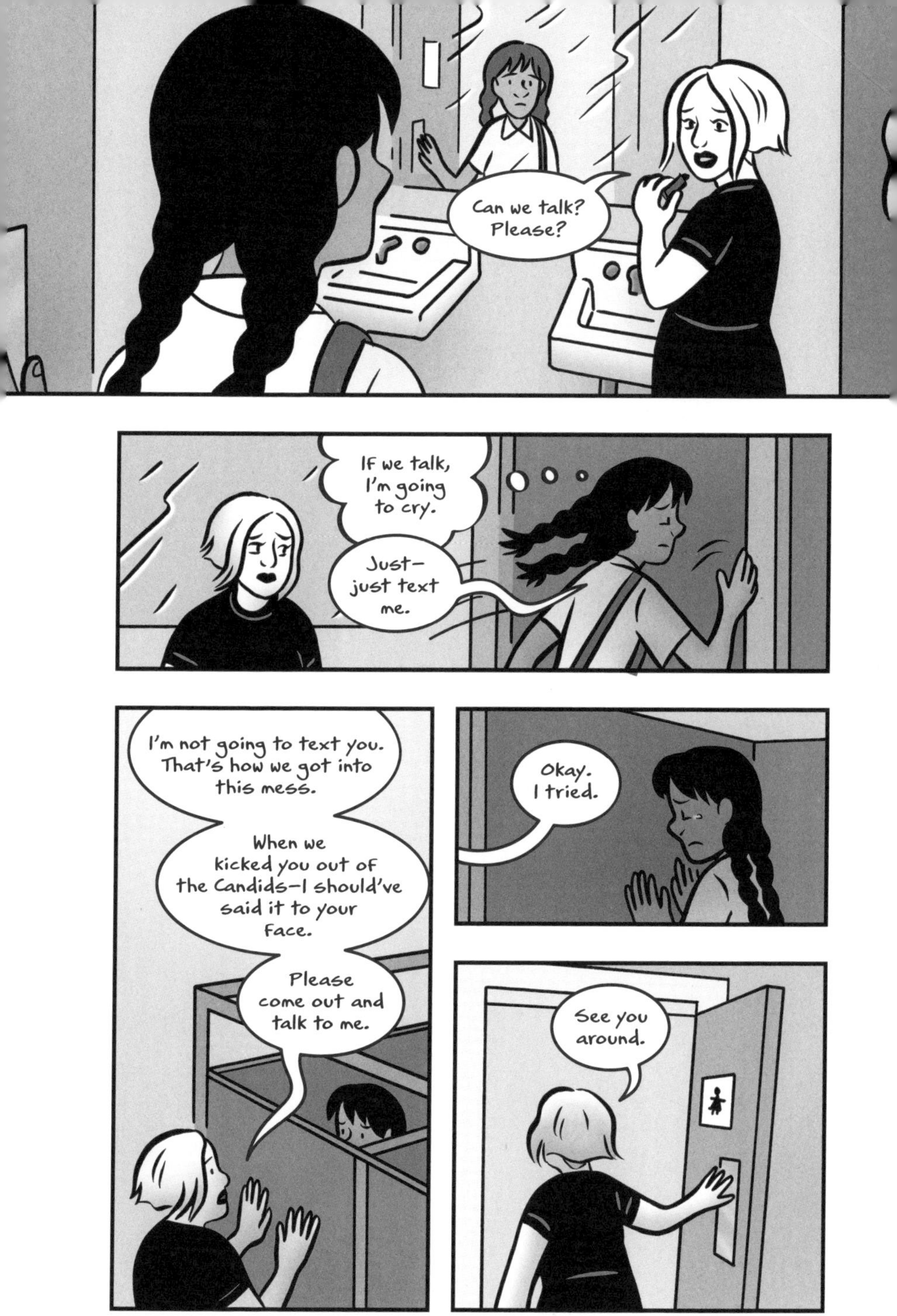
Can we talk? Please?
If we talk, I'm going to cry.
Just– just text me.
I'm not going to text you. That's how we got into this mess.
When we kicked you out of the Candids—I should've said it to your face.
Please come out and talk to me.
Okay. I tried.
See you around.

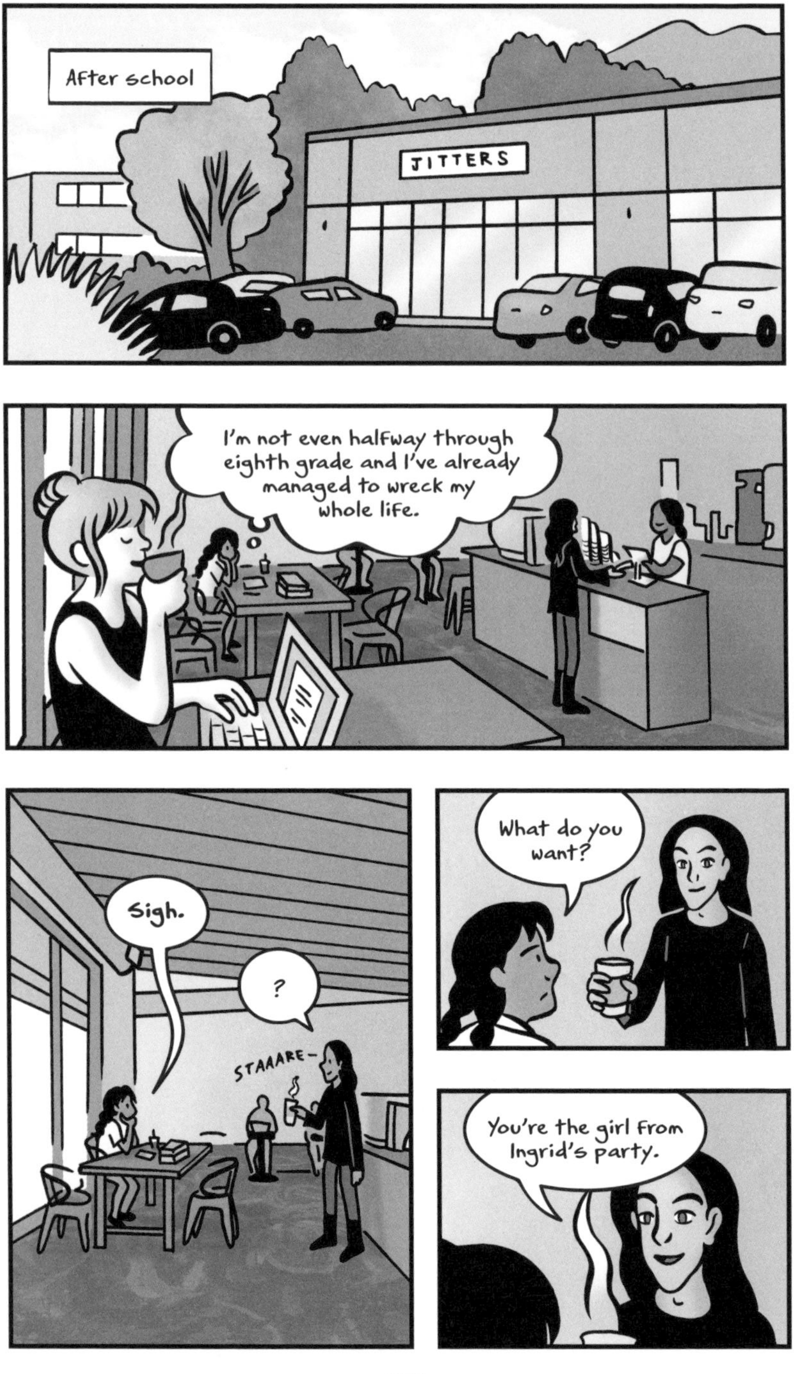
After school
JITTERS
I'm not even halfway through eighth grade and I've already managed to wreck my whole life.
Sigh.
?
STAAARE-
What do you want?
You're the girl from Ingrid's party.

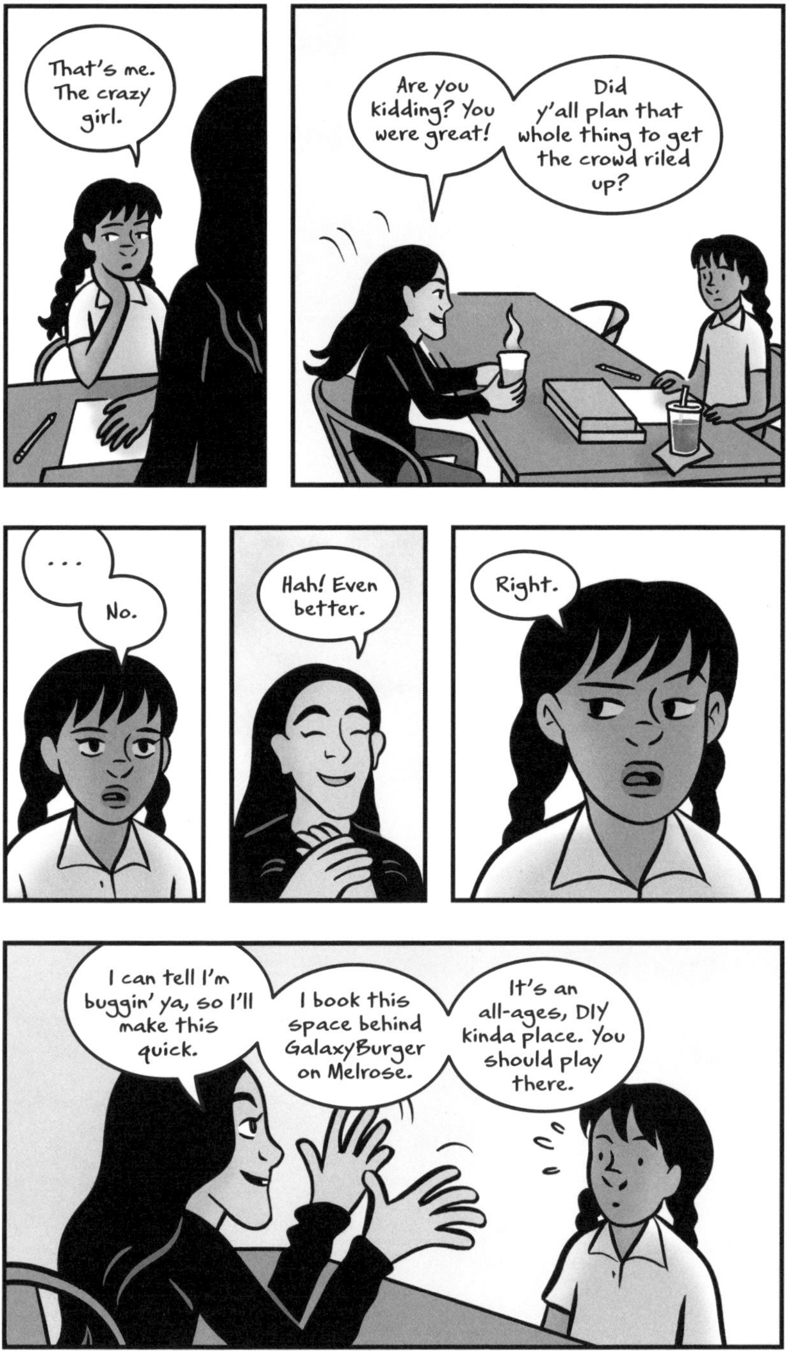
That's me. The crazy girl.
Are you kidding? You were great!
Did y'all plan that whole thing to get the crowd riled up?
...
No.
Hah! Even better.
Right.
I can tell I'm buggin' ya, so I'll make this quick.
I book this space behind GalaxyBurger on Melrose.
It's an all-ages, DIY kinda place. You should play there.

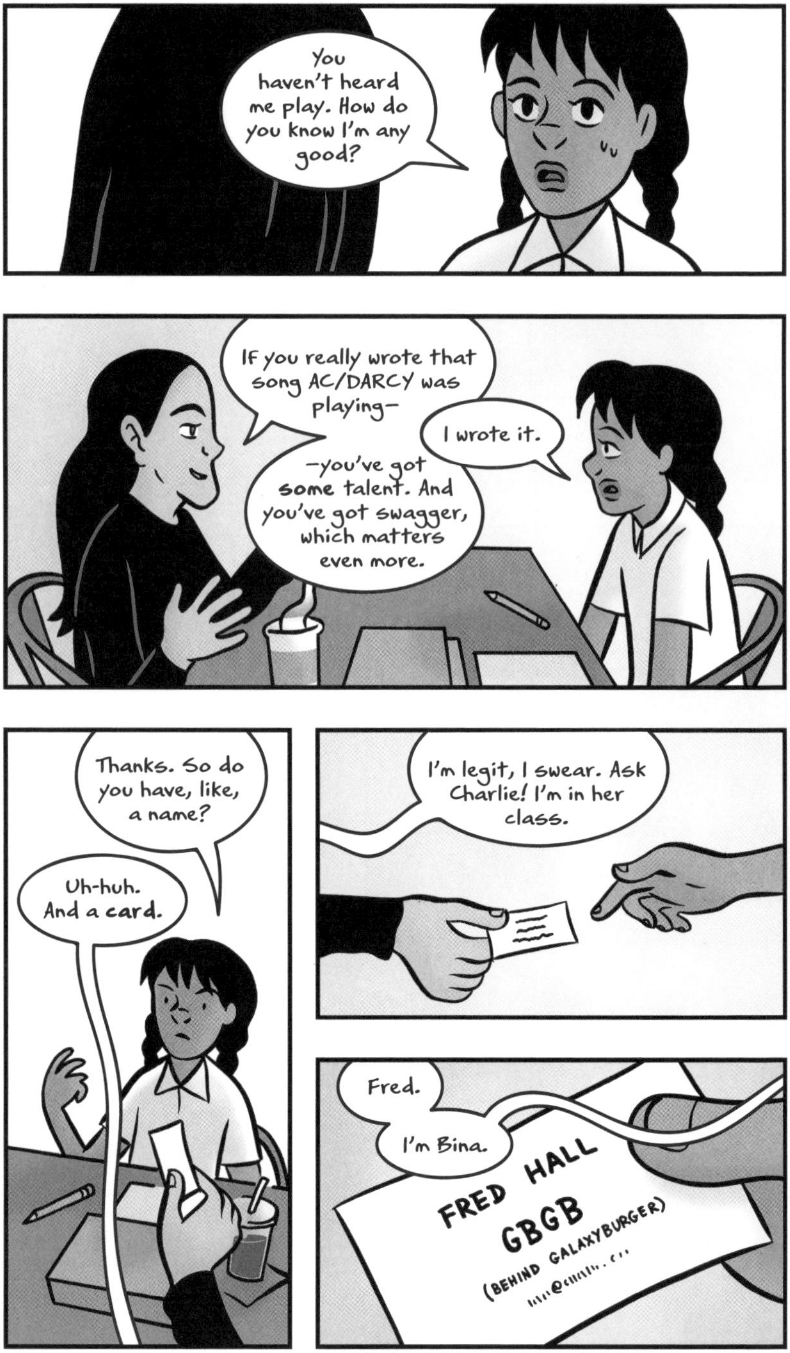
You haven't heard me play. How do you know I'm any good?
If you really wrote that song AC/DARCY was playing—
I wrote it.
—you've got some talent. And you've got swagger, which matters even more.
Thanks. So do you have, like, a name?
Uh-huh. And a card.
I'm legit, I swear. Ask Charlie! I'm in her class.
Fred.
I'm Bina.
FRED HALL
GBGB
(BEHIND GALAXYBURGER)

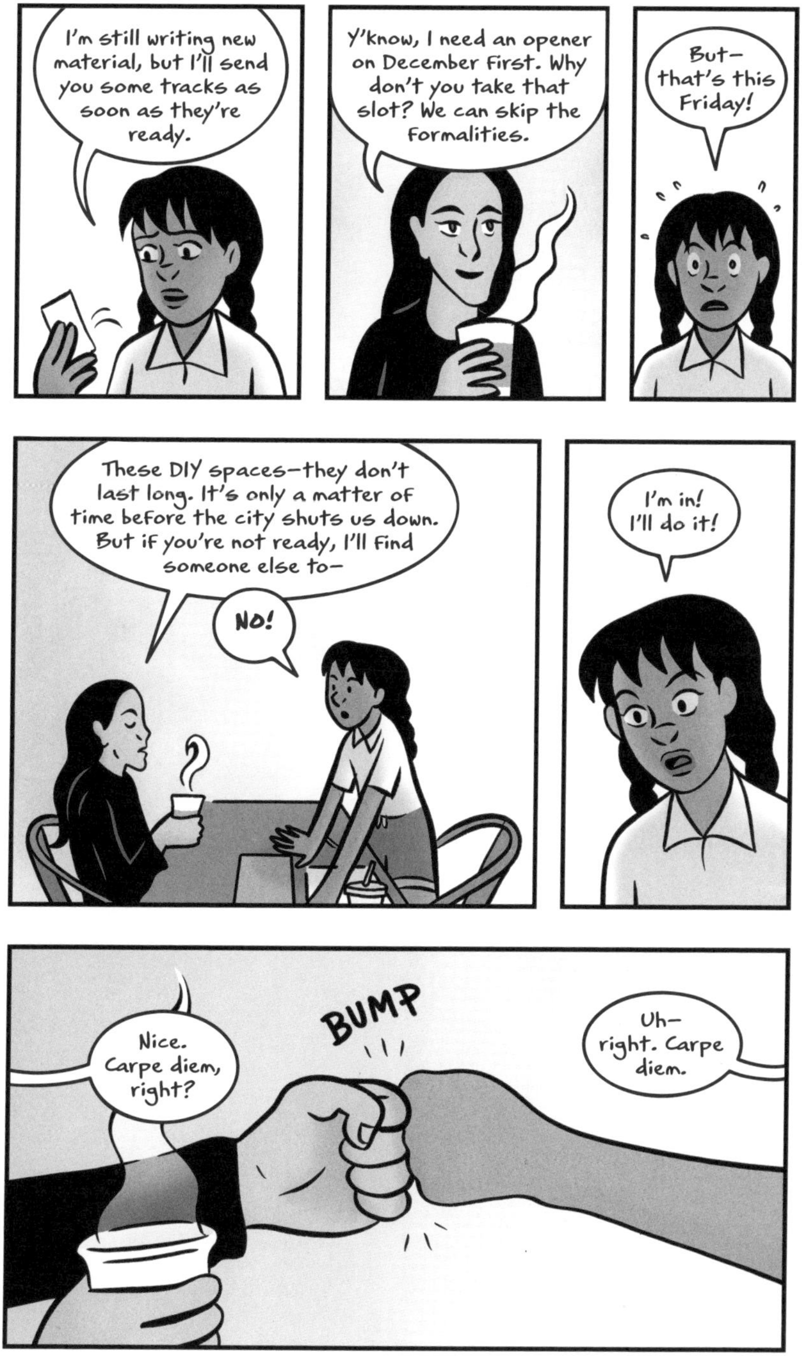
I'm still writing new material, but I'll send you some tracks as soon as they're ready.
Y'know, I need an opener on December First. Why don't you take that slot? We can skip the formalities.
But— that's this Friday!
These DIY spaces—they don't last long. It's only a matter of time before the city shuts us down. But if you're not ready, I'll find someone else to—
NO!
I'm in! I'll do it!
Nice. Carpe diem, right?
BUMP
Uh— right. Carpe diem.

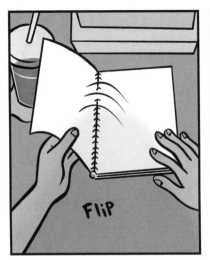

FliP

New Song 2

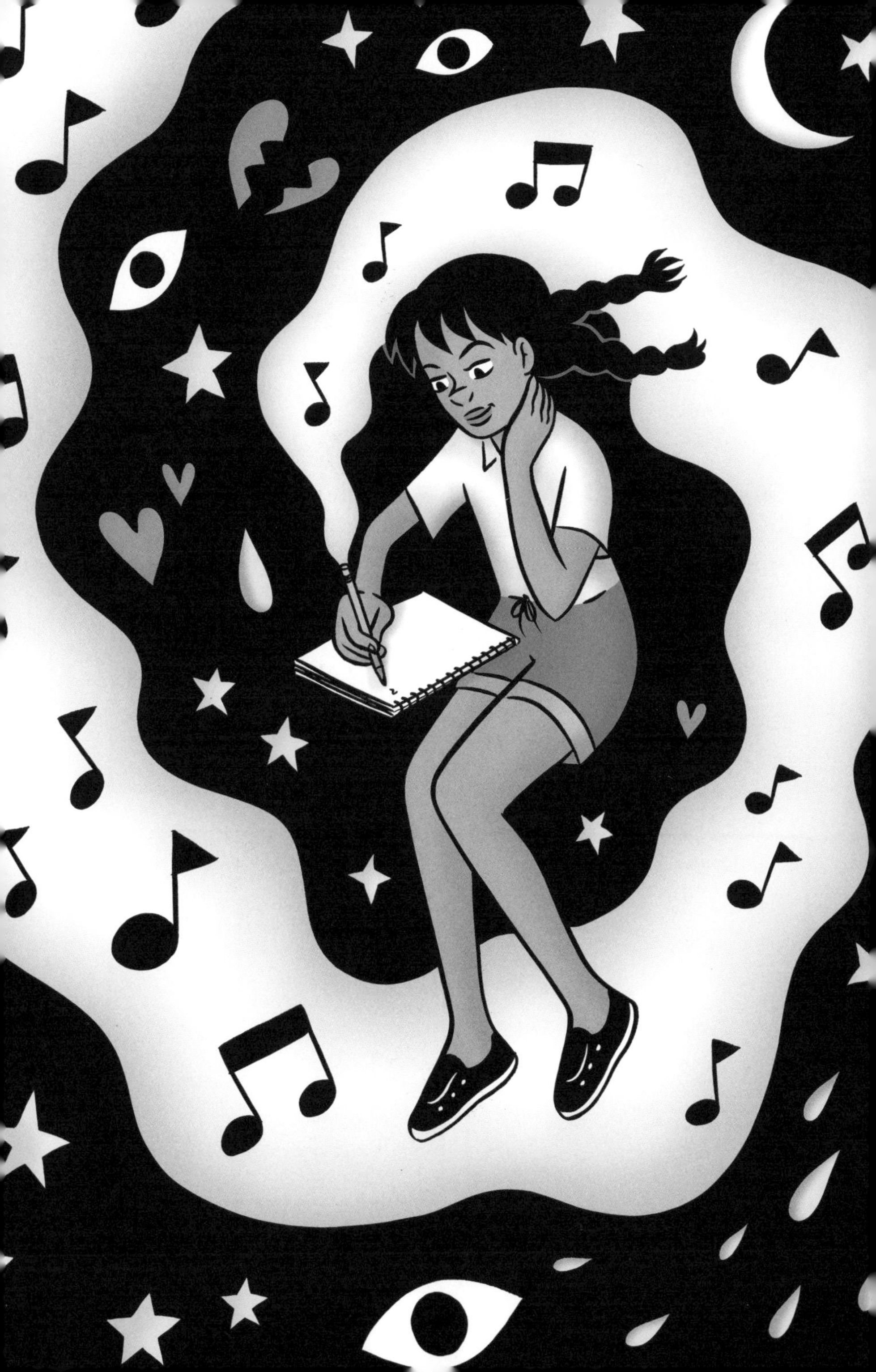

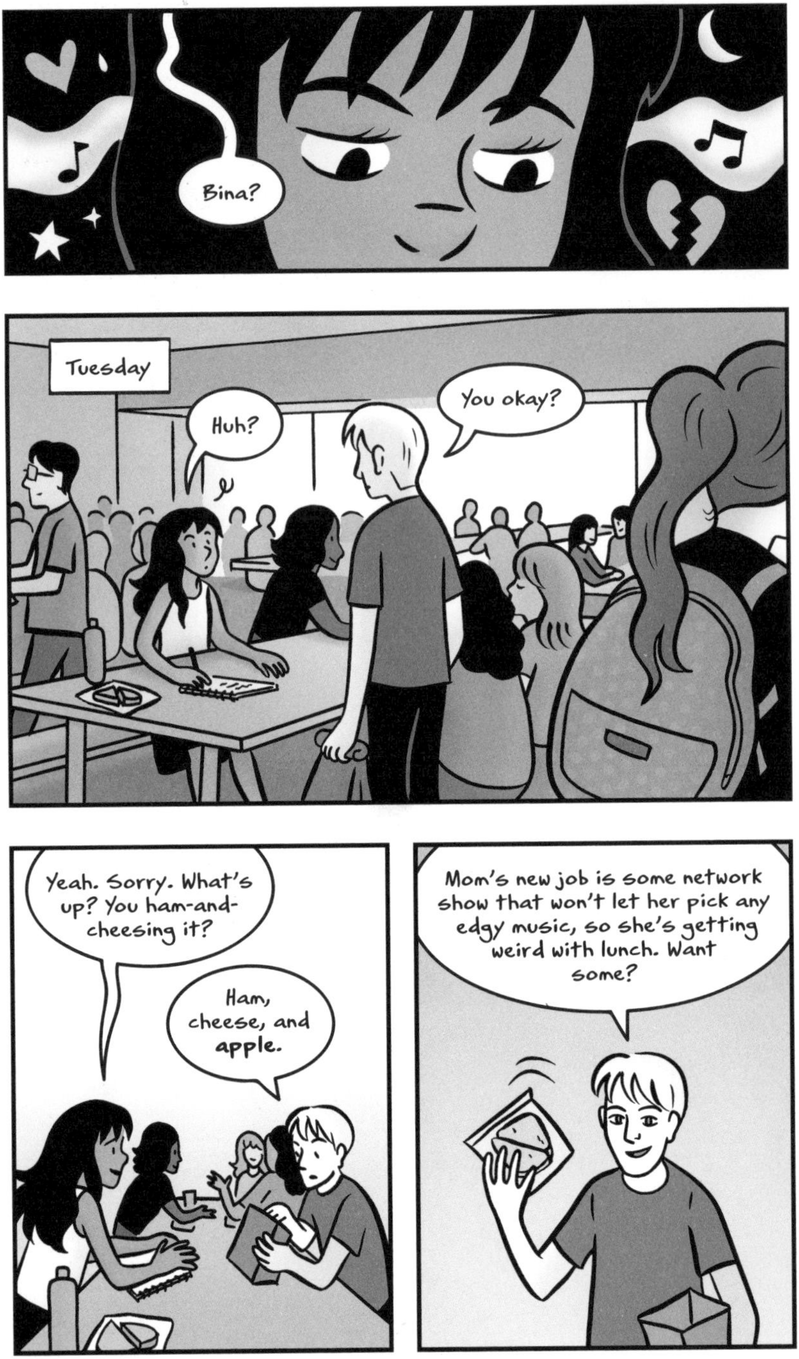
Bina?
Tuesday
Huh?
You okay?
Yeah. Sorry. What's up? You ham-and-cheesing it?
Ham, cheese, and apple.
Mom's new job is some network show that won't let her pick any edgy music, so she's getting weird with lunch. Want some?

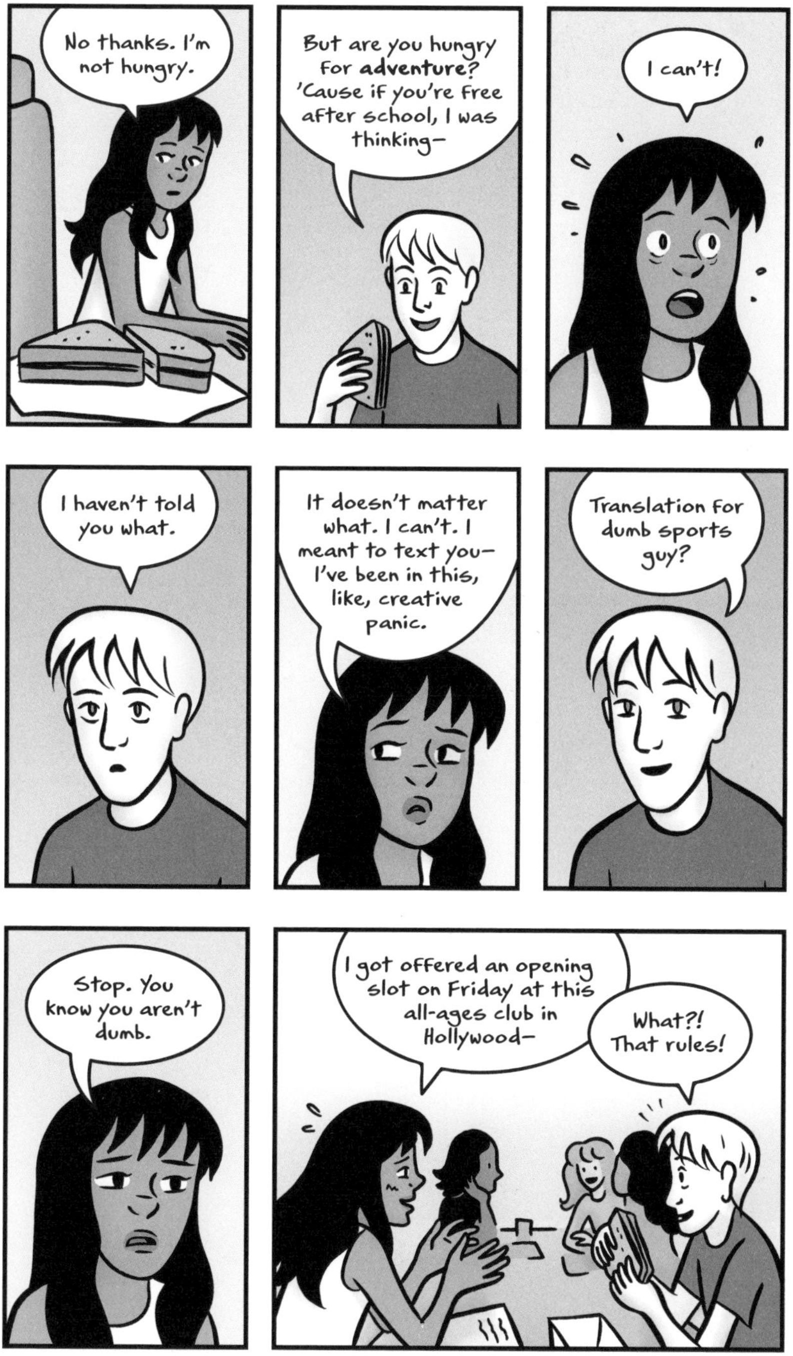
No thanks. I'm not hungry.
But are you hungry for **adventure**? 'Cause if you're free after school, I was thinking–
I can't!
I haven't told you what.
It doesn't matter what. I can't. I meant to text you– I've been in this, like, creative panic.
Translation for dumb sports guy?
Stop. You know you aren't dumb.
I got offered an opening slot on Friday at this all-ages club in Hollywood–
What?! That rules!

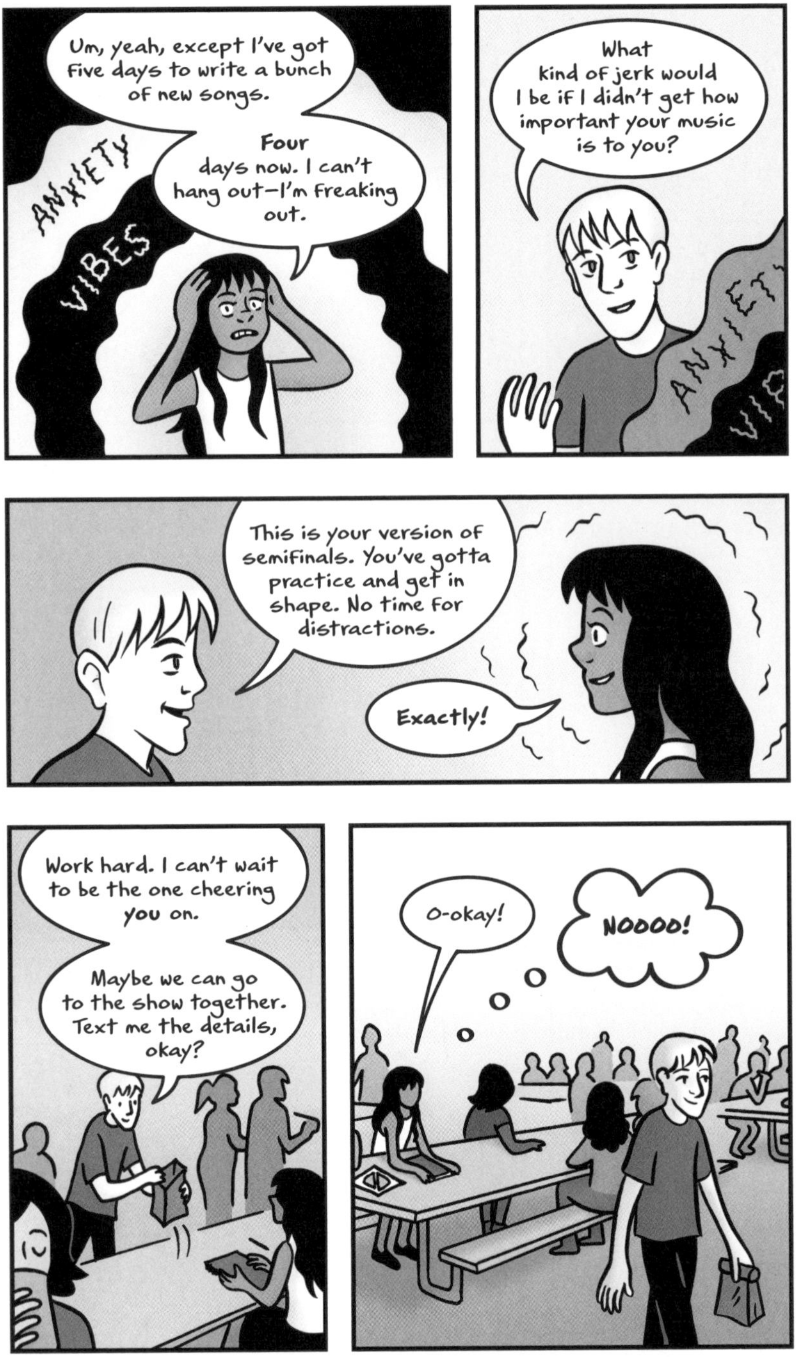
Um, yeah, except I've got five days to write a bunch of new songs.
ANXIETY
VIBES
Four days now. I can't hang out—I'm freaking out.
What kind of jerk would I be if I didn't get how important your music is to you?
ANXIETY
This is your version of semifinals. You've gotta practice and get in shape. No time for distractions.
Exactly!
Work hard. I can't wait to be the one cheering you on.
Maybe we can go to the show together. Text me the details, okay?
O-okay!
NOOOO!

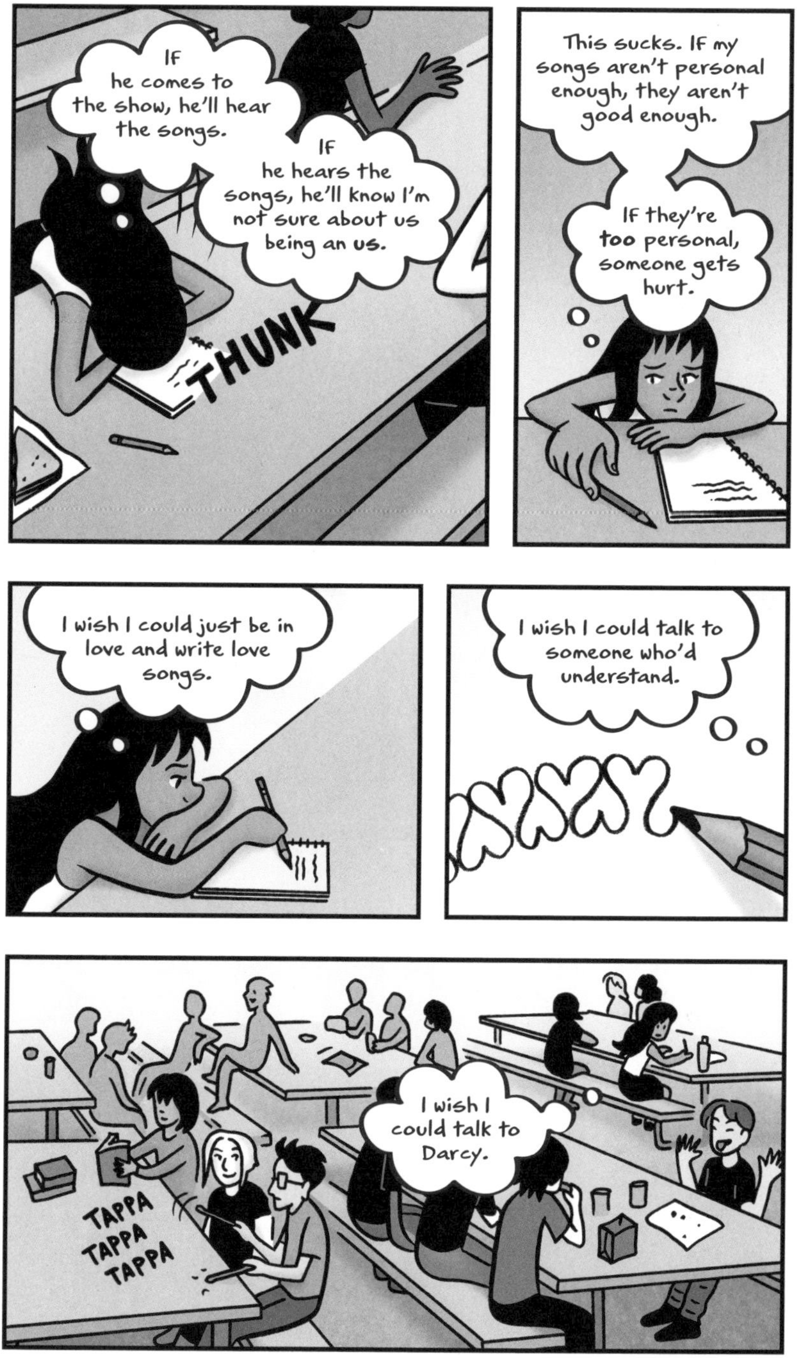
IF he comes to the show, he'll hear the songs.
IF he hears the songs, he'll know I'm not sure about us being an us.
THUNK
This sucks. IF my songs aren't personal enough, they aren't good enough.
IF they're **too** personal, someone gets hurt.
I wish I could just be in love and write love songs.
I wish I could talk to someone who'd understand.
I wish I could talk to Darcy.
TAPPA TAPPA TAPPA

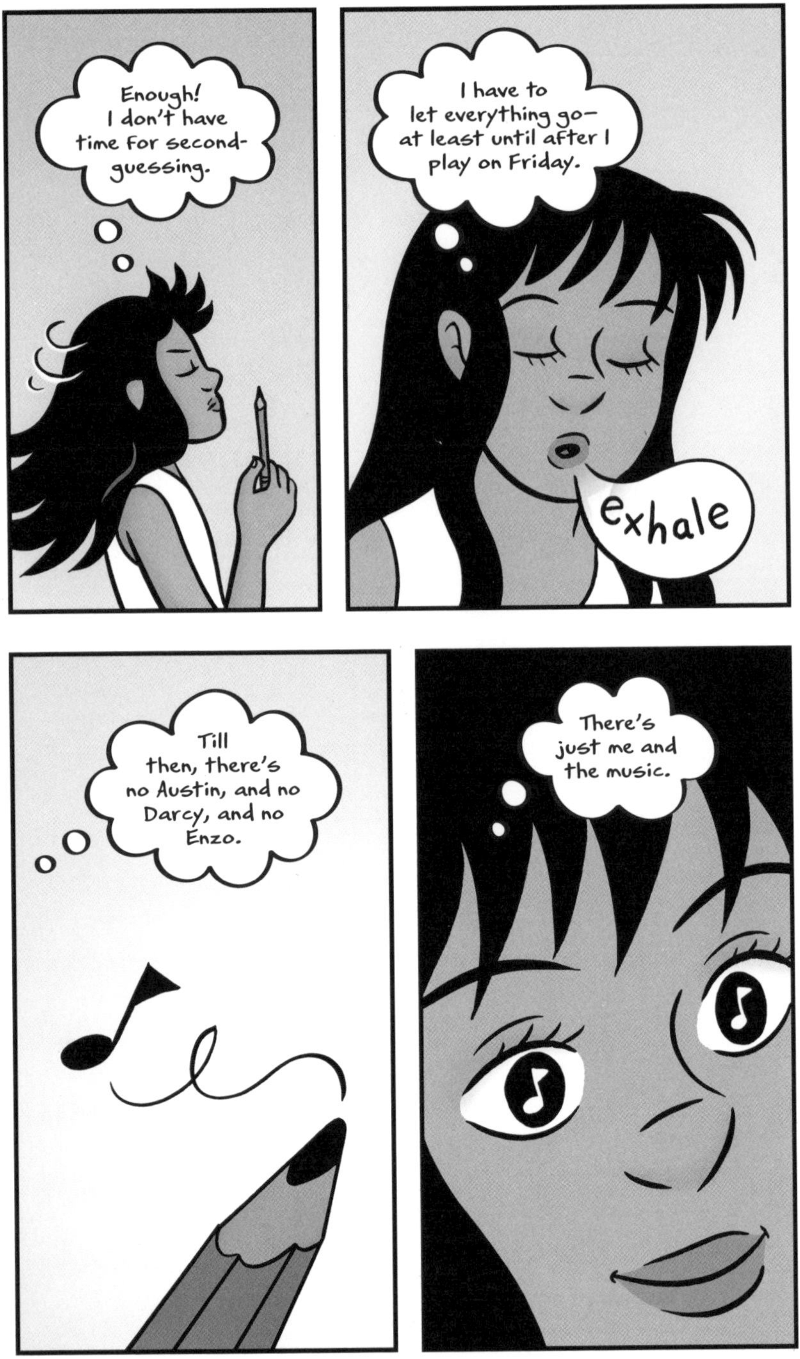
Enough! I don't have time for second-guessing.
I have to let everything go—at least until after I play on Friday.
exhale
Till then, there's no Austin, and no Darcy, and no Enzo.
There's just me and the music.

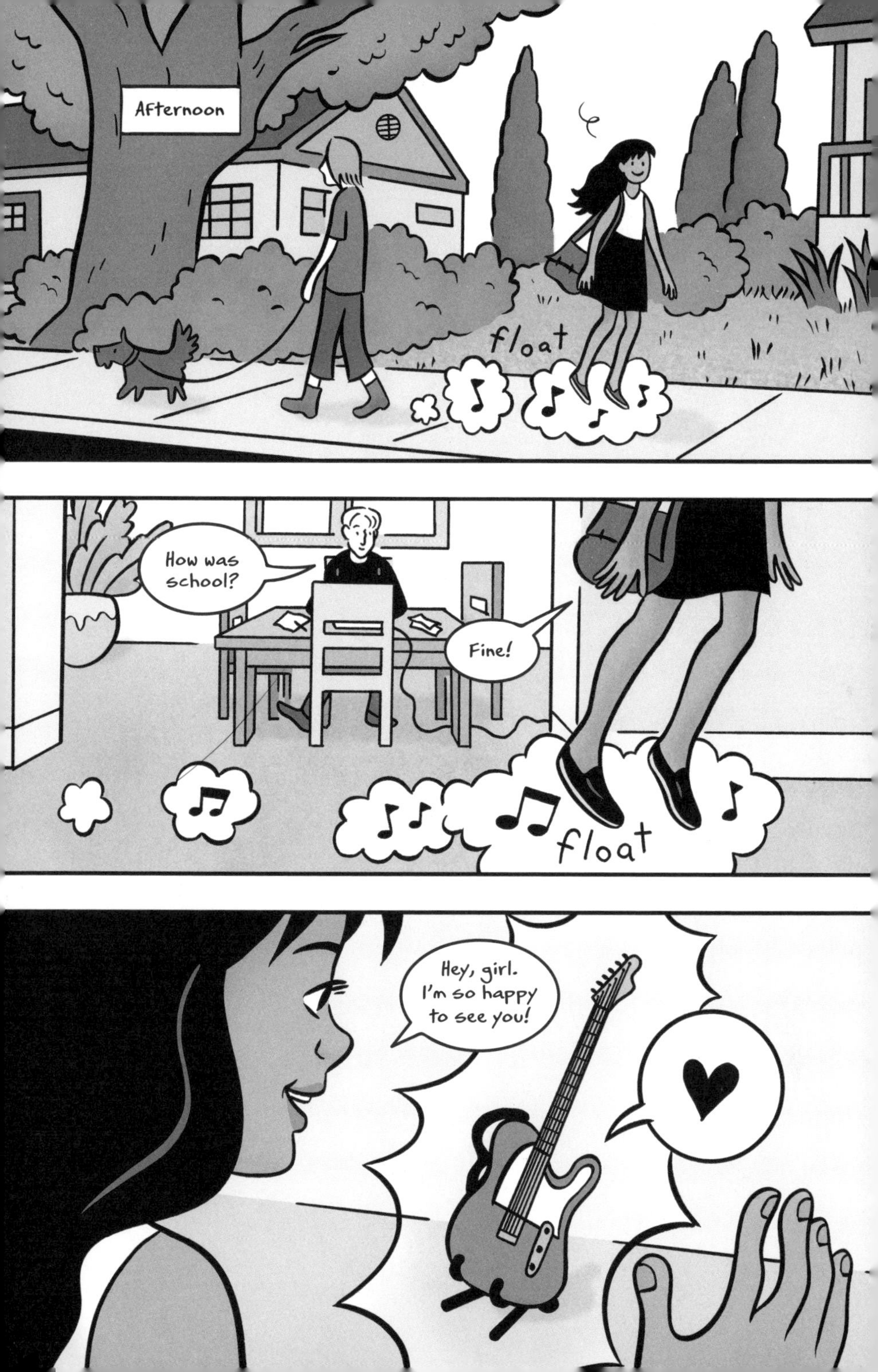
Afternoon
float
How was school?
Fine!
float
Hey, girl. I'm so happy to see you!

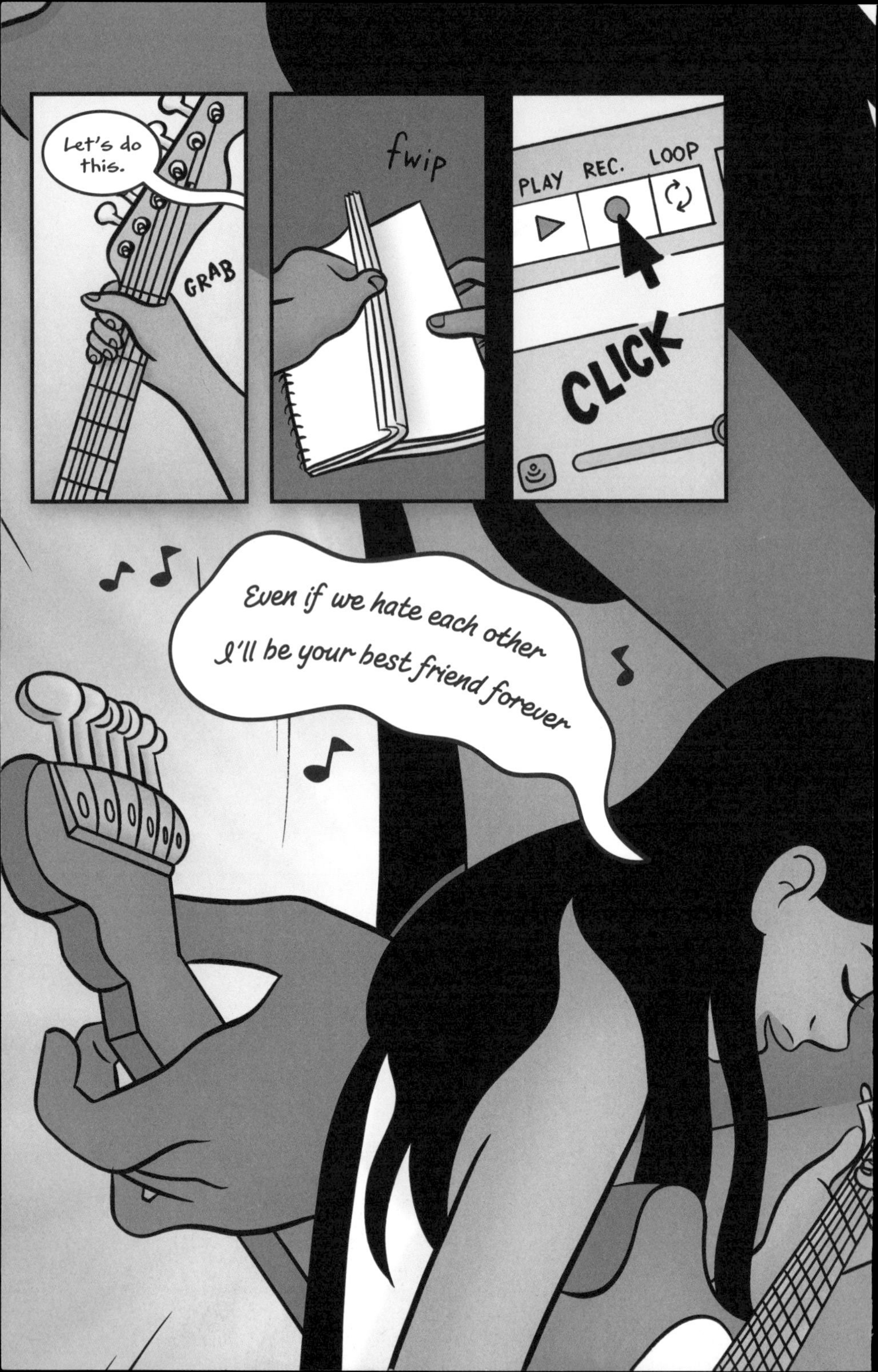

Let's do this.
GRAB
fwip
PLAY
REC.
LOOP
CLICK
Even if we hate each other
I'll be your best friend forever

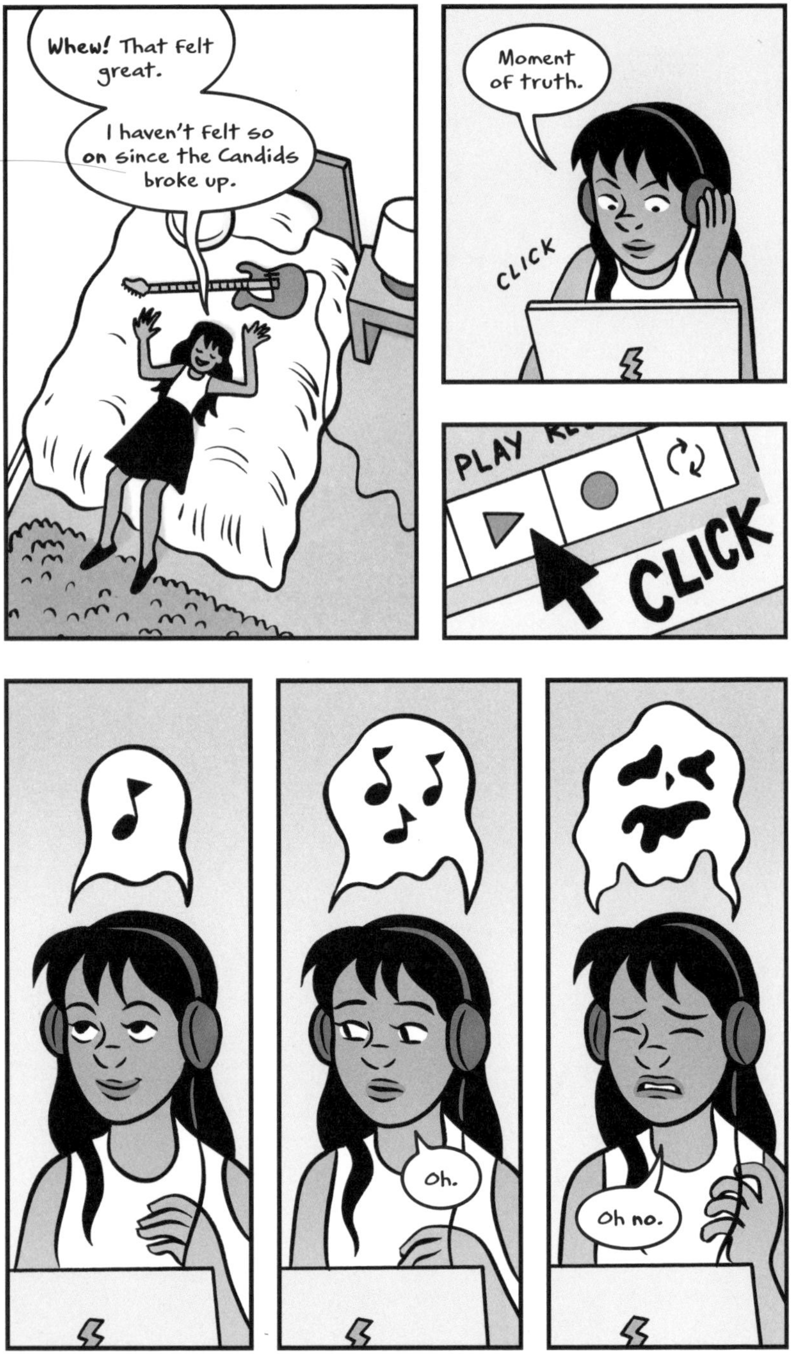
Whew! That felt great.
I haven't felt so on since the Candids broke up.
Moment of truth.
CLICK
PLAY
CLICK
Oh.
Oh no.

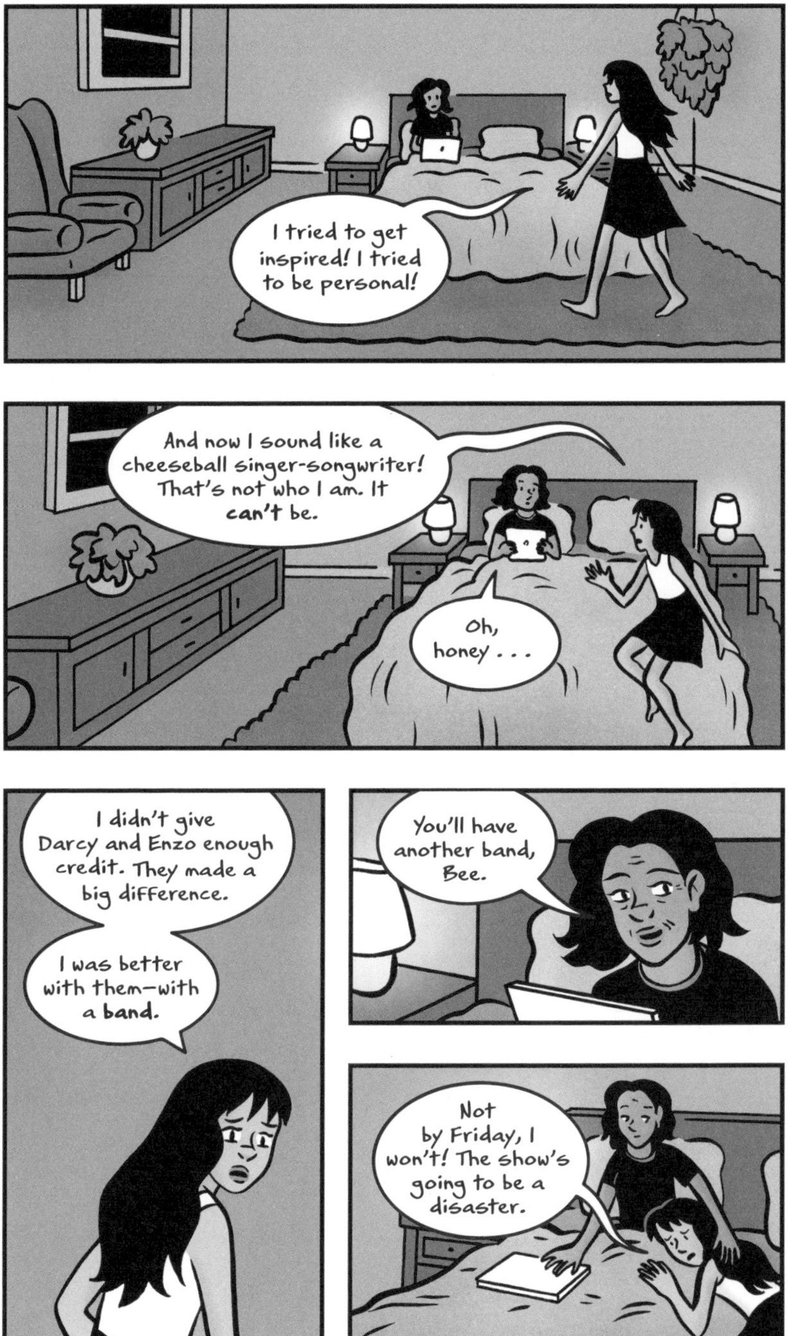
I tried to get inspired! I tried to be personal!
And now I sound like a cheeseball singer-songwriter! That's not who I am. It **can't** be.
Oh, honey . . .
I didn't give Darcy and Enzo enough credit. They made a big difference.
I was better with them—with a **band**.
You'll have another band, Bee.
Not by Friday, I won't! The show's going to be a disaster.

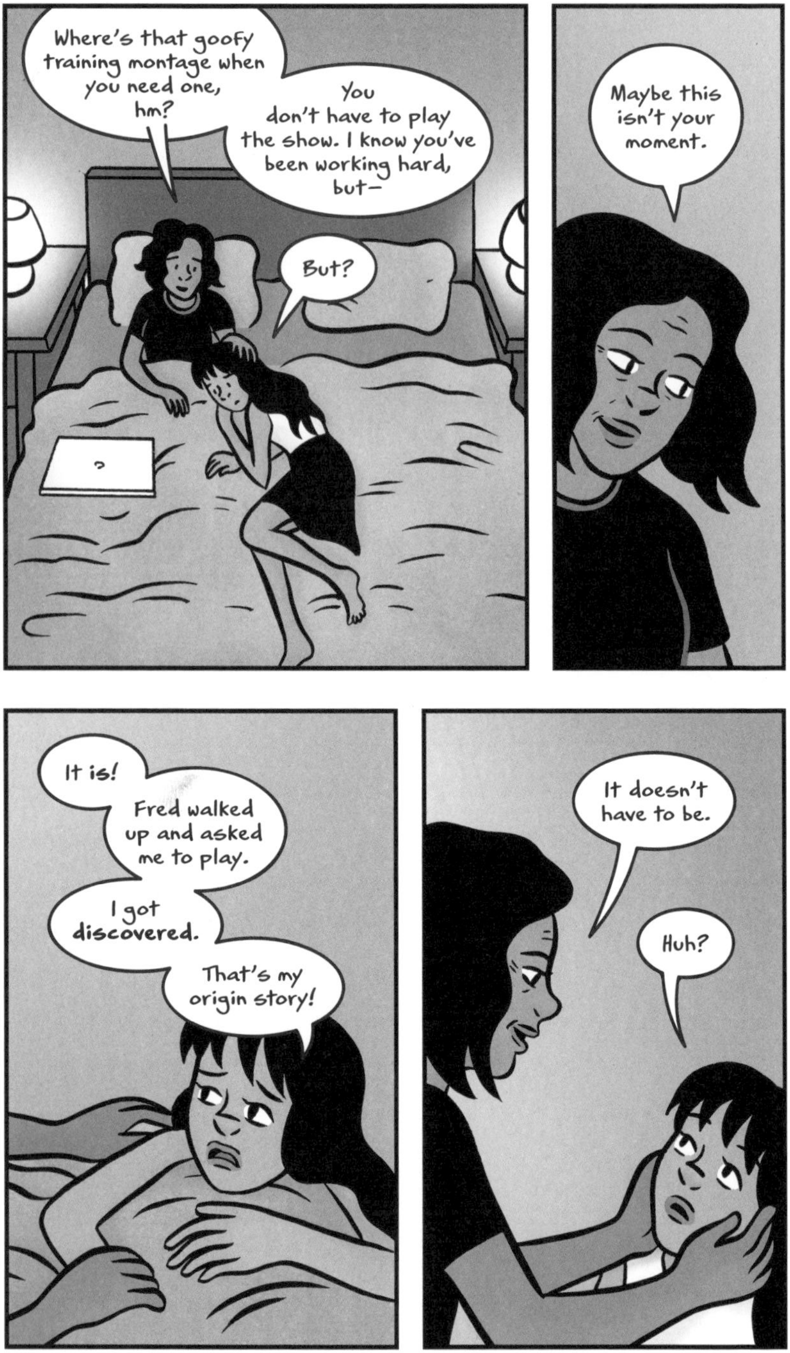
Where's that goofy training montage when you need one, hm?
You don't have to play the show. I know you've been working hard, but–
But?
Maybe this isn't your moment.
It is!
Fred walked up and asked me to play.
I got discovered.
That's my origin story!
It doesn't have to be.
Huh?

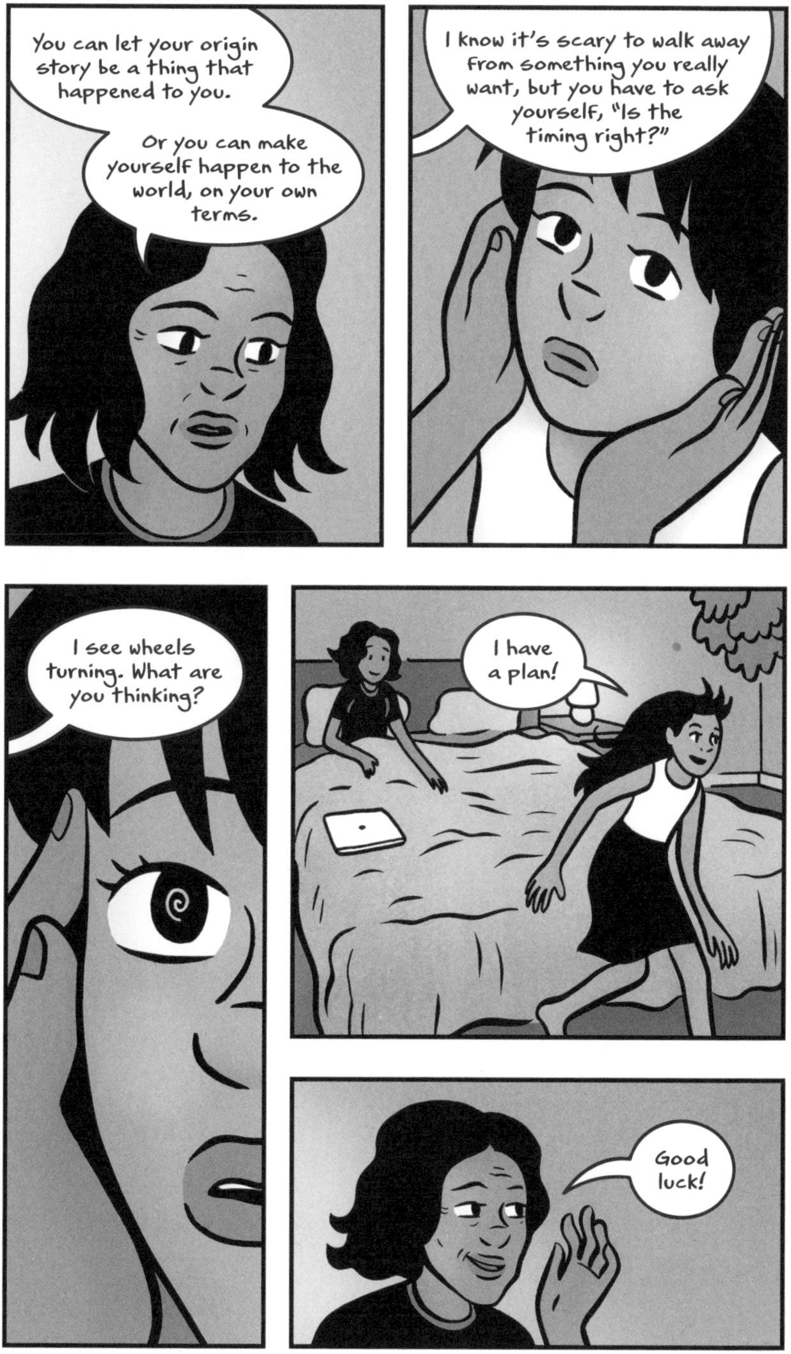
You can let your origin story be a thing that happened to you.
Or you can make yourself happen to the world, on your own terms.
I know it's scary to walk away from something you really want, but you have to ask yourself, "Is the timing right?"
I see wheels turning. What are you thinking?
I have a plan!
Good luck!

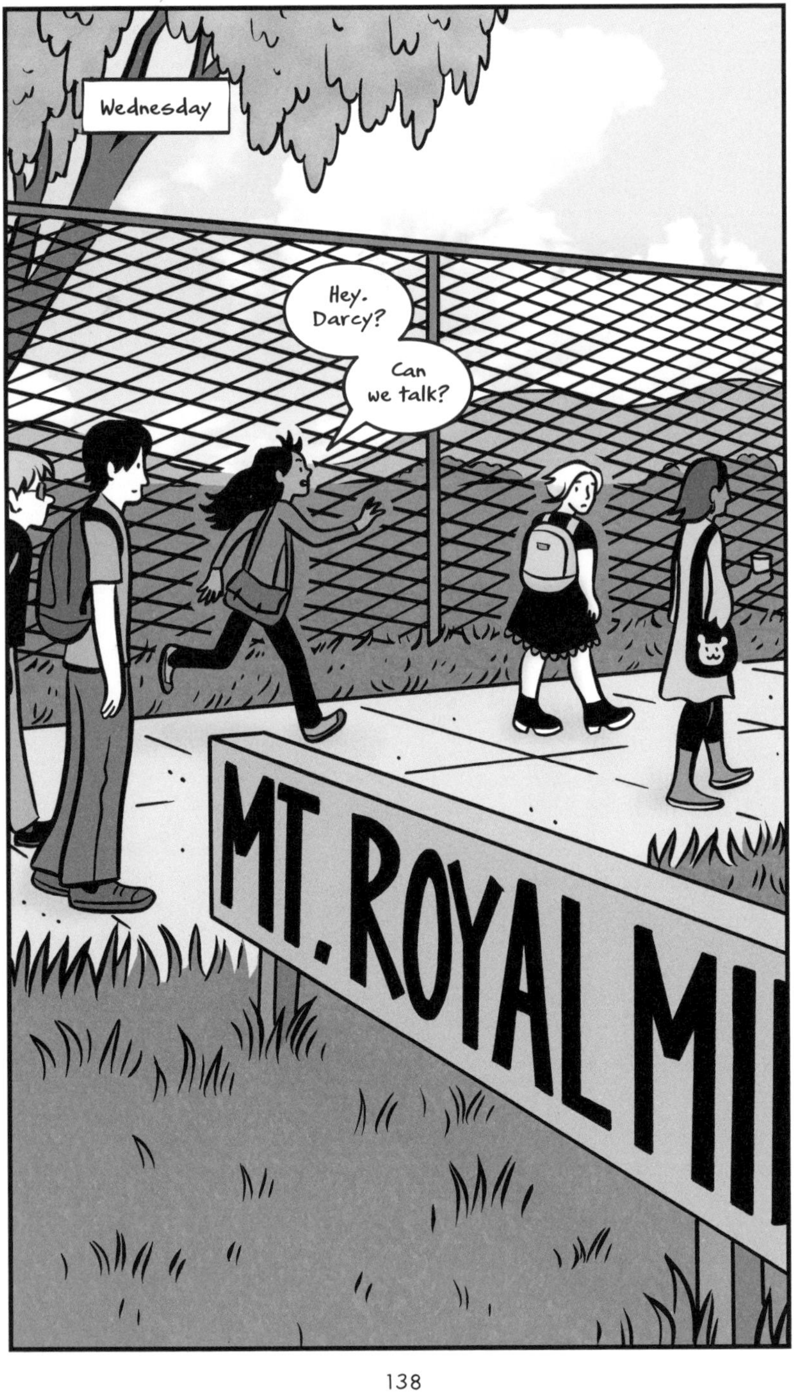
Wednesday
Hey. Darcy?
Can we talk?
MT. ROYAL MI

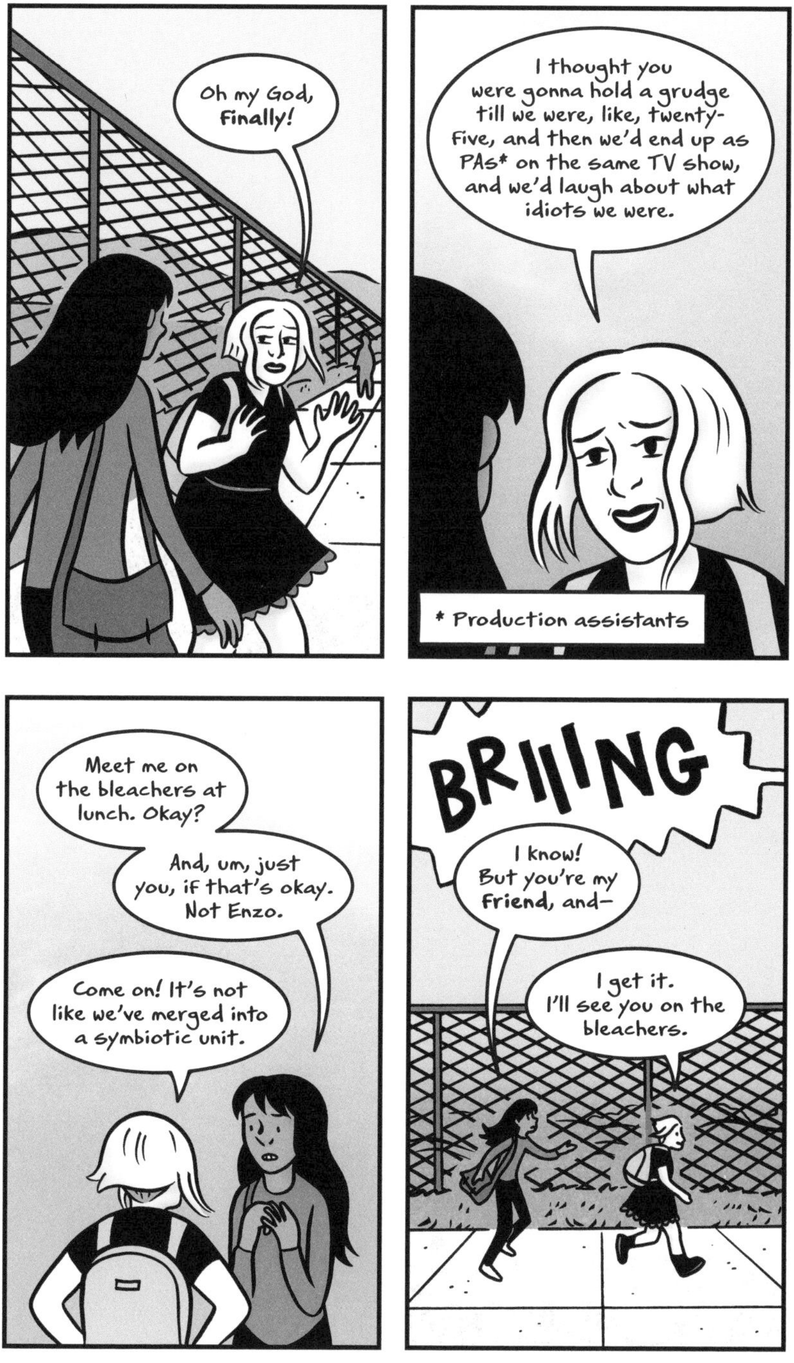
Oh my God, Finally!
I thought you were gonna hold a grudge till we were, like, twenty-five, and then we'd end up as PAs* on the same TV show, and we'd laugh about what idiots we were.
* Production assistants
Meet me on the bleachers at lunch. Okay?
And, um, just you, if that's okay. Not Enzo.
Come on! It's not like we've merged into a symbiotic unit.
BRIIING
I know! But you're my friend, and–
I get it. I'll see you on the bleachers.

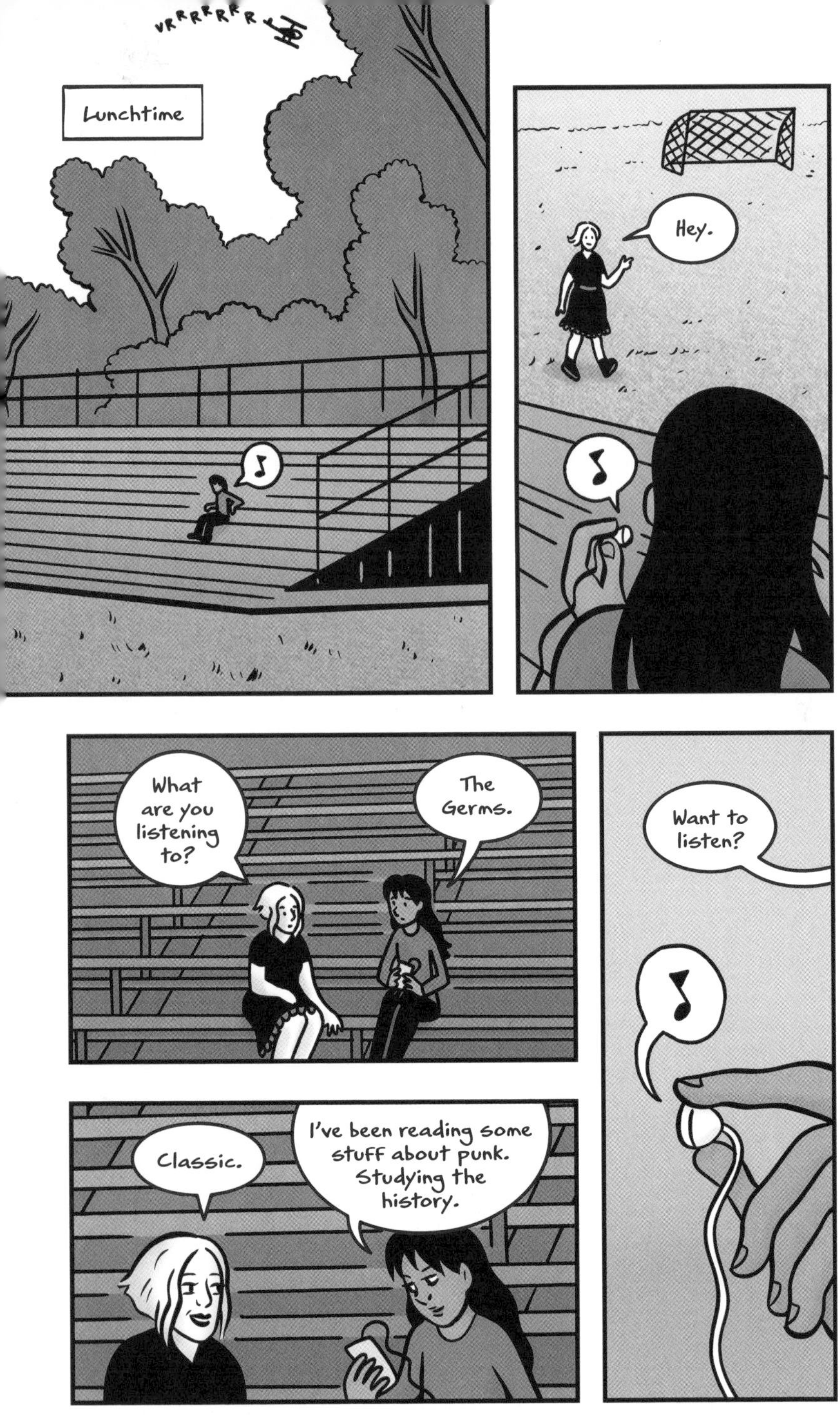
VRRRRRRR
Lunchtime
Hey.
What are you listening to?
The Germs.
Want to listen?
Classic.
I've been reading some stuff about punk. Studying the history.

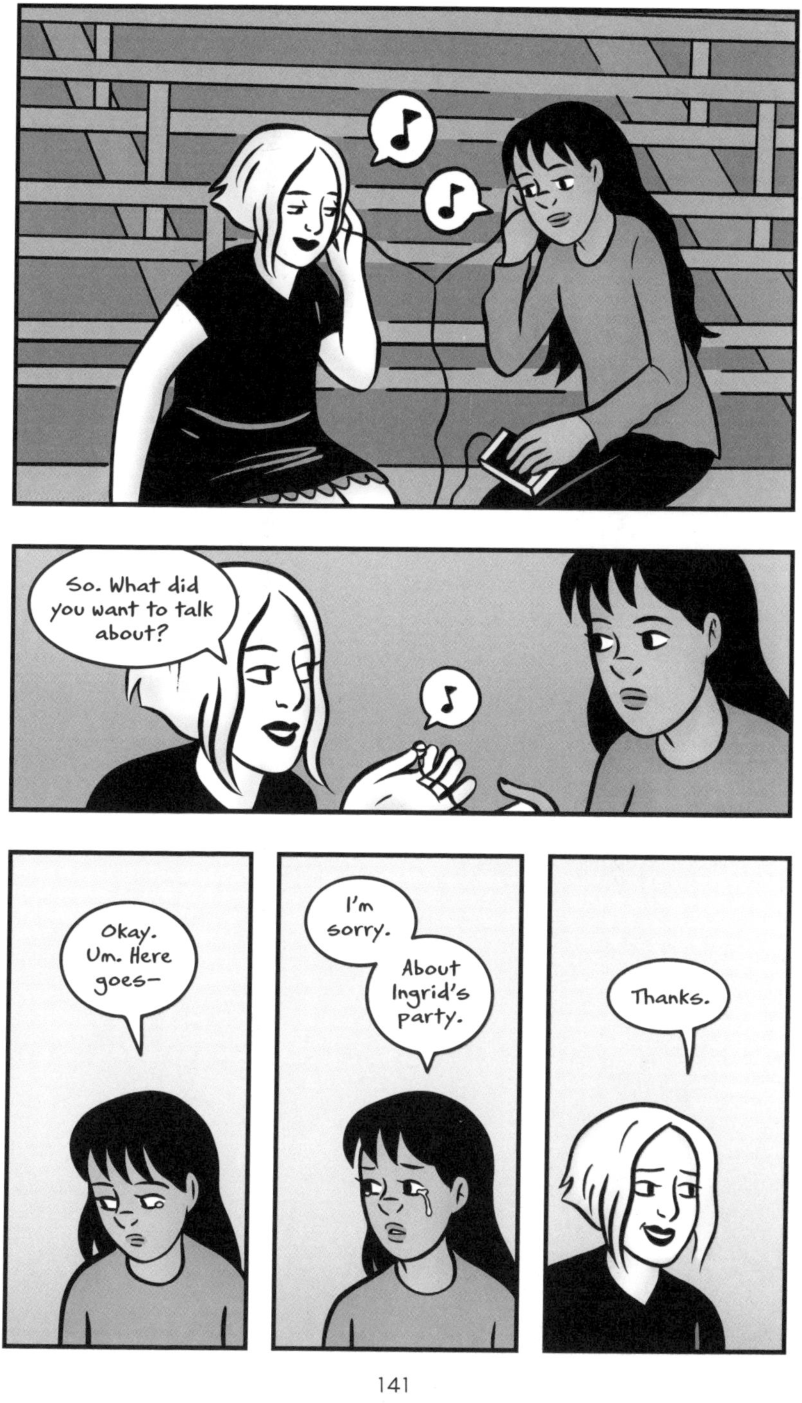
So. What did you want to talk about?
Okay. Um. Here goes—
I'm sorry.
About Ingrid's party.
Thanks.

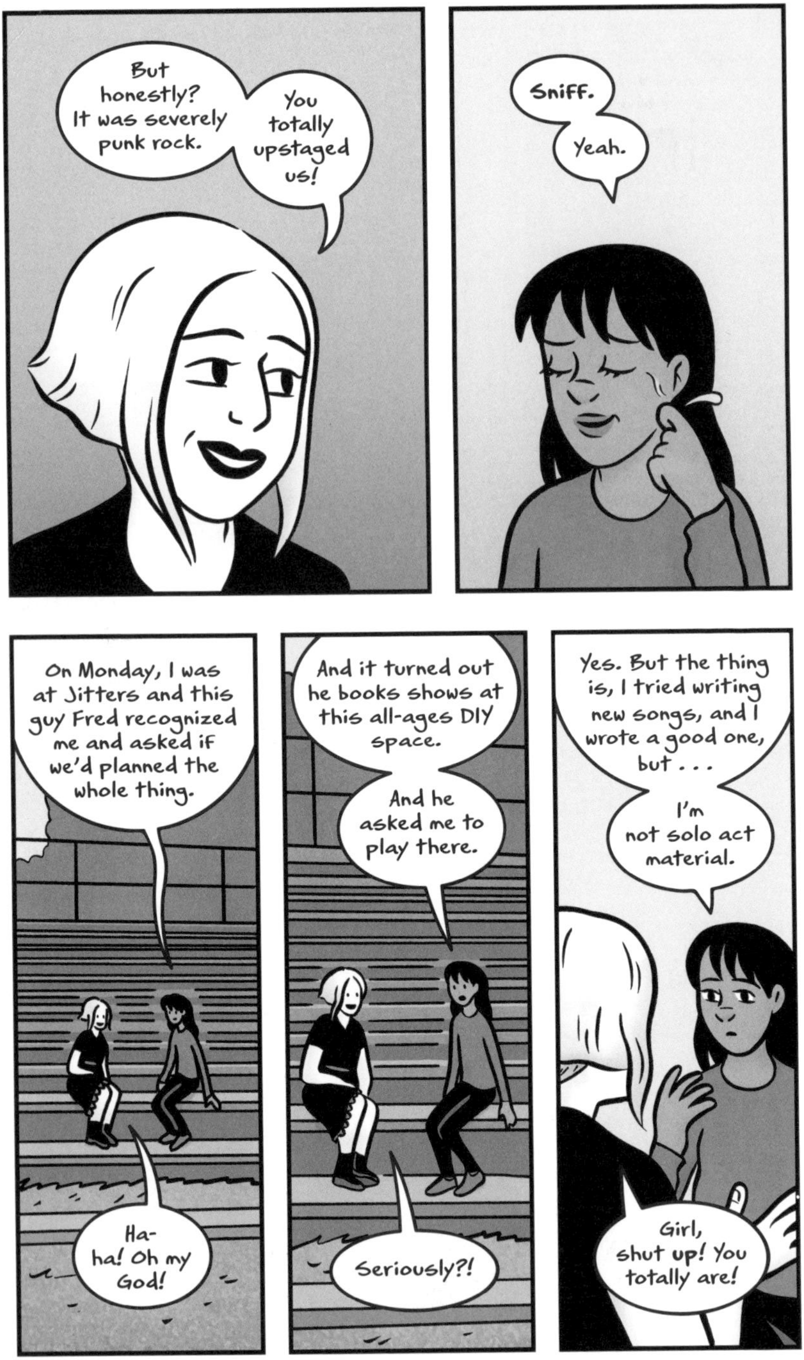
But honestly? It was severely punk rock.
You totally upstaged us!
Sniff.
Yeah.
On Monday, I was at Jitters and this guy Fred recognized me and asked if we'd planned the whole thing.
Ha-ha! Oh my God!
And it turned out he books shows at this all-ages DIY space.
And he asked me to play there.
Seriously?!
Yes. But the thing is, I tried writing new songs, and I wrote a good one, but . . .
I'm not solo act material.
Girl, shut up! You totally are!

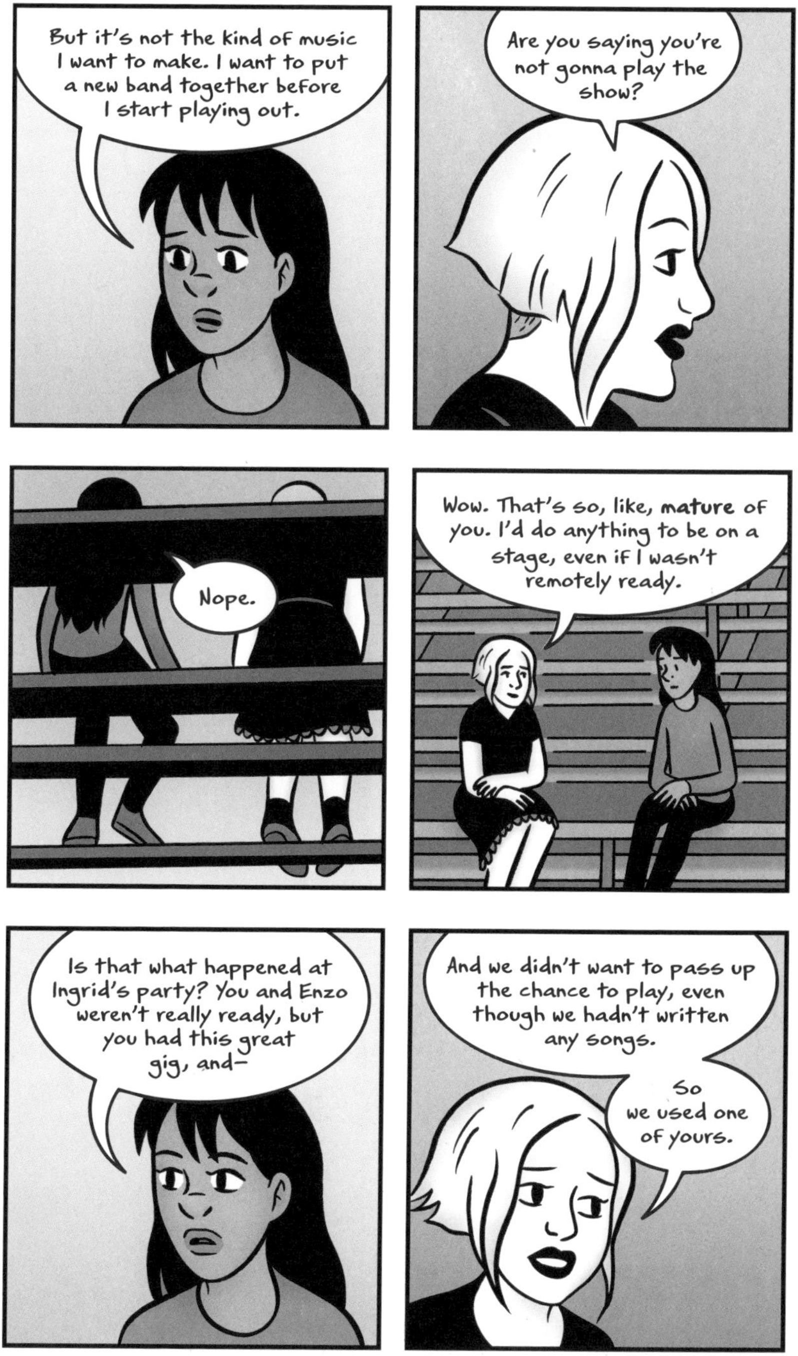
But it's not the kind of music I want to make. I want to put a new band together before I start playing out.
Are you saying you're not gonna play the show?
Nope.
Wow. That's so, like, **mature** of you. I'd do anything to be on a stage, even if I wasn't remotely ready.
Is that what happened at Ingrid's party? You and Enzo weren't really ready, but you had this great gig, and–
And we didn't want to pass up the chance to play, even though we hadn't written any songs.
So we used one of yours.

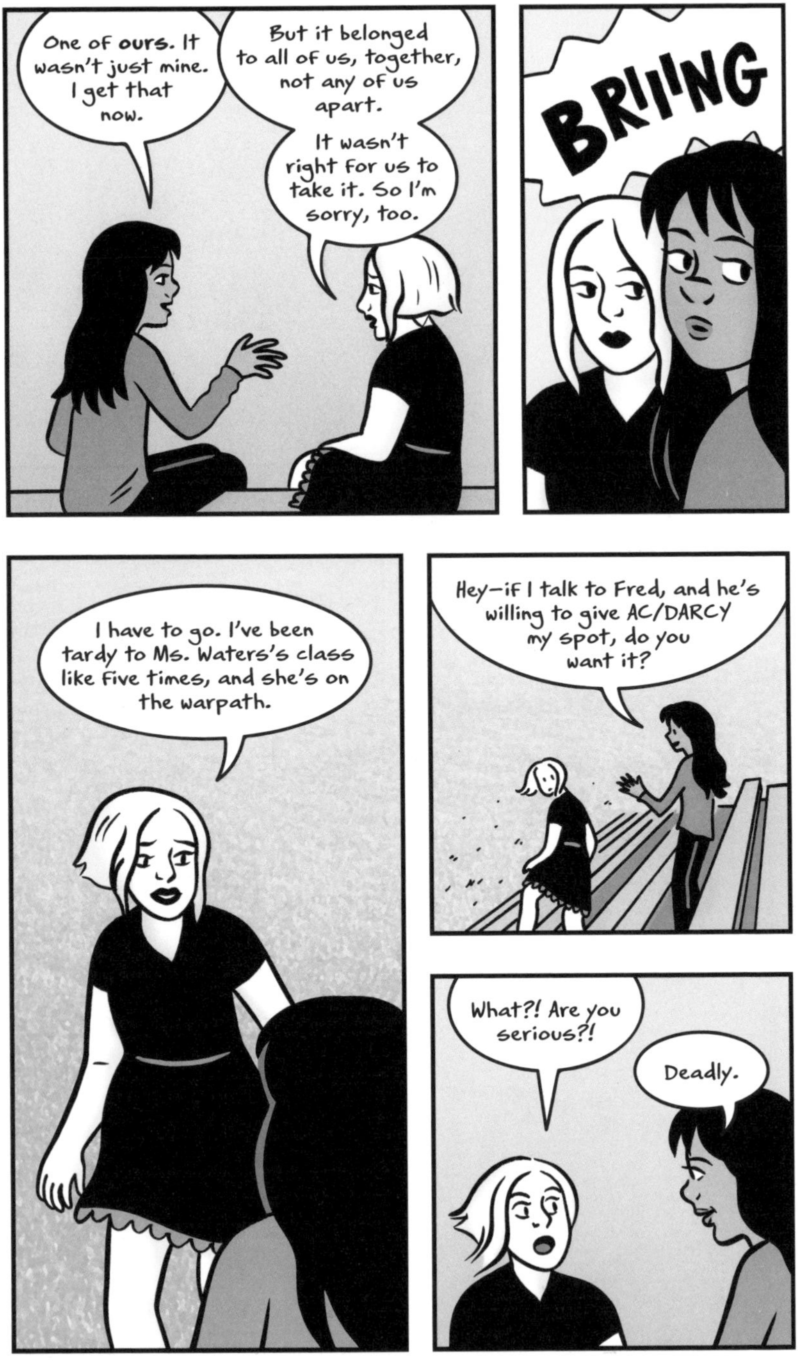
One of ours. It wasn't just mine. I get that now.
But it belonged to all of us, together, not any of us apart.
It wasn't right for us to take it. So I'm sorry, too.
BRIIING
I have to go. I've been tardy to Ms. Waters's class like five times, and she's on the warpath.
Hey—if I talk to Fred, and he's willing to give AC/DARCY my spot, do you want it?
What?! Are you serious?!
Deadly.

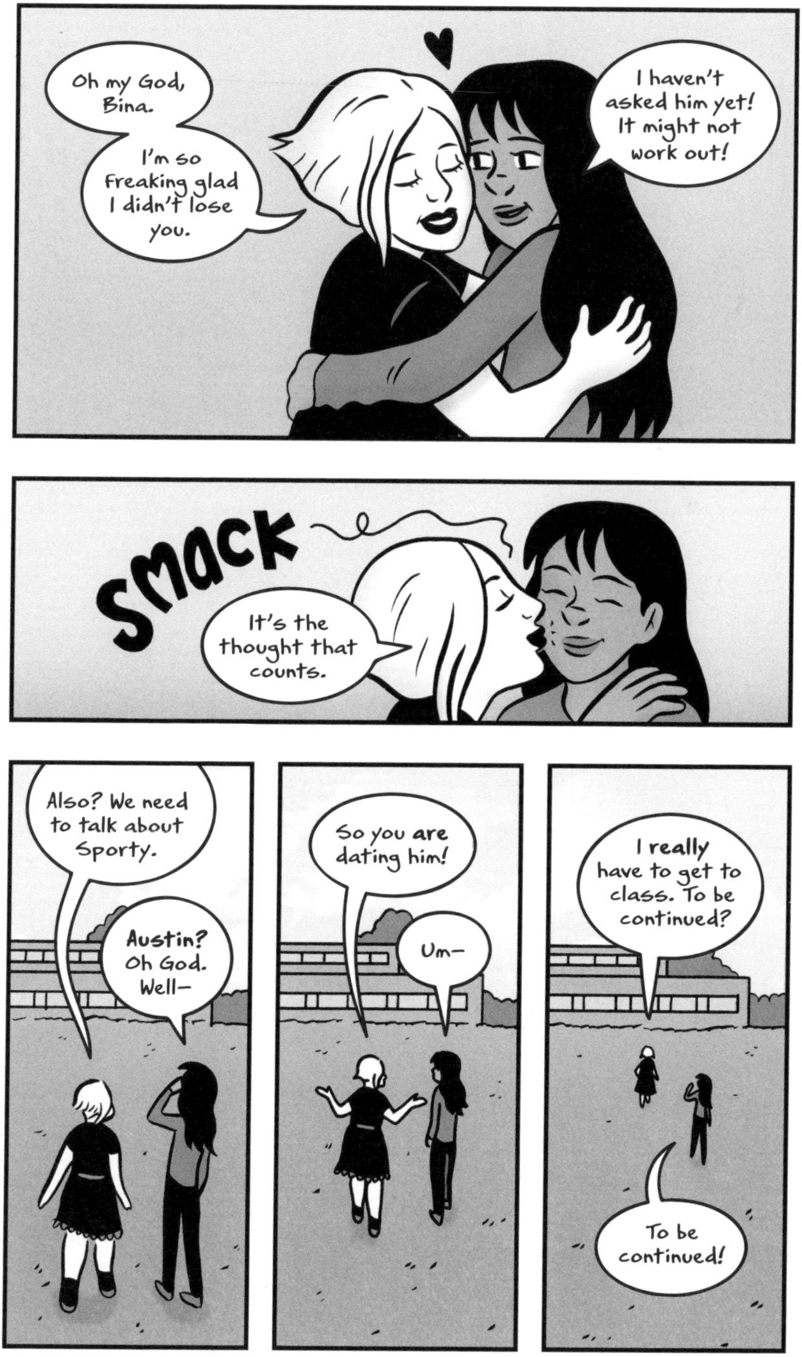
Oh my God, Bina.
I'm so freaking glad I didn't lose you.
I haven't asked him yet! It might not work out!
SMACK
It's the thought that counts.
Also? We need to talk about Sporty.
Austin? Oh God. Well—
So you are dating him!
Um—
I really have to get to class. To be continued?
To be continued!

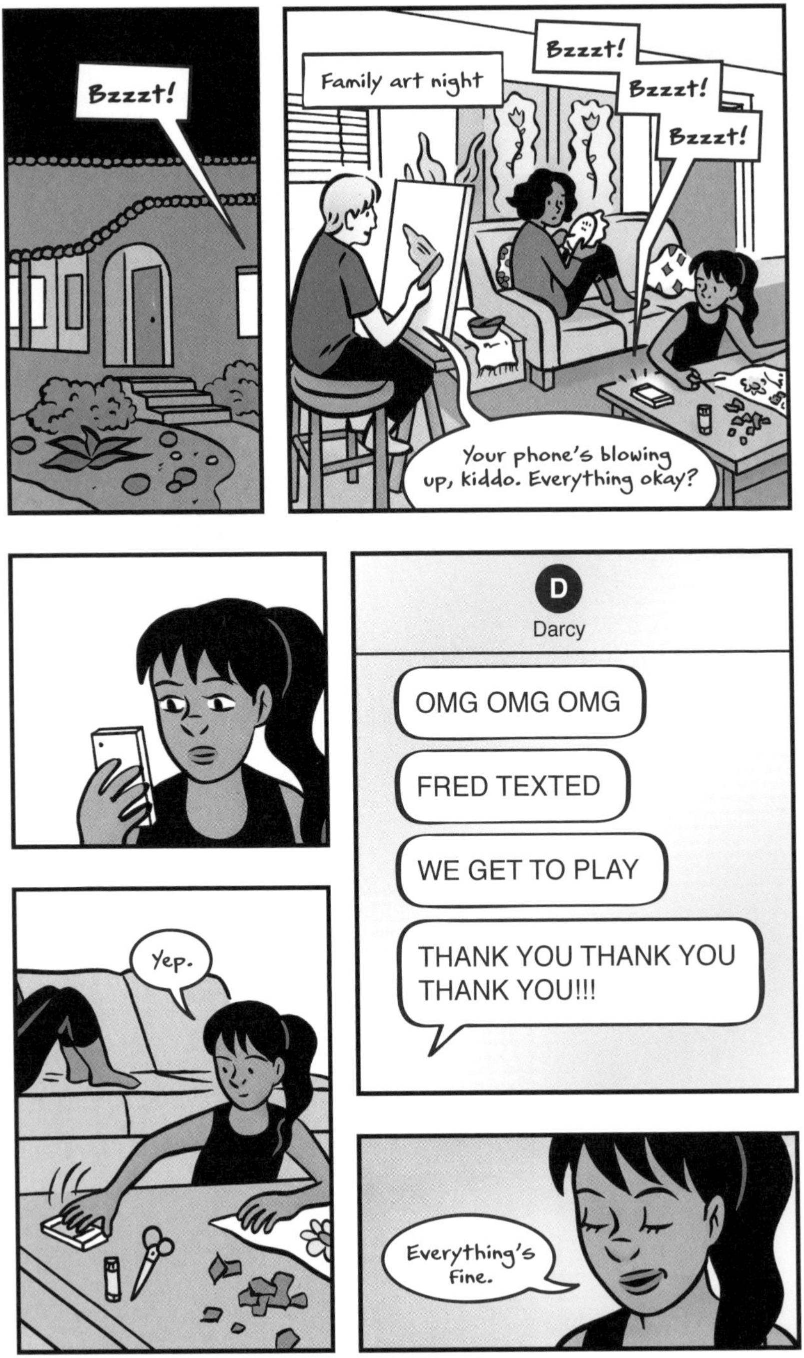
Bzzzt!
Family art night
Bzzzt!
Bzzzt!
Bzzzt!
Your phone's blowing up, kiddo. Everything okay?
D
Darcy
OMG OMG OMG
FRED TEXTED
WE GET TO PLAY
THANK YOU THANK YOU THANK YOU!!!
Yep.
Everything's fine.

December

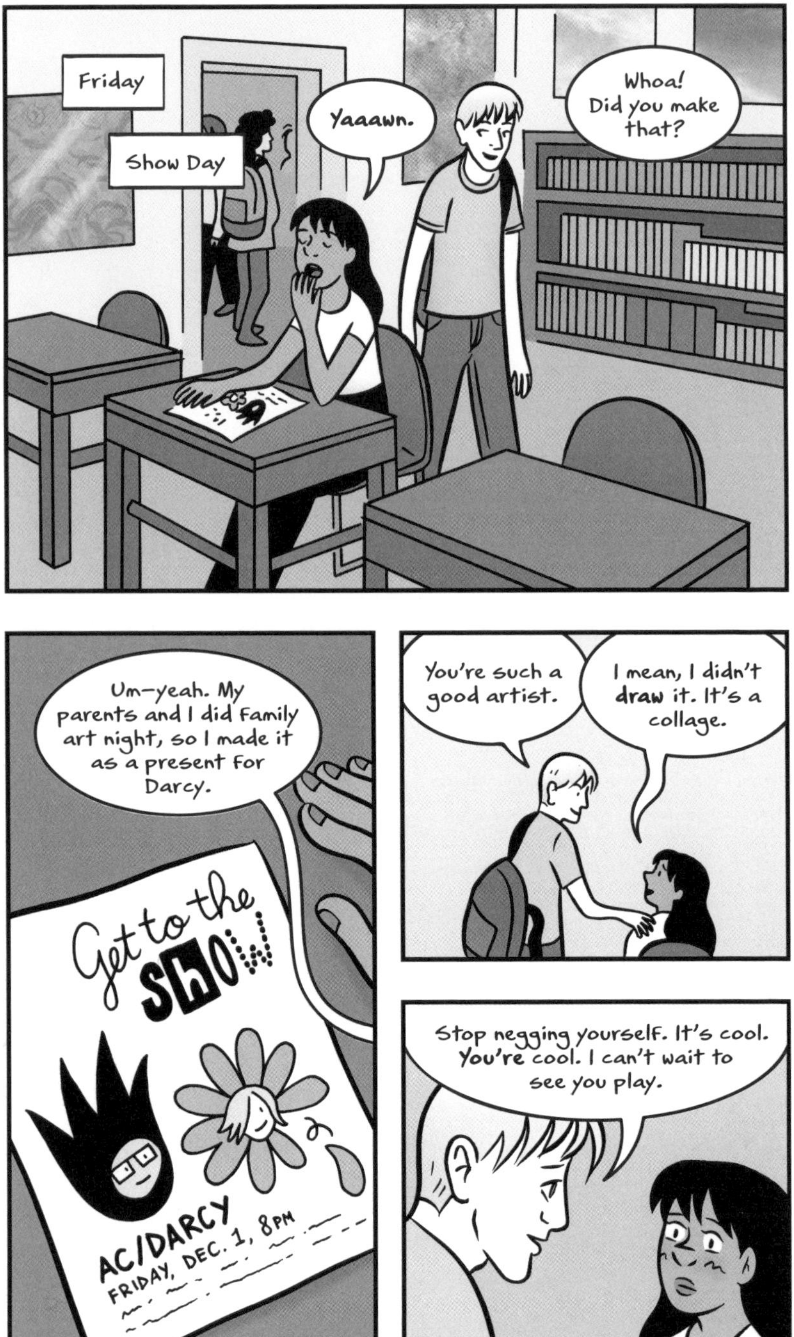
Friday
Show Day
Yaaawn.
Whoa! Did you make that?
Um—yeah. My parents and I did family art night, so I made it as a present for Darcy.
Get to the ShOW!
AC/DARCY
FRIDAY, DEC. 1, 8PM
You're such a good artist.
I mean, I didn't draw it. It's a collage.
Stop negging yourself. It's cool. You're cool. I can't wait to see you play.

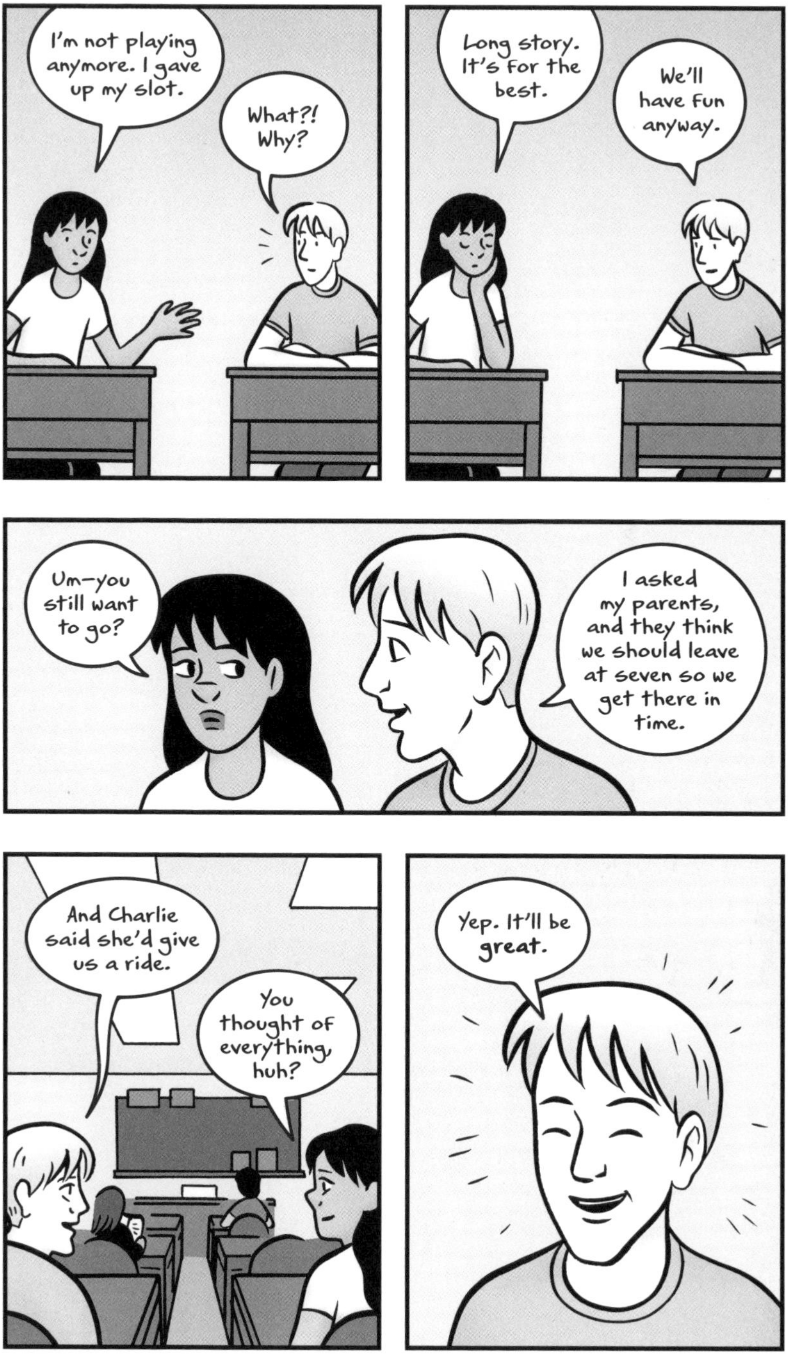
I'm not playing anymore. I gave up my slot.
What?! Why?
Long story. It's for the best.
We'll have fun anyway.
Um—you still want to go?
I asked my parents, and they think we should leave at seven so we get there in time.
And Charlie said she'd give us a ride.
You thought of everything, huh?
Yep. It'll be great.

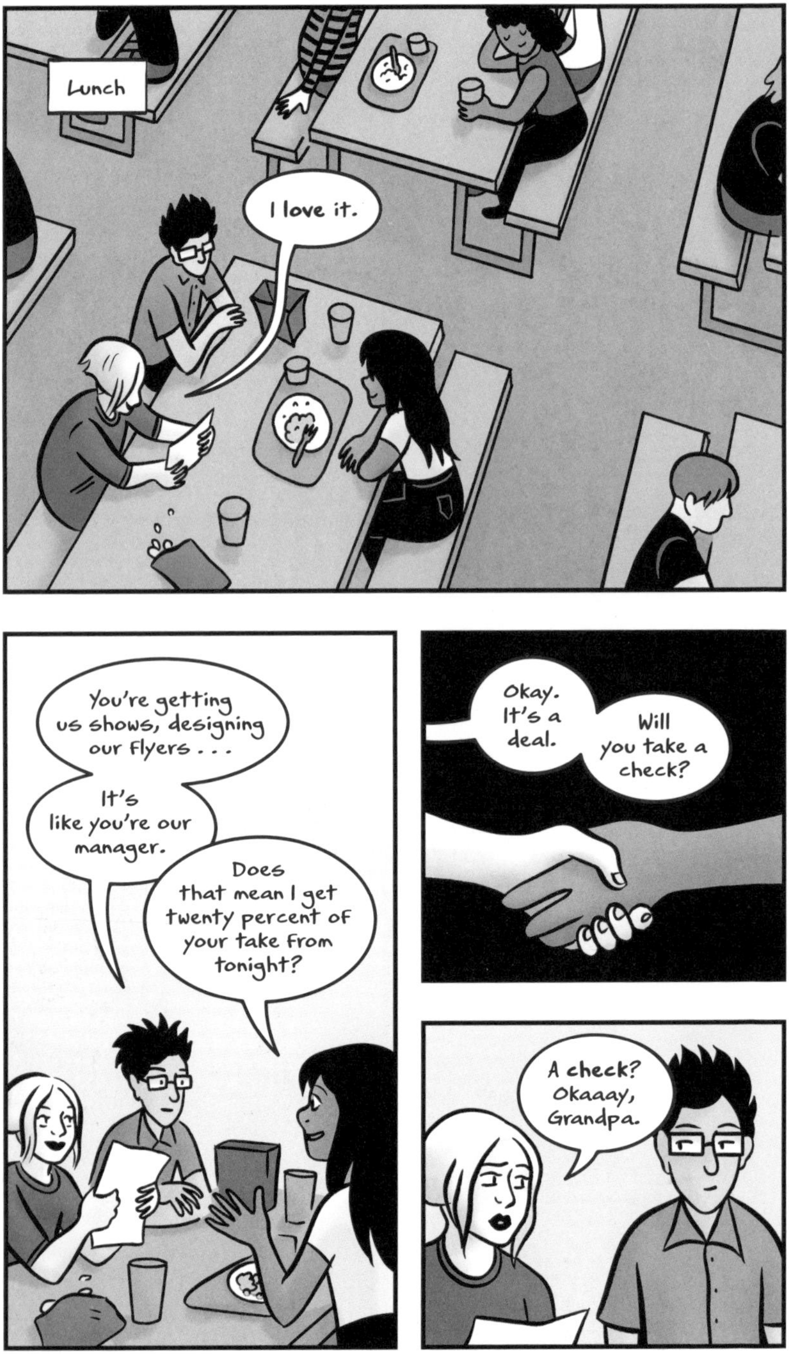
Lunch
I love it.
You're getting us shows, designing our flyers . . .
It's like you're our manager.
Does that mean I get twenty percent of your take from tonight?
Okay. It's a deal.
Will you take a check?
A check? Okaaay, Grandpa.

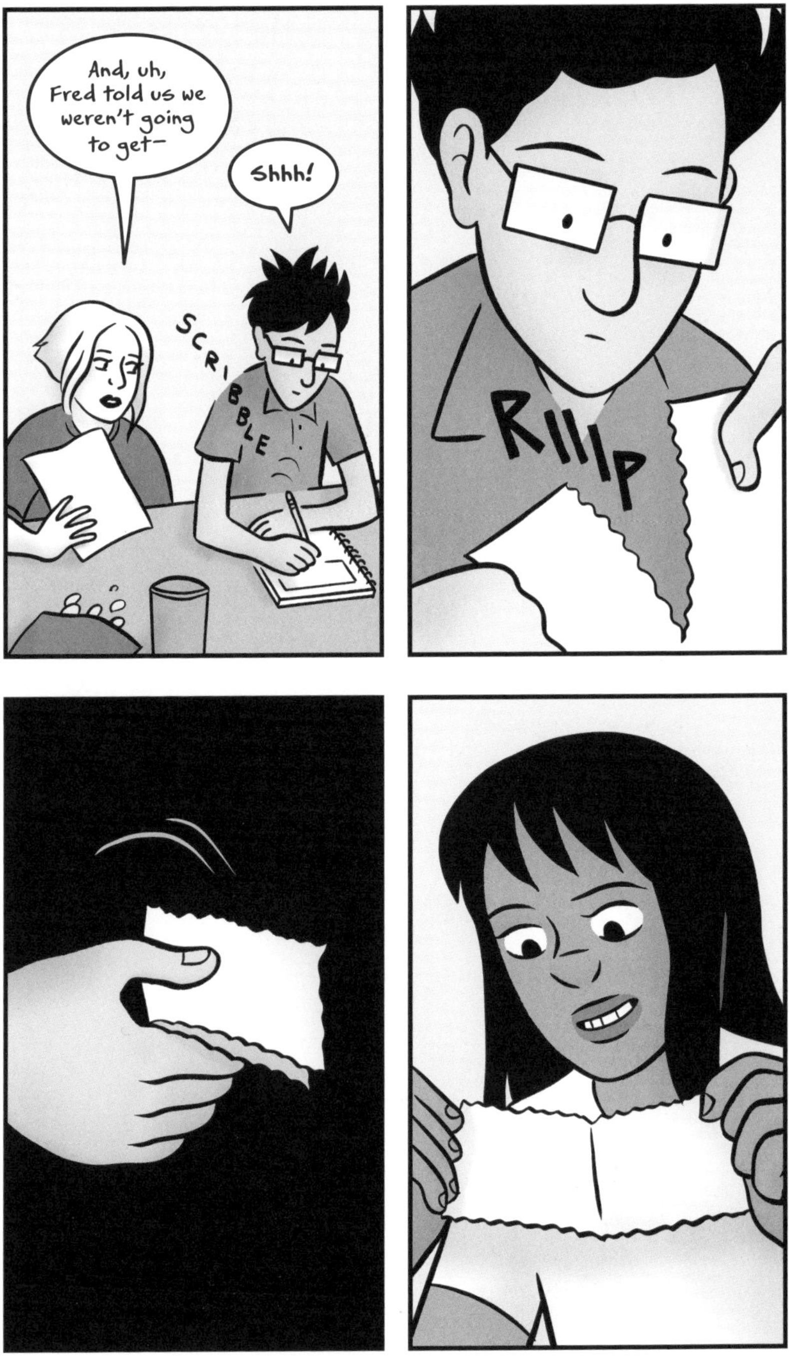
And, uh, Fred told us we weren't going to get–
Shhh!
SCRIBBLE
RIIIP

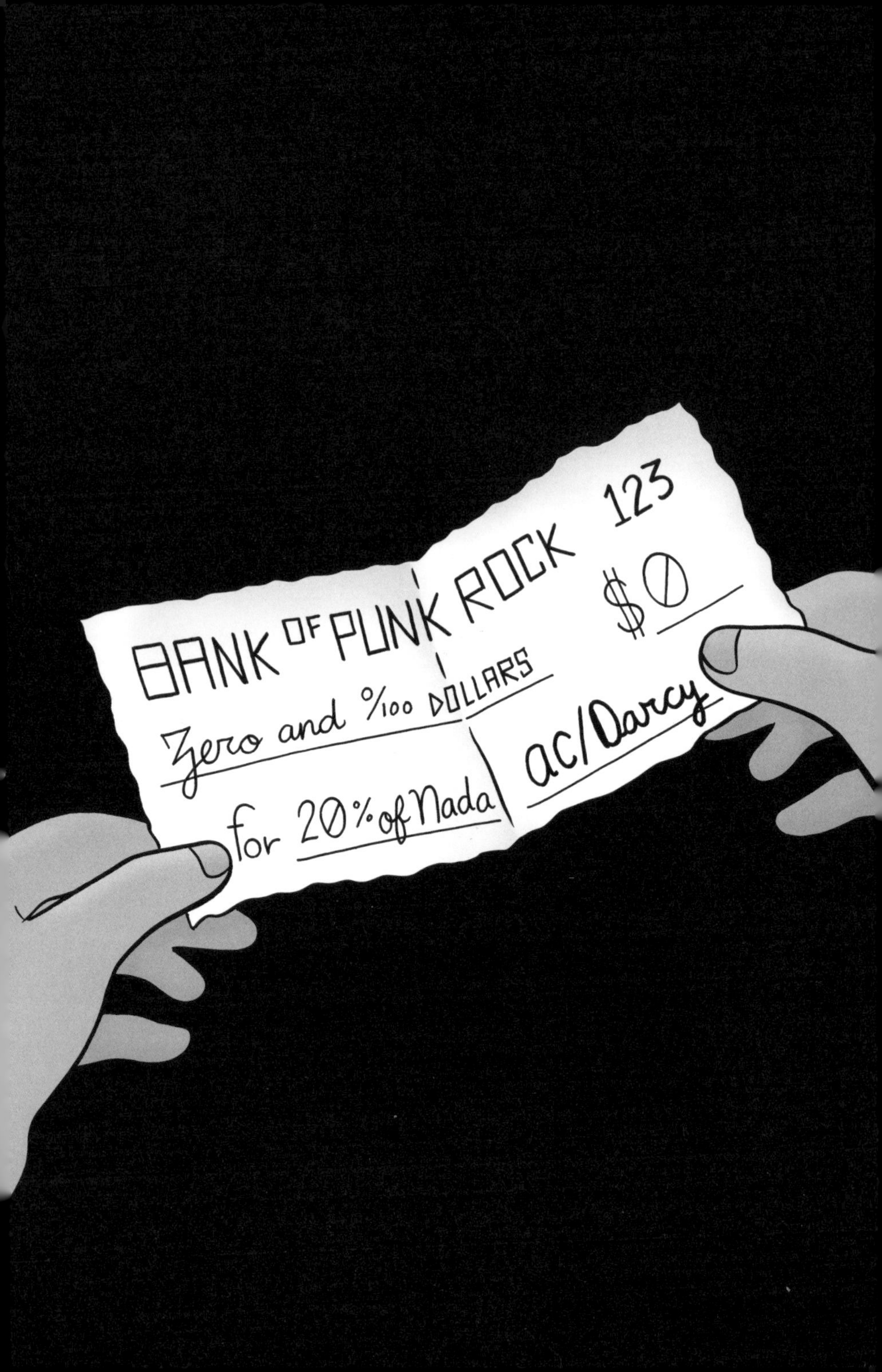
BANK OF PUNK ROCK 123
$0
Zero and 0/100 DOLLARS
for 20% of Nada
ac/Darcy

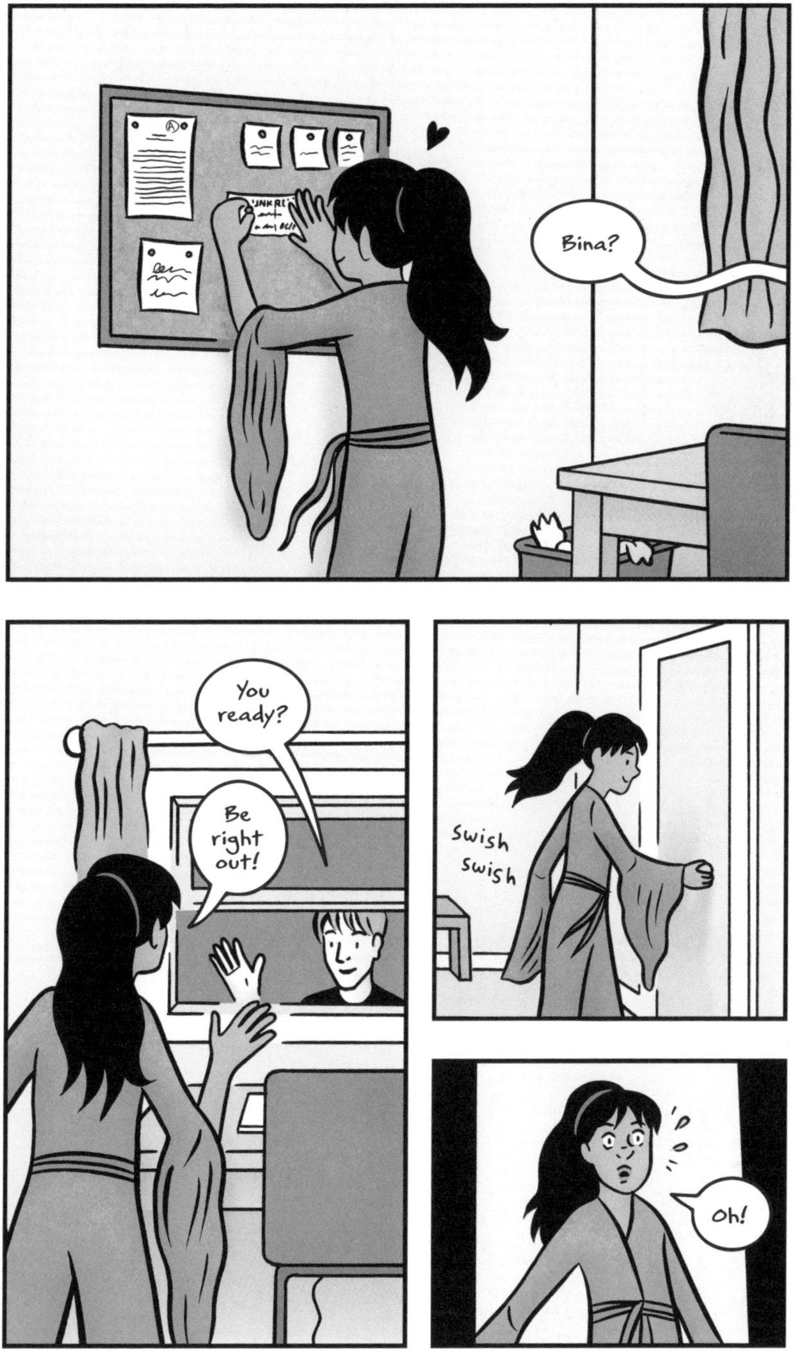
Bina?
You ready?
Be right out!
swish swish
Oh!

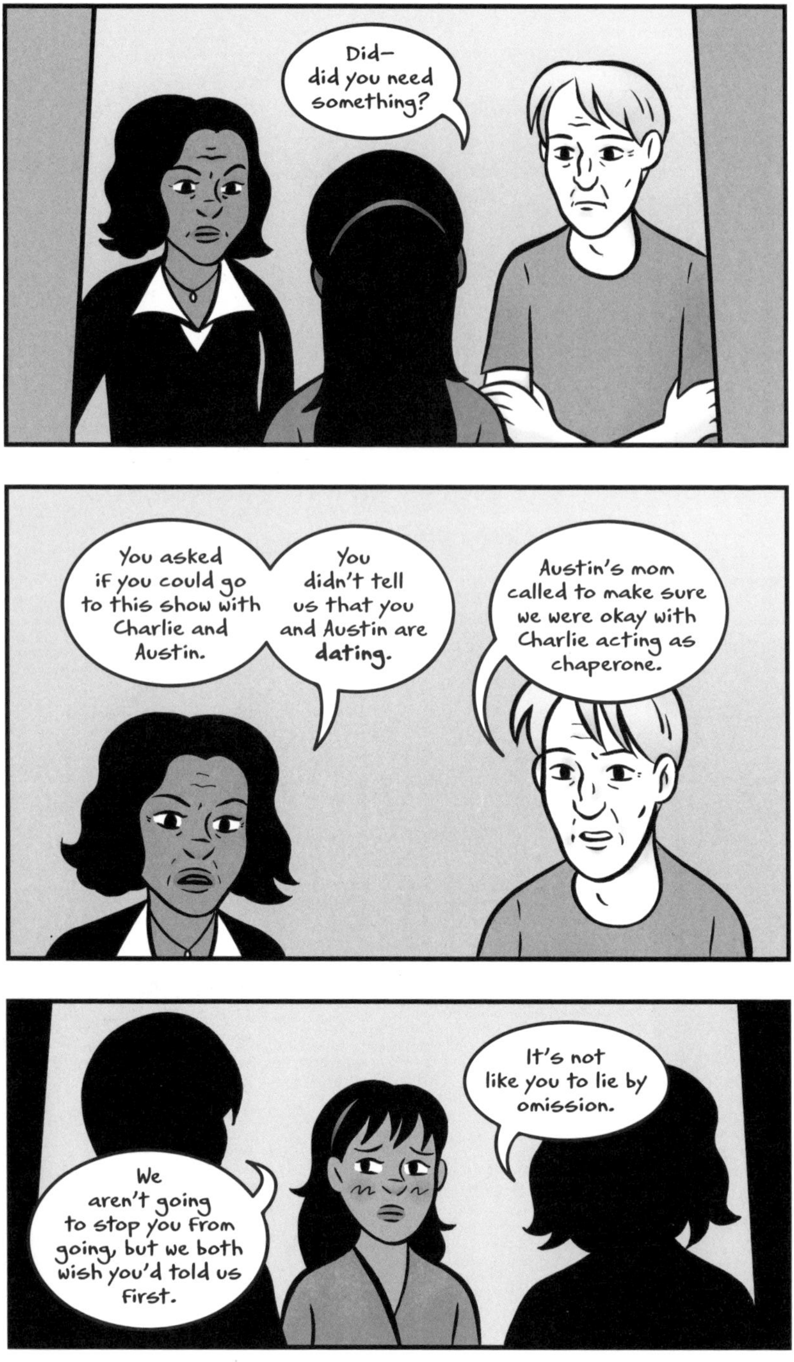
Did— did you need something?
You asked if you could go to this show with Charlie and Austin.
You didn't tell us that you and Austin are **dating**.
Austin's mom called to make sure we were okay with Charlie acting as chaperone.
It's not like you to lie by omission.
We aren't going to stop you from going, but we both wish you'd told us first.

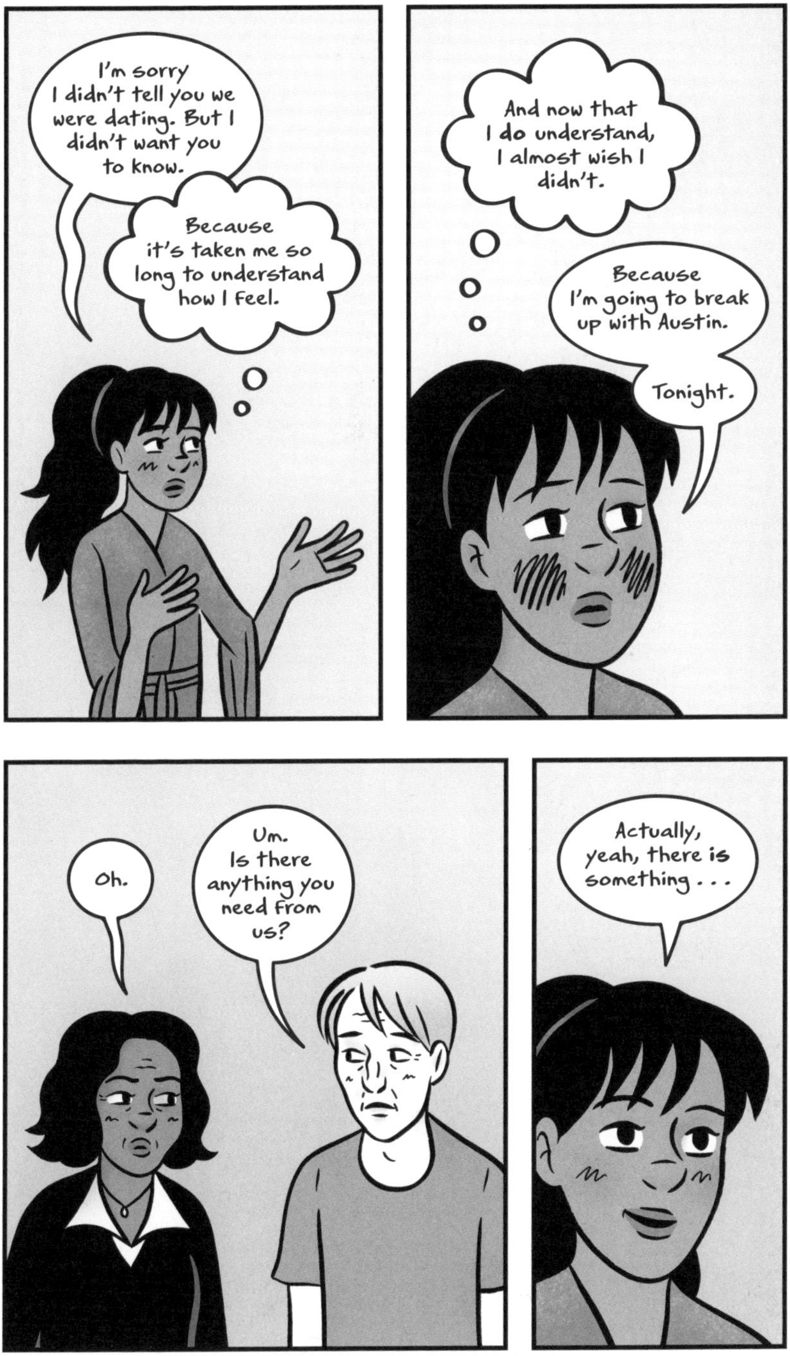
I'm sorry I didn't tell you we were dating. But I didn't want you to know.
Because it's taken me so long to understand how I feel.
And now that I do understand, I almost wish I didn't.
Because I'm going to break up with Austin.
Tonight.
Oh.
Um. Is there anything you need from us?
Actually, yeah, there is something . . .

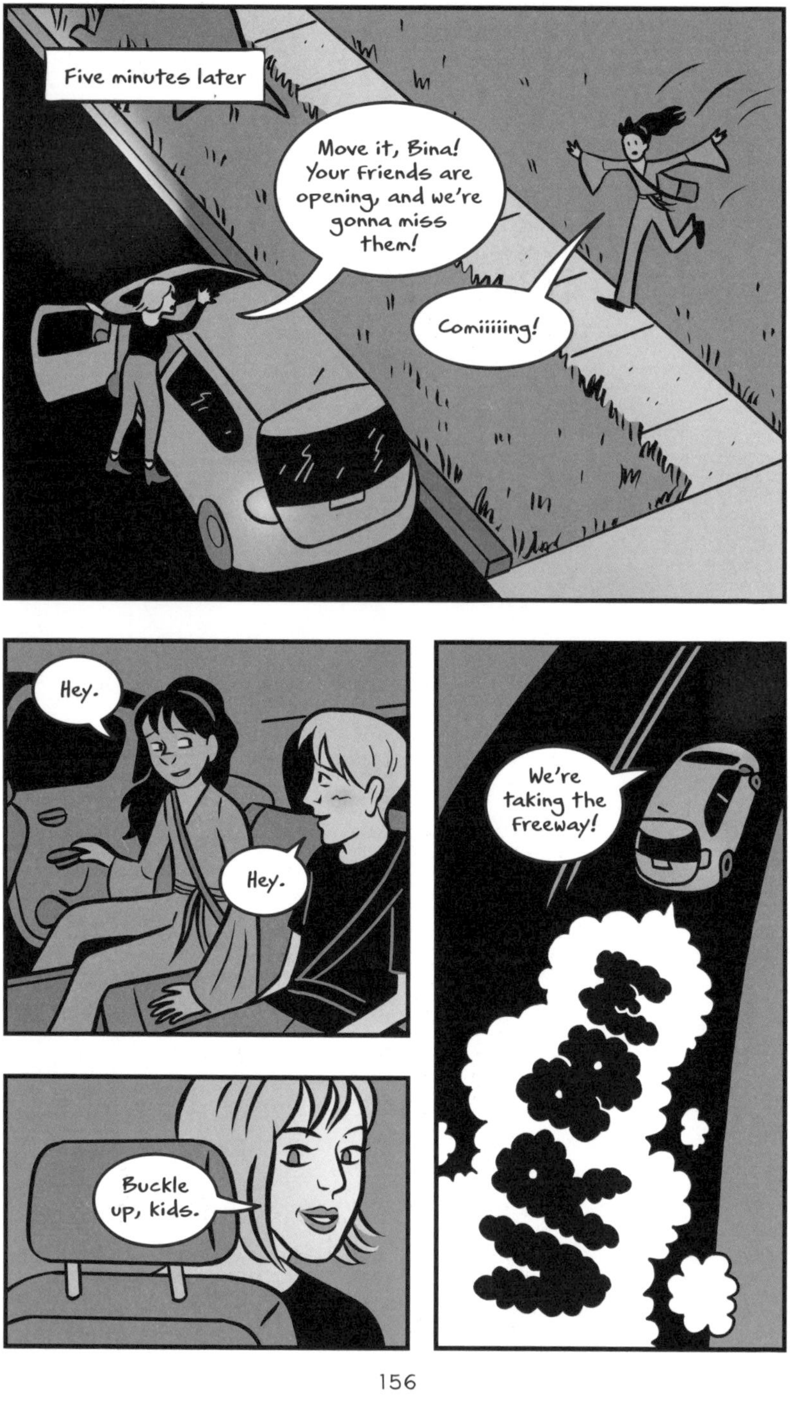
Five minutes later
Move it, Bina! Your friends are opening, and we're gonna miss them!
Comiiiiing!
Hey.
Hey.
Buckle up, kids.
We're taking the freeway!

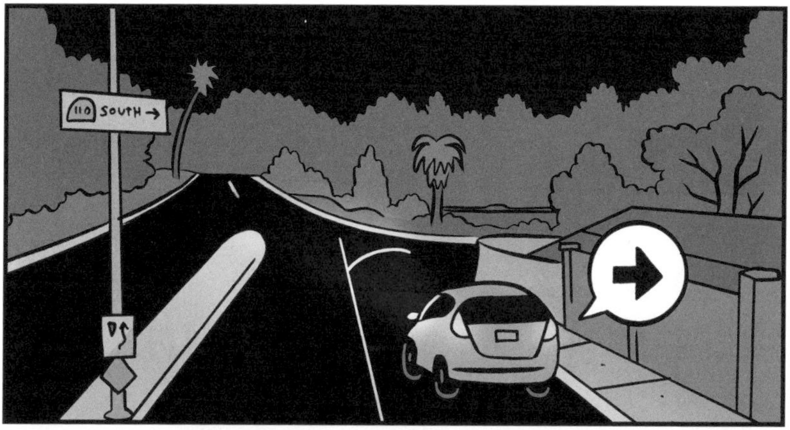
110 SOUTH

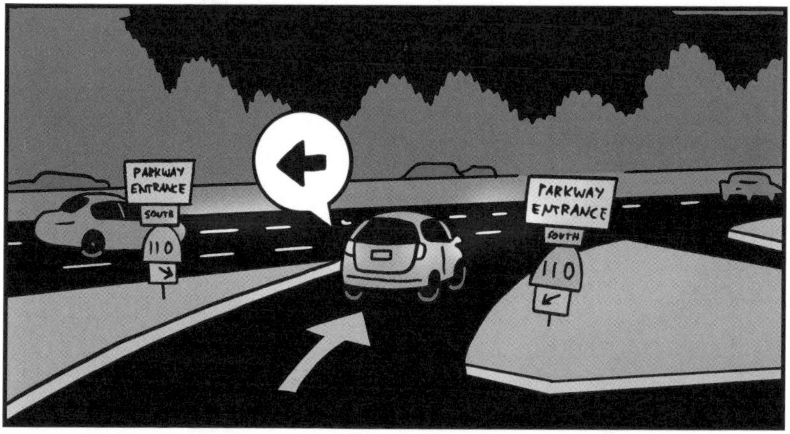
PARKWAY ENTRANCE
SOUTH
110
PARKWAY ENTRANCE
SOUTH
110

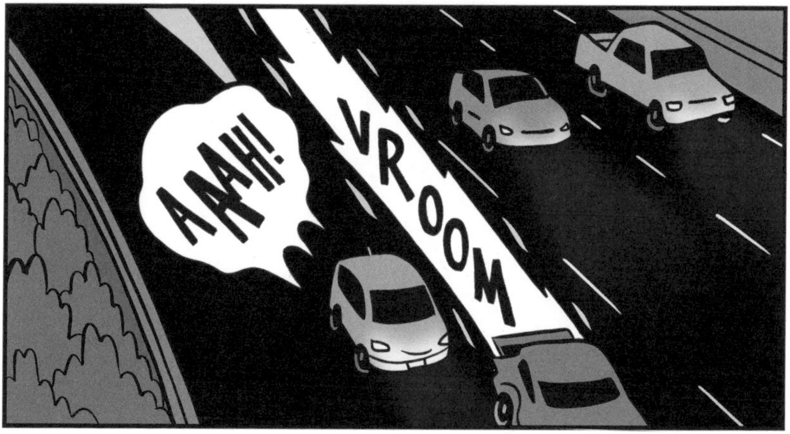
AAAH!
VROOM

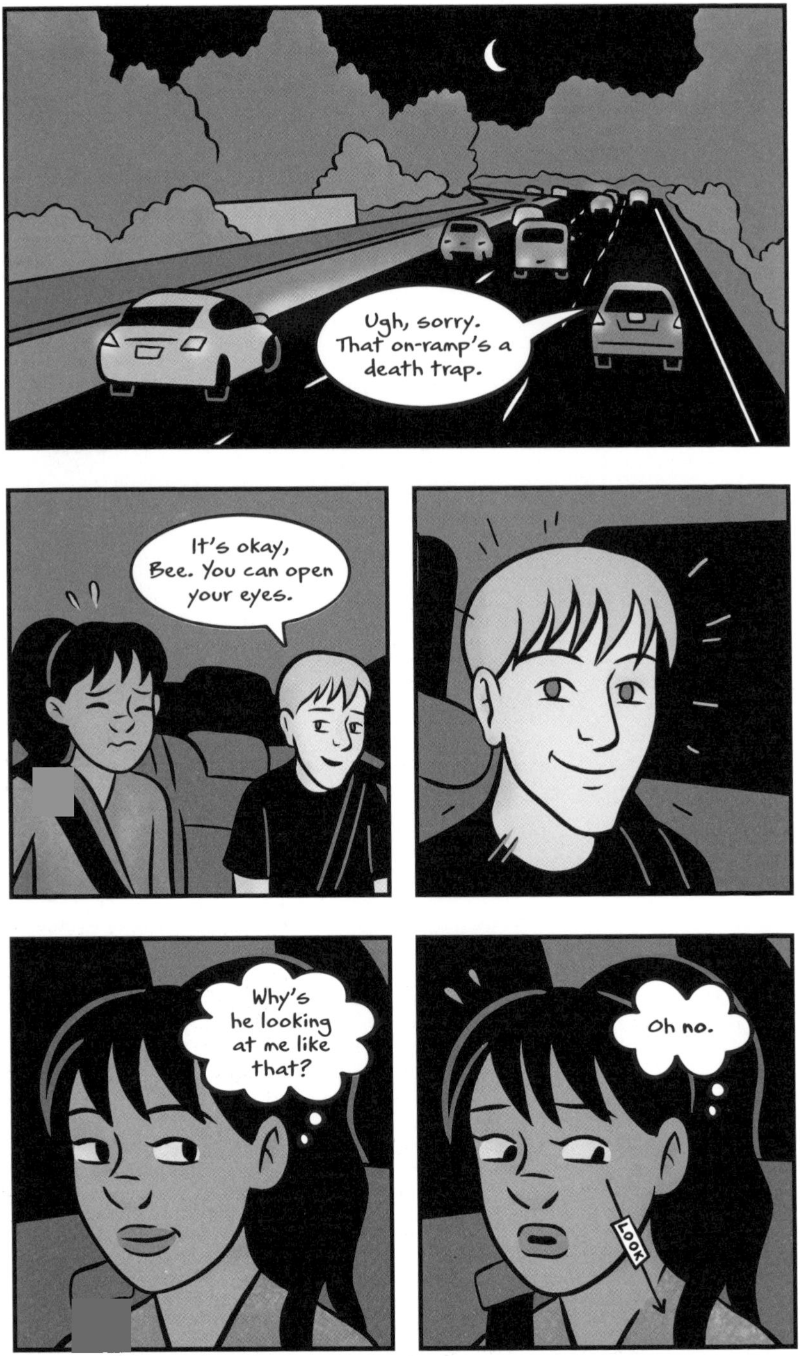
Ugh, sorry. That on-ramp's a death trap.
It's okay, Bee. You can open your eyes.
Why's he looking at me like that?
Oh no.
LOOK

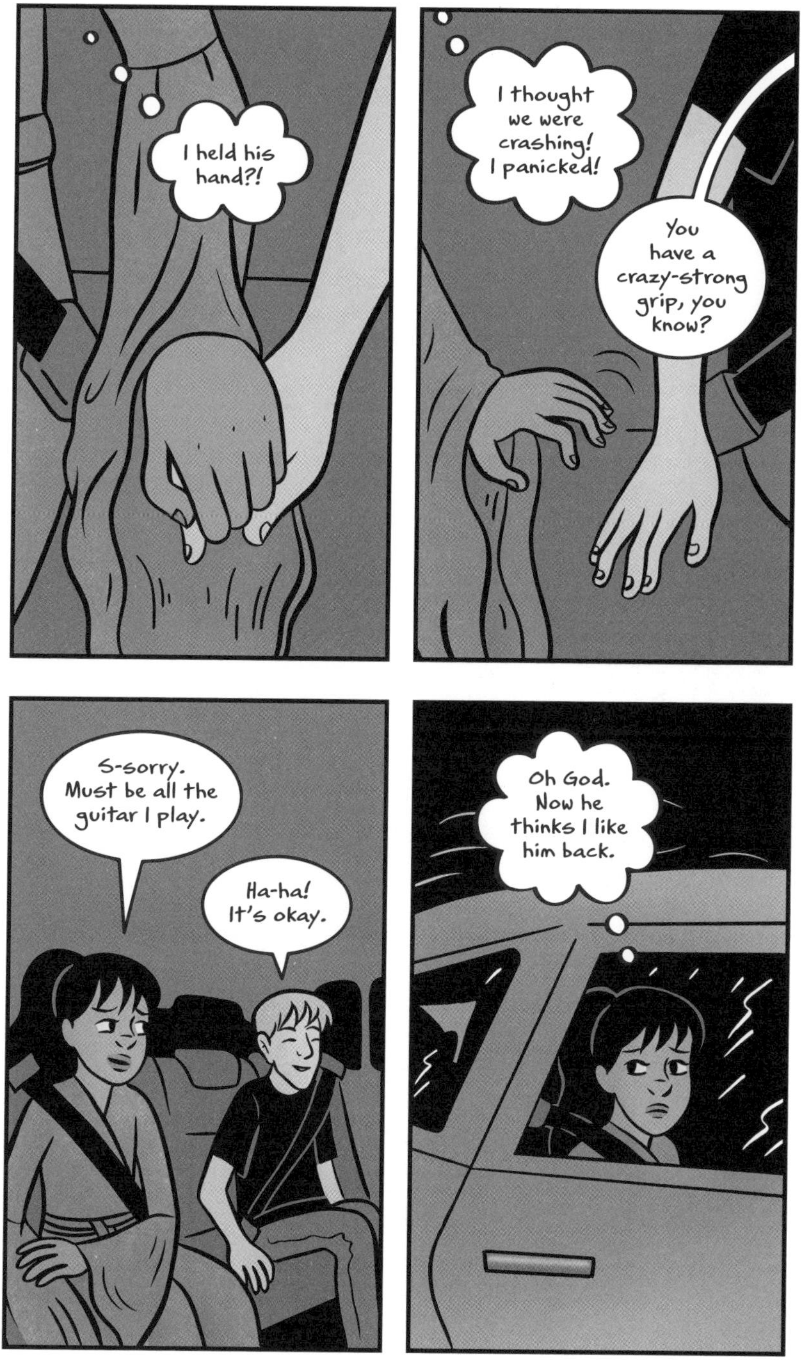
I held his hand?!
I thought we were crashing! I panicked!
You have a crazy-strong grip, you know?
S-sorry. Must be all the guitar I play.
Ha-ha! It's okay.
Oh God. Now he thinks I like him back.

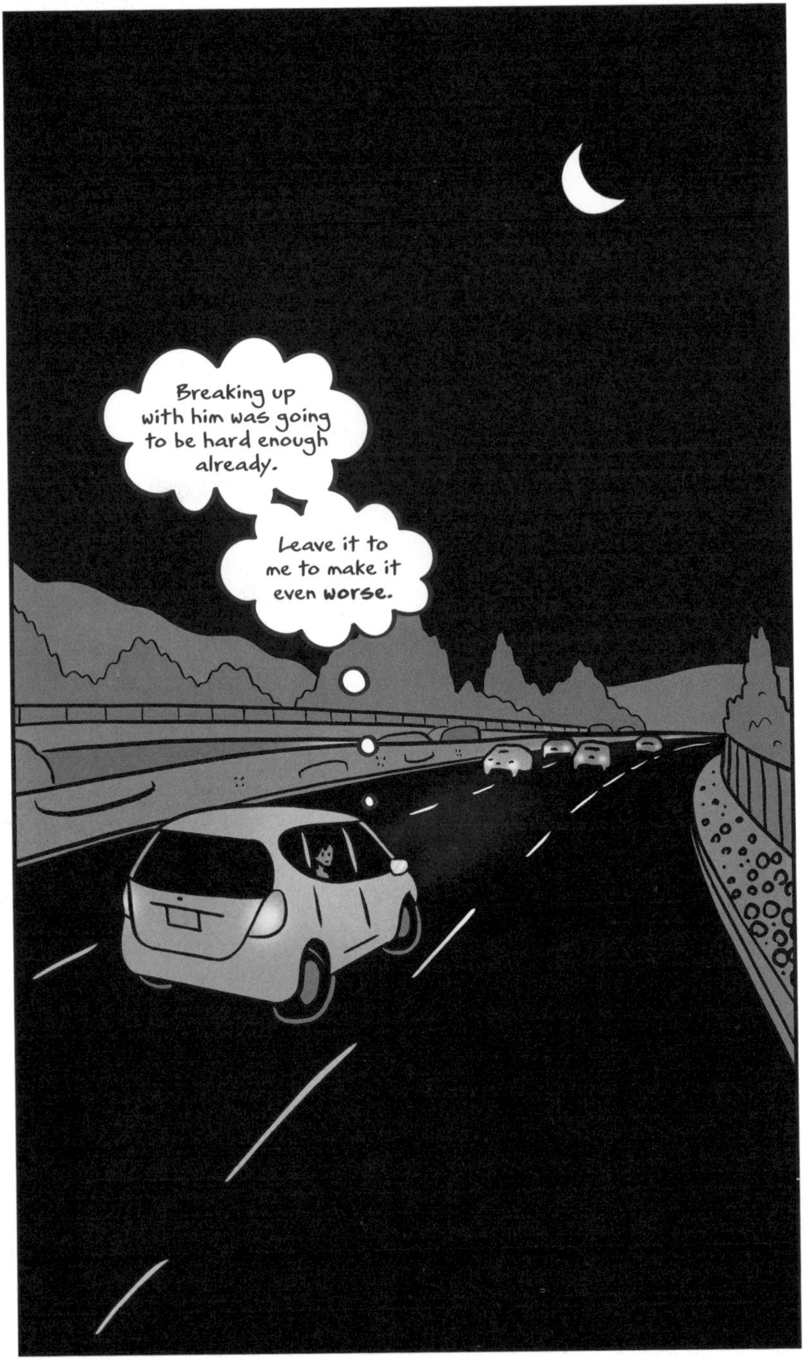
Breaking up with him was going to be hard enough already.
Leave it to me to make it even worse.

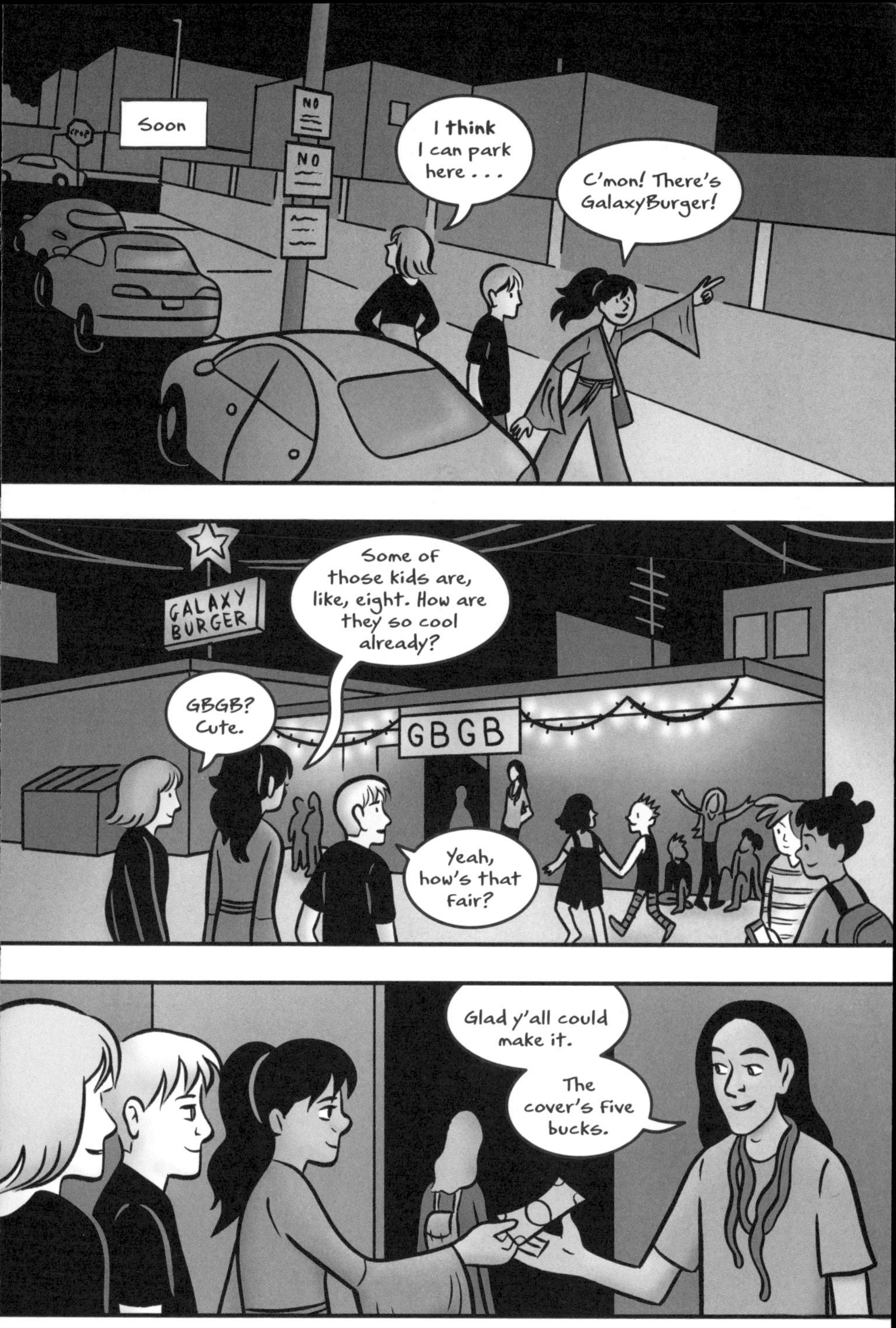
Soon
I think I can park here . . .
C'mon! There's GalaxyBurger!
GALAXY BURGER
Some of those kids are, like, eight. How are they so cool already?
GBGB? Cute.
GBGB
Yeah, how's that fair?
Glad y'all could make it.
The cover's five bucks.

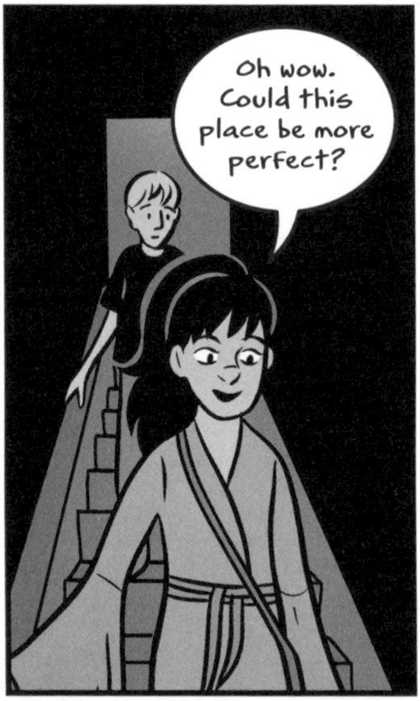
Oh wow. Could this place be more perfect?

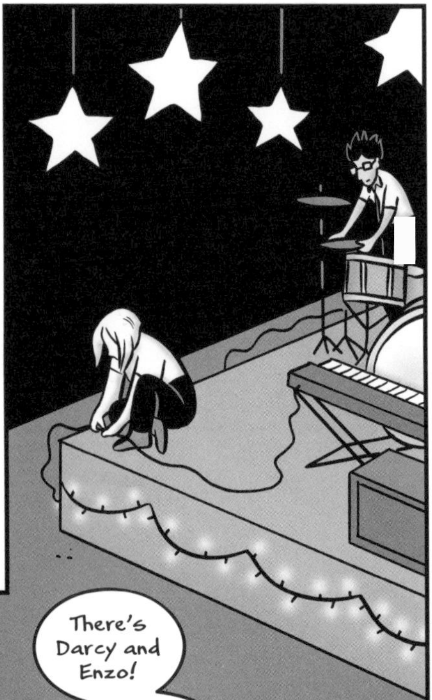

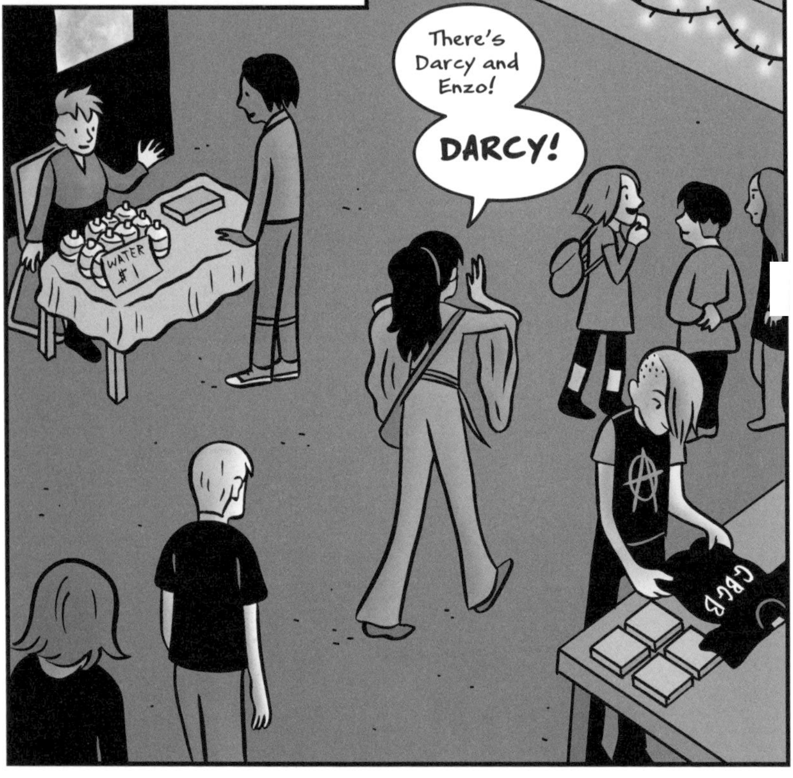
There's Darcy and Enzo!
DARCY!
WATER $1
CBGB

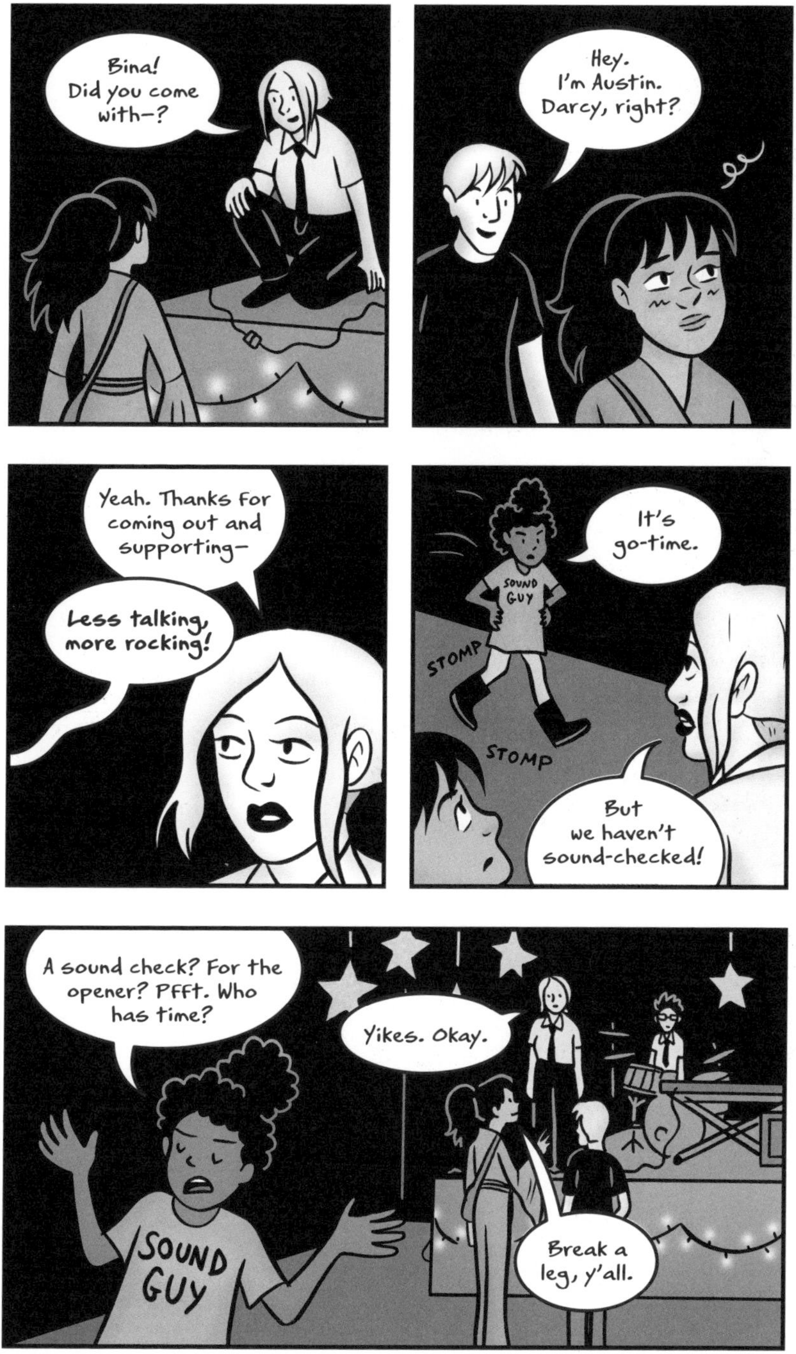
Bina! Did you come with–?
Hey. I'm Austin. Darcy, right?
Yeah. Thanks for coming out and supporting–
Less talking, more rocking!
It's go-time.
SOUND GUY
STOMP
STOMP
But we haven't sound-checked!
A sound check? For the opener? PFFT. Who has time?
Yikes. Okay.
SOUND GUY
Break a leg, y'all.

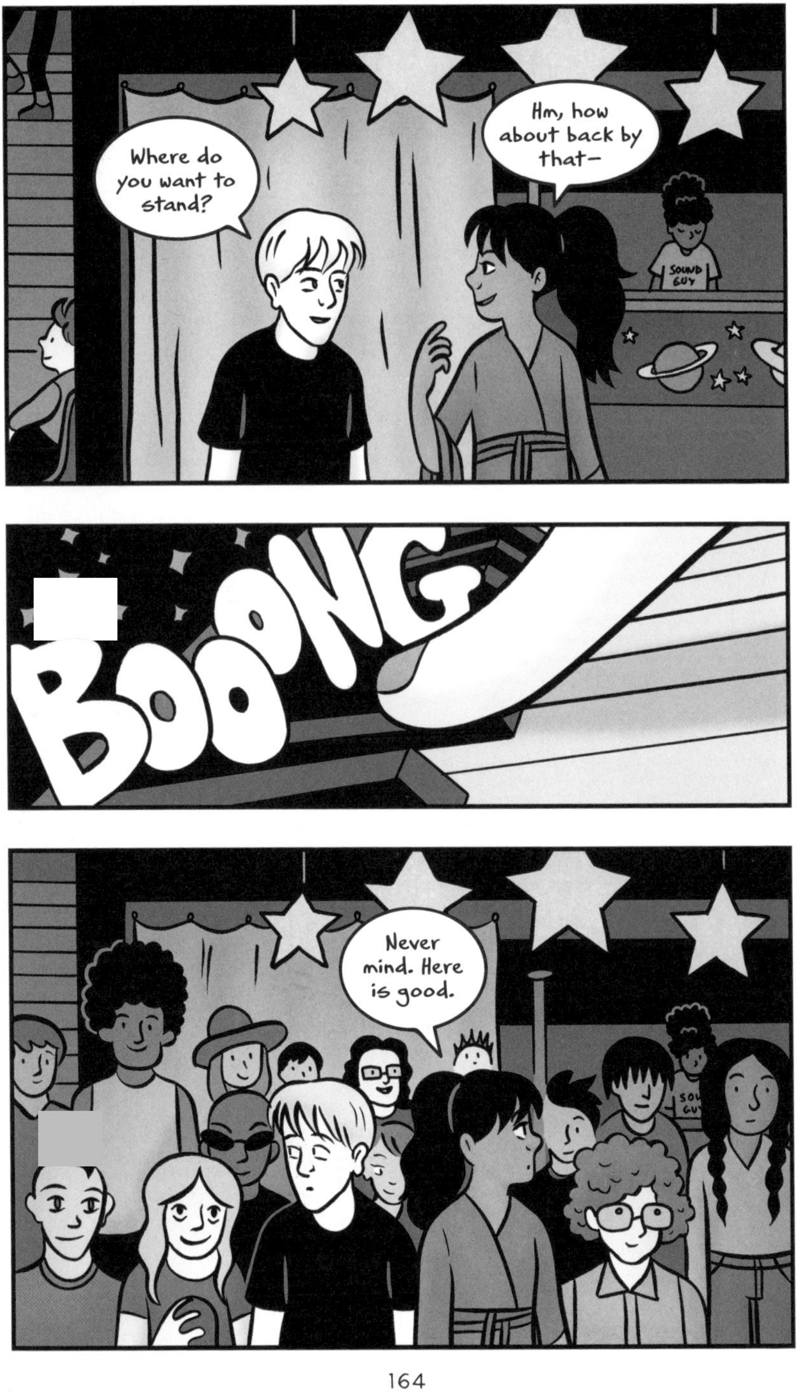
Where do you want to stand?
Hm, how about back by that—
SOUND GUY
BOOONG
Never mind. Here is good.

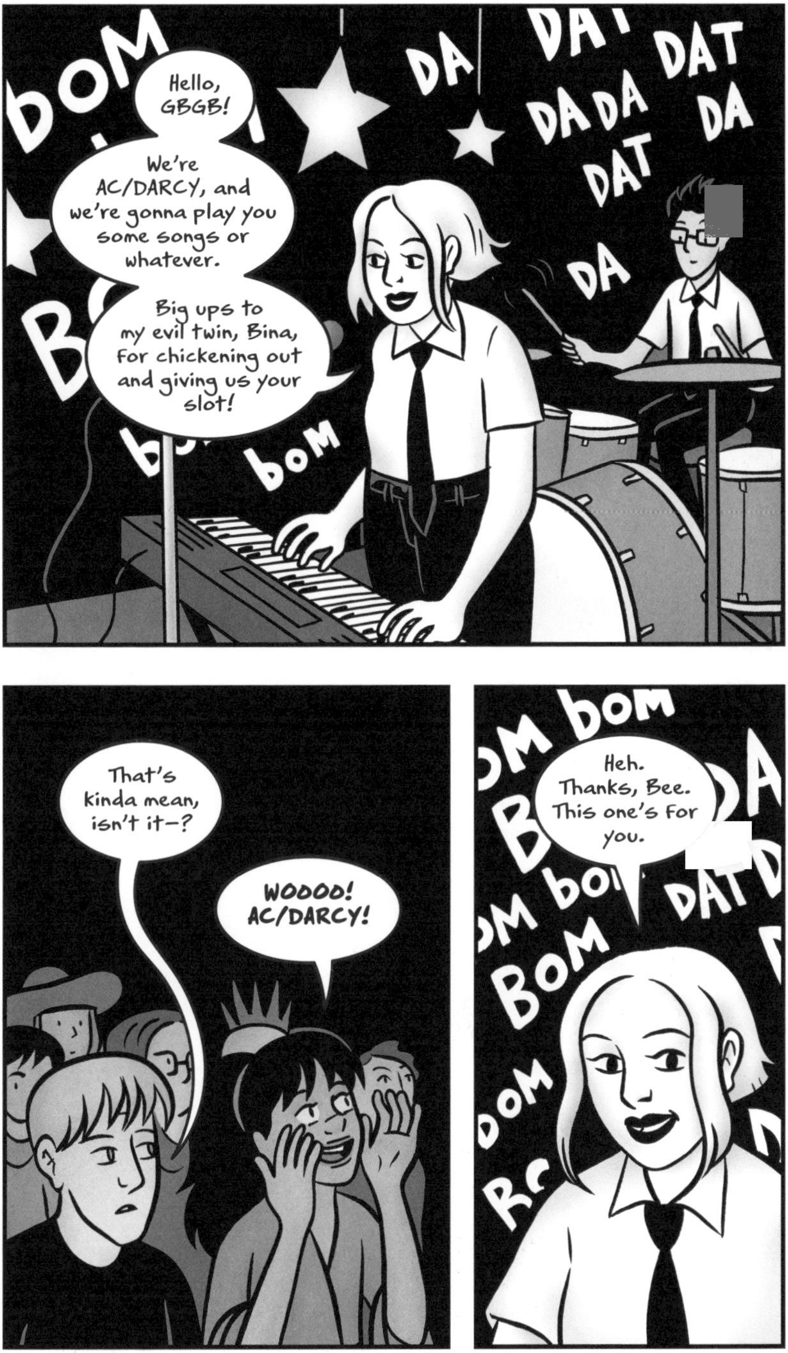
bOM
Hello, GBGB!
We're AC/DARCY, and we're gonna play you some songs or whatever.
Big ups to my evil twin, Bina, for chickening out and giving us your slot!
DA
DAT
DAT
DA DA
DA
DAT
DA
bom
That's kinda mean, isn't it—?
WOOOO! AC/DARCY!
bom
Heh. Thanks, Bee. This one's for you.
BOM

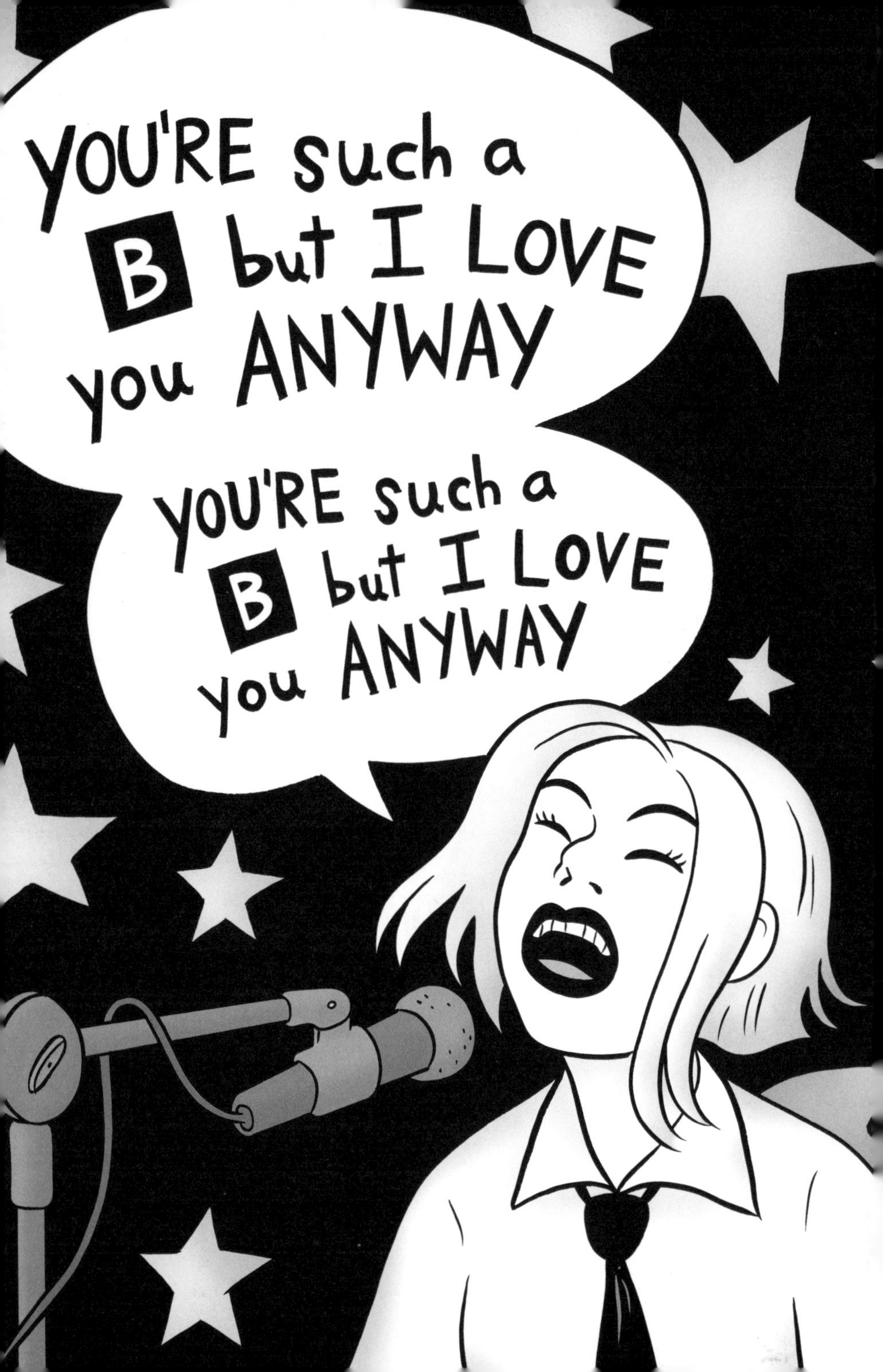
YOU'RE such a B but I LOVE you ANYWAY
YOU'RE such a B but I LOVE you ANYWAY

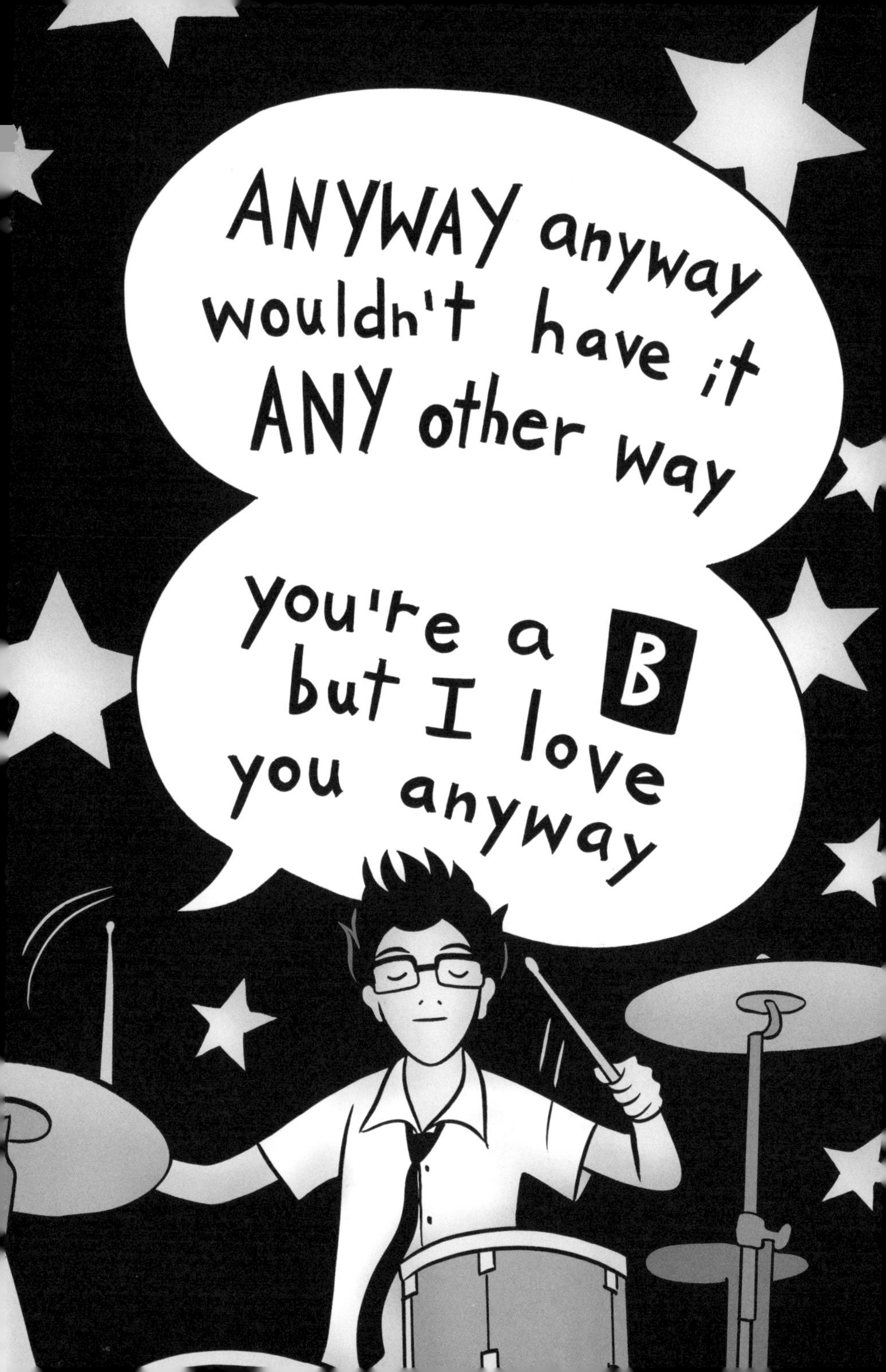
ANYWAY anyway wouldn't have it ANY other way
you're a B but I love you anyway

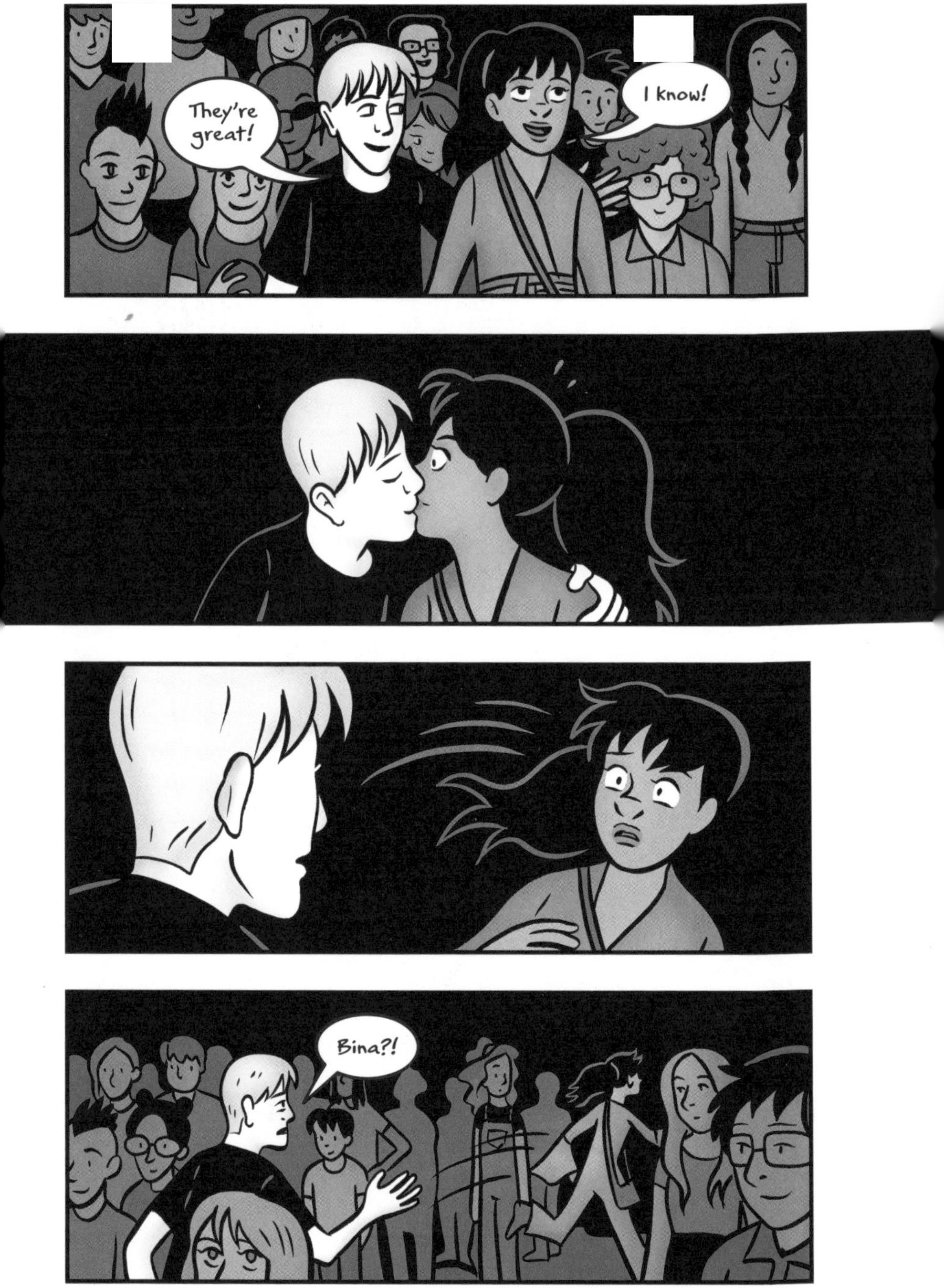
They're great!
I know!
Bina?!

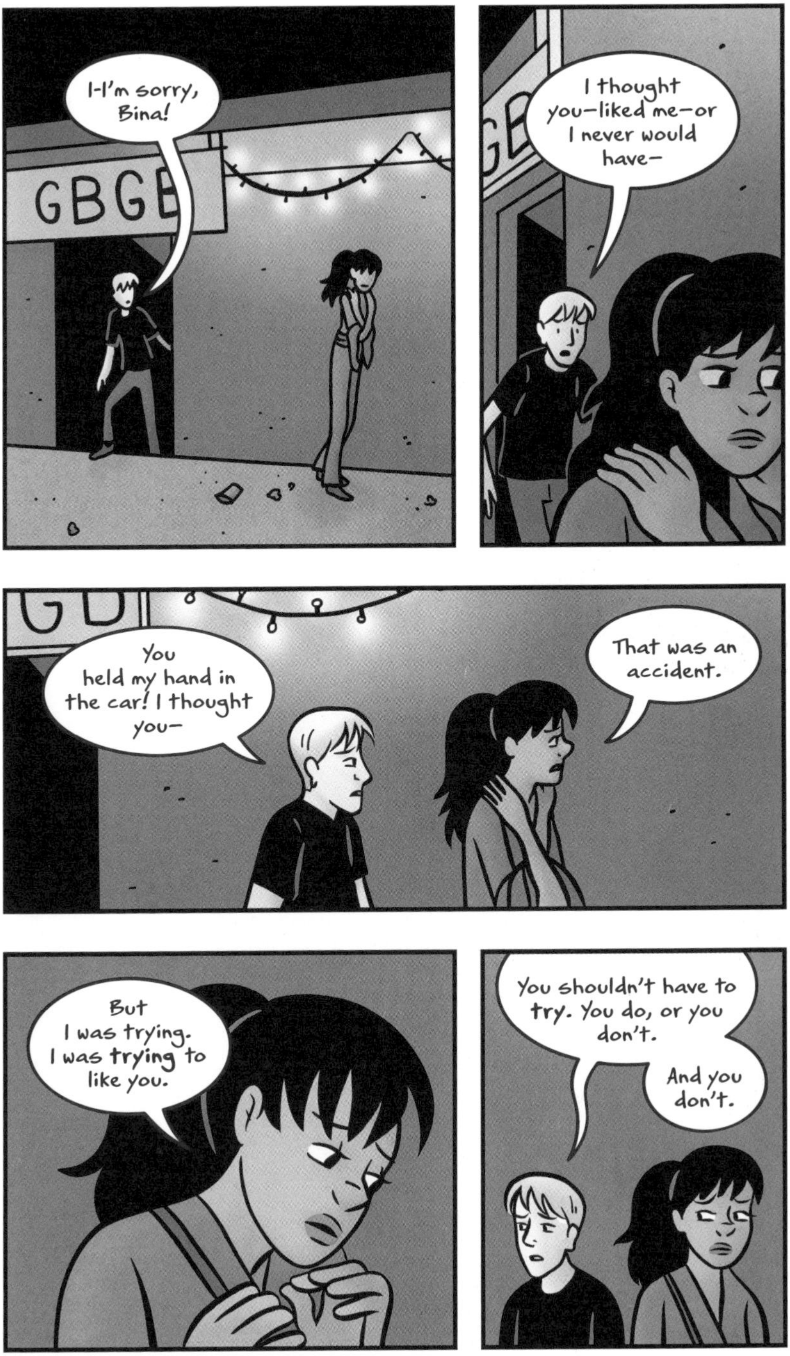
I-I'm sorry, Bina!
GBGB
I thought you—liked me—or I never would have—
You held my hand in the car! I thought you—
That was an accident.
But I was trying. I was trying to like you.
You shouldn't have to try. You do, or you don't.
And you don't.

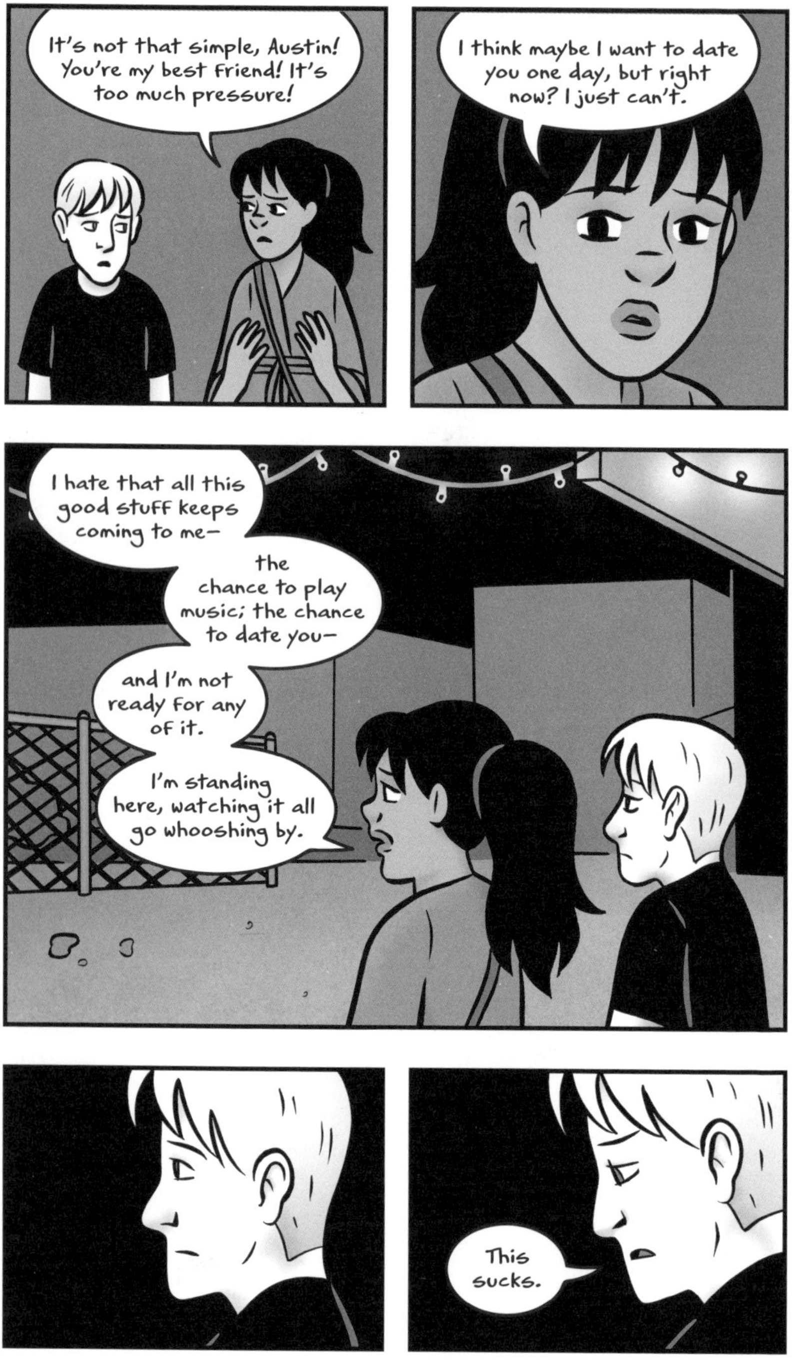
It's not that simple, Austin! You're my best friend! It's too much pressure!
I think maybe I want to date you one day, but right now? I just can't.
I hate that all this good stuff keeps coming to me—
the chance to play music; the chance to date you—
and I'm not ready for any of it.
I'm standing here, watching it all go whooshing by.
This sucks.

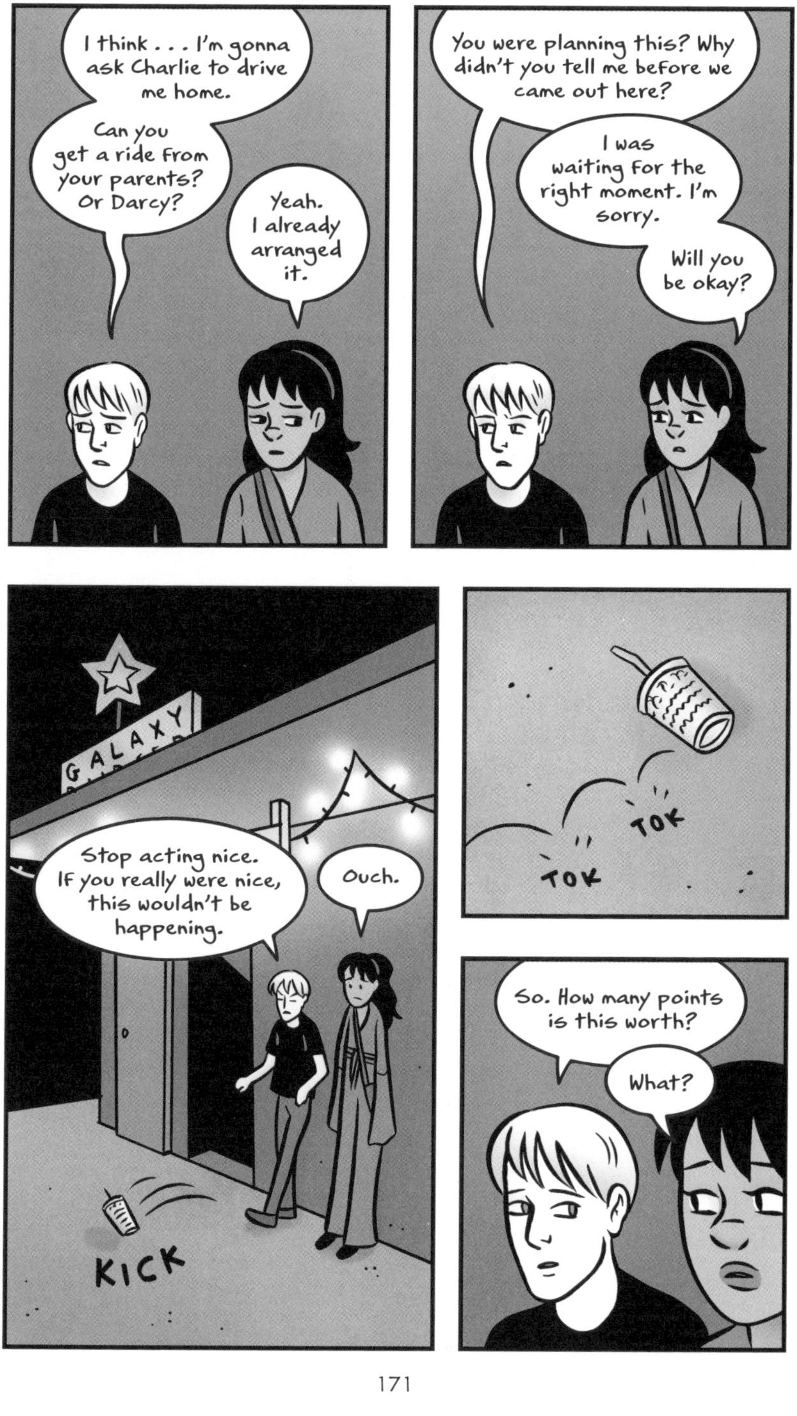
I think . . . I'm gonna ask Charlie to drive me home.
Can you get a ride from your parents? Or Darcy?
Yeah. I already arranged it.
You were planning this? Why didn't you tell me before we came out here?
I was waiting for the right moment. I'm sorry.
Will you be okay?
GALAXY
Stop acting nice. If you really were nice, this wouldn't be happening.
Ouch.
KICK
TOK
TOK
So. How many points is this worth?
What?

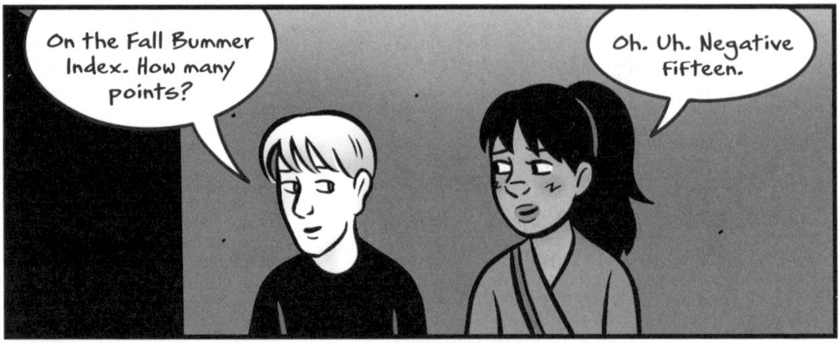
On the Fall Bummer Index. How many points?
Oh. Uh. Negative Fifteen.

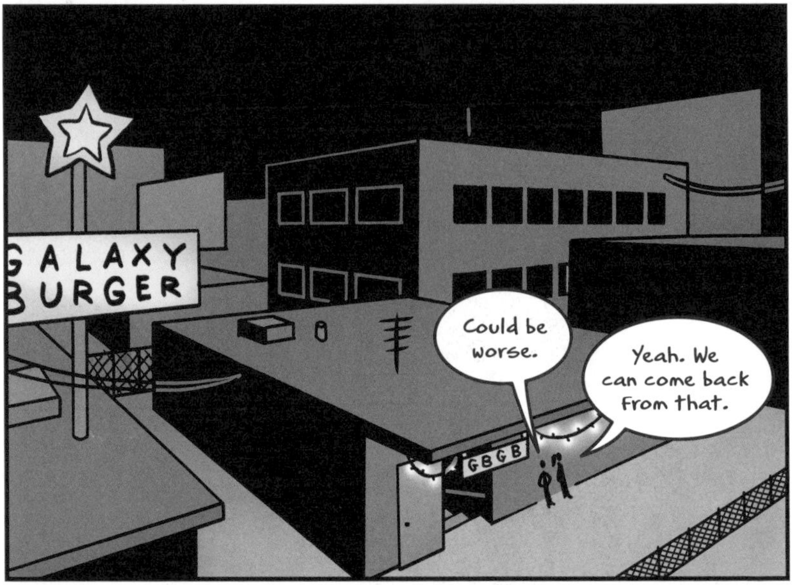
GALAXY BURGER
GBGB
Could be worse.
Yeah. We can come back from that.

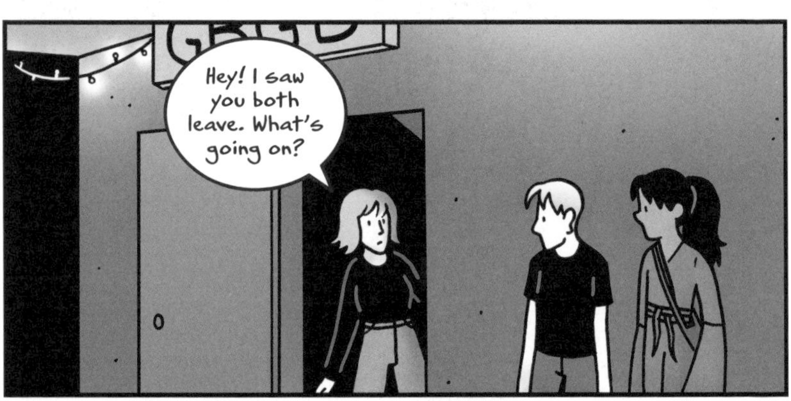
Hey! I saw you both leave. What's going on?

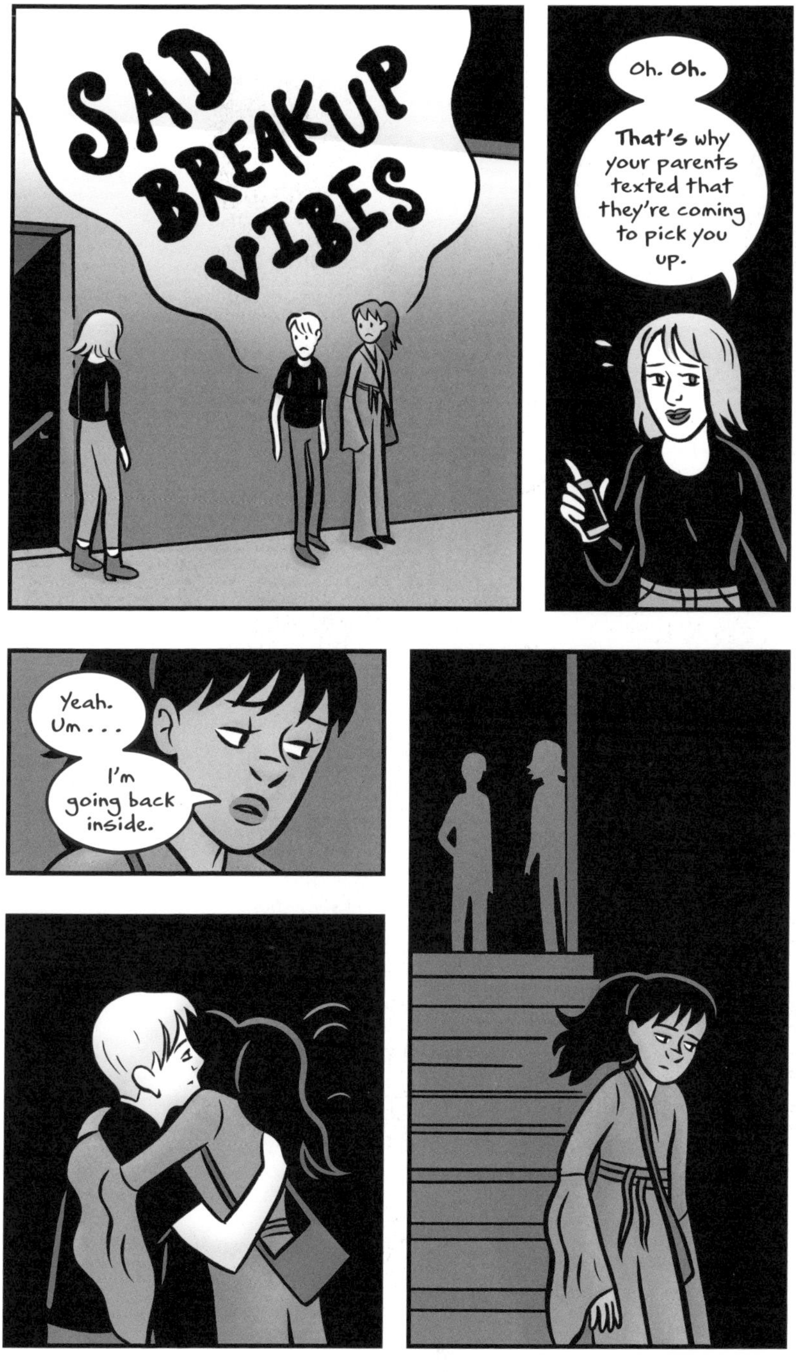
SAD BREAKUP VIBES
Oh. Oh.
That's why your parents texted that they're coming to pick you up.
Yeah. Um . . .
I'm going back inside.

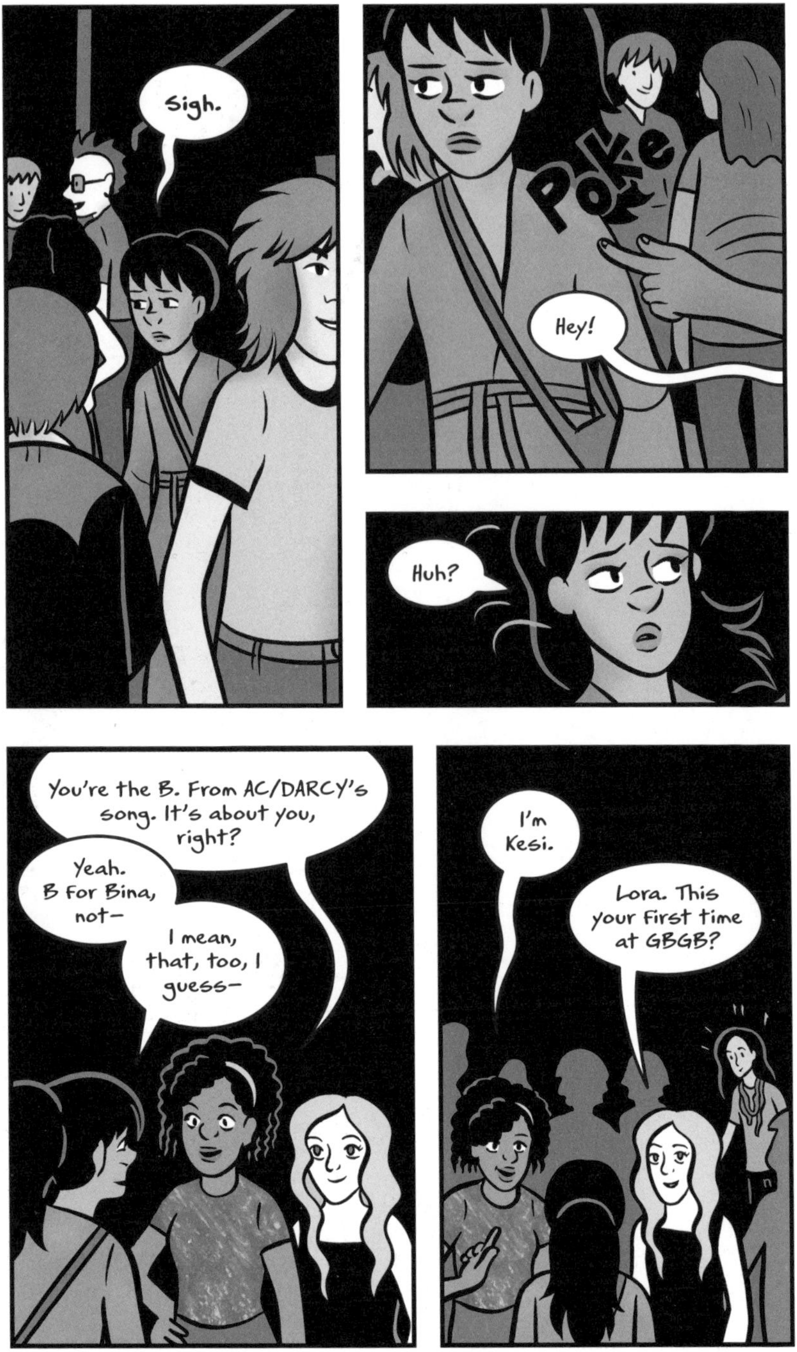
Sigh.
Poke
Hey!
Huh?
You're the B. From AC/DARCY's song. It's about you, right?
Yeah. B for Bina, not—
I mean, that, too, I guess—
I'm Kesi.
Lora. This your first time at GBGB?

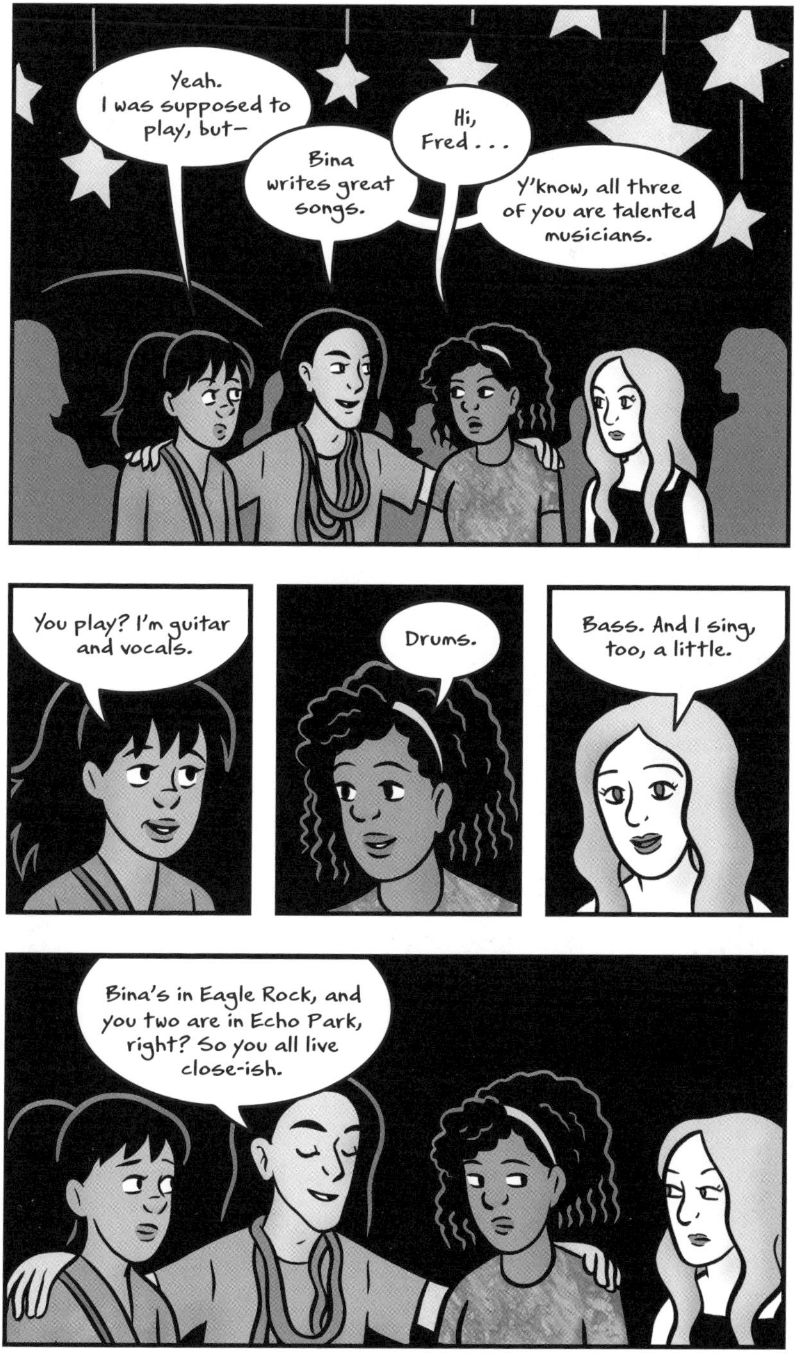
Yeah.
I was supposed to play, but—
Bina writes great songs.
Hi, Fred . . .
Y'know, all three of you are talented musicians.
You play? I'm guitar and vocals.
Drums.
Bass. And I sing, too, a little.
Bina's in Eagle Rock, and you two are in Echo Park, right? So you all live close-ish.

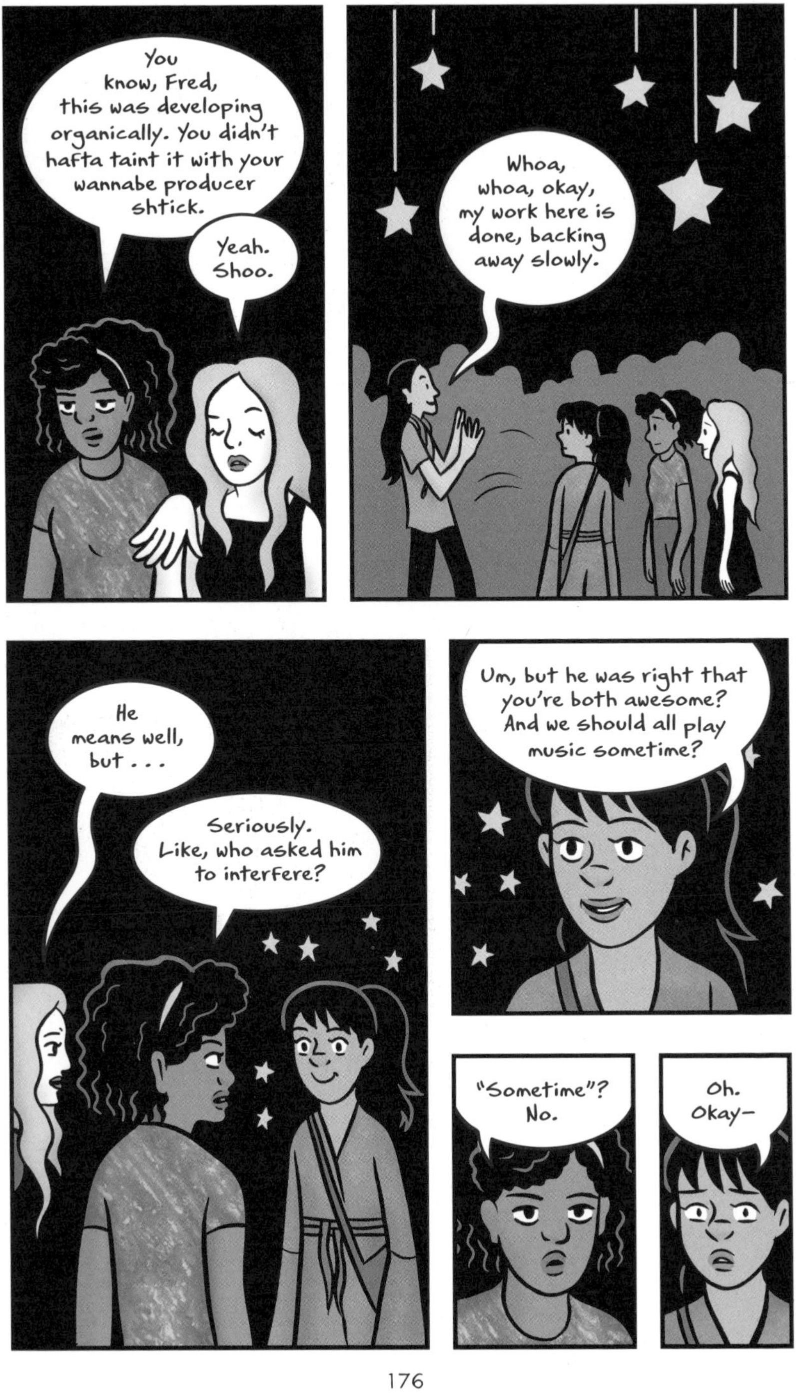
You know, Fred, this was developing organically. You didn't hafta taint it with your wannabe producer shtick.
Yeah. Shoo.
Whoa, whoa, okay, my work here is done, backing away slowly.
He means well, but . . .
Seriously. Like, who asked him to interfere?
Um, but he was right that you're both awesome? And we should all play music sometime?
"Sometime"? No.
Oh. Okay–

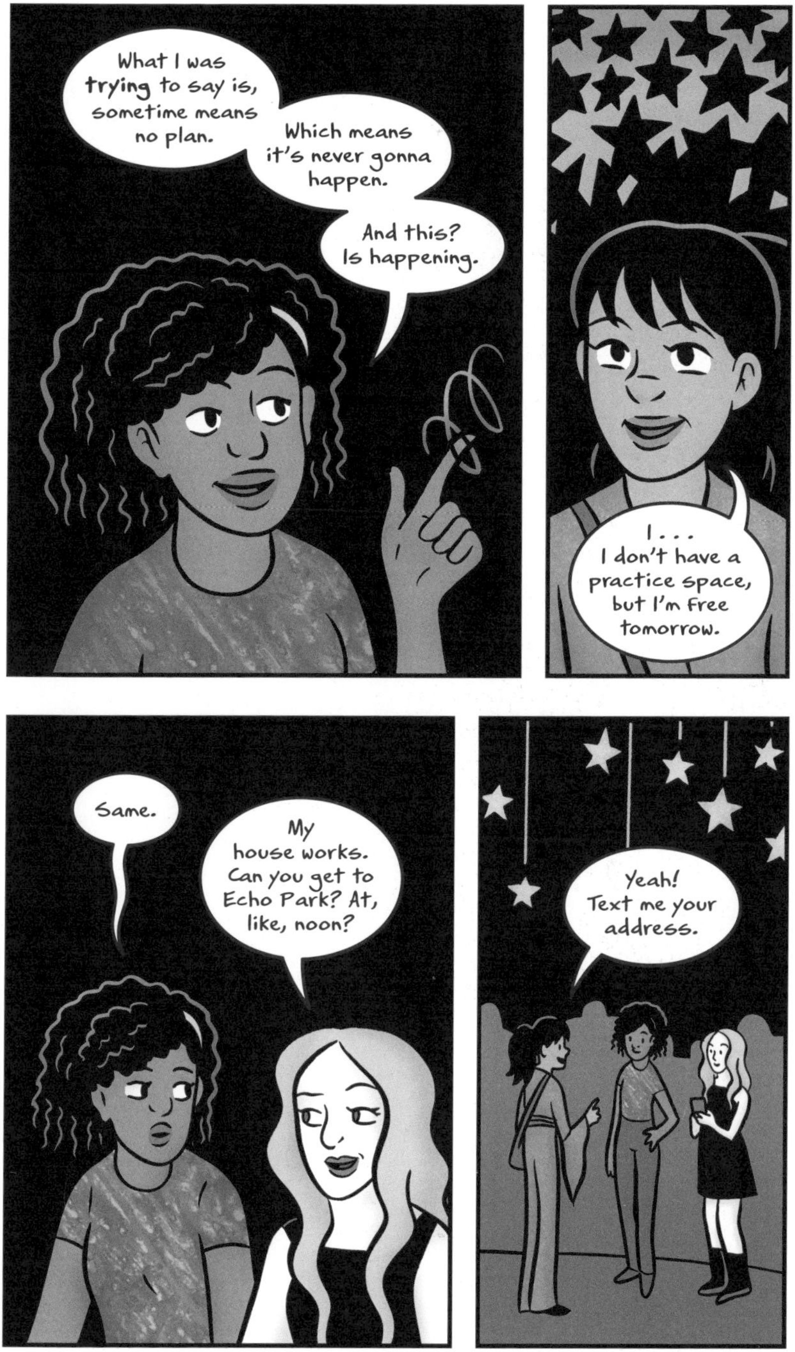
What I was trying to say is, sometime means no plan.
Which means it's never gonna happen.
And this? Is happening.
I . . . I don't have a practice space, but I'm free tomorrow.
Same.
My house works. Can you get to Echo Park? At, like, noon?
Yeah! Text me your address.

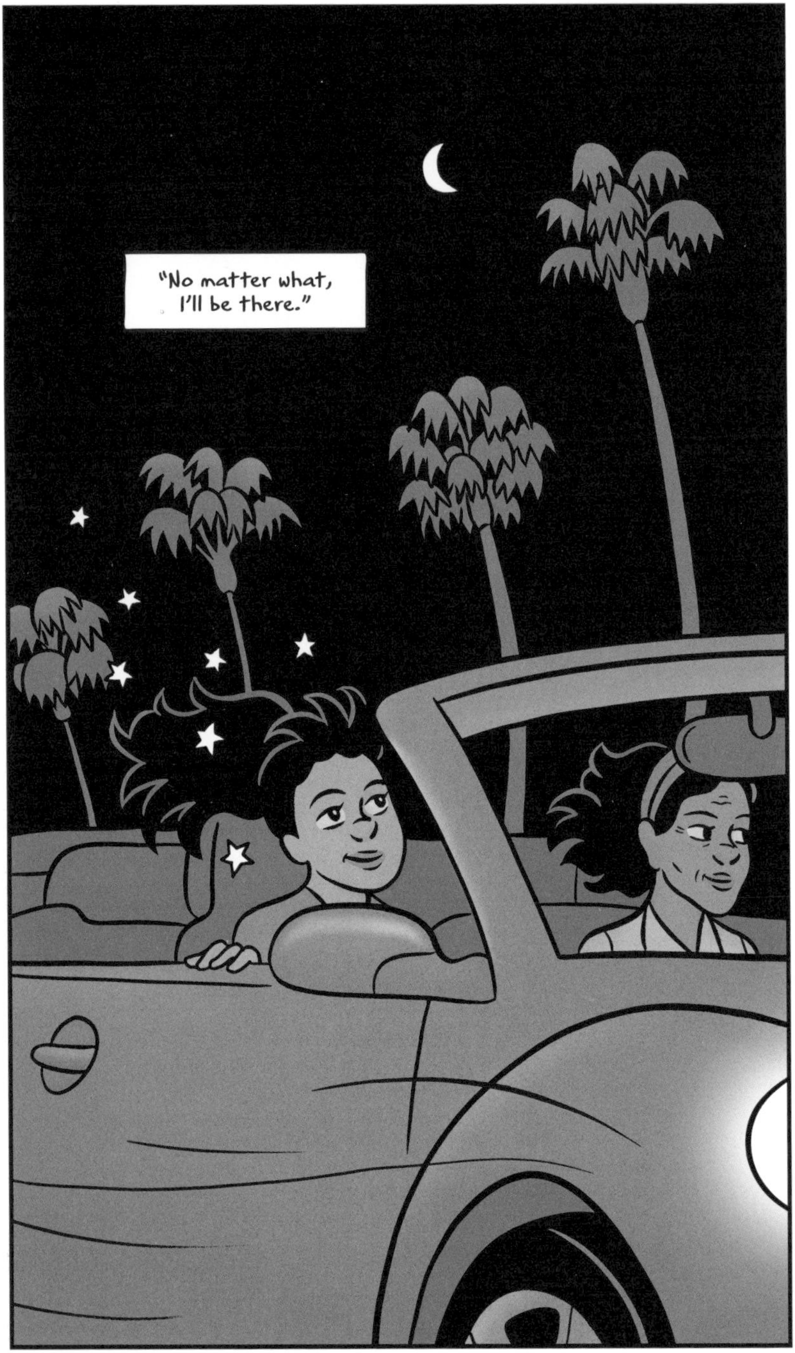
"No matter what,
I'll be there."

HOW I MAKE COMICS

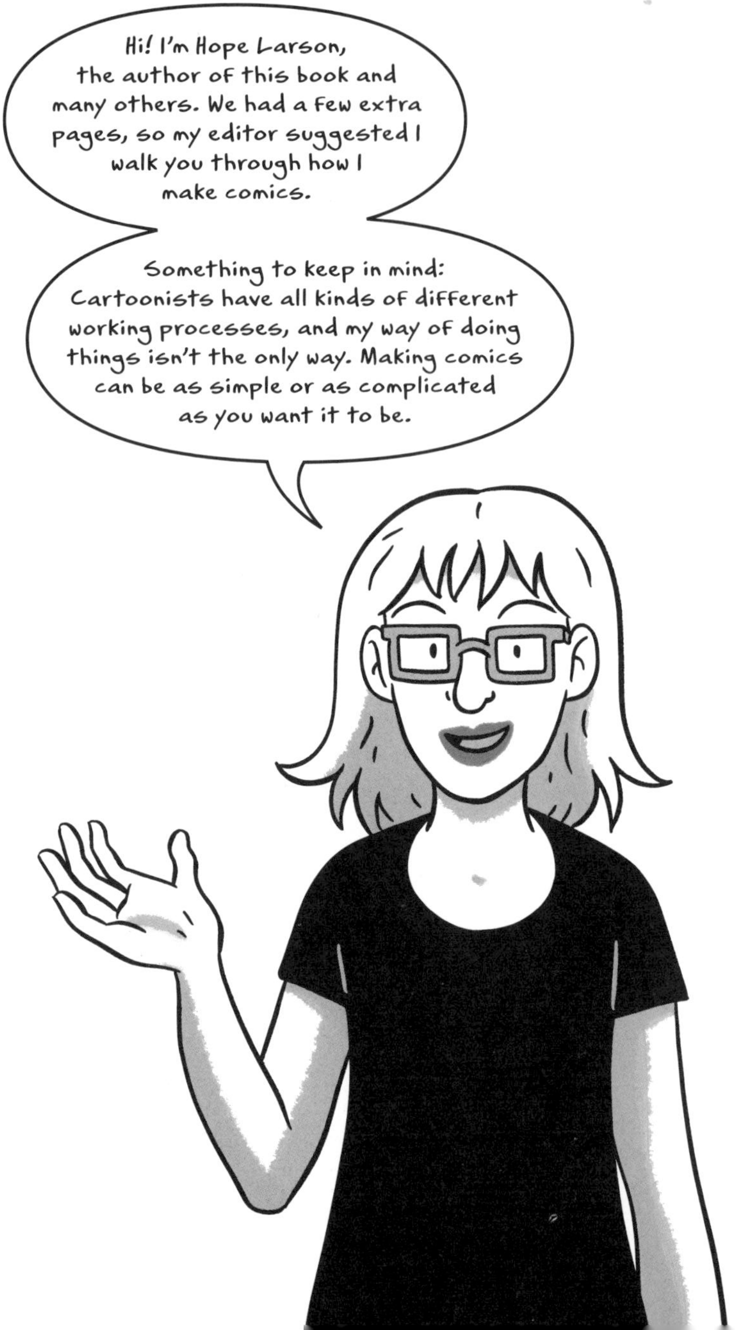
Hi! I'm Hope Larson, the author of this book and many others. We had a few extra pages, so my editor suggested I walk you through how I make comics.
Something to keep in mind: Cartoonists have all kinds of different working processes, and my way of doing things isn't the only way. Making comics can be as simple or as complicated as you want it to be.

THE SCRIPT

All my comics start with a SCRIPT. It's easier and faster for me to visualize the comic through words than to draw it all out while simultaneously figuring out the plot, characters, and dialogue. Writing a script also helps me figure out how long the book will be.

Important elements of comic scripts include:

HEADING
At the top of each page, I write the page number and the number of panels on the page. The more detailed the panels, the fewer there should be.

PANEL DESCRIPTION
I explain what's happening in each panel, including where we are and what time it is, what the characters are doing, and what emotions they're feeling.

DIALOGUE
This is anything the characters are saying or thinking.

SOUND EFFECTS
Not every page has sound effects, but I usually write these down, too.

PAGE 161: 5 PANELS
HEADING
Panel 1: The Fit's parallel parked along an industrial-looking street. Bina and Austin are getting out. Charlie's squinting up at a confusing mess of parking signs.
PANEL DESCRIPTION
CHARLIE
We should be able to park here.
(continuing)
I think.
Panel 2: Charlie leads the way down the sidewalk. The GalaxyBurger sign is sticking up above some buildings.
CHARLIE
C'mon. There's GalaxyBurger.
Panel 3: They approch the mouth of an alley behind the burger joint.
BINA
Fred said to go down the alley.
(continuing)
This must be it.
DIALOGUE
Panel 4: A larger panel. There's an entrance to a basement behind the restaurant, or in the building right next door. Kids their age and younger, and a few awkward parents, are milling around outside. The sign over the door reads GBGB, in the same font as the CBGB sign. Charlie, Austin and Bina head toward it.
CHARLIE
GBGB? Cute.
AUSTIN (WHISPER)
Some of those kids are, like, 8. How are they so cool already?
BINA (WHISPER)
I know! It's not fair!
Panel 5: They stop at the entrance. Fred's taking money. Bina and Charlie and Austin are handing over cash.
FRED
y'all. Glad you could make it.
(continuing)
The cover's five bucks.
DIALOGUE SPLIT INTO MULTIPLE BALLOONS

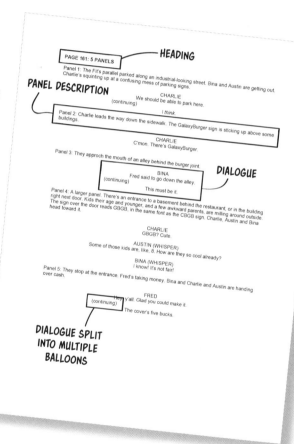

The script goes through several rounds of revisions before my editor, Joy, decides it's ready to be drawn. But even then, nothing in the script is set in stone. Things always change once I sit down to draw.

LAYOUT

I scripted five panels on this page, but when I did my LAYOUT, I decided that was too many. To make sure the environments (aka backgrounds) got a chance to shine, I reduced the panel count to three.

I do my layouts on an iPad Pro, in an app called Procreate. I like being able to move elements around, and that's easier to do while working digitally.

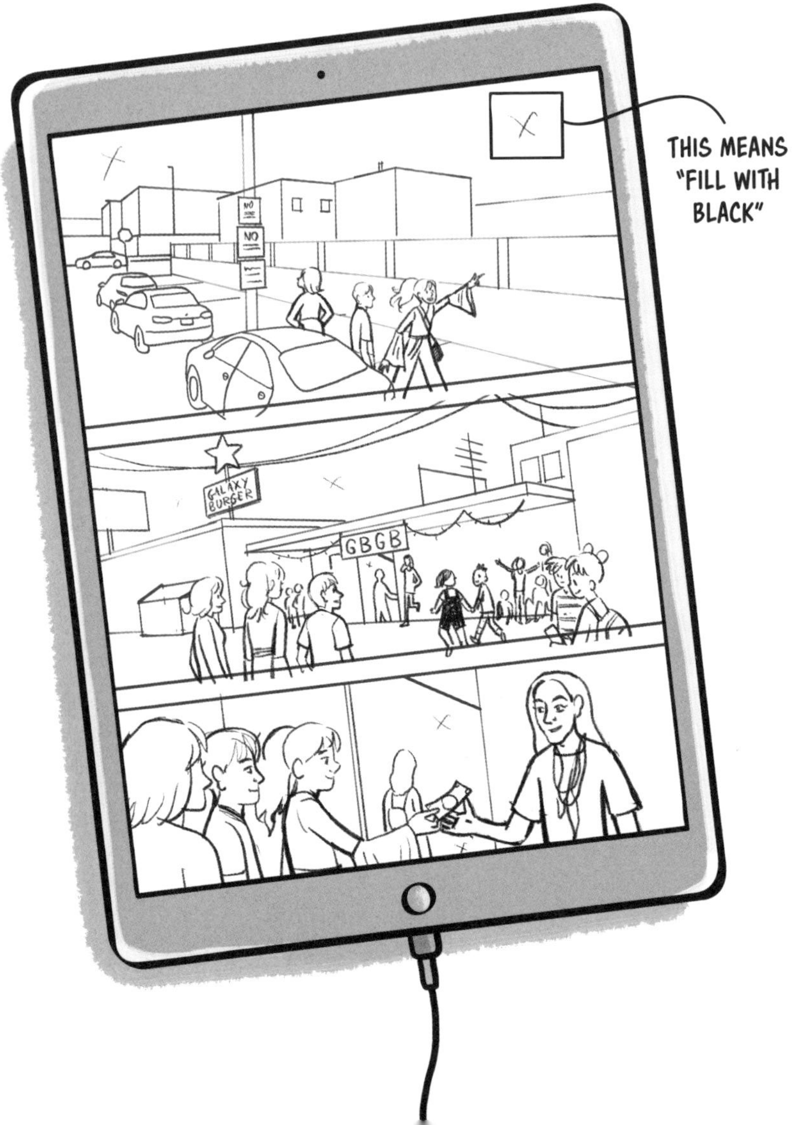
THIS MEANS "FILL WITH BLACK"
NO
GALAXY BURGER
GBGB

PENCILS

Once I'm happy with the layout, I move on to PENCILS. I bring the layout into Photoshop and tint it a very light blue, then print it out on Bristol board, a kind of thick drawing paper.

I trace over the layout with an orange Col-Erase pencil—an erasable colored pencil—and tighten up parts of the drawing that weren't clear. Then I scan it back in and add the speech balloons, or "letters."

I do a whole draft of the book that looks like this, then I go over it with my editor again. She makes suggestions for improving the book even more, and I fix as many problems as I can before I move on to the next step.

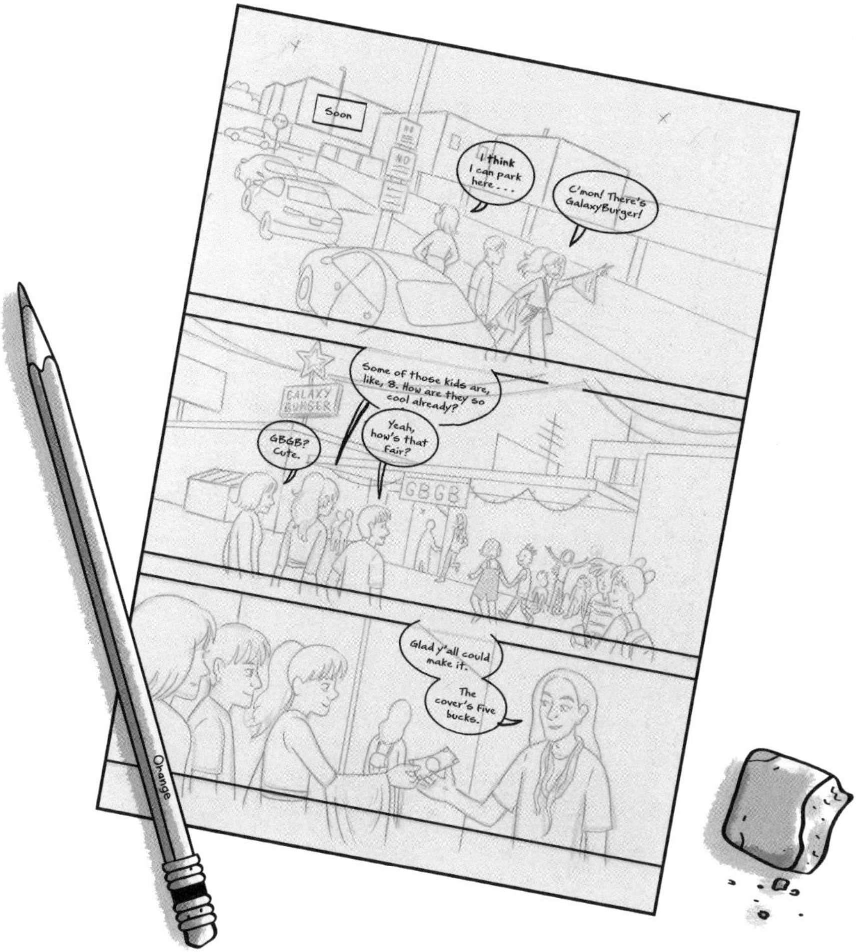
Soon
I think I can park here . . .
C'mon! There's GalaxyBurger!
GALAXY BURGER
Some of those kids are, like, 8. How are they so cool already?
GBGB? Cute.
Yeah, how's that fair?
GBGB
Glad y'all could make it.
The cover's five bucks.
Orange

INKS (UNCORRECTED)

We've finally reached one of my favorite parts of the process: inking! This is when the book starts coming together and looking how I imagined it would. I throw on a podcast or audiobook, pull out my stack of orange-penciled pages, and start inking right over the top of them. I use a small watercolor brush and a bottle of ink for almost everything but straight lines, which require a felt-tip pen and a ruler.

Below is a scan of a page as it looks on paper, before I correct it on the computer. The blacks aren't very dark yet, and I'm still using those little *X*'s to indicate which areas will be black. I like to fill those areas on the computer, because it's faster and it uses less ink.

I leave the orange pencil lines right where they are. I can remove them on the computer without needing to erase them.

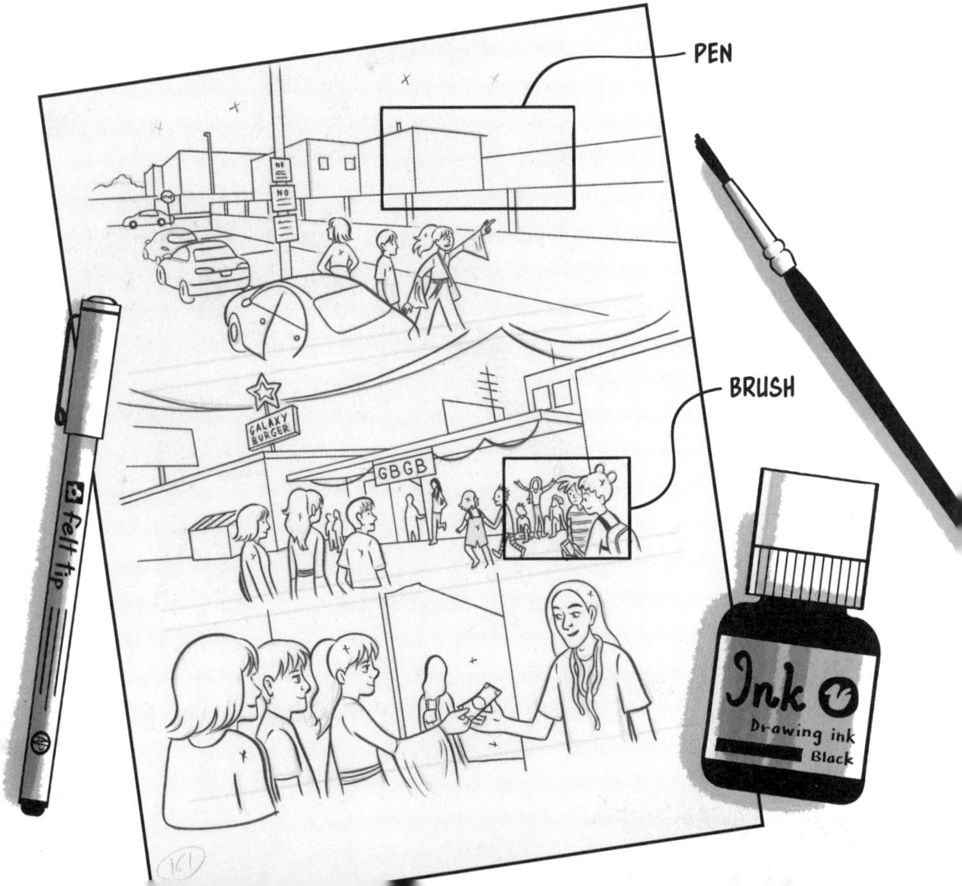
PEN
BRUSH
GALAXY BURGER
GBGB
felt tip
Ink
Drawing ink
Black
161

INKS (CORRECTED)

I scan my inks into Photoshop and make lots of changes. I adjust the image to be black and white. I fill any solid black areas. I fix and digitally redraw any parts of the image that look wonky.

I add the letters back in. I rethink speech balloon placement, draw final balloon tails, and send the page off to the colorist!

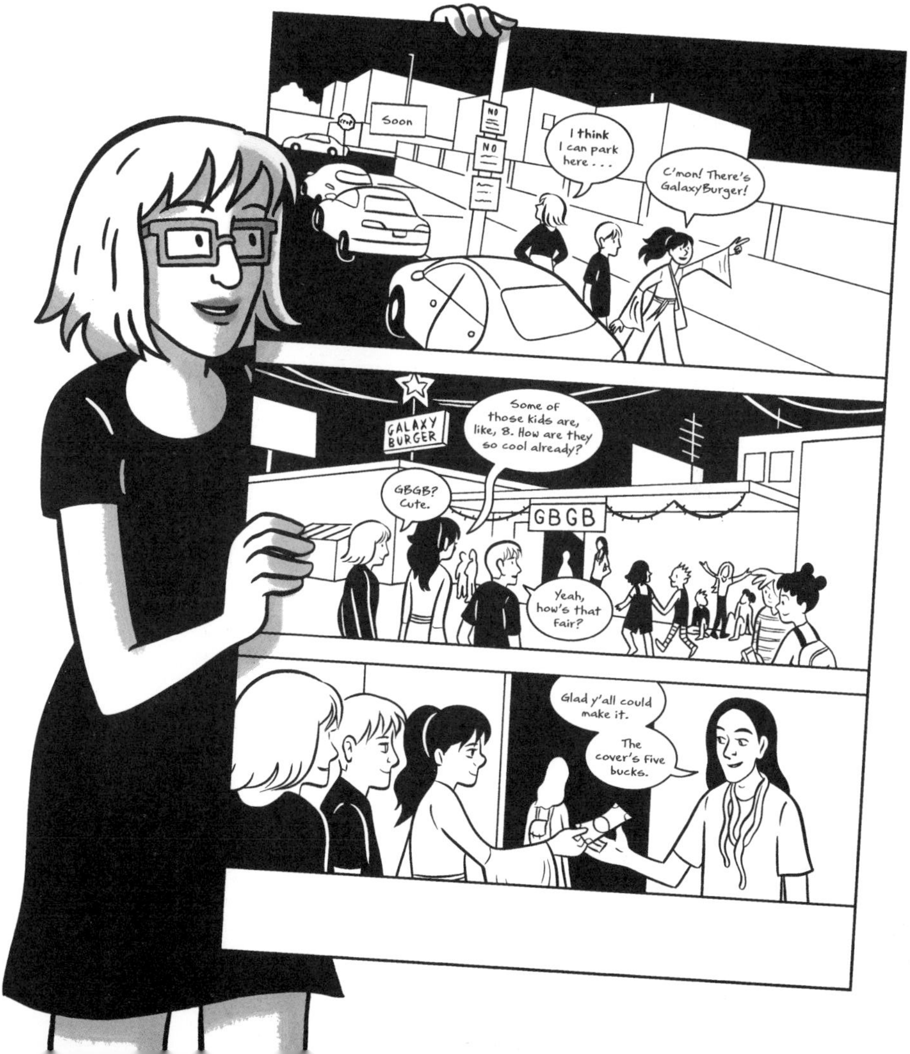
Soon
NO
NO
I think I can park here . . .
C'mon! There's GalaxyBurger!
GALAXY BURGER
Some of those kids are, like, 8. How are they so cool already?
GBGB? Cute.
GBGB
Yeah, how's that Fair?
Glad y'all could make it.
The cover's Five bucks.

COLORS

It takes a long time to draw a graphic novel, so having someone else to help with colors is wonderful. On *All Together Now*, I worked with colorists Hilary Sycamore and Karina Edwards. They add the tones and shading that bring the artwork fully to life.

I don't want to say I *couldn't* color a book by myself, but I would be a grumpier, more frazzled person. I'm so glad Hilary and Karina are on my team!

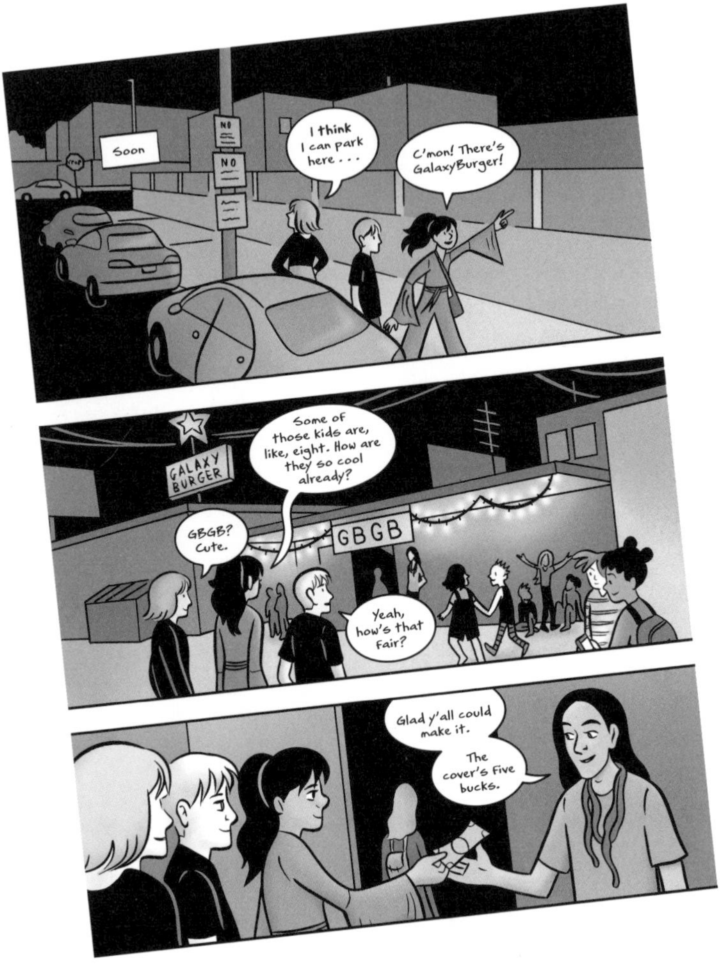
Soon
NO
NO
I think I can park here . . .
C'mon! There's GalaxyBurger!
GALAXY BURGER
Some of those kids are, like, eight. How are they so cool already?
GBGB? Cute.
GBGB
Yeah, how's that fair?
Glad y'all could make it.
The cover's five bucks.

AND THAT'S IT!

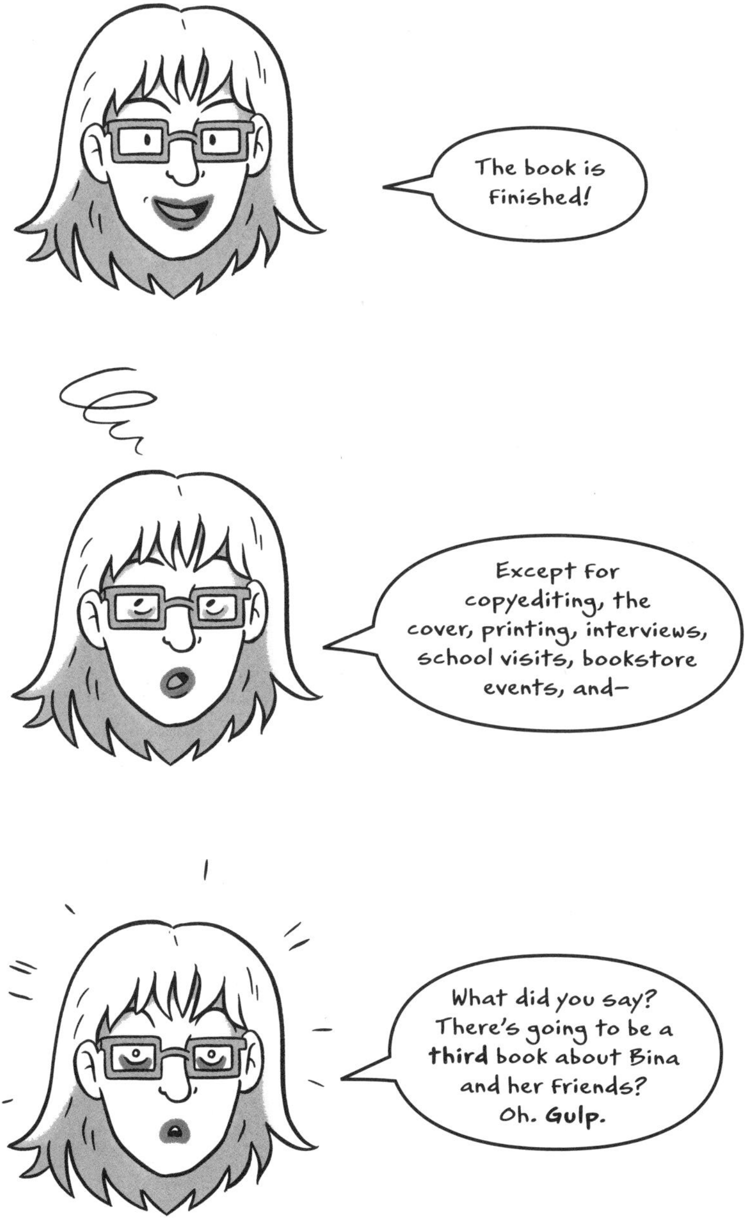

The book is finished!
Except for copyediting, the cover, printing, interviews, school visits, bookstore events, and–
What did you say? There's going to be a **third** book about Bina and her friends? Oh. **Gulp.**

OKAY, THEN.
BACK TO WORK!